PRAISE FOR *BENEATH THE MOTHER TREE*

Soulful and dreamlike, and utterly original, Cameron's Beneath the Mother Tree, *is a story about love – what bonds us to each other and the land we share. Here is a slice of Australia as you've never seen her before.*
Kim Kelly, author of *Lady Bird & The Fox*

Cameron has crafted a compelling page-turner that will transport readers to a world populated with characters who are as mysterious and gripping as their Australian landscape. Beneath the Mother Tree *is a captivating debut and genuine love story that will electrify.*
Tiffany McDaniel, author of the Not-the-Booker Prize winning novel *The Summer that Melted Everything*

A seductive, dark, contemporary fairy tale thrumming with a fierce, beguiling energy.
Kim Lock, author of *The Three of Us*

From the first page, this book held me in its thrall. As sultry and immersive as a tropical night.
Ilka Tampke, author of *Skin*

BENEATH

the

MOTHER
TREE

D.M. CAMERON

MidnightSun

First published 2018 by MidnightSun Publishing Pty Ltd
PO Box 3647, Rundle Mall, SA 5000, Australia.
www.midnightsunpublishing.com

Cataloguing-in-Publication entry is available from the
National Library of Australia.
http://catalogue.nla.gov.au

ISBN 9781925227390

Cover design by Kim Lock
Internal design by Zena Shapter

Typeset in Garamond, American Typewriter and Gills Sans.

Printed and bound in Australia by Griffin Press. The papers used by MidnightSun in the manufacture of this book are natural, recyclable products made from wood grown in sustainable plantation forests.

This project is supported by the Regional Arts Development Fund. The Regional Arts Development Fund is a partnership between the Queensland Government and Redland City Council to support local arts and culture in regional Queensland.

Even though the island of Moondarrawah is fictitious, this story takes place within the landscape of Quandamooka country. Moondarrawah is a Ngugi word granted to me by revered Ngugi Elder, Uncle Bob Anderson. All Indigenous content was written under the guidance and encouragement of Uncle Bob who decided upon the spelling of the Ngugi words phonetically because he learnt through an oral tradition. Please accept this as my love song to a place that formed me, written with deep respect for the three clans who belong to the Quandamooka past, present and future – the Ngugi of Moorgumpin, and the Nunukul and Gorenpul of Minjerribah.

For Loom

Strongly I feel your presence very near
Haunting the old spot, watching as we
Disturb your bones. Poor ghost,
I know, I know you will understand.

Oodgeroo Noonuccal

Get up from the stool, through the lattice step lightly
And we'll rove in the grove while the moon's shining brightly.

The Spinning Wheel
(Traditional Irish song)

1.

On the wind, Ayla heard a tune so sweetly mournful it made her toes curl in the sand. Had she imagined it? She glanced behind her to see the world had turned a sickly green. Even the rich red of Mud Rock was tinged.

The pied cormorant's heart pounded against her wrist through the stained pillow case. She placed its webbed feet gently on the shoreline, uncovering the head last. Freed, the bird skittered up the deserted beach. The only remaining sign of its ordeal with fishing line was a featherless patch on its curved neck.

'Go Buster.' Ayla knew not to name rescued wildlife, but a name always came.

Buster opened his yellow beak and cried to the sky at the injustice, before uncurling his oily blackness to glide over the water and behind the headland.

'Bye Buster.'

Even my voice sounds green, she thought, as she heard it flop onto the sand. She looked down to see her voice had turned into khaki seaweed – faded and brittle. She stood on it, imagining vocal chords crunching underfoot. The stench of rotting seaweed clung to the roof of her mouth.

Moving out of the sinister shadow of the Rock, she saw the source of the strange coloured light was the sun caught behind boiling black clouds, miles out to sea. The storm that passed over earlier, still lingering.

A ripple came across the water, reaching the shoreline as a breeze, filling the air with electricity. Her hair stood on end as the eerie music came again, twining itself around her, drawing her up the beach into the pigface — its feathery flowers closing on the day. A thrill coiled through her as she followed the melody into the trees, creeping as lightly as soldier crabs scuttle across sand.

She paused in the thick stand of bent she-oaks.

He was sitting, his bare back to her, on a dead banksia in the clearing, a strange wooden flute dancing in his hands. The colour of his jeans blended with the faded log so he became part of the tree. The spirit of the old banksia, perhaps? Ayla enjoyed the fantasy, peering through the she-oak's prickly curtain at his hair, so black it looked blue in the sun. He turned his face to the sky and she saw it was a gentle profile. His music reached out, took her by the hand and she danced with him in her mind.

He stopped, flute poised, staring toward her clump of trees.

Ayla merged with the she-oaks she had known since childhood, when she had rested on their horizontal trunks bent by the wind, murmuring her grandfather's stories.

The stranger's dark eyes were unblinking. He blew one low solitary note. She felt the ends of her hair split. Was it the music, or the eerie green light that was so bewitching? She considered stepping into the clearing, but backed away, stumbling onto the beach. Where the sand was wet and firm, she danced, eyes shut to let her body connect with his rhythm, slow, deep, divine. She lost herself in the pulse of him.

He paused. She ran, exhilarated, leaping on the tide line to notes on the wind then running again for sheer joy along the empty beach. Who was he? Where had he come from and why was he here on her little island in the middle of the wild old sea? She scrambled to the top of Mud Rock. Little Beaudy bobbed on the water of the next bay. Her grandfather's launch, a ruby floating in the turquoise inlet. Hibiscus Bay curved in a crescent moon: the headland jutted out to protect the calm water from open sea.

She cooeed. Her grandfather emerged from the cabin, barefoot and bare-chested. He waved, unhooked the dinghy and rowed to shore.

'Getting in or am I getting out?'

She was already in. The small row boat felt safe and familiar and the stranger with his music could not touch her here.

'What?' He rested his oars for a moment. The hem of his favourite shorts frayed now, the strands of white matching the hair on his chest.

'Hey?'

'Usually go round the Rock, not over it.'

She shrugged. 'Felt brave for once.'

Her grandfather rowed and said the wind was unsettled. She agreed and felt tingly all over.

Climbing from the rowboat into Little Beaudy, the mixture of smells she had known all her life – kerosene, fish guts and whisky – wrapped comforting arms around her. They sat at the table that folded to a bed and he put the kettle on. 'You look flushed.'

She felt her hot cheeks and picked at the sand under her nails. He threw tea bags into chipped enamel cups, slurping a dash of whisky into his. They waited for the water to boil, listening to the waves lapping against the boat, as they always did.

Ayla's heart began to settle. 'Tell me one of your stories, Grappa?' Grappa had been the first word she had spoken, a failed attempt at Grandpa. Because Grappa was a form of alcohol, the island community thought it apt, so the name had stuck.

'Why?'

Ayla's heart tightened at the sad look on his crinkled face. It had been too long since she had asked for a story. 'You told me about a dark-haired man once. Far...something?'

'Dorocha.'

'Far Dorocha.' She repeated it like a secret.

'God help those who fall under his spell.'

'You said he played an instrument?'

'Can do. A flute, a pipe, sometimes a drum. The one I met didn't play anything.'

'You met one?' Ayla acted as if she hadn't heard the story. When she was a child, this technique could always draw the tale from him.

'Up at the hall. The Stop Progress Association's Annual Masked Ball was on. You know the rest.' Grappa was wise to her. She was twenty now, too old to get away with it.

'Tell me again.'

He looked at her sideways.

'Please?'

His voice dropped so there was a dangerous edge to it. 'No moon that night. I remember 'cause he appeared from nowhere – stepped straight out of the blackness. Not a soul had seen him catch the barge across. No water taxi back then. Barge was the only way on and off. Nettie and I weren't long married, but he took her under his spell. Last thing I remember was her twirling round with him – couldn't take her eyes off the bugger, like she was in a trance or somethin'.'

'What do you mean, the last thing you remember?'

'Dunno. Lost time. Woke up on Three Mile with sun in me eyes, sand in me ears and couldn't for the life of me remember how I got there. Thought he'd taken her for sure. Ran all the way home, but there she was sweeping the kitchen with the kettle on, waitin' like nothing had happened. 'Course she denied everythin'. But I knew she was under his spell. Counted the hours 'til he came back.'

'He came back?'

'Nup. Must have known Nettie's heart was part of mine. She could never truly leave me. One thing about 'em...they respect love.'

'And usually they play an instrument?'

'That's what Gran said. They pull you towards 'em with their music.' On the word, pull, he gestured with his hands, drawing in an anchor. 'Once you're under his spell, then he takes you down into the black abyss, into his realm, never to return.'

'What did he look like?'

Grappa watched her. 'Why?'

'Maybe I just saw one.'

His eyebrows jumped. 'Maybe it's the same one?'

Grappa was so serious, she hid her smile. 'Can't be. He looked my age.'

'Ayla, they don't age. Where was he?'

'Beyond the she-oaks. I heard this music and had to follow it. Couldn't help myself.' Her laugh escaped.

'It's not funny. What was he playing?'

'A strange wooden carved looking thing, curved at the end but held at the side like a flute. It had markings burnt into the wood. Never seen an instrument like it.'

Grappa looked like he was about to explode. 'And he had pitch-black hair?'

'Black as.'

'Holy Mary, Mother-of-God.' He poured more scotch into his tea.

'Don't worry, he didn't see me. I hid in the she-oaks.'

'They don't need to see you. They can feel you.'

Grappa was scaring her now, not because she believed him anymore, but because something had happened. The stranger's music had woken something in her. Something dormant deep inside was alive again. She glimpsed herself as a child, sitting here at this table with a head full of possibilities and a fist full of Smarties – rainbow colours smudging her palms.

Grappa peered through the porthole towards Mud Rock. 'Unless...'

'What?'

'The she-oaks hid you.' His rumpled features sharpened. 'Those trees know you. They would've protected you. That's how you escaped.'

She smiled. He always brought it back to the trees.

'Now I know why you went over the headland 'stead of round it. Scared you, didn't he?'

'No. It was fun, running. His music, and the way he looked in the clearing, he...' She felt herself blush under Grappa's glare.

He shook his head. 'Jesus Ayla.' All colour had drained from his face. 'Knew today was gonna be a bad day.' He covered her fine hand with his spotty clump of a thing. 'Not to worry. You're safe now. Those old she-oaks saved you, girl. Don't forget to thank 'em.'

She marvelled at how his eyes lit up at the thought of the trees saving her. His hand was shaking. She had upset him to amuse herself, an attempt to momentarily recapture the magic of her childhood. Her guilt had her gulping the rest of her tea. 'Thanks for the cuppa.'

'Got some whiting you can take. I'll walk you home.'

'I'll be fine.'

'Go straight home, hear me? Long way, via the road. Not goin' past the she-oaks again.'

As Grappa rowed her back to shore, Ayla thought of a time when his words were intoxicating. She wanted to believe in the ominous encounter with his black-haired demon, but the flute player was probably a tourist. A backpacker who had come to the island for the day. Everything was so easily explained away now. Adulthood already felt stale at its threshold. Where had all the wonder gone?

Reaching the road, she glanced back to see Grappa in the late afternoon glow at the shoreline, scratching his bum. Grappa, who still believed in magic, guarding, watching until she was out of sight. She waved and blew kisses, envying his blind faith in it all.

He headed up the beach behind the Rock into the tangle of cottonwood trees, towards his 'Far Dorocha'. She hoped the young man had gone so Grappa wouldn't make a fool of himself. Remorse shot through her. She had set him up for more ridicule. Only yesterday she had overheard locals joking about him. 'Great old bloke, but mad as a cut snake once he's had a few.'

They misunderstood. He wasn't a ranting drunk. He was simply living his life through the stories his grandmother had crowded his head with. Stories carried from the other side of the world, precious gifts from a childhood in a cold green country, adapted to suit this bright tattered land. Grappa had seen it as his duty to fill Ayla's head with the tales.

I'm the only one who really understands him.

This lonely thought made her pace quicken. The darkness of early evening fell on the dirt road of Hibiscus Beach Drive – abandoned holiday houses at one end and the old Johnston place on the mangrove swamp at the other. Most islanders believed the old house was haunted.

Ayla crossed Hibiscus and swung left onto the bitumen of Long Street, the main road bisecting the island. The air felt heavy and the frogs in the swamp started grumbling. Perhaps the storm had changed direction? She began to run.

At the top of the rise, she slowed to a walk as the breeze from the sea caressed her, bringing to mind the flute player.

Turning left into her street, she heard women laughing. Mandy's mother, sister and grandmother lived on the corner in a ramshackle Queenslander that often wobbled on its stumps from women's laughter. The island felt empty without Mandy.

At home, she found her mother in the kitchen, an easel on the bench, wooden spoon in one hand, paintbrush in the other, painting as she cooked. The canvas covered yet again with a watery green background.

Please, not another drowning.

It had been months since her mother had painted. 'Grappa sent whiting.' She jammed the parcel of fish in the freezer.

'Hmmm?' Her mother lowered the skyline with a stroke of the brush and wiped her face with the back of her sleeve.

Ayla saw now, she had been crying.

Her mother's head jerked towards the back window. 'Bloody

chickens. Would you mind, darling? Bugger.' She lifted the pan as the scent of burnt milk pervaded.

Ayla walked behind the chickens, clapping to a beat in her head. 'I often hear rhythms,' she told Grappa once. He said that was the Irish in her and that his Gran had hated Australia, claiming, 'There's no music. At home, there's music all around. How can you thrive in a land without music?'

Clapping, Ayla shooed the chickens out of the vegetable patch into the bracken fern. The black Bantam darted down the sandy track to the beach. She cut it off, sending it toward the coop.

Pausing in the messy softness of the paperbarks, she leant against a spongy trunk, breathing in the tea tree balm. The clearing was close enough, if the handsome musician was still there she might hear him. The lone honk from a peacock pierced her hope. She knew she would never see him again.

The seductive tone of a wind instrument wound its way through the maze of cottonwood limbs. Grappa broke into a sweat at the sound of it.

So help me Mother-of-God.

The events of the day now made hideous sense. The dead dugong on Three Mile Beach at dawn, propeller cuts still wet with blood, a lone crow pecking viciously at the milky eye. It filled him with the memory of the last time he'd found a sea cow's carcass washed up. The day Nettie died. He couldn't shake the premonition that today was akin to that day – death had closed in on the island. All morning he'd noticed birds acting up, then the unnatural storm that blew in from nowhere, lurking out at sea, turning the light peculiar. Grappa knew now, none of this was coincidence. Far Dorocha had returned.

Grappa stepped into the clearing at the banksia log. The only thing staring at him was a hairy cone of eyes: a spent seedpod from the old tree.

The flute sound drifted in from the ocean. He pushed his way through the she-oaks, whispering, 'Thank you for protecting her,' caressing their rough trunks, drawing courage from their solid presence.

The beach too appeared empty. He waited in the papery grass that grew where scrub met sand.

The same melody began to waft out of Mud Rock itself. As Grappa listened, the haunting tune faded away. The demon was playing with him, leading him on into the night, if Grappa were silly enough to follow. 'Leave her alone. Hear me? You don't stand a chance. She knows what you are.' He felt moronic calling to no one.

For a time, the only sound between waves was the wind through the grass tickling his feet. He looked at the disappearing sun and farted. I too can be musical, he thought.

If he hurried, he could reach the Nor Folk Tree to ask protection for Ayla before night fell. The Nor folk, according to his Gran, were 'faeries, nature spirits. Call them what you will.' Gran had convinced him they lived in the circle of Norfolk pines on the southern end of the island. 'See lad? See how the old fig grows smack bang in the centre of the pines? That's no coincidence. That's a sign. This Moreton Bay fig is easily the oldest tree on the island. Has to be here. I'm sure of it.'

'What has to be here, Gran?'

'The way into their realm. What else would I be talking about?'

Grappa walked toward Dead Tree Point as fast as his tired heart allowed, dodging sea sponges, faded coral and mangrove seeds washed up after the storm. The sharp whiff of it all caught on the wind. He was breathless when he arrived at the sandbank full of half-buried trees lying on their sides, roots reaching to the sky. The jumble of petrifying limbs pushed over years ago by a cyclonic wind was a graveyard of bones in the ghoulish twilight.

Grappa detected movement near the cave half way up the cliff. He peered into the dark opening. Something large shifted in the scrub nearby and he almost messed himself.

'Wallaby. Idiot.' The sound of his own voice was comforting.

The curve of a swollen yellow moon crept from the ocean. He paused at the sight of it. Gran always said the Fey were at their most potent when the moon was full. The foreboding that had been building all day swamped him. 'No time to go to the tree – dark soon,' he mumbled to the ghost crab at his feet before it turned to sand.

Hurrying back to Little Beaudy, he knew in his coward's heart, more than anything, he needed a drink.

Grappa struggled up Mud Rock. Little Beaudy waited in Hibiscus Bay, as did the dinghy, floating now on the incoming tide. No sign of any creature, not even a bird. He listened for the faint sound of a flute.

'Where are you' – the words poison on his parched tongue – 'Far Dorocha?'

2.

Marlise turned at the flap of wings to see a scraggly bird with a bald patch in the middle of its arched neck peering through the glass, judging her worthiness, giving her the creeps. She slid the door open. 'Shoo.' It flew over the endless mass of mangroves out to sea.

Intoxicated by the view, she stepped onto the verandah. The sun was so low in the sky now, it nestled like an egg in the tops of the trees, yolk dripping into the water. She adored this hour of day, dusk, the swamp mosquitoes' favourite time, and delighted in their frenzied buzz. She listened for the whine of them in the mangroves, wondering if her brood in the insectary were aware of their surroundings yet, so proud of the way they had travelled, arriving full of life. She had fed them on live pathogens before leaving in case something happened to the liquid nitrogen during transit. Looking into the large room transformed into her laboratory, she almost purred with a sense of accomplishment at the neatness. The portable humidified booth, made to order years ago, had survived the move without a scratch. It hummed as it worked to keep the insectary at eighty percent humidity, just how her darlings liked it. The large canister of liquid nitrogen which preserved her live pathogens – thankfully intact – along with the small cupboard hiding her cage of mice, the jars of petri dishes, incubators and tissue culture flasks, the centrifuge and microscope, were all methodically placed, ready for work.

The rest of the house lay in disarray, a life packed in boxes.

Again, the faint bark of a dog destroyed her mood. She had moved to the island for solitude. That dog had irritated her all day. Burrawang had been so isolated, Marlise was unaccustomed to sharing her soundscape with anything foreign. She stormed downstairs and trudged up the dirt road toward the barks, fighting an overwhelming fatigue.

The shadows were long in the uncanny light. Riley should have been back by now. Marlise had yet to ascertain what type of people lived here.

'Could be full of all sorts of weirdos,' she whispered, arriving at a junction with a bitumen road to the right and a beach to the left. The street sign said Long Street. She was about to walk the beach to search for Riley when the dog barked again.

In Long Street, two faded fibro cottages sat side by side separated by a chain-link fence. An old cattle dog in the front yard of the first one growled at her.

She approached, hissing. 'Shut-up. Stop that barking. It's got to stop.'

The pungent doggy odour hit her as she became aware of a thin figure of a man behind the screen door of the house. She forced her friendliest voice, 'Does it always bark?' Even though night was falling, the man was wearing dark sunglasses. She could feel him watching her. 'I've heard a dog barking all day. I...I was just wondering if it was this dog?'

'Hardly barks at all.'

A torn plastic blind in the neighbour's house moved. Someone was watching. 'Sorry...my mistake.' Throwing her hands up in apology, she backed away.

At the start of the dirt road, she heard Riley approaching from the beach. Once again, she was surprised by the sight of him; her baby boy had grown into a broad-shouldered handsome man so like his father, it took her into buried memories.

He spotted her and stopped playing, slipping the flute into his back pocket.

'Don't wander off again until we know what kind of people live here.'

The look he flashed hushed her. She saw his fists clench. He hated it when she treated him like a child. She wondered, not for the first time, if he would ever hit her. His temper lately had been frightening.

Falling into step with him, they walked along the dirt road towards their new house. She watched him from the corner of her eye. Poor baby. He was miserable. Maybe she had made a mistake bringing them here to start again. But David had kept reminding her Riley would be twenty-one soon, that it was time for her to let go, that he needed to get out into the world and meet friends his own age. At least here, there was a chance that could happen.

'So, what do you think?' She made her voice sound bright.

'Of what?'

'The island? Did you look around?'

The old wooden house loomed in front of them, hanging askew over the gloomy swamp. 'I miss Burrawang.'

'It's not Burrawang you miss.'

He looked at her as the words hovered, suspended. Even here on new ground, the unspoken fact that David was dead still saturated each shared moment.

Unable to hold his accusing gaze, she glanced toward the house, wishing the stink from the mangrove mud wasn't so invasive. 'You'll get used to it.'

'Truth is, Mum, I don't have to.' He went inside, not bothering to hold the screen door so it slammed in her face.

Always this threat that he would leave. A hot flush unleashed itself as she leant against the door frame. Surely she was too young for menopause? She heard him thumping up the internal staircase as if climbing to his doom. The harder she tried to hold him, the further he slipped away.

The urge to jam the sharp wooden flute into her eye-socket terrified Riley. Whenever she made reference to David being dead, he wanted to hurt her. What was happening to him? He had read that a stage of grief was anger, but this was an uncontrollable rage taking hold. He could feel it gaining strength. The only place he found relief was in his music. But at what cost? He had seen proof now that he could touch people through his music. By pouring his pain into his flute playing, the other day he had reduced that old woman in the park to tears, and that drunk had screamed at him to stop. Riley had done it on purpose. The memory that he had played wanting to inflict his pain on others, so all those smiling people idling in the park would feel as bad as he, doused him with shame.

Riley drooped through the queer house with the slanting walls, depressed at the extent of the unpacking that remained. Even the kitchen was still full of sealed boxes. Typically, his mother's laboratory had taken precedence, and she had chosen the large front room that opened onto the verandah. He had pleaded with her to make her workspace at the back of the house in a less public location. She had only laughed, 'What I'm doing is totally legal. I'm a practising entomologist. You're such a worry wart.'

But he knew from her whispered arguments with David that an aspect of her research was not legal. He suspected it had something to do with the mice she bred for experiments, hidden away in that stinky cupboard. On hot days, he predicted, the pissy rodent smell would permeate the whole house.

Walking down the uneven hallway, he realised it was the house itself that was oppressive. A heaviness seeped from the unpainted weatherboards.

He missed the airy tree house he had built with David at Burrawang, missed the moist earthy smells of the rainforest and the customary crack of whipbirds. When David had told him the whipbird's call was created by two birds, Riley had spent years listening for the lone unanswered whipbird, but it never happened. David was right. There were always two.

Riley stared into the ugliness of the green-tiled bathroom and remembered how hysterical she had been when he attempted to leave, how she had begged, 'Please? Things will be better there. You'll see. All we need is a change.' But nothing would change. Nothing would bring David back. Nothing would alter the fact that he and his mother were stuck with each other like a pair of strange whipbirds who didn't belong with other birds. Why on earth had they moved to a small island full of people? The pit of his stomach contracted. Something terrible could happen here if they weren't careful.

He stepped into the room he had chosen for himself, the one furthest from the smell of the swamp where the morning light would flood in, and opened a cardboard box containing his flutes. He arranged them on the shelf that ran the length of the space, and came across the first flute he had made, with David's help, of course. Twirling it in his hands, smiling at its crudity, he missed the man who had been a father to him, who had showed him the possibility of surviving in the world on his own, who had secretly helped him earn money.

The money. Where was it?

He scrambled through the box until he found the flute case lying at the bottom. He lifted the lining and counted the stash. Still all there. His mother hadn't found it.

Something shattered over the kitchen floor. She was exhausted. Riley felt a pang of guilt for all he had done to her today. She had deserved it though, insisting she leave her car on the mainland. It meant they were forced to ride in the cabin of the removalist truck with those awful men. As a form of punishment, instead of climbing into the front beside her, Riley had asked if he could jump over the back to lie in the sleeping compartment, feigning tiredness.

'Go for it mate, we'll take care of your mother, won't we Rick?'

'Too right we will.' Rick had patted his mother's leg before driving the big lorry with their life's possessions onto the barge.

She would have hated being stuck alone in that small space with those two men who kept ogling her. David had always said she was too beautiful for this world and Riley had noticed the way certain men stared. He shouldn't have left her alone with them. He couldn't understand what made him do things to purposely annoy her.

It was the way she had spoken to him later though, when they were unloading, addressing him like a precious child, causing the men to snigger under their baseball caps, that had embarrassed him so he had stormed off. What angered him most was that she gave him no choice, crowding him until he was forced to escape in order to breathe, in order to not smash his fist into a wall.

The sound of her sweeping up shards of porcelain caused him to sigh as he stood and readied himself.

When Riley entered the room, Marlise made an effort not to look up. 'Don't fuss. You suffocate him.' She could still recall David's intonation.

He was searching for something to eat.

'There's a can of baked beans and a loaf of bread. That's about it. I'll go across and get groceries in the morning. You eat. I'm not hungry.'

'You're never hungry.'

True, she seldom had an appetite, but why say it like an insult? She watched him slice the bread and felt a wave of weariness. 'I need to lie down.'

'Mum?' He was struggling to find the right words.

'Yes?'

'Doesn't matter.'

Marlise waited in hope, but the silence became stifling. 'I miss him too you know.'

His face softened as he moved to hug her. 'I'm sorry.'

Such a good boy. She wanted to hold him forever, but he pulled away and resumed buttering his bread. She ran her fingers through his hair – still as soft as the day he was born – before heading for her bedroom.

Sitting on the bare mattress, she reached for the closest box, wondering what memories lurked inside waiting to be exposed. The packing had been rushed, done by the removalist company. Marlise had barked orders to throw everything into boxes, deciding to sort through their lives when she arrived at the other end. At Burrawang, the imperative had been to escape David. He was everywhere there. Even when she opened the fridge, he was there in the contents, in the worn embroidery on his favourite chair where he had sat every morning to read, the smell of him on the sheets which she had washed and washed, and thrown out in the end.

She ripped the packing tape off the box, then paused, looking around the room. Something important was missing. The beat of her blood intensified. Her old metal chest.

Marlise stood too quickly, legs almost buckling. She had instructed the removalists to carry it in here. Had they mistakenly placed it in Riley's room? Her stomach rolled over as she darted across the hallway.

No sign of it.

She switched on the living room light and saw the chest sitting benign against the wall, as if it didn't contain anything that could harden Riley's heart against her, as if it didn't contain a lifetime of lies. She tried to lift it. It was too heavy. She tried to pull it along the floor towards her room. It wouldn't budge. To move it, she would need to unpack it. Curse those removalist men with their leering smiles. The latch was rusted together and had folded in on itself where the lid of the chest had buckled during transit. To open it, she would need a file that could cut through metal.

Why would Riley bother? It was of no interest to him. She allowed herself to breathe again, calling out, 'leave the unpacking, we'll tackle it tomorrow.'

'Uh huh,' he managed through a mouth full of food.

Marlise returned to her room. This was what frightened her most about moving. It meant disturbing layers of dust and memories, exposing artefacts hidden away safely for years. With the need to rearrange their lives, the risk of unwanted discoveries surfaced.

Her priority in the morning would be to buy a file. Then she could rid that chest of what was lying buried at the bottom. If Riley unearthed it, the web of deceit she had carefully woven around him, cocooning him from the truth, would be torn apart, ripping his heart open, too wide for forgiveness.

The cardboard box beside her bed was full of clothes she hadn't worn in a decade. Burrawang had been so private and humid, Marlise had spent twelve years lolling around in sarongs. She pulled out a skimpy crocheted swimsuit and laughed.

Probably too old for that now.

At the side of the box, her hand slithered into something cool and silky. The black halter-neck dress David had bought her the weekend he had taken them to Port Douglas. A replica of the famous white garment lifted by the wind when Marilyn Monroe stood over a subway grate. Marlise remembered the way David looked at her when she put it on. 'Maybe we shouldn't go to dinner.' He had joked. 'Stay here and order room service instead, in case some young buck tries to steal you away.'

She pressed the dress into her eyes. It hadn't mattered that David had been fifteen years older. His desire for her had been immeasurable. Such a generous lover, she hadn't felt the need to stray. Why had he never been convinced of this? She was sure that was why he agreed for them to live so alone and cut off, even though he worried about the effects such isolation would have on Riley. She ran the satin material down her throat, pretending it was David touching her. Her loving David who had embraced her son, becoming the father Riley needed. Their life together had been ideal. Until the end. She could never forgive him for supporting Riley in his increasing desire to venture out and explore the world, undermining her authority, continually taking the boy's side, making her feel left out, or worse, like the big bad mother.

Her knuckles had turned white from clutching the dress so hard. Best not to think of David, too much pain lurked there ready to knock her sideways.

She dropped the dress and opened the large window to stare into the endless twist and turn of the mangroves, their pale lichen-covered trunks rising from the black mud alive with things breathing, bubbling, popping. The sharp putrid tang of it cleared her head. She could feel the pull on her weary body of a full moon rising, somewhere.

The sky was bleeding pink. 'Like watered down blood,' she murmured and wondered at the beauty of the world as mosquitoes swarmed toward the window. They could smell her. She pressed her face against the screen. 'Starving. You poor darlings.'

In the distance, a dog barked again.

3.

Ayla stood at her window, naked, watching the dawn fog twisting around the paperbarks; a mythical creature silently stealing toward the house. She longed for this time of year when the fog came in across the sea, so thick the ferry couldn't run until the heat of the sun lifted it. She watched the mist hovering in the trees, waiting for something to happen. But nothing would happen. This was the island. Nothing ever happened. She was curious as to what it would feel like on her bare skin.

What the hell.

She tiptoed down the hallway past her mother's soft snores, smiling at herself. Is this what her life had become, cheap thrills by streaking naked in the fog at dawn? In the kitchen, the half-finished painting made her pause. Her mother had added a tiny fishing trawler on the watery horizon. The familiar hard-boiled egg of grief slid up to stick in her throat. Why couldn't she paint something else?

Her mother's last painting was desperate: two men clinging to an upturned hull as waves engulfed it. She saw her fourteen-year-old self with Mandy before the cruel hand of death stroked them, marking them for life. They were coming home from school on the ferry, giggling hysterically over the day's events, when half way across the strait they became aware of distress in the air and surreptitious stares. Ayla leant across the aisle. 'What's happened, Mrs Parker?'

Mrs Parker burst into tears as the boat slowed to tie up. Their mothers were standing at the end of the jetty, grasping onto one another as if trying to find the strength to face their daughters. The girls knew immediately. Something had happened to their fathers.

Ayla tore her gaze from the painting to halt the memory and snapped the back-door lock, almost breaking it. Her mother really needed to move on.

She ran down the stairs and along the sandy track through the paperbarks, the crisp air turning her skin to goose flesh. The sensation made her think of the flute player, his face turned toward the sky as if paying homage.

The fog became so thick, she inched her way along, the dewy smell of eucalypt, intoxicating. She crossed through the goat's foot, its soft leaves tickling her feet, then the line of jumbled sea wrack — seaweed, sticks and pumice — until her toes sank into the softer sand. All around was whiteness, permeated by the loud breaking of waves. She couldn't see her outstretched hands, lost in a cloud, spinning, dancing in it, making a silly deal with herself — once I touch the water, I'll turn back.

Riley lay in bed listening to the mosquitoes working themselves into a frenzy, wired to get through the net and suck his blood. Awake all night, spooked by the continual creaks of the house, he now watched a purple sky fading into day and questioned if his mother was capable of change. Or would he be forced to leave, to prove to her he could survive on his own? If he left, she would be devastated, but surely she would cope? She had her precious mosquitoes, her obsession to the point of madness.

Grabbing a flute, Riley scrawled a note to his mother to avoid the search helicopter — she had done that once — and raced out of the house toward the beach, running to escape the swarm of mosquitoes that followed him from the swamp and the grief that followed him everywhere.

He sat in the dawn on the wet sand watching the fog drift over the water, eerie and silent. Too silent to disturb with music. What was this exotic place his mother had brought him to? The living creature of mist curled toward the island, filling him with awe.

In his idleness, the mosquitoes swarmed, the empty landscape making him their only meal. He ran towards the giant cliff looming at the end of the bay, wondering if the fog would be rolling in on the exposed beach he had discovered yesterday, where the waves crashed in. The tide was low enough that he was able to skirt the front of the headland, and there it was, the impenetrable whiteness devouring the surf. His run slowed to a walk until the mist engulfed him. Unable to see, he sat on the damp sand and waited, feeling lonelier than he had ever felt on Burrawang, trapped on a deserted island in the middle of a fallen cloud.

He heard the soft laugh of a woman. Or had he imagined it?

Eyes straining through the cotton wool curtain, he was greeted only with the repetitive folding of waves on the shore.

There it was again. Someone was laughing at him.

Maybe he should play a trill, echoing her laughter back? He pulled his flute from his pocket and placed it against his lips. The curtain of mist parted to reveal a naked woman, a mermaid washed in on the tide who had grown perfect legs, testing her new limbs by twirling in a cloud. It swallowed her up.

A mermaid? Was he going insane? Longing to see her again, he blew a ripple and heard her gasp. She was no apparition. He played another.

Nothing.

He had learnt he could affect people through his flute, but could he control the elements? He walked blind towards where he thought she was, breathing a melody from the depths of his soul, a song for clarity, calling the wind to lift the fog.

Ayla's body went cold when she heard the enticing voice of his flute piercing the air.

She spun, disoriented by the sound, straining to see through the misty blanket, losing all sense of direction.

Where the hell was the track?

The melody was closing in. Through the drifting fog, she glimpsed a tall ragged shadow. The angophora; its sunburnt skin hanging in strips around the 'No Trespassers' sign. Stumbling blind, hands held out, she fled.

The mist suspended in the paperbarks hadn't yet drifted into the yard. The white Silkie hen stared through the chicken wire, head cocked to one side, perplexed. Grabbing a sarong off the washing line, Ayla fell up the rickety stairs into her bedroom. She hid at the corner of her window to spy and listen and catch her breath.

A playful breeze danced in, lifting the fog as the heat of the rising sun hit the earth. She straightened up. Grappa's Far Dorocha explanation was becoming irritating.

She found her mother in the laundry, ironing a blouse for work.

'Grappa's black-haired man – what was Nana Nettie's version?'

Her mother gave her customary snort of disgust whenever one of Grappa's stories was mentioned. 'Why bring that up?'

'Just wondering...what was Nana's take?'

'Nothing like your grandpa's.' She turned the blouse over.

'What, then?'

Her mother held up the iron. 'Those days, the island was lucky to have fifty residents, so someone new always made a stir. This stranger turned up who happened to be an amazing dancer, and Mum loved to dance. You remind me of her when you dance. There's an idea – you could study dance if you don't want to go back to veterinary –'

'So, what…Nana danced with this guy and that was enough for Grappa to call him Far Dorocha?'

'Dad can't put one foot in front of the other. Mum claims he felt threatened and proceeded to get drunk, so drunk she went home in disgust. She said he got that drunk he blacked out and couldn't remember a thing. God knows where and how he spent the night. When he arrived home the next morning, he was raving about this Far Dorocha'. She resumed ironing. 'And he's still raving. Why you insist on indulging him, I'll never understand. The more people take him seriously, the more he keeps it up. I know the islanders love to egg him on to entertain themselves at his expense, but I don't get why you do it.'

Ayla shrugged. She didn't know either.

Walking onto the back deck, she caught herself listening for a flute, and wondered if she didn't want to grow up. Is that why she hadn't handled life in the city? Not mature enough yet? She remembered feeling nothing as she grew accustomed to watching friends off their face on drugs and stumbling drunk. She had slowly become a numb observer, detached and alone.

A gust of wind brought with it a memory of the first time she had seen a storm blow in from the open sea. Her Dad had buried her in sand up to her neck, and her Mum, lying on the towel beside them in a red bikini watching the horizon, observed. 'Big storm gathering out there.'

'Just a squall,' her father had said, too busy patting the sand around Ayla's protruding head to look up. 'See if you can move, Aylee.'

Surprised at the strength of the sand cementing her in place, she could only wiggle her fingers and toes.

'That's more than a squall.' Her mother, half up on elbows, poised.

Her Dad's pale blue eyes, as he studied the direction of the clouds, and the loudness of his voice were still vivid in Ayla's memory. 'Help me dig her out.'

She remembered their hands scrambled, scratching the sides of her five-year-old body as the wind hit the land and the sand became needles in her eyes, blinding her. The terror of being trapped as they tried to pull her up while the earth sucked her down, until her father's strong arms wrenched her to the warmth of his chest. Like all precious memories of her Dad, Ayla had replayed the sequence so often, she questioned how much of it was real and how much was embellishment by grief's only cure: time.

Riley gazed along the abandoned beach. The fog had dissolved and a breeze blew the last of it away along with any persistent mosquito. Nothing but footprints in the sand. He followed them to a track. Tacked on a tree was an old sign: *Private Property. No Trespassers, please.* Someone had painted a smiley face after the 'please'. Not wanting to trespass, he found a boulder to sit on and watched the trail. As the sun rose, people began to walk on the beach: a middle-aged couple, a pimply teenage boy with a greyhound.

He lay down on the sand with his head against the rock and fell asleep.

The whinny of a regal white horse carrying an elderly lady in a straw hat woke him. '*Buon giorno,*' she called out.

He waved, feeling sunburnt and hungry in a foreign land.

After examining the footprints in case his naked mermaid had returned while he slept, he headed home, turning to look back at the track until he could see it no more.

Maybe it won't be that bad living here after all, he thought. A smile stuck in his throat.

4.

Grappa slept in, missing his usual dawn walk because he'd stayed up crabbing most of the night. Once he'd seen the size of the king tide dragged in by the fat orange moon, turning the water mercury, he knew it'd be a perfect night for crabs. To his disgust, every pot had come up empty.

Holy Jesus, another sign.

He rowed into Hibiscus and set off to ask the ferrymen if they'd seen a black-haired stranger catch the boat over. They'd seen nothing, but the bargemen might've.

When he reached the barge ramp, it was mid-morning. The mass of Blue Blubber jellies washed up on Three Mile, turning rancid in the sun, disturbed him. Something was wrong in the order of the universe.

The one car waiting to be loaded was Henry Pickler's. Henry had been trying for years, without success, to design a bicycle that could become a boat, then transform back into a bicycle when on land. Grappa told him he was mad, so Henry had called Grappa an arrogant bastard.

A few walk-on passengers waited. Poor McClelland's missus with her tribe of children and a little tucker riding her hip. The only other person was by herself. A striking looking woman Grappa had never seen before: thick black hair framing dark eyes too big for her face, pale skin untouched by the sun, as if she'd lived all her life where only shadows grew.

The bargemen signalled for Henry to reverse on. As he drove past Grappa, they exchanged wary nods. Everyone turned to watch the stranger walk on. There was a fragility about her that made all of them stare. The oldest of the McClelland children was so busy gawking as he ran past, he slipped. The crunch of the child's elbows on the metal ramp was loud enough to make Grappa cringe from where he stood on the shoreline. But the woman merely glanced at the screaming child and kept walking. Other adults ran to the bleeding child's assistance as the stranger sat down on a bench, smiling. Was she taking delight in the distraught child? The idea made Grappa shiver. As if sensing him, she turned and stared with those black eyes, forcing him to look away.

He signalled to the barge boys. They sauntered toward him and hung over the boat rail, rolling cigarettes for their next smoko. The smell of fresh tobacco washed over him with their hushed conversation. They were joking about who'd be the first to get into her pants, glancing back at her, trying to guess the woman's age. She wasn't young, that was certain, but she wasn't what you'd call old either. The barge boys knew all about her, as was the island way.

'Filthy rich widow – bought the old Johnston place on the swamp.'

'Probably a bit old for me, but who gives a shit – check out the tits on her.'

'Ranga, you got no idea, mate. Older women know what they want and how they want it. Sexiest thing I've delivered to the island in a long time.'

'Wouldn't go near her if I was you, boys.'

They both looked at Grappa who had been in this world long enough to have earned their respect. He knew the best spots for fish and crabs and could pick the weather and a person's character.

'Why's that?' snorted Grunter.

'A feeling I got.'

'Reckon she's got a dick?' Ranga blurted, and Grunter guffawed.

'You boys see a black-haired man carrying a flute or something catch the barge across in the last few days?'

'Nothin' but locals.'

Grunter pointed to the woman. 'Me wet dream came over yesterday in a removal truck. Two removalist guys with her, but they left on the three o'clock.'

The barge driver up in the tower blasted the horn.

'Alright, already.' Ranga yelled and signalled the driver to lift the ramp.

'Bloody Macka. Any excuse to play with his horn.' Grunter winked as the barge reversed away from the beach.

Grappa looked at his bare feet in the sand. Bright blue suicidal jellyfish decorated the shoreline for as far as he could see. He had a bad feeling in the ends of his toes. None of the boat boys had seen the stranger arrive. This confirmed it. Holy Mary. Far Dorocha had returned, coming via supernatural means during the storm yesterday, bringing that strange light from another realm.

He pulled his flask from his pocket and took a swig. The whisky burn soothing on the back of his throat. The barge with that woman on board swung round and chugged toward the mainland. Her amusement at the child's pain had sickened him.

Maybe she was smiling for another reason? You can't read a woman's mind, silly old fool, he reprimanded himself as he headed up the beach, negotiating the intricate maze of blubbery jellies putrefying in the sun.

Marlise refused to let the banality of the shopping centre destroy her mood. She was so proud of herself, she couldn't stop smiling. On finding Riley's scrawled note in the kitchen this morning – 'Gone for walk' – she had resisted the urge to search for him. Instead, she too had written a note: 'Grocery shopping.' She hadn't waited until he arrived home to fuss over him, trusting him to return safely of his own accord. This is what she needed to do to keep him from leaving, she kept reminding herself.

Gliding down the aisles of the supermarket with a newly-purchased metal file tucked in her handbag, she became subdued by the variety of choice on the crammed shelves, randomly selecting things they might need and cringing when she remembered Riley's exasperation with her after her last grocery trip.

'Mum, why did you buy five jars of pickled anchovies?'

David had always done the shopping because David had always done the cooking. With each new aisle, full of too many choices, she cursed herself for relying so heavily on him for all those years. The supermarket was a labyrinth, every aisle seemed increasingly complex and more protracted than the next. But she could endure it, feeling refreshed and vigorous today. Once that damn dog was finally silent, she had slept long and deep.

Appalled at the aisle devoted to lollies and chocolate, she wilted in the next at the sight of acres of canned food, stocking up on a selection to ensure she wouldn't need to return too soon. She loathed shopping centres because they were crammed with people. People confused her. She found them difficult to read and always said something inappropriate, upsetting and offending and never understood why. It was easier to avoid contact. This shopping centre was full of gargantuan women with oafish children and hoary pensioners wanting to gnaw on trivialities. She encountered one waiting in line at the checkout.

'My granddaughter is pregnant with twins.' The geriatric beamed.

Marlise nodded politely, feigning interest in the magazine rack.

'Through IVF. I don't know what's wrong with young people today. In my time, we fell pregnant at the drop of a hat.'

Realising there was no escape, Marlise espoused her theory. 'Maybe the decline in the fertility rate is the planet's way of coping with the fact that there are too many humans in existence. We're the most destructive species that ever lived. The world would be a better place if we all died off.'

The crinkled slits for eyes widened in shock.

Uncertain how to react, Marlise unpacked her trolley. She hadn't meant to offend but was gratified to hear the old biddy harrumph off to another checkout. There was something about the papery skin on the back of her hands that reminded Marlise of her mother. A vision of the last time she had seen her mother overpowered her in the bright lights and piped muzak, forcing her to clutch the trolley. Her drunk mother, dried out and aged before her time, staggering up the road behind the taxi, shrieking like a banshee, one futile fist raised in the air.

This memory so affected Marlise, when she drove to the barge office with her car full of groceries, only to discover the barge was fully booked, she burst into tears.

The myopic girl behind the counter didn't know where to look, her concern magnified by thick glasses. 'There's vehicle space on the next barge after lunch, if you're willing to wait two hours?'

Unable to speak, Marlise raced to her car, scrambled into the driver's seat and hid under her sunglasses. She tuned the radio until a voice announced, 'Mozart's Requiem in D Minor'. Usually she couldn't tolerate any form of music, particularly in Riley's presence, but in this instance the sound of all those human voices harmonising calmed her.

She reversed to unload her shopping. The waiting walk-on passengers, all silently watching her, clutched wheeled upright trolleys which carried their goods. She made a mental note to buy herself one. Forced to leave her purchases exposed by the side of the road for all to examine, she drove to the long-term car park.

The barge was already at the ramp when she arrived back and the lucky pre-booked vehicles were driving on. As she struggled to pick up her groceries, the red-faced bargeman came to her aid. 'One of the downsides of living on the island', he grunted, taking most of the bags, leaving her looking stupid carrying one.

'Me name's Stewart by the way. Feel free to call me Grunter. Everyone else does.' He placed her shopping on a bench at the side of the boat.

'Thank you.'

'Happy to hold your bags anytime.' He winked, then weaved through the cars to the opposite side of the boat where a group of locals gathered on the only other seat. Between the cars, she spied them sneaking glances. Were they discussing her?

As the barge pulled out, they yelled and waved at the driver in the tower. The boat ground to a stop with the ramp part way up. A thin man wearing sunglasses, torn jeans, and a black t-shirt leapt onto the ramp. He slipped as he landed, his long greasy hair flying out like rope. In unison, the group ran forward, wrenching him to safety. The gracefulness of their coordinated movement struck her. Like mosquitoes when they swarm, she thought.

Marlise stared at sunglass man, almost certain it was the dog owner. She couldn't remember the hideous scar running down his right cheek, but he had been standing behind a screen door in the dark. Wanting a clearer look, she pushed her sunglasses to the top of her head in the hope he would do the same. Grunter moved toward her and she handed him her money.

'Thanks, Marlise.' He appeared to enjoy the shock on her face.

'You know my name.'

'You bought the old Johnston place. Everyone knows who you are. Everyone, this is Marlise.'

To her dismay, the group of locals had followed him over. They began to introduce themselves. Only sunglass man remained seated on the other side of the boat. She couldn't see his eyes but swallowed when she suspected he was staring at her.

By the time they reached the island, she had four offers of a lift and the promise of home grown pumpkin. Tilly the real estate agent, whom Marlise had bought the house through, was dropping someone at the barge ramp. She called out, 'Need a lift, love?'

'That would be great.' Marlise turned to Bob who was waiting in his ute. 'Actually, I'll go with Tilly. Thanks anyway.'

They all welcomed her to the island again and joked with each other as they parted. Unused to people en masse, the general camaraderie made Marlise so uncomfortable, she had a silly smile frozen on her face.

Grunter had to wake sunglass man, who walked gingerly off the barge as if it was an effort to place one foot in front of the other.

Tilly called, 'Want a lift Harley? Going right past your place... Harl?'

'Hey?'

'Need a lift?' Tilly closed the boot on Marlise's shopping.

'Yeah thanks, man, if it's not too much trouble.'

Marlise was already in the passenger seat when Harley slid in behind her. A sharp mixture of dog and body odour filled her nostrils. She wished now she had gone with Bob.

Tilly squashed the butt of a cigarette and lit another before starting the car. 'Harley, this is Marlise. You guys are almost neighbours. Harl? You awake back there?'

'Hey?'

Tilly gave up. 'How you settling in, Marlise? Tell me if there's anything you need or want. "Fix it", is my middle name.'

'I love the house, the view over the mangroves. And from initial observations, the mosquito population looks vibrant.'

'Vibrant? One way to put it.' Tilly laughed so hard she started to cough.

In the side mirror, Marlise watched the dog owner, his sunglasses too dark to decipher if he was asleep or staring. Tilly was asking if she wanted a regular gardener or cleaner.

'A cleaner would be handy. I hate housework.'

'I'll send her along next Friday then, love. See how she goes.'

David had always done the housework and now David's money would pay for a cleaner. Bless his soul. She turned her face toward the window, horrified by the sudden lack of control. When would these stupid tears end? Marlise noticed his sunglasses in the mirror again. Was he watching her? She felt like she couldn't breathe and wound down the window as Tilly pulled up in front of the fibro cottage with the dog lying on its side in the yard.

'There you go, Harl.'

'Thanks, Till. Shit.'

'What?'

'Jip. Wasn't himself this morning when I left. Now look.' He slammed the car door too hard and raced to the dog who wagged its tail but didn't lift its head.

'Hope he's okay. Harley would be lost without Jip.' Tilly drove off puffing smoke as Marlise glanced back at the prone dog. She caught Tilly watching her and saw pity settle in the large woman's face. 'I know you're still in a state of grief, but I won't take no for an answer. You're coming down to the Resort tonight to meet the girls.'

'There's a resort?'

'Sounds fancier than it is. Just a restaurant and bar, few units attached, but it's the only place to go on a Friday night. 'Fact, it's the only place to go any night. Us locals lovingly refer to it as "the last resort."' She stopped in Marlise's driveway. 'But don't let that put you off. I'll come back on dark and pick you up. How does that sound?'

'Thank you but I'm not up for socialising. I was awake half the –'

'It's Friday, love. You've got the rest of the week to sleep. Told you, won't take no for an answer. Everyone's dying to meet you. See you tonight.' She drove off, leaving the vile smell of her cigarette lingering in the air.

Ayla searched the cloudless sky for the moon as she pulled the trolley of cleaning equipment along the dirt road. Grappa called days where the sun and moon shared the sky 'sun moon days'. He claimed, 'Good things happen on a sun moon day.' But the moon was nowhere to be seen. She checked her pocket to ensure the key was there and not left in the door like last time. Only one house cleaned and already her hands were itchy. She couldn't understand – all the products she used were organic, fully bio-degradable. Her Mum, as always, was right, she needed to wear gloves.

Her mother had been appalled at Ayla's decision to defer from veterinary science to become a house cleaner. But the monotonous physical repetition suited Ayla for now. The last year at uni had left her jaded. Her curriculum didn't seem relevant, the ice caps were melting, species were dying out by the minute, and it appeared to Ayla that no one seemed to care; too obsessed with their earning potential, they wanted to party and shop. Ayla knew money was necessary – here she was cleaning houses for money – but surely there was more to life? She had even joined a radical young activist group hoping to discover answers but found their angry meetings pointless in the end.

She listened to the rattle of her trolley as she pulled it along the gravel, remembering the moment she had seen footage of the plastic islands floating in the oceans. How it had unleashed a tsunami of questions within her. Would all the sea be covered in plastic one day? What was the point of studying when the planet was dying? These thoughts weighed her down until she couldn't drag herself out of bed to attend lectures. She had no choice but to come back to the island. On the ferry trip, dolphins had played in the wake of the boat, jumping until she was laughing and wiping tears from her cheeks. She knew then, it had been right to come home.

Ayla parked her trolley in front of the faded sign: 'Tilly Little Real Estate. We Make Big Things Happen.' This was the epicentre of the island. If anyone had a problem, they called Tilly who always knew who was where on the island and what they were doing when. All sales and rentals went through Tilly. No one could come or go without her knowing. The mother hen of the community, she thrived in her position, and even though she perpetuated most of the gossip, her heart was as big as an island.

Ayla heard Tilly on the phone as she entered the small office thick with cigarette smoke.

'She's a recent widow.' Tilly waved her cigarette at Ayla without a pause. 'Yes, I know…a short version of Angelina Jolie, don't you think?…Nice skin. I said that to Wayne. He said, "I didn't notice her skin I was too busy looking at her you-know-whats"…Darlene you're awful…trace of some accent. Can't pick it…Wayne reckons she's American…One thing I do know, she's loaded. Bought the place sight unseen and paid cash…I know…Moved down from up north, huge property that backs onto a national park near the Atherton Tablelands…I searched it on the net – beautiful house… god knows what she sold it for…I know…I said to her, I've got much better properties. That place hangs over the swamp, it's filthy with mosquitoes. "That's exactly what I want", she said…I know…She's an antiologist or something or rather. A mozzie expert.'

'Entomologist,' Ayla offered, embarrassed she had been listening, and placed the key on the desk.

'Entomologist…I know.' Tilly gestured for Ayla to wait. 'Can I call you back, Darl?' She took a quick puff and hung up. 'Harley Mangleson's dog's sick. Would you mind, love? Harley's beside himself. Called me twice in half an hour.'

'Me?'

'Stan's still away caravanning.'

'Just because Stan's away, I'm suddenly the island vet.'

'You're the next closest thing we've got. Told Harley I'd send you down. Would you mind, love? Never heard him so wound up.'

'Of course, I'll have a look, but caring for injured wildlife is one thing, domestic pets is a whole different –'

'Forget number ten Three Mile, that can wait 'til tomorrow if you get caught up. Oh, and I've got some more work for you. Woman that's moved into the old Johnston house wants a regular cleaner every fortnight on a Friday.'

'Sure. I'll have to leave my trolley.'

'I'll give you a lift, love.' She grabbed her car keys and lit another cigarette to smoke on the way.

Ayla had known Harley Mangleson most of her life but had rarely spoken to him, he was that shy. She had never forgotten the time she and Mandy approached Harley's house, selling chocolates for a school fundraiser. The door was wide open with the TV blaring, while Harley, sitting in a chair, slept with his head almost resting on the floor as if someone had folded him in half. He looked so unnatural they thought he was dead, until Mandy noticed he was breathing. Too young to understand the sharps kit on the coffee table, Ayla recalled how Harley's greasy hair stuck to the side of his pale neck like a stick insect.

As they pulled up, Harley was in the front yard bent over Jip. June was with him. June lived next door to Harley with Trev. Trev and June didn't have a last name on the island. They were simply known as Trev and June. At twenty, Trev had been conscripted and sent to Vietnam. He never spoke of it and most of the time the rum and coke held it at bay. When it didn't, June understood, so she stayed. Try as she did, she never quite managed to hide the bruises. Ayla was with a freshly bruised June once on the end of the jetty when she heard the whispering: 'Why doesn't she leave?' June pretended she hadn't heard.

Ayla watched as June tugged her cardigan tighter, waved, and hurried toward her house, letting her hair drop over the side of her face.

'Leave you to it. Got to meet a potential buyer off the next barge. Don't know why I bother. They come, they look, but they never buy. Still, one lives in hope.' Tilly attempted to laugh but it turned into a coughing fit.

'You should really stop smoking, Till.'

'Tried to once, almost killed me.' Smoke trailed from the window with a wave of her hand as she drove off.

Harley was on his knees with his head against Jip's chest, listening to his heart. Jip was his heart.

'Thanks for comin', man. Sorry to put you out.'

'Not at all. Just hope I can help.'

'He can't stand for long and when he does he's all unco.'

The dog was listless and didn't respond to her voice or touch.

'Hurts to even lift his head, and check this out.' Harley pointed to a circular welt on Jip's underbelly where the skin was naturally free of hair. 'What the hell's that?'

Ayla examined the perfectly round mark, the skin inside the circle full of lumps. 'Maybe some kind of allergic reaction?' She pulled her phone from her pocket and searched: *round lumpy welt dog's underbelly*, to no avail. She searched Jip's other symptoms, but the possibilities were endless. She felt Jip's nose again. The poor dog had a fever. 'Has he been off his food or lethargic?'

'Nup. Good as gold. I was down volunteerin' at the youth hut most of yesterday. When I come home, he seemed fine. Noticed this mornin' before I went to the mainland...' Harley paused and stole a glance at Ayla. It was common island knowledge that each morning Harley went to the Rocky Point Pharmacy to swallow a paper cup of methadone, his legally prescribed amount, in front of the chemist. 'He was actin' like he'd had a rough night or somethin'. Kept pressin' the top of his head against the fence post. Thought he might have a tick. Didn't find nothin'. When I got back, he was like this. Yesterday he ate all his dinner. Happened overnight, man.'

'Has he eaten anything different to what he normally eats?'

'Nup, unless someone threw somethin' over the fence.' Harley's forehead creased. 'Woman that moved into the old Johnston house complained he was barkin' too much. Maybe she...? Fuck...' He rubbed his temple.

A spasm racked Jip's body.

'Has he vomited?'

'Nup.'

'Then it's not a bait. Looks viral, with the temperature. We need to take him to the mainland, to a vet.' There was a long pause. 'Harley?' A tear rolled from under his sunglasses.

'No money.' He said it so fast, she almost didn't catch it.

'I could lend you –'

'Nup.'

Jip struggled to his feet, gave up and pressed the top of his head into the earth instead, whining. 'Wish Stan was back. We really need to get him to a vet.'

Harley stood up. 'Just caught a bad head cold or somethin'. Not a spring chicken no more. He'll pull through.' He folded his arms, unfolded, then folded them again.

She thought for a minute. 'Where's Jip's favourite spot on the island?'

'Hibiscus, man. Loves that beach.'

'Let's get him there. Might cheer him up, at least.'

Harley brightened, handing her Jip's water bowl. He took a towel and wrapped it around Jip, picking him up with such care, Ayla's heart went out to Harley for all the possibilities a different life would have allowed.

He carried Jip the short distance to the beach and laid him under a large scribbly gum. The markings on the trunk like drawings of a mad man, strangely echoed Jip's incessant whine.

Harley soothed him. 'Come on, man. Don't want to miss your next Whale Welcoming Day. Whole island's counting on you.'

Ayla remembered the year Jip became famous for riding at the head of the gigantic whale float which led the annual parade around the island each Whale Welcoming Day. Everyone on the island was expected to take part in the parade and Harley had been allocated to old Bob Morgan, whose ute was transformed into the whale float, obscuring Bob's visibility. Harley's job was to lie on the hood of Bob's ute, hidden under the fibreglass whale, and call out for Bob to stop or turn as required. Jip, who always wanted to be where Harley was, unbeknown to Bob or Harley, climbed on top of the whale above Harley's head and sat there utterly still, leading the parade. The following year Bob placed an old sailor's hat on the dog and Jip became the official Whale Welcoming mascot.

Harley sat with Jip and Ayla on the beach but kept nodding off. He shook himself awake, cursing under his breath. 'If you need to lie down for a bit Harley, I'll sit with him until you get back.'

The unspoken acknowledgement of his drugged state lay thick in the air between them.

'Nah, can't leave him like this, man.'

Ayla stared at the angry scar running from the top of Harley's cheek bone to the corner of his mouth.

'Ex-girlfriend pushed me through a glass door.' Harley said, in answer to her stare. 'Don't ever deal with anyone in a psychotic state, man. Their psychosis gives them the strength of ten men.' Harley almost nodded off again, then scratched his arm. 'Just popping home. Back in a tick. Sorry.'

'It's fine, Harley. Why don't you ring a few vets? Just ask about the price?'

Ayla couldn't see his eyes for sunglasses. She wasn't sure if anyone had seen Harley Mangleson's eyes, but everyone had seen his shame. She could feel it now, pouring out of him as he shuffled away, arms crossed, fingers tucked under his armpits.

At the end of the beach, Mandy's grandmother, Aunty Dora, was gathering morning glory off a Bribie Island pine. Since retiring from nursing, she weaved baskets out of weeds to supplement her pension, selling them through the tourist gift shop at the resort. Dora had accepted that she couldn't rid the native landscape of exotics. They were here to stay, and some of them were quite useful, like her asparagus which popped up in the same spot every year to feed her. But Ayla knew, for Aunty Dora, it was about balance. That's why she worked every day to help keep the weeds under control and give the native flora a fighting chance.

She approached, arms full vines. 'What's up with Jip?'

'Not sure.'

'Don't look too good. Hey, you heard from Mandy?'

'Not for a while.'

'Her Mum's dirty on her for not ringing.' Dora giggled. 'Mandy's too busy uptown with her new mates, living the high life. Good for her, I reckon. Get off the island, live a bit. What are you doing back here, girl? Should be out there strutting your stuff. Only young once.'

'There's something wrong with me, Aunty. Missed the island too much.'

'The island will always be here. Not going anywhere.' Dora shaded her eyes. 'Here comes trouble.'

Grappa walked towards them pulling his hat off out of respect for Dora.

Ayla enjoyed watching Grappa relate to Aunty Dora. He went all puppy eyed and soft around the edges.

'How you going, ladies? That Harley's dog?'

Ayla nodded. 'Not feeling too well. Are you, Jippy?'

Dora squinted at the sun. 'Just finishing your morning walk now? Running late today, old man?' A cheeky smile slid across her face.

Every morning at sunrise Grappa rowed to the island and walked the perimeter like a guard keeping watch. He unofficially thought of himself as the island's official protector. Aunty Dora and Grappa often crossed paths of a morning, collecting rubbish. They had both seen enough of what plastic could do to birds and sea creatures.

Grappa hid his smile. 'Slept in. Awful night's sleep. Moon was too bright.'

'Yeah, big moon last night. Had some bad dreams myself. Hasn't happened in a long while.'

Jip whimpered and rolled onto his back, shaking his head in the sand. 'Poor old feller. Better get him to a vet.' Dora gathered her morning glory. 'Well, this basket isn't going to weave itself.'

'Heard some fancy arse from down Melbourne way's offerin' to pay big money for your baskets.' Grappa fiddled with his hat.

'Yeah. Should make me happy, hey? But I kind of feel ashamed when I think of those poor old Grannies on the mission when I was a kid, sitting there smoking their pipes, weaving the traditional reed baskets all day for nothing but baccy money.' She looked out toward Big Island as if she could see the remnants of the mission with its three-sided tin huts and banana trees, then turned and walked away.

Grappa watched her big hips swaying from side to side. He called to her. 'That moon's gonna be just as bright tonight. Come for dinner?'

Dora waved without looking back, 'Might just do that.'

Ayla smiled at Grappa smiling.

Irritated, he changed the subject. 'Why isn't Harley here?'

'Popped home for a sec. Hopefully ringing a vet.'

'Harley's off his head most of the time. Probably got home and passed out.' Grappa's disgruntled snort reminded Ayla of her mother.

'Want me to sit with Jip? Got stuff to do?'

'Nothing that can't wait.'

Grappa pointed at two large ospreys circling over the water. 'They never come over this side this time of year. That's because of your Far Dorocha. Has he tried it on again?'

Ayla wavered.

'When?' Grappa knew her too well.

'This morning in the fog, I heard him, but I didn't see him.'

'Where?'

'On the beach.'

'On the beach, where?'

'Where our path comes out.'

'So, he knows where you live.'

'Grappa, he's just some tourist –'

'The crabs aren't running, the jellies are suiciding, the birds are jittery.' He watched the dog shudder through laboured breathing. 'Now Jip,' he said, and walked away.

'Where you going?'

'To find out what's happening.'

'The Nor folk?'

He tapped the side of his temple and strode off with purpose, placing his hat firmly on his head.

Ayla's smile broke her face in two remembering herself as a child, lying on one of the Nor Folk Tree's branches, listening to Grappa whisper. 'The only way you'll ever see them is if you believe in them. I saw one once, when I was your age...sittin' at the base of the buttress root there, starin' like he'd been waitin' all his life for me to notice him.'

'What did he look like?'

'Almost human, but they can shape shift into anythin'...a dragon fly, a sparkle of light.'

'Did he?'

'Nup. But he was hard to keep in my vision because he was the same colour as the skin of the tree, like he was part of the tree...'

'What did he say?'

'It was only after, when he'd vanished. I shut my eyes and a voice came into my head...knew straight away it was him, whisperin' in my ear.'

'What did he say?'

Grappa searched her little face. 'He told me...one day I would have a granddaughter called Ayla, that I was to tell her about the Nor folk. He gave strict instructions to pass on all I knew.'

'Why?'

'Because they're the spirit of the land. It's important each new generation remembers to love and respect them, watch for them, listen for their guidance. If they die, then the land dies. If the land dies, we die.'

Ayla caressed Jip as she scanned the water and remembered what it was she had seen that day as she lay in the Moreton Bay fig, looking up through its twisted branches, wallowing in the sweetness of the fermented seed pods rotting on the ground. She had glimpsed a solid flash of gold, a momentary sparkle as big as Grappa's thumbnail. Grappa had convinced her it was one of the Nor folk. For many years she carried that miracle with her as proof there was a shimmering beneath the surface of things. Life beyond life. She knew now it had been a trick of light.

Two orange butterflies fluttered around her head before landing on Jip. Her younger self would have viewed this as a healing gift sent by the Nor folk. She fell into her old habit of pretending. 'Come on, Jippy. Draw on their energy.' Jip's tail wagged.

The butterflies flew off, circling higher and higher, heading west towards the mangroves. 'Come back.'

Jip shuddered uncontrollably. 'Such an idiot, Ayla.' She spat the words through clenched teeth. As if butterflies could help. The faery myth didn't even belong here. It came from the other side of the world. This was dugong dreaming country. Aunty Dora's stories were full of sea creatures, not bloody faeries. Why hadn't she pointed this out to Grappa? Her anger mounted each time Jip's muscles shook. 'Face it Grappa, you're nothing but a –' she tried to think of Mandy's word for white feller. 'Degga. Nothing but a degga, and so am I.' Degga meant 'a stranger.'

Three metres from where she sat, Ayla knew there was a midden. Mandy had revealed to her the shelly layers of remains stuck in the red clay of the earth. In the bush to the right was one of several 'canoe trees' on the island. Ayla stared at the canoe shaped scar left by the men who had prised its bark off in one thick slab. The place was saturated with evidence of an ancient blood line.

We have no right to pretend we have a spiritual link here.

This new thought brought tears as she stroked Jip. If she were a fully qualified vet she would know what to do instead of sitting around like a waste of space. Her mother was right. She was throwing her life away cleaning houses. Cleaning houses on an island where she didn't even belong. She felt so lost and useless as Jip whined in pain, she wanted to scream.

Grappa arrived at the tree sticky and thirsty, stopping at the brook which ran down to the beach to wash his face. It had been months since a good rain, so it was nothing more than a trickle, but still crystal fresh. In all the years, he had never seen it run dry.

'Purest water on the land.'

He looked up. The wind had risen, and the clouds were moving too fast. The she-oaks whispered as the circling Brahminy kite cried out, warning that something dark had disturbed the island's peaceful equilibrium.

Always impressed by this arrangement of trees dominating the skyline – not native to the island, the pines had been planted in a protective circle like guards standing to attention around the ancient fig – he took a deep breath and entered the sacred grove. A private living, breathing room that often smelt of nectar. He knew it was the perfume of the Nor folk, impossible to define and as elusive as their presence. The sand was thin here, only a sprinkling over the hard, grey bones of the earth. Leaning against the knotty trunk, he lowered himself to the ground and spoke his greeting to the aerial roots cascading from the horizontal branches.

'*Dia dhuit.*'

On saying this he often heard Gran's reply, '*Dia is Muire duit.*' She had insisted he always say two things to her in Irish: hello and thank you. After she died, he only ever spoke these sacred words here, to the Nor folk. The strangeness of the language on his tongue felt powerful. In this simple act, he was calling them out from the tree.

'I come with a heart full of love and gratitude. Never a day goes by I'm not aware of your presence.' Captivated by the light dancing in the space, he cleared his throat. 'Think Ayla might be in a spot of trouble. Far Dorocha's returned. Got his eye on her, he has. Tried to get her again this mornin' in the fog. Have no doubts it was him called up that fog. He knows where she lives. What would you advise me to do?'

He pulled his flask from his pocket and toasted the old fig. The hot fire of pure whisky quenching his thirst. Soon, sleep rested his chin on his chest, his snores wafting up through the gnarled limbs, disturbing the hovering Brahminy kite.

His Gran was sitting outside in her old striped-canvas beach chair near the edge of the circle, where the goat's foot petered out, butterflied leaves curling in the sun. Delighted to see her, he ran like a boy onto the sand, dropping to his knees at her feet. The castle he started to build was effortless. Feeling too young and lively, he did a forward roll and fell into the impish sparkle of her eyes as she settled into her chair. He'd forgotten how she'd loved that time-worn chair.

'The poor O'Ryan family, they never lived it down.' The familiar sound of her voice with the soft lilt of her accent was almost unbearable.

'Lived what down, Gran?' he whispered, scared she would evaporate.

'Maeve O'Ryan was a bit odd I always thought.'

He cherished the way she pronounced thought as taught.

'Such a pretty lass. Beware the pretty, pretty ones.'

The woman on the barge came to mind.

'Prettiest in our village everyone claimed, but odd.'

'In what way, odd?'

'When Maeve was a wee one, she went from being a bonny baby to a nightmare of a ting who wouldn't stop bawlin' cryin'. Her Mammy was full sure it wasn't her Maeve. She believed the faeries come and put a changelin' in her place. Because everyone knew, at the bottom of the graveyard behind the church at the end of the village there was a faery mound. Father Kearney hisself was saying he had seen lights there of a night and heard strange music. Come evenin', no one would go near the place. But one dark summer night, so dark even the moon was hidin', Mrs O'Ryan picked up her screamin' baby and carried her to the end of the village and left the poor wee ting at the bottom of the faery mound. Left her there all night. At dawn she returned, and there was her baby Maeve lyin' as quiet as a church mouse.' Gran leant forward in her chair. 'But Maeve O'Ryan grew up to be a queer one, ne'er a kind word for anyone but always a laugh for other's misfortunes. Some even say she caused them. A fine trouble maker. People said it was the time she spent with the faeries. Others claim it was the cause of a mad mother. But my theory is...she was a changelin'. Her eyes were too black. To look in her eyes was like looking into the end of nothin'.'

The wind began to howl and the sky turned an unnatural colour. Grappa saw something moving too fast to be human, charging through the blinding sand towards them. As it closed in, he knew it was the woman from the barge. Her serpentine tresses of hair had grown a life of their own.

'Stop her,' Gran cried, struggling to get out of the chair. Her terror made him jump, blocking the path of the woman who was focused on his Gran.

'What do you want?' His scream a whimper.

He looked in to her eyes and saw the end of nothing as the world was sucked into blackness.

Waking with a start, he was drenched in sweat.

I've got to stop drinkin' in the middle of the day. This thought made him thirsty, but his flask was empty. His body was so stiff, it took him a minute to get to his feet. He hugged the old tree and gave thanks.

'*Maith thu.*'

A loud group of approaching teenagers forced Grappa in the opposite direction. Trying to remember where he had anchored Little Beaudy, images from the dream flashed through his mind. He clutched his head as the piercing headache spread rapidly.

5.

Riley sat on the back deck, devouring a croissant stuffed with pineapple. He wasn't fond of tinned pineapple, but for some reason his mother had bought five cans.

The view over the mangroves was markedly different to the one from his tree house. The vast scale of the swamp was distinct in its lonely, twisted beauty. Beyond the sea, a watermelon sun was being swallowed by the mainland, casting a pink light on the breeze which made the whole swamp shimmer. It was a pity about the smell. Riley had learnt to breathe only through his mouth out here, where on certain days the mud became a ghastly brew resembling rotting fish and faecal matter.

He counted the crows sitting in the mangroves, glaring at him. Twelve. Carrion eating birds of doom, David called them. Riley detested the murder always hanging around the house, watching. What were they waiting for?

The mosquitoes here were smarter and smaller than the fat lazy ones he was accustomed to up north. These vicious nasties were so numerous that he was driven inside, where he met his mother who was clad in a black-satin gown which revealed too much of her breasts.

'Are you going out in that?' The shock made his voice squeak.

She threw her hands up in distress. 'I don't know what to wear. This came from a resort so I thought it might be appropriate. I wish...'

David was here. He finished the sentence for her in his mind. Riley couldn't remember the last time she had seemed so nervous. 'You look fine. Calm down.'

She followed him into the kitchen and started slamming cupboard doors.

'What are you after, Mum?'

'Glasses.'

'Above the sink.'

'Thank you for organising the kitchen.'

'Thanks for buying food.' He decided not to ask about the pineapple. The rapport between them felt unusually healthy. He considered telling her about the money, but decided it might be safer to broach the subject of work. 'I might see if there are markets on the mainland. I could run a stall, maybe sell my flutes and busk or something...?'

She choked on her water. 'Why?'

'To make money.'

'We don't need money. All of David's investments...believe me, money is not an issue.'

'It's not that Mum, it's.... I'm an adult. I want to make my own money. Prove to myself –'

'Why? If you need anything, tell me. I'll buy it.'

'I don't like you having that power over me.' There. He had said it.

'Power? What do you mean, power? I've never denied you anything. Tell me what you want, and I'll buy it for you.' She banged her empty glass down on the sink.

'What if I want to go to university –'

'University? You can't. There's no uni here.'

'Exactly. I'd have to pay for somewhere to live. I'd need money for food, transport.'

'You've never told me this.'

'Maybe I could study music.'

'Music?' Her laugh was brutal. 'If money is what you're after, I wouldn't become a musician.'

He exhaled. There was no point. She was incapable of seeing life from anyone's perspective but her own.

A car came up the dirt road.

She squeezed his hand. 'Leave the unpacking in the living room. I'll do it tomorrow.' She picked up her handbag. 'I don't want to do this.'

David wasn't around to protect her anymore and her dress was so revealing. 'Please be careful. You know how you are…with people.'

'With people?'

'Maybe I should go with you? How do you intend getting home?' He followed her downstairs.

'Don't worry, darling boy, I can protect myself.' The look on her face…was she laughing at him?

He felt embarrassed as the car drove off. He had sounded like David.

In the dark stairwell, the creaking house filled with menace. He ran upstairs into the brightness of the kitchen and through to his bedroom, flicking lights on.

Another creak.

What was it with this house?

He began to unpack books.

Someone was creeping down the hall.

He peered into the empty passage and shivered. Maybe the mermaid girl was on the beach? If not, he could sit by her 'No Trespassers' sign and seduce her with his music. A more attractive proposition than staying here alone in this house at night.

Ayla let out her frustration on the chopping board. 'I even offered to cover the vet bill or said the community could donate.'

'Of course they would. Jip's the Whale Welcoming mascot.' Her mother sat at the kitchen table, painting her toenails purple.

'He refused.' Bits of carrots flew into the air.

'Too proud, bless his soul.'

'He insisted I go in the end. There was nothing I could do. It was godawful.'

'Poor little Jippy.'

'The more he deteriorated, the angrier Harley got. He's blaming some woman that moved into the old Johnston house.'

'Someone bought that ghastly place?' Her mother disappeared into her bedroom.

Ayla called out. 'God help her if Jip dies.'

'Poor woman. Welcome to the island.'

'I've tried ringing Stan all day. Must be out of range.'

Her mother reappeared. 'Ayla, it's not your responsibility. If Stan were here, he probably couldn't do anything either. He's retired. People seem to forget that.'

'He's got a few supplies left, could give Jip some painkiller at least.'

'Well he's not here and you're not the island vet. You can't fix everything.'

'Hate seeing animals suffer.' Ayla threw the knife into the sink so hard, it bounced out and landed near her feet, spinning.

'Ayla.'

'Sorry.'

Her mother presented the painting she was holding. 'What do you think? I'm giving it to Rayleen.'

The seascape with the fishing trawler now had two men in the underwater foreground, her Dad and Mandy's, both with tails. She had made them mermen, looking as if they had just shared a joke. Her mother had brought her Dad to life, the way he was laughing. Ayla heard his loud distinctive laugh. She touched him in the painting. 'Oh, Mum.'

They hugged.

'I can't start crying. I've just done my face.' She pulled away.

Her mother seldom wore make-up. 'You going somewhere?'

'Guess.'

'The Resort? Why?" Her mother wasn't a regular at the Resort.

'Catching up with Ray. Seven years ago, to the day.'

Ayla felt guilty for not remembering.

'Sometimes I still think he's going to walk through that door, sunburnt and smelling of fish.'

Ayla took the painting, studying it. 'Best one you've done yet, Mum.'

'It's about time I worked towards another exhibition. I've been stuck on the moment of his death. With this painting, something opened in me, I was able to move past that, capture them as I remember them. I'm going to do a whole series titled, "The Mermen."'

'Good for you.' Ayla's smile faltered. As they hugged, she breathed in her Mum, the comfortable scent of childhood.

'Oh God, I will need to re-do my make-up.'

Ayla looked out into the night. 'I think Jip's dying, Mum.'

But her mother had gone.

The resort was a faux Spanish-mission, besser-block building, rendered in ochre with arched doorways; even the toilet signs proclaimed Señors and Señoritas. The restaurant boasted a water feature with goldfish and fountain, the sound of which kept the clientele running to the Señors and Señoritas.

Marlise felt stupidly overdressed. Why the hell had she let herself be coerced into coming? Tilly mistook the expression on her face for disappointment.

'Looks a bit abandoned now, but you should see this place at the height of the tourist season, love. Can't move in here.'

A tourist season? There were already too many damn people on this island. The room didn't feel abandoned, it felt claustrophobic. 'When is the tourist season? Summer?'

'God no. Place is filthy with mozzies then. Holiday housers come for a while around Christmas but never stay long now. Mozzies drive them away. Main tourist season is when the whales start coming through. The island is at its best then. Summer used to be a good money spinner, until some dickhead greenie in council decided spraying the wetlands was bad for the environment.'

'They sprayed the mangroves?' Marlise knew this occurred the world over, but it horrified her to think it had happened here, literally on her own doorstep.

'Shit yeah. They'd fly over in a chopper and dump a whole load of insecticide. Worked a treat. Few years ago, they stopped it. Mozzies came back in droves and the property prices dropped. Total catastrophe. That's why the community is pushing for council to start it up again.'

Marlise had the sinking realisation that perhaps she had made a mistake moving here. The decision had been quick and irrational, picking the house from an on-line real estate site accessed from an internet café two hour's drive from Burrawang. The photos of the endless swamp and the description of the house as isolated had convinced her. She had bought sight unseen, knowing from research on the island's temperature and humidity, it would be an excellent mosquito habitat. She wished now she had also researched the local council's policy on mosquito management.

Tilly led her to a coffee table, around which sat a group of women. One of whom, a red-head called Samantha, she had met on the barge. Tilly was forced to yell to be heard over their prattle. 'Girls, this is Marlise who I was telling you about.'

They all said hello, admired her dress and resumed their conversation.

'Have a seat, love.' Tilly pushed her into a chair and waddled off to the bar.

Marlise surveyed the room as the women reminisced over a surprise birthday party and guffawed at each freshly remembered detail. There were two other women, sitting at the bar, one dark as the other fair, discussing a painting propped between them. Grunter, the bargeman, was standing near a pool table at the far end of the room with a cluster of men. Marlise slipped quietly out of her chair.

She interrupted the men who also appeared to be in the middle of reliving a group memory. 'Grunter, I was wondering if jobs for deckhands ever came up?'

A silence followed as the men stared, making her acutely aware of the shape of her body pushing through the clingy dress.

'If you're the one looking for a job, sure. Start tomorrow.'

Their laughter sounded threatening.

'No, for my son...he's...twenty.'

'Come off it, you're too young to have a twenty-year-old,' said a guy with a shaved head, his eyes gorging on her half-exposed breasts like they were an all-you-can-eat buffet.

'Why not try the passenger ferry? We have more shifts than the barge, so a higher turnover.' This came from a short man with glasses who managed to maintain eye contact despite his head being at the same level as her chest.

'I forgot there was a ferry.'

'Runs on the hour, every hour, 'til midnight. Those barge arses are slackers, stop just after sundown. Don't have the night shifts like we do. I'm JK.' He held out his hand so she was obliged to shake it. They all held their hands out then and introduced themselves, even Grunter.

'Do you think there's a possibility of a job then, JK?'

'Let you know if something comes up. What kind of work has he done?' JK gulped his beer.

'None yet.'

'Kids these days. By the time I was twenty, I'd done a shitload of jobs.' Stevo, covered in tattoos, chimed in.

The group rumbled agreement.

Marlise decided to stop talking about Riley. She didn't want him bullied.

Tilly approached with two glasses of wine. 'Here you are, love. See you've met everyone.'

'Sorry, Tilly. I don't drink.'

The room went quiet. Marlise had the distinct impression she had grown three heads.

'Not to worry. Just saved me a trip to the bar.' Tilly grabbed the wine back.

The women from the coffee table stood behind Tilly. Some of their faces closed to her now. Marlise realised too late, she had crossed a boundary. Why had she abandoned them to talk to their men?

'Dressed in that skimpy dress.' The tail end of a whisper.

Sharon, a tall, pretty blonde, put her arms protectively around the shaved-headed man, whose name Marlise had forgotten.

'Tilly said you study mozzies?' Sharon's nasal tone was eerily reminiscent of the insect.

'Yes'.

'Hope you're studying how to make the little fuckers extinct'. A group guffaw made Sharon look pleased with herself.

Marlise took an instant dislike. 'Extinction of the mosquito would be disastrous. They're an essential part of the web of life. Didn't you listen in high school biology? Or sorry, didn't you finish high school?'

Sharon's eyes hardened. 'Couldn't think of anything more boring.' She squeezed her man tighter, as if she was frightened he was going to run off with Marlise.

Noting this, Marlise lowered her eyelids at him. 'They're far from boring. Mosquitoes are the biggest killers of human beings on this planet. One lone female, by merely sucking on you –' she let the phrase linger in the air, 'has the ability to inject a live pathogen that can make you so sick it can kill you.' She turned to Sharon, knowing what she was about to say was unsupported by any scientific evidence, but wanting to scare the silly woman. 'With the temperature of the atmosphere changing, these diseases are mutating, becoming even deadlier and spreading much further afield. If I were you, I wouldn't be bored, I'd be frightened.'

Tilly huffed. 'Now, love, I know you being a scientist, you know what you're talking about and all, but I don't want you repeating none of that, ever again. That goes for the lot of you. Imagine if stuff like that got out, what it would do to our –'

'Property prices.' The group teased in unison.

Tilly herded Marlise toward the restaurant, unimpressed.

Ayla lay on her bed watching Peach, an orphaned ringtail-possum she had hand-reared, explore her room. 'Almost time to release you back into the big wide world, Peachy.' She held out a piece of carrot, contemplating whether to ring Harley as Peach stuffed the carrot into her mouth with her tiny paws.

Over Peach's crunching, she thought she heard a distant flute. She lunged up, frightening Peach who scampered back into her box. Ayla snapped her bedroom light off to stand at her window and peer out.

Was that a figure she glimpsed at the end of the track? It merged into a shadow. Or was it a tree? She stared so hard her eyes hurt. The flute sounded again, sinuous, seductive. Thoughts of Far Dorocha turned the light from the misshapen moon bleak and grey. The crooked clothesline seemed to menace the chook pen so it cowered, and the track opening became a sinister cavern into which something ghastly could step.

The music came to an abrupt halt. Ayla listened so hard her pulse was deafening. The noise she heard next made her skin crawl. Grappa's childhood Banshee tales of an old demon woman wailing in the dead of night bombarded her.

It's just him mucking around on the flute, blowing to clear it out, she told herself. Or a curlew? Unconvinced, she pulled her curtains shut and raced through the house, locking doors and switching lights on.

Whatever it was out there began playing that enticing melody again, raising the hairs on her arms. At least it wouldn't be able to get in. Unless of course it could walk through walls?

Ayla observed her own silliness. Grappa would be impressed. She imagined how much fun it would be with him here, gulping from his silver flask, working up the courage to confront 'Far Dorocha' and the subsequent confusion on the poor tourist's face. She supressed a giggle. Of course, he was just a tourist, staying in one of the holiday houses. Recalling his pale torso in the sunlight, she unlocked the sliding back door and pushed it open far enough to stick her head out.

Silence. A maroon eucalypt leaf landed at her feet. An arrow shot from a bow. A secret message?

The sudden lack of music was disturbing. At least when he was playing she knew vaguely where he was. Meeting him in the bright of day would be preferable than meeting him at night on an isolated beach, she decided, locking the door and closing the curtains.

She had definitely glimpsed a figure on the track. Forget Far Dorocha. What if he's some sicko rapist? He had seen her naked and knew she lived here. Hopefully Grappa was close by, anchored in Hibiscus. As she picked up her phone, it rang, making her drop it.

Mandy's picture flashed on the screen. 'Hey, Mand.'

'What are you doing tonight, Aylee?' Mandy yelled over loud background noise.

'Nothing. What are you doing? I can hardly hear you.'

'Speak up, Aylee. I can hardly hear you.'

'Nothing. I'm doing nothing.'

'Hold on, I'll find a quieter spot. This place is pumping. Wish you were here. What are you up to tomorrow night?'

'Nothing.' She was still half-listening for the flute.

'Then get your sweet little arse over here and come to a party with me. It's going to be awesome. Warehouse up on a hill overlooking the city. Everyone's going to be there. Whole bloody campus has been invited.'

'Your Mum wants you to ring her.'

'Did, this arvy. Come on, Aylee, it'll be fun. You can stay at mine for the night. Can't hide away on that island for the rest of your life, girl.'

'You've been talking to your Nan, haven't you?'

'What's that got to do with nothing? It'll be Saturday night. Come on. What are you going to do instead? Go to the Resort?'

'I'm not that desperate.' They sniggered.

'How you going to meet anyone if you don't get off the island, woman?'

'Actually, I did meet someone. Well we haven't officially met, but he's a musician.'

'What? You are going to get your butt on that boat tomorrow girl and get in here and tell me all about him.'

'There's nothing to tell, but okay.'

'Text me when you get here.' Mandy hollered before disconnecting.

In the silence, Ayla listened, deflated now the flute had stopped. Mandy's phone call had normalised the situation. He was human. He had seen her this morning, so had returned in the hope that she might reappear. Nothing more, nothing less.

At first light, she would search for his footprints in the sand, just to be certain, then she would check on Jip. There was no way she could go to the mainland if Jip's condition had deteriorated.

She opened a packet of popcorn and nestled in front of the TV. A movie was starting, nostalgic piano music to the tune of 'Hush Little Baby' filled the room, blocking out any possibilities of a distant flute. White letters appeared on the screen: Jessica

Lange, Gwyneth Paltrow. Ayla snuggled into the couch, wishing her mum was home. They always watched the Friday night movie together.

Her thoughts returned to the flautist. Had he really seen her naked? She stared at the vase on the table, full of wild freesias half open in anticipation, and quivered.

Marlise endured the night, impressed by Sharon's subtlety. The insinuating smile that sat on Sharon's face as she looked her up and down, signalling certain codes of dress and conduct to be adhered to, the indistinct references to being a long-term local, the continual exclusion – so understated, no one else seemed to notice. Marlise was fascinated: such a small mind, such thirst for attention. Sharon was a shiny golden fish trapped in a stagnant puddle.

In comparison, everyone else was too friendly. By the end of the night, Marlise found the tight-knit community so welcoming she felt suffocated. When she made noises about leaving, a very drunk Grunter offered to drive her home. Luckily, Tilly intervened. 'No worries, Grunter, got this one covered.'

Walking out, Tilly leaned into her, 'Wouldn't touch him with a barge pole. Pardon the pun. Nice guy, but he's slept with that many women, he's sure to have some kind of STD.' She stopped to introduce the two women sitting at the bar.

'Helen and Rayleen? Marlise. Just moved into the old Johnston house.'

Rayleen's dark face grew darker. 'If you can live in that house, you're a stronger woman than me.'

On the drive home, Marlise asked Tilly what Rayleen had meant, but Tilly dismissed it in a hurry to gossip. 'Samantha the redhead, she's an interesting one. One of her closest friends is Sharon – the tall blonde. A few years back, Sam had a one-night stand with Sharon's partner Josh – the good-looker with the shaved head. They were both pissed as farts and sore and sorry the next day. Of course, the whole island knew about it. That's how it happens here. You'll get used to that. But you know what? To this day, Sharon still doesn't know about that little misdemeanour. She adores Josh and Josh loves her to death. No one wants to see her heart break, and not a day goes by that poor Sam doesn't go out of her way for Sharon, she feels that guilty. It was an unspoken pact. We all decided it was best Sharon never found out. That's how we are here. We look after each other. Need anything, love, you just ask.'

Tilly pulled up in front of the house and turned to Marlise with tears in her eyes. Her hand on Marlise's arm felt clammy.

'I know you've just suffered a terrible loss. You need to know, you're not on your own here, Marlise. You've moved to the right place. Wouldn't leave this island if you paid me. I love these people. You'll grow to love them. Know you will.'

Marlise shrank from Tilly's wine and cigarette breath, opening the car door, desperate to get away. She never knew how to react when people became emotional.

'Thanks for the lift.'

'Won't come in, love. Wayne wasn't feeling well when I left. Better get back and check on him.' Tilly weaved away and Marlise listened for movement in the house. She knew instinctively he wasn't home. She called out anyway as she walked through rooms, switching lights off.

'Riley?'

He had promised to always leave a note. They had made a deal. Where the hell was he in the middle of the night? Maybe he had walked to the resort, looking for her? She would give him an hour, then ring Tilly and ask her to help search for him. At least he had no money, which meant he couldn't catch the ferry. Marlise understood in that moment why she had moved to an island.

She slipped the metal file out of her handbag. All day she had been waiting for Riley to leave the house. She lifted the table cloth thrown over the chest and started to file the latch. After a minute, her hand cramped up and a wave of anger rose at the stupid removalist men. She whacked at the latch with the file. Noticing it moved slightly, she hit it again and again until it became the hand of the removalist man who had touched her on the thigh, and the two bits of metal snapped apart.

She was greeted by reams of yellowed documents, articles, old press clippings of her as a young medical entomologist lauded as 'someone to watch', draft after draft of papers she had written, research documents kept to prove her theories were her own. Images tumbled over her, facts, lies, snippets of memories, causing her to whisper involuntarily to the empty house, until her gaze landed on the small, intricately carved wooden box at the bottom of the chest. She fell silent with the need to hide it before a world cracked open, before a heart could run dry of love. She ran her fingers over the carvings, recalling the feel of it, the smell of sandalwood. Unable to stop herself, she lifted the lid. Only to find the interior empty.

Where were all the photos? The letters?

She remembered the tiny latch at the side of the box, twisted it then pulled out the false bottom to reveal his face, so like Riley's it jumped out across the years and stole her breath. There they were, the three of them, happy and young, Riley still a baby. Such a beautiful baby. She felt the grip of his tiny hand in that cramped apartment with the rats in the walls, the broken toilet, the pot plants they painted themselves that sat on the windowsill. Far in the back of her mind it occurred to her that it was the only time she had been truly happy. Before the thought could solidify, she heard a flute.

She rushed to hide the box and dropped it, spilling the contents over the floor so an image landed on her shoe. Cramming the letters and photos under the false bottom – no time to wipe tears – she raced to her bedroom, the carved wooden box a time bomb in her hands. He was almost at the house. She pushed the box under her bed and saw the tiny latch holding the false bottom had broken off. 'Damn'. Frantic for a safer hiding place, she heard the screen door slam and footsteps mount the stairs. 'Is that you, Riley?'

'Uh huh.'

She stuffed the box as far under the bed as she could reach, dried her face and walked into the kitchen, resolving not to berate him for the missing note.

'Went for a walk on the beach. Sorry, remembered after I left about the note.'

'Must have been a long walk.'

'Played my flute for a bit, then sat and watched the waves.'

'I spoke to one of the ferrymen. You might be able to get a job as a deckhand if a position becomes available.'

He stood there nodding, too surprised to speak, then he was hugging her. 'Thanks Mum.'

She savoured his hugs, so rare these days. 'If you did want to go to uni, maybe we could look at an online course. Lots of universities are online now.'

He pulled away to see her face, then embraced her again, lifting her off her feet, twirling her in the air.

For the first time in what felt like years, Marlise found she couldn't stop laughing.

6.

Riley knelt amongst empty cardboard boxes on the floor, finding solace in the familiar nutmeg smell of David's books. He was absorbed by two orange butterflies that had landed on the windowsill to mate. So bright in the shadow of the house, they shone without edges, fallen fragments of light stuck end to end in an ancient dance. The colourful sight made him hopeful. Maybe things would work out with his mother. Maybe he could lead a normal life, like the young people he had met at the markets, enjoying the freedom to do whatever they wanted. Maybe he would make friends here, people his own age. At this thought, his heart fluttered in time with the butterflies' wings, remembering how shy he had been with the market crowd, and that girl from the incense stall who had tried to kiss him. How frightening that was. He could still see her slightly crooked front tooth and the black smudge of make-up around her eyes.

The toilet flushed. His mother had slept in. The butterflies flew off, taking his optimism with them, leaving the hollow part that didn't quite trust her.

She poked her head through the doorway. 'You darling boy.'

As a surprise, he had organised the lounge room.

'Nearly finished.'

'I'm going into the mangroves to collect samples. If you need me, call out.'

He couldn't recall relating this well to his mother in a long time, and had never seen her so – he searched for the word – normal. Shards of memory of how she was before David's death kept piercing his fragile bubble of hope, fragile as a plant being hacked by a grafting knife.

After David died, he had withdrawn from her as she converged on him, but something had shifted since moving here. The smothering intensity between them was dissipating.

He reached for the last box and spotted a photo lying face down on the floorboards: a picture of him at the age of two or three in the arms of a strange man. His mother as a young woman had her head on the man's shoulder, gazing up at him. She looked so happy, Riley almost didn't recognize her. But the man wasn't looking at her, he was beaming at him, the young Riley. The man's face so like his own, for a moment, Riley thought he was looking at a picture of his father.

Impossible. His father was dead. He knew this from his earliest memory, the jolt and sound of a car crash through embryonic fluid. David has said it was impossible to retain pre-birth consciousness, but his mother had argued she had heard of several cases, and Riley remembered it so clearly. Or he imagined he did. As he stared at the man in the photo, it dawned on him: was this a lie his mother had planted in his young mind which had grown to be real over time, so real he never questioned it? Is it even possible to hear sounds from the womb? What David said the last time he saw him jumped into his head.

'Your mother is frightened she'll lose you if she tells you the truth.'

'About what?'

'Not my place to say. Your mother needs to tell you.'

He had asked her what David meant, but she had been flippant. 'Poor David. So feverish, he's delusional. Didn't even know who I was this morning.'

'We should get him to hospital, Mum.'

'Do you know how far away the hospital is from here? It's the same flu I had last month. Once the fever breaks, he'll be fine. I don't want you catching it. How many times do I have to tell you? Stay away from him.'

But David died that night while Riley slept peacefully in his tree house.

The memory galvinised him. Assuming the photo had fallen from a book, Riley pulled apart every volume he had neatly stacked on the shelves, holding each one open from the spine and shaking the pages in the hope that more faded secrets would flutter out. When they didn't, he threw the book and grabbed the next until he had searched them all.

He collapsed onto his haunches and stared at the photo. The man looked so like him he continued to gaze into the image until doubt coiled like a snake in his gut. Her voice shattered his thoughts.

'Riley?'

He struggled to stand, legs all pins and needles. Leaning against the windowsill, he stomped to bring the circulation back and saw her below in the swamp. She waved. He imagined stomping hard on her beautiful face and watched her smile float into the air. A lone crow caught what remained of her smile and flew off with it, over the house towards the sun.

His face stopped her. Looking up at him from this angle, he looked older. An angry stranger glaring down at her inadequacies. What the hell had happened? He disappeared from the window.

'Riley?'

She rushed inside and climbed her way upstairs, panicking. What had she done now? Pausing halfway up, light-headed from the adrenalin shock of seeing him so angry, Marlise realised she was starving. She had forgotten to eat again today.

She couldn't comprehend at first what had happened to the room. Her son, with that murderous face, was standing in a sea of books so thick she couldn't see the floor. He was holding a photo in his outstretched hand. The faded image sucked the breath out of her. Had he found the box? She scanned the room. The walls started to sway. It must have fallen out when she dropped the box last night. The thought stabbed at the side of her temples as their eyes met. The hot flush felt like it began in her feet, by the time it reached her head, she had lost grip of the door handle. Before blacking out, she heard him say, 'My father isn't dead, is he.'

It should have been a question.

The look on his mother's face before she collapsed told him the truth. He waded through the books to check she was breathing. 'Mum?' He carried her into her room and laid her on the bed. She was feather light and too hot.

'Mum?' – worried now – 'Mum?' He moved her onto her side, unable to feel a breath. 'Mum.' He shook her. She was breathing. Thank God. He should ring someone – that real estate agent. He scrambled through her handbag for the number.

She came to and traced the shape of his face with her eyes while he counted their breaths. He pulled the photo from his shirt pocket and watched her face light up. His heart felt so big and confused he had to sit back to make more room for it. 'You lied.'

'To protect you. He didn't want anything to do with you. He hates us.' She shut her eyes on the image.

'He's still alive?'

'I don't know.'

'Where is he?'

'How would I know? He abandoned us. I've had no contact since.

I'm sorry. Thought it would be less painful if you thought he was dead.'

Riley sat with his heart so swollen he couldn't breathe for the size of it. Surprised at the power of his sobs, between spasms he spat the words out. 'It is not less painful.'

'Oh, Riley.' She sat up, but he sprang away and ran out of the house. He heard her call from the verandah. 'Where are you going?'

'Off this island. Away.' He didn't look back.

Halfway up the road, he heard: 'You won't get far.' The tone of her voice – she was mocking him. He had missed something obvious.

Money. Of course. Money was essential.

He stomped back into the house.

'What are you doing?' She followed him into his bedroom. He grabbed a flute and stuffed it into his pocket. 'You can't go anywhere. You don't know anyone. You have no money.'

She was wrong. He had plenty of money, taking the wad of it from under the inner lining of his flute case.

'My God. Where did you get that? Answer me. Riley?'

She tailed him down stairs, trying to grab hold of him. 'Answer me. Please don't leave. Please. Don't leave me.' He kept pushing her off. 'You're all…I've got. I'll be alone, all alone without you. Riley?'

He tore free and slammed the door. His sense of direction never failed him. The barge ramp was to the southwest, and the road went north. He looked toward the mangroves. There must be a way through.

She was behind him again, trying a different tactic, her voice full of threat. 'I'll call the police like last time. You won't get far.'

When he headed into the swamp, her screeching doubled in volume. 'Don't go in there. What the hell are you doing? Riley. Get out of there. Come back. Riley.'

The further he walked, the more she screamed until her voice, ringing through the mangroves, woke the mosquitoes from their midday slumber.

In the end, it was only his name she repeated over and over, until she lost sight of him, until her voice grew hoarse from fighting the eventuality she had struggled against. So, it had happened. He would leave her now. A sharp stone lodged itself in the base of her heart.

The police had been unhelpful last time, once they had discovered his age. She remembered the condescending tone of the senior officer: 'He's a grown man. If you had a fight and he's taken off, there's nothing we can do.'

It was only when she explained he had no money and no access to money that they had been willing to co-operate. This time he had money and there was only one possible source for that money. More proof of David's betrayal brought a bitter taste to her mouth.

'People always end up disappointing me.' Her voice sounded small against the limitless backdrop of the mangroves. The wind blew and her cheeks felt cold. This was the last time she would cry for him. David had stolen enough tears now.

She wiped her face, deciding to give Riley twenty-four hours. Then she would ring the police. Her heart drifted out, weaving its way through the mangroves to her poor nervous son who was still learning how this cruel world operated.

He'll be back before bedtime. He knew how she felt about bedtime, about tucking him in, checking he was safe. It was her job to keep him safe. That's what good mothers do, keep their children safe.

Marlise only realised she had walked into the swamp when her shoes grew heavy with mud. The day was so stagnant, she heard the mosquitoes before she saw them starting to swarm. She let them suck from her.

'Hello, girls. Have you seen my son?'

They had seen him. They had even tried to feed on him. Her screeching had pushed him further and further into the mangroves until the mud was above his knees and he was lost, with mosquitoes attacking mercilessly. Driven to insanity by their biting, he rubbed his exposed skin with the rancid mud. Discovering they couldn't suck through if caked on thickly enough, he feverishly applied it everywhere, including his face and in his hair, trying to protect his scalp.

The knowledge that she had lied to him his whole life fed his rage, giving him strength to struggle against the sinking gunk and trip wire mangrove roots. He had known somehow. He had always known. He couldn't believe his father hated him. That photo was full of love, not hate. He would find a way out of this quagmire, find his father and learn the truth.

But the swamp had no end and his conviction seeped out of him until the resonant shriek of the barge ramp scraping on cement made him fall backwards into the slippery sludge. Harnessing his strength, he moved toward the noise. The mud so deep now, he used branches of the mangroves to pull himself forward. When he reached hard sand, and saw the barge through the trees, he charged in jubilation onto the beach, arms in the air, a primeval roar escaping him.

'Swamp monster,' came the cry from a group of children in scout uniforms walking onto the barge. Several screamed as one of the adults stepped forward, protectively. Riley retreated, continuing past the barge, further up the beach. He could still hear one of the smaller children wailing from fright and felt dreadful.

Finding a flat rock where the sand was dry, he took the photo from his shirt pocket, placed it on the rock with his flute on top, and waded into the water. Unable to wash the mud out of his clothes, he surrendered to the sea and floated face down like a dead man.

The water was calm on this side of the island and cooler than the ocean he had swum in up north during the weekend David had taken them to a resort. The water seemed saltier too, it was easy to stay buoyant. Striped fish darted above the sand and a stingray glided past, sneaking a shy look at him. Occasionally there were pale rocks with red tide-line markings running through them. When touched, pink clay dissolved into the water. He floated on his back and admired the flat-bottomed clouds, fluorescent white against the powdered blue sky. After the nightmare of the swamp, he had landed in paradise. Two birds circled, probably white-bellied sea eagles. He had read about them in David's *Birds of Australia* book. The male was smaller than the female. He remembered David's face the day he realised Riley's ability to store facts, calling out. 'Marlise, I think Riley has a photographic memory. I show him something once and he recalls it verbatim the next day.'

His mother didn't look up – 'Of course, I was like that' – as if it was perfectly natural.

David had leaned in, 'I think you're remarkable. You'll be able to do whatever you want in life. Don't ever forget that.'

Riley lay on the hot sand to dry out. The remaining mud in his clothes and hair hardened, releasing a foul smell. He stared at the man in the photo and pondered how he would find him in such a large world when he wasn't even sure of his name. Riley knew now, he couldn't trust anything his mother had said.

The barge was long gone. He decided to walk in the opposite direction and explore around the bend.

From a stand of ironbark trees, their black trunks splattered with grey lichen, the magnificent white horse appeared, minus its elderly rider. It galloped up the beach – a ghostly apparition gleaming against the indigo water. Riley half expected it to grow a horn.

He kept walking, stopping to marvel at a piece of driftwood bleached by the sun to the colour of bone, in the shape of a human foot.

In the distance, a jetty appeared. Near the jetty was a Hacienda he recalled from David's *Encyclopaedia of Houses Almanac*. The books he had spent his childhood studying had prepared him well for this new world that tasted of salt and sunlight.

Coming closer, he read the sign over the jetty, 'Welcome to Moondarrawah Island,' the faded outline of the stolen letters still visible. It now read, 'come to Moondarrawah land.' Moondarrawah sounded Indigenous. He wondered what it meant.

The courtyard of the Hacienda was cool and inviting with an in-ground pool encompassed by potted palms, cacti, tables and chairs. There was a booth selling ice-cream. His mother didn't let him eat ice-cream. Only then did he remember the money, damp and muddy in the pocket of his jeans. He attentively unfolded some notes.

The pretty blonde behind the counter was studying her only customer.

'Cor, I think you've stood in something.' She held her nose.

'No I...sorry. I....got lost in the mangroves.'

'That explains it. The island's septic systems are so old, I'm sure they're all bleeding into that bloody wetland.'

He took a step back to read the sign above the counter. 'Can I have a triple scoop in a cone thanks?'

'What flavours, mate?'

He was so hungry, he picked the first three flavours on the left, deciding to work his way through the lot and discover which was his favourite.

The ice-cream was soft and sweet on his tongue. For some reason, it brought to mind the naked girl in the fog. He looked around hoping she would walk past. Would he recognise her clothed?

The sugary coldness was addictive. After the fourth time he ordered, the woman said, 'You really like ice-cream, don't you?'

'My mother never let me eat it. Now I can do what I want.'

'Some mothers need their heads checked. Eat up then, mate. Make up for all those years.'

He went to hand her the money.

'Nup, this one's on the house.'

He was pleased with himself over this exchange. It wasn't hard communicating with people, only a matter of practice.

He recalled David berating his mother. 'He should be at school. Being brought up in such isolation will give him a fear of social interaction.' How right David had been.

Riley couldn't finish the last ice-cream but knew nothing could surpass mango sorbet.

A ferry had arrived at the jetty so he decided to catch it. A chorus of complaints met him as he entered the confined space of the boat. He had grown accustomed to his smell, so had forgotten.

'Sorry,' he said, disoriented, floundering around the cabin like a fish trapped in a bucket.

The decky grabbed him by the elbow. 'Upstairs, mate. You're stinking the boat out.'

Riley clambered up the ladder to an open deck and stepped into the fresh air. The sun, about to disappear behind the mainland, had become a red eye bleeding into the ocean, turning the water liquid gold. Now he was further out from the island, he perceived it as a crouching creature, its red rock face looking toward the open sea, glowing in the golden light. A pod of dolphins glided past, playing in the wake. Riley had lived in a shady, wet jungle most of his life. This place was open light and water. He cried out, temporarily awed by the utter beauty, rejoicing in the dolphins as they swam off into their golden world.

Half-way across the strait, the remainder of the sun melted into the mainland, and his stomach churned and bubbled. As the ferryman came to collect his ticket, Riley vomited ice-cream into the wake.

'Seasick?'

Riley wiped at a dangling string of spit, embarrassed. 'I...no...I ate too much ice-cream.'

'That'll do it, every time. That combined with a nice steady swell like we got this evening. Return? Single? Multi? What?'

'What's a multi?'

'Twenty trips.'

'Oh um…single?'

'Six eighty, please.'

'I…where does this boat go?'

'The mainland.'

'Australia?'

'No, fuckin' China. What you reckon, mate?'

Riley kept his face neutral. Unused to people, he never knew if they were serious or joking.

'Christ, even your money stinks. What the hell you been doing? Rolling in dog shit?' The ferryman disappeared down the ladder, shaking his head.

Riley watched as the mainland grew closer, recognising the barge ramp and the car park where his mother had left her car.

As he walked up the jetty, the street lights came on in a magical welcome. The timing gave him hope. He didn't know where he was going or how to find his father from one snapshot taken years ago, but the idea of returning to his mother repulsed him.

Endless cars zipped past square houses in varying shades of grey and brown, crammed side by side in tiny rectangular yards, high fences marking their boundaries. He considered how people could exist with no space between them and longed for Burrawang's 200 hectares, where he had roamed the rainforest for hours without encountering a soul. He remembered himself as an eight-year-old, the day he had arrived at Burrawang, how David had tried to walk him through the forest, how rude Riley had been, how untrusting. He felt a welling of tears and swung left into a laneway, determined to stop the electric train of thought that always led back to David.

It was pleasant to be away from the main road. The streets were quieter, with only the occasional car. He started to run, free and wild on an unknown adventure in a new land. 'I'm Huck Finn,' he shouted.

David would be proud of him for leaving: 'It's your journey now. Claim it.'

Riley roamed the back streets, staring into houses lit from within, fascinated by the people who were unaware they were being watched. Most families sat mesmerised in front of giant screens. He could understand this. The small amount of television he had encountered held him transfixed. Television was another thing his mother never allowed.

He came across a family singing happy birthday as the father carried a cake with three candles to the table. The little boy blew the candles and they cheered and hugged. Riley couldn't hear what they were saying but their elation propelled him to jump a low fence and hide behind a bottlebrush bush to gain a better view. The father threw the little boy into the air, making him squeal, begging his father to do it again. Riley pulled the photo out of his pocket and tilted it toward the light from the window. Had his father thrown him into the air like that? The way he was looking at him, Riley suspected he might have. The possibility filled him with an unaccustomed longing.

An outdoor light flooded the yard and an old woman from the neighbouring house gathered her garden hose. 'You pervert! Jim. Pam. There's a perv in your yard. I've called the police. They're on their way.'

The happy family stopped smiling and looked toward the window as their neighbour sprayed him with the hose. Riley jumped the fence and bolted. Turning left at the end of the street, he glimpsed a police car. Minutes later, he heard its siren. He ran down a lane way as the insistent wail grew louder, frightening him into a thickly hedged yard, the house silent and empty, where he hid and waited until the siren faded and long after.

He knew about police and their sirens, remembering the day the police came to Burrawang after a neighbour had lodged a complaint against his mother. They wanted to talk to David and his mum in private, so the lady officer took him out to the police car and let him operate the siren. After they left, David was fuming. His mother had lied about something again.

Riley's last encounter with police had only been months ago. Two officers had woken him from where he was sleeping under a bridge and asked him his name. 'Your mother's worried about you, son. We'll give you a lift home.'

Riley drifted down streets randomly, not knowing where to go or what to do to find his father. How could there be so many houses and people jammed into one world?

On discovering a Lilly Pilly tree, he gorged on its citric fruit, and at an abandoned play-ground he drank and drank from a tap. Climbing onto a platform with a slippery slide down one end and monkey bars on the other, he realised he would be screened from the road if he lay down. Thinking it would be a safe place to rest, he didn't mean to fall asleep.

7.

The doof-doof music vibrated through each corner of the massive warehouse, leaving Ayla hoarse from trying to be heard. Every way she turned someone had questions for her. What had she been doing? When was she coming back? She pushed her way through the dancers, towards a door that led onto a balcony, equally crowded, but at least the music dulled to a muffled thud. The cloying smell of marijuana hung low in the air. She checked her phone again for a message from Harley, wishing now she had insisted on visiting Jip before leaving the island. On the phone, Harley had been adamant, 'all good, man.' He was such a reserved soul, Ayla hadn't wanted to invade his privacy.

She drank from her cider and spied the one she was hoping to avoid: Harry Anderson, bare-chested and holding court. She had asked once why he never wore a shirt. He had ripped her top off and said, 'If you've got it, flaunt it honey,' before sinking to his knees in mock awe of her naked torso.

He had his arm draped over the shoulder of a pretty brunette. The gathered crowd hung on his every word. Ayla was surprised at her body's reaction as he spotted her mid-sentence.

'Baby-face,' he rushed over, wrapping himself around her.

She pulled away. 'Hi, Harry.'

'How the hell are you?' He tried to kiss her on the lips but she tilted her head. Ayla had lost her virginity to Harry, and most of her self-worth. Harry Anderson, drama major aspiring to be a literature major, had wooed her with his perfect body and bad poetry. The lust he aroused had sent her to the point of addiction. Harry became her drug. She thought she would die when he withdrew to start writing worse poetry for Clarissa, a virginal arts major. There had been three other virgins since. Mandy had kept her informed. He was known on campus as the Virgin Slayer. Ayla felt humiliated she had been his initial conquest. Her only source of pride was that she held the record for maintaining his interest the longest. Their relationship lasted exactly fourteen months.

The brunette came over and slipped her arms around him, sizing Ayla up. 'Hi.'

'Sonya, this is Ayla. Ayla, Sonya.'

Ayla couldn't help herself. 'What happened to Clarissa?'

'Psycho bitch. Had to take a DVO out on her, wouldn't leave me alone.'

Sonya pulled at him. 'Come on, let's go.'

'Soon, okay? What have you done to your hair, Aylee? Looks sexy,' he reached to touch it. 'Rrrrringlets,' he said, growling his R.

She moved away. 'Goes like that from swimming in the sea every day.'

'And women pay hairdressers big bucks to get sprayed with bottled salt water to achieve the same effect.' He smiled his winning smile, but she was no longer charmed by it.

'I need to widdle,' Sonya said in a child's voice and placed his hand between her legs.

He pushed her off. 'Then go widdle.'

Sonya sulked off unsteadily on her platform heels, her tube of a dress riding up to expose her underwear.

'God, it's good to see you, Ayla.'

She couldn't speak, feeling the pure physical energy of their past rising between them.

'Want an eccy? Got one left. We could split it and cut this scene, go back to my place, relive old times? What do you reckon?' He fished in his pocket for the tab.

'Aren't you here with Sonya?'

'She wouldn't care, she's that pissed.'

'Yes she would. When are you going to stop being an arsehole, Harry?' Even Ayla was surprised at the snarl in her voice.

He blinked.

She sipped on her cider and spotted Paul, a long-haired science major. 'Paul,' she called and waved.

'Ayla, honey,' he held up a joint and motioned for her to join them. 'Guys, look who's here.'

Ayla was embraced by friends from her old faculty and Harry sulked off into the crowd. They passed around the joint. Ayla was reluctant.

'Don't tell me you're out of practice, honey?'

'Afraid so, Pauly,' she took a small puff and coughed out the hot smoke. 'Have any of you seen Mandy? I've lost her.'

'No, you haven't.' Mandy snuck up behind her. She dragged Ayla inside where they danced and giggled like teenagers again until Mandy's housemates, four of them, all majoring in law like Mandy, signalled they were leaving.

Falling outside into the fresh air – it was such a perfect night – they decided to walk home, past crammed restaurants and pubs seething with drunks. So different to the island, for Ayla it was a visual feast. She was so busy taking it all in, she collided with Evie.

'Fuck, move over. Think you own the pavement?' Evie growled.

Ayla had asked Mandy about Evie once because she never felt comfortable around her. 'I'm sure she hates me.'

'Nah. She's from a mob out west. Had a crap childhood. She assumes all whites are racist. Where she's from, most of them are. Can't blame her for being angry. More she learns about the history of our people, the angrier she gets.'

'What?' Evie was glaring at her.

Ayla looked at the time and caught Mandy's eye. 'I might get going, actually. If I catch the next bus, I'll make the last ferry home.'

The others, with the exception of Evie, called out in protest, wanting her to stay. Mandy dropped behind. 'Don't let her get to you, mate. She's like that with everyone. I'd offer to deck her but look how bloody big she is.' They held hands. 'Please stay. I'll cook pancakes for breakfast.'

Ayla felt ashamed she didn't have the endurance to stay and 'suck it up', as Mandy would put it. Evie was a blip in Ayla's life compared to what she had seen Mandy endure: years of inherent and casual racism. Like the time in their first year of uni, while waiting for Mandy to buy a coffee, Ayla had walked into an expensive gift shop where the shop assistants glanced at her but continued their conversation. When Mandy entered a few minutes later, Ayla was appalled to witness their suspicion as they followed Mandy around the store, assuming she was going to steal something. Mandy thought it was a big joke the way Ayla had become outraged on her behalf. Mandy dealt with that kind of occurrence on a regular basis.

'Pancakes are tempting, but I'm too worried about Jip.' Which was true. 'Got to go or I'll miss this bus. Love you.' She hugged her friend.

'Love you too. Hey, thanks for coming in.'

Ayla ran fast through the late-night traffic of cabs and throngs of lurching drunks, but missed the bus, which meant she would miss the last ferry home. She caught the next bus, deciding to ring Grappa and ask him to fetch her in his boat. Anything was better than dealing with Evie. Evie made her feel ashamed. In Evie, she saw the generations of resentment. The whole big unspoken mess of it, an open wound still bleeding. Growing up alongside Mandy, Ayla had not only witnessed the racism, but the indelible effects on Mandy's extended family from a generation of stolen children. A death in custody of Aunty Dora's favourite nephew, which almost destroyed her. She had watched some of the mob on Big Island not able to cope with the reverberations of trauma, falling into the narrow cracks of substance abuse, and marvelled at the ones who endured with dignity. She had heard whispers of childhood memories of the Bullyman from the mission on Big Island and the horror stories passed down of the massacres; the landscape reverberating with the cruelty of it all. It made her think of the initial moment she had ever felt guilty about the colour of her skin. She and Mandy were seven. Unbeknown to Helen, they had crept down to the beach.

'We can pretend we're mermaids and this is our rock we sing from. Come on, your Mum's not here.' Ayla insisted as she climbed Mud Rock.

Mandy's little face clouded over. 'There's a bad reason my Mum won't let me on that headland.'

'What bad reason?'

'White soldiers with guns pushed them like cattle my Mum said.'

'Pushed who?'

'My ancestums.'

'What are ancestums?'

'Like my great, great aunties and uncles.'

'Your relatives?'

'Yeah, my relatives. They herded them up, those soldiers with guns, and pushed them over the edge. They all got smashed on the rocks and died. Even babies, Mum said. My cousins, they don't call it Mud Rock, they call it Blood Rock. So, if I was you, I'd get down right now.'

Ayla stood her ground, undecided, hands on her hips jutting out in defiance.

Mandy waited, scowling. 'My ancestums, their skin was dark like my uncle Freddie. The soldiers had white skin...like yours. Maybe they were your ancestums.'

Ayla looked at her skin and wondered why people had different coloured skin. 'You're lying. Grappa tells me all the stories and he hasn't told me that one.'

'Not his to tell.' Mandy pegged a stone hard against the rock so it splintered into pieces. 'If you think I'm a liar, I'm not playing with you no more.' With that, she ran off crying. Their first fight.

Ayla stared through the bus window at the dark suburbs, remembering how she had climbed to the top and crawled to the very edge. In the white foam of the waves below, blood began to swirl and what at first she thought was a large chunk of brown seaweed, became the body of a dead baby smashing against the rocks. It wasn't words that spilled out of her mouth. She didn't know what it was, but it came from somewhere deep within her seven-year-old self. She sang to Mandy's dead ancestors and felt them listening. She sang until the tears ran down her windblown face and the dead baby dissolved into the crashing waves.

The memory made her shiver in the almost empty bus, speeding through the endless suburbs in the night towards the water's edge.

Riley woke up disoriented on the playground equipment, with no comprehension of how long he had been asleep. Busting to urinate, he slid down the slide and headed for the clump of trees at the edge of the park.

Wondering if he had broken the record for the longest pee in the world, he saw a beach through the low-lying branches, and beyond that the shape of the island in the middle of the bay. In the distance, he could see the silhouette of the jetty. A bent moon hanging above it. Dejected, he walked towards it, knowing the only option was to return to his mother. To find his father, he needed more information and she was the only one who could give him that.

The massive houses with yards that ran down to the water contained large dogs with blood curdling barks. The beach turned into boulders at one section, which he scrambled over to escape a Rottweiler.

Nerves shattered, he arrived at the end of the jetty, relieved to find the shelter shed empty. He walked to where the pier ended to dip his feet into the water, curious at how the cement steps continued descending into the murky sea.

'A mermaid's staircase?' he asked the dark liquid gently lapping his toes.

The image of the girl in the fog returned. He imagined her ascending from the bottom of the ocean, walking naked up the steps in the moonlight, glistening wet, and became so aroused he had to sit on the cold metallic seat to calm himself.

The day's heat had dispersed and a chill rose from the water. There was no sign of the ferry. A bus pulled up, then drove off, but no one came along the jetty. To warm up, he decided to play his flute, squatting on the bench to test the sound. With the night so still and the water like glass, the acoustics bouncing around in the shed were sublime. He played his song for David until David was conjured, standing there beside him, listening; the lines in his face, full of pride. Riley could hear David's foot tapping along, as it sometimes did.

The bus driver was talking to her. 'Rise and shine. Last stop.'

Ayla stepped onto the pavement as the briny sea tang welcomed her. The bus sped off. Still half asleep, she pulled her phone from her pocket.

'Hi, Grappa....sorry if I....I've missed the last boat home...if that's not too...thanks. You're the best.' She stared at the long jetty that ribboned into the darkness. At least the shelter shed at the end was lit up, even though from here it was impossible to see if anyone was in it. The lack of human life in the car park felt wrong. She decided to stay under the cold comfort of the street light, until she caught sight of Little Beaudy.

Two ciders, one puff on a joint, and that old empty feeling was visiting again. What was wrong with her? Why couldn't she thrive on the city life, the socialising, the networking sites, the partying?

'I'm abnormal,' she told the warped moon.

The night was so still she could hear the crabs breathing in the mud. The wind sighed. Her scalp tingled. It wasn't the wind. From the end of the jetty, the tantalizing melody danced across the water.

'What the...?'

She slipped off her shoes and crept down the pier. Her world had become black and silver: the moon against the sky, the liquid flash on dark water, and the shed shining silver in the moonlight. There was no colour anywhere. Maybe he was a dark faery lord after all? Why else would he be here on the end of the jetty playing his flute when all the boats had stopped? Why else would the night look as if it was made from celluloid?

As she reached the shelter shed, she could hardly hear the music over the pounding of her heart. She smelt him before she saw him, squatting barefoot on the seat, eyes shut. His whole body seemed to be playing the instrument. He looked like he had been soaked in mud. Had he crawled out from under the earth?

Ayla stood transfixed, uncertain as to what to do. If she could sneak past to hide where the steps led down to the water, she would feel safer. That's where Grappa would pick her up, and if forced to, she could jump. Swimming to the island might be possible on a still night like this.

The melody changed – his playing became frenetic. She ran and ducked down. The tide was rising, soon all the stairs would be covered. To stay hidden she would need to stand in the water. He hadn't seen her...or was he pretending? His eyes were still shut. She peeped from her hiding place at his splayed and hairy feet as the unearthly smell overwhelmed her. Was the stench coming from his feet? He stopped playing as his eyes opened on hers. She strangled the sound that leapt up her throat.

The smooth tip of the flute dangled from his mouth, fingers still now, as he glimpsed something golden on the steps. Craning his neck, he saw it was a head of blonde hair framing two startled eyes.

As he stood, she stood. The girl in the fog. Where had she come from?

His blood thickened as he considered she *was* a mermaid who had used the cement staircase to climb out of the sea. He had read about mermaids in David's *Mythological Creatures* book. They grew legs on land. Her legs were lovely. All of her was lovely. She couldn't possibly be human.

'There is always a logical explanation for everything,' David often said. Riley clung to this. The silence of the night beat down on them while time moved in slow motion. The logical explanation came.

'You snuck past me when I was playing.'

A slight nod and he saw how frightened she was. He sat down to appear less threatening, combing his matted hair with his fingers, trying to make himself presentable.

'Sorry. I stink I, I got stuck in the mangroves…'

She was looking at him, deciding whether to trust him or not, her voice soft and husky when she spoke. 'Why are you here in the middle of the night, playing a flute?'

'I…I'm waiting for the ferry.'

'It stopped at midnight.'

He looked up the jetty, embarrassed, then back at her. 'Looks like I'm stuck here then.' He was struck once again by her presence. 'Why are you here?'

'My grandfather's coming to pick me up in his boat.'

He had an uncontrollable urge to laugh. 'I seriously thought you were a mermaid for a second'.

'A mermaid?'

He nodded through his laughter which, to his dismay, turned into a sob. Here she was, the girl he had been thinking of all day, and he looked and smelt atrocious. He felt his face go hot. 'Sorry, I, I've just found out my father's alive, and my mother's a lunatic who has lied to me my whole life, and…and I miss my stepfather.'

He could sense she didn't know what to do. 'And you're in a strange place you're not used to?'

He nodded.

Tentatively, she approached and sat beside him. 'When did you move to the island?'

He held his breath, waiting for the spasms in his chest to subside and wiped his face with the back of his dirty sleeve. 'Two days ago – no, yesterday? Ha. I've lost track of time…so tired. My mother bought this hideous house that hangs over a swamp. Find it hard to sleep there.'

'The old Johnston house?'

'Johnston house?'

'There was a family called the Johnstons. They built it, lived there for years. Generations of them. My name's Ayla.' She held out her hand.

It seemed too tiny in his large palm. 'I'm Riley. Nice to meet you, Ayla.' The smooth touch of her skin sent a spark through him. He pulled away, feeling shy, wiping his face again with his sleeve, fiddling with the rustic flute, spinning it on the end of his fingertips, showing off, wondering if it would be rude to play, anything to fill the screaming silence.

'You're very talented. Think I've heard you a couple of times on the island.' She blushed.

I've seen you naked, he thought and blushed back. 'I can't play at home. My mother can't tolerate music.'

Her eyes widened in astonishment. 'I could listen to you for hours.'

They stared at each other as another silence engulfed them. He liked the way her cheeks lifted, making the sides of her eyes disappear when she smiled. She turned at the sound of a boat.

'Here he is. We can give you a lift if you want.'

'Thanks.'

'Probably best you hide that, he's…a bit funny sometimes about… stuff.'

'The flute?'

'I'll explain later.' She looked uncomfortable. Time was moving too fast now. He wanted to sit here talking all night but she was already shifting away, focused on the red wooden boat trailing a small tin dinghy in its wake.

Grappa had been lying naked in the arms of Dora, admiring the silver colour of her hair in the patch of moonlight through the sun roof, enjoying the gentle rock of the boat, when his mobile rang. Dora had been in a rare talking mood. He ached to hear more of her stories but they were seldom shared. When it happened, he felt like he was receiving a precious gift.

From where they were anchored, Dora could see the black mass of Big Island on the far horizon. He watched her watching it, knowing she had spent the first seven years of her life on the mission there.

'They've got a new section at the Big Island Museum, about how the mission came to be. Got some real old government documents on display.'

'Yeah?' He stroked the outside of her thigh up to her waist, loving the feel of her ample hip under his hand.

'In one of those documents, it talks about the policy of 'clearing the land', to open it up for new settlers.'

'What – clearing the scrub?'

'Nah, that's what I thought. But clearing the land meant killing anyone that was already living there. After they 'cleared the land', they realised they hadn't really 'cleared the land' because there were survivors, too many of them, so they decided to round them up and dump them all together on an allotted piece of dirt. That's what became the Mission, three different countries of people with three different languages, all forced together –'

The shatteringly modern phone tone of Grappa's mobile interrupted. He almost threw the damn thing in the drink. When he heard Ayla's distinctive voice through the little speaker, he thanked the Lord for such devices.

'Ayla's stuck on the mainland.'

'Better drop me back to the island then. Don't want tongues wagging.'

'They wag anyway.'

'Yeah, wag if you do, wag if you don't. If you don't, they just make it up, so it's better if you do.' She winked.

Grappa chuckled. His passion for this woman had led him to ask for her hand in marriage ten years after Nettie's death.

Dora had replied, 'You're a drinker. You'll always be a drinker. Why would I go marry me another drinker? Had enough drinkers in my life. Let's keep things the way they are, hey?'

'I could stop?'

'Let me know when you do. But if you can't, promise me, when it all catches up with you and you start getting sick, take this boat of yours and go park it off some other island a long way from here, because I'll be damned if I'm going to sit by and watch another person I love die from the stuff.'

The tears he had seen in her eyes that day made him secretly stop, but only a month went by before the brown liquid touched his lips, coated his throat and gurgled in his belly again.

'Thanks for dinner.' She stood in the shallows and pushed the dinghy out.

'Thanks for the company.' He rowed toward Little Beaudy.

'My pleasure, frisky old sea dog.'

'You can't talk, woman.'

Her laughter rang out in the night. He called between strokes. 'You keep me young, Dora. You keep me young.'

By the time Little Beaudy arrived at the mainland, there was a coolness hanging in the air. He could see Ayla wasn't dressed warmly enough. She had a friend with her. A scruffy looking bloke he had never seen before. Least it's not that wanker Harry, he thought, glad to see the back of him.

Grappa killed the engine and drifted into the jetty as he threw the rope for Ayla to tie off.

'This is my friend, Riley. Mind if we give him a lift?'

'Not at all. In you hop.'

Ayla jumped in and turned to untie the rope. As the boy went to step down, something slid from under his shirt and came to a stop at Grappa's feet. The boy stayed frozen on the jetty when he saw Ayla, horror-stricken.

Grappa picked the flute up, examining the strange symbols carved and burnt into the wood. He recognized the markings as runic. After his Gran died, Grappa had borrowed every library book he could source on faeries and Irish folklore. He remembered reading about runes and discovering the official title for Gran's black-haired man, Far Dorocha. The night felt lethal.

'Where'd you get this?'

'I made it.'

'Then these carvings, you know what they say?'

'They're patterns I made up.'

'Think I was born yesterday? They're ancient symbols. What do they mean?'

'I...I don't know. They're just random patterns. Honest.'

Grappa took in the creature, only half listening. Something had been rubbed into its hair to make it less black. He stepped closer and smelt the ungodly stench. Then he saw the large hairy feet.

Holy Jesus, Son of Mary.

'You smell rotten. Like the livin' dead.' Grappa threw the instrument at it. The flute almost rolled off the jetty. As the creature ran to grab it, Grappa snatched the rope from Ayla and untied. He couldn't get her away quick enough.

'No Grappa. Please?'

Thank the lord the engine caught first go. 'Leave my granddaughter alone, hear me? Go back to where you came from. We don't want you here.' He pulled out in to the bay, his heart beating wildly.

'Grappa –'

'Didn't you smell him? Didn't you see his feet? They're not human.' He hadn't meant to scream at her.

Ayla called to the thing. 'Sorry. I'm so sorry.' No denying it, she was in the grip of its spell.

Grappa watched the monster as distance made it appear smaller. He waited for it to fly out across the water and attack, but it stayed motionless at the end of the jetty.

Ayla was pleading. 'Please – he doesn't know anyone here. He was crying.'

'That's how he sucked you in, turned on the tears. Oldest trick in the book. Throw that rug over you, you're shivering.'

'What about him? He's going to freeze stuck on the jetty all night. Please? He's not Far Dorocha, I swear. His name's Riley. His mother bought the old Johnston house.'

'His mother...?' Grappa needed a moment to process this. His dream appeared more vividly than before. 'I've seen his mother. Ayla, listen to me. Look at me.' He turned her toward him. 'His mother – the Nor folk sent me a warning about her. If he's her son, then you need to stay right away from him.'

Ayla let out a frustrated shriek into the star peppered sky.

'The Nor folk tried to tell me...makes perfect sense...she's sending him out to do her dirty work.'

She bellowed it, 'You are a stupid old drunk. You know that? You're just a stupid old drunk.' Bursting into tears, she went and sat at the back of the boat.

They rode in silence for the rest of the trip. At the island jetty, Ayla jumped out without tying off, then fled, not looking back.

'Didn't even say thank you,' he muttered, reaching for his flask. He stopped himself from unscrewing the lid and threw it to the floor of the boat. He wasn't going to allow himself to be hurt by this. She wasn't herself. She was under a spell.

Still, her last words became a morbid echo bouncing round in his skull.

Ayla ran down the jetty, past the resort, up the hill and by the church. The slap of her sandals on the hard ground too loud in the sleepy island night. She didn't give a stuff. The faster she could get away from Grappa, the better.

'He's lost his mind this time. He's really lost his mind.'

When she reached Aunty Dora's house at the top of the rise, she leant against the front gate to catch her breath. The idea of poor Riley stuck on that lonely jetty made her hit out in frustration. A light near Hibiscus Bay caught her eye. At the bottom of Long Street, opposite the paperbark swamp, a house was lit up – Harley's.

'Jip.'

She was running again, towards the light, towards Jip lying comatose on a towel behind the screen door, Harley huddled beside him looking up with his small eyes – such tiny eyes – too close together, swollen and bloodshot.

'Ayla, what the fuck? It's the middle of the –'

'Is he dead?'

'He's still breathing...just.'

'You promised you'd ring.' She slammed the screen door so it rattled on its hinges.

'There's nothing you can do. Nothing anyone can do.'

'Harley, you promised.' She knelt by Jip and lifted the dog's eyelid. 'His eyes have rolled back. He's in a coma. How long has he been like this?' Her accusatory tone filled the quiet house.

'I don't fucking know. Kept having these seizures and...he messed himself...and...' Harley's face puckered in pain, making his small eyes disappear. Before Ayla could say anything, he was bawling like a child. 'He's dying, man, he's dying. Just know it.'

'It's not your fault, Harley. Hey?' He was inconsolable. 'I'm sorry.' She patted Harley on the back with one hand and stroked Jip with the other as the poor dog's breath caught and then stopped, sounding like a human sigh.

Harley let out a strangled moan as he hugged the dead dog, rocking and babbling. The moment was so private, so full of grief, Ayla quietly slipped out the door. She wanted to smash her head against the verandah post and scream; 'Useless Ayla. You are useless.' Instead, she began the long walk up the hill, every muscle in her body aching with sadness and shame. When Harley had first asked for her help, she should have taken control of the dog. That's what Stan would have done, taken Jip straight to a mainland vet. She had failed Jip. She had failed Harley. She had even failed Riley. Because of her he was stuck on the mainland for the night. If only she hadn't planted that stupid Far Dorocha seed in Grappa's alcohol-riddled brain. She turned the corner into her street and spat viciously. The salt from her tears tasted angry.

'Cry as much as you want, idiot. Won't change a thing.'

8.

Marlise woke from pain in her neck, unable to place where she was. A rectangular patch of sunlight on the floor blinded her.

David? No. David was dead. She had fallen asleep on the couch last night waiting for Riley. The house was empty. She could feel it. He still wasn't home.

Quickly showering and dressing, she decided the first step would be to discover if he had left the island, which meant talking to the boat drivers.

When she walked past the dog owner's house, she was relieved to see all was quiet. No sign of the dog and the house looked abandoned.

At the top of the hill, on the opposite side of the road, people were spilling out of a small wooden church. She was crossing the street in the hope to ask someone for directions to the ferry, when she spotted the dog owner. He was standing with his back to her, the dead dog in his arms, holding it out like a sacred offering to the parishioners who gathered round. Mumbled words of condolence rippled through the air.

In the church yard was a large hoop pine with a white horse tied to it. She hid between the horse and the tree, listening.

'Least he looks at peace, Harl.'

'Sorry Bob, can't be no mascot no more. Gone and died on me, he has.'

'Not to worry, matey.'

'Know what he died of, Harl?'

'Wasn't natural causes, man.'

'What, you think someone –?'

'I'm sure no one would want to hurt Jip,' the priest interrupted.

'No one who knows him would, no one who's seen him as the Whale Welcoming mascot, but maybe someone who's just moved to the island would.' The look on his face frightened Marlise.

'Someone who doesn't like dogs,' said a child.

'We haven't had any newcomers in a while.'

'There's new renters moved in next to me at Three Mile,' an old man said.

'And new people in the old Johnston house,' a teenage girl piped up.

'That house is not far from yours, Harl. Maybe Jip disturbed their idea of a quiet island life?'

'The woman came round and complained about his barking the day before he got sick. Doesn't take much to join the dots, does it?' Harley hissed.

There was a general murmur after this statement. Marlise felt cornered, not knowing whether to run or stay hidden.

'We don't want to go accusing people when we have no proof,' said the priest, then pointedly changed the subject.

Marlise sank behind the tree and thought of Harley's face with sunglasses for eyes in the car mirror, watching. Surprised at how she had broken into a sweat, she dared another look.

Harley was speaking to an older couple standing to his left. 'I don't have the strength to bury him Trev, June I...' He almost dropped the dog.

June stepped forward. 'We'll take care of him for you, won't we, Trev?'

'What are neighbours for? Here, let me carry him, Harl.' Trev held the dog out with a respectful formality.

June took Harley by the elbow. 'Come on, Harl, let's go home.'

Organ music continued to drift from the church as the parishioners watched the odd little funeral procession disappear down the hill. There was a murmured consensus: it was a sad day. The island had lost its favourite dog.

As people dispersed, Marlise, trapped, stayed close to the tree, pretending to pat the horse. A short elderly lady in a big hat addressed the animal, untying it. 'Did you see, Toto? Our friend Jip is dead.' She spoke with a thick Italian accent.

The tears in the woman's eyes surprised Marlise but she persevered. 'Excuse me, do you know where the ferry comes in?'

'The jetty. Straight downhill. Easy. No turn left. No turn right.'

'Thank you.' The old lady had no idea she was the suspected dog killer.

At the jetty, a few tourists lingered outside the resort around the ice-cream booth. When she saw that bitchy Sharon woman serving behind the counter, Marlise kept walking up the pier where a group of despondent teenagers sat fishing.

'Jip was a legend.'

'I reckon.'

She nearly tripped over in shock at how quickly word had travelled. A pelican perched on the stump at the end of the jetty glided off at the sound of the ferry approaching. She saw Riley sitting by himself, on the top deck, his head bowed.

Poor baby.

He stepped off the boat and looked through her, walking straight past, making her feel as inconsequential as the stinky fish scales stuck to the jetty under her shoes. She fell in beside him, wanting to ask where he had been all night. By the look on his face, questioning was not the right tactic. He waved at Sharon in the ice-cream booth who waved back with a smug smirk.

'You know that woman?'

'She said you need your head checked.' He powered up the hill.

She had to run to keep up. 'Why did she say that? Riley? Talk to me.'

He increased his pace, forcing her to catch her breath between words. 'I'm sorry I lied, but it wasn't far from the truth. He might as well be dead. He only stayed for a couple of years, then left. That's it, end of story.'

He stopped. 'It's not the end of the story if he's still alive. Where were you when he left? America?'

'Yes.'

'So, he's still in America?'

'Need a lift?' It was Grunter, hanging out the window of a beat-up Holden station wagon, one hand on the wheel.

'Grunter.' Her voice betrayed her embarrassment at being caught in such an intimate exchange. 'This is my son, Riley. Grunter works on the barge. He's keeping his eye out for a job.'

Grunter sized him up. 'Come down sometime. We'll give you a try. Nothin' goin' yet, but never know your luck.' He winked at her.

'Okay. Thanks.' Riley mumbled, studying his dirty feet.

Grunter watched her. 'So, need a lift?'

'If it's not out of your way?'

'I'll just spin her round.' He did, before the exhaust fumes had left the pipe. 'Jump in.'

She climbed into the back, forcing Riley to sit in the front. Grunter twisted to look at her, disappointed. 'I don't bite you know, unless you're into that sort of thing.' He winked again. Alarmingly, he kept turning back to talk to her. 'I'm on the first of me days off. On the barges, we have seven days on, three days off. Great job if the weather's good. If the weather's crap, it sucks. Poor old Harl.'

He slowed to take in the scene. The dog owner was digging a hole in his front yard. The dead dog at his feet. His two neighbours stood beside him, beer in hand. Marlise slid down the seat as they stared at the passing car. This was why she had accepted the offer of a lift.

She saw Grunter give them a nod. 'Won't know what to do with himself now Jip's gone. Poor bugger.' He manoeuvred the corner. 'Like fishing, Marlise?'

'It's something I haven't had much experience with.'

'We better get you some experience then. Free this arvy? Thinking of taking the tinny for a spin, drop a line. What you reckon?' He pulled up outside their house and turned his sun red face to her, pockmarked and hopeful.

'We're barely unpacked...maybe next time? Once we've settled in. Thanks for the lift.' She smiled graciously then slammed the door as he opened his mouth to protest. Riley murmured a thank you. They watched Grunter reverse, swinging the big car around, tooting as he drove off.

Riley frowned. 'Are you really going fishing with him?'

'Absolutely not.'

'Then why lie?'

'I didn't. I said maybe.'

'You touched him on the arm as you said it, leaning in, smiling, teasing. That man now thinks you're going fishing with him.'

'Well, I'm not.' She held the door open.

'You lie continually. You don't even know when you're doing it.' He scowled as he went past.

'I was being polite. He gave us a lift. He might give you a job. What did you want me to say? I find you very unattractive?' He headed up the hallway, looking worn out by life, making her wish he was still small enough to rock to sleep in her arms. 'Aren't you hungry? Why don't you have a shower? Freshen up?'

Grateful to have him home, she ignored the slam of the bathroom door. He was safe again here with her, where she could protect him from the rest of the world, like a mother should. There were people out there with the potential to hurt, to take him into dark places. She knew that darkness. It would give him nightmares for the rest of his life. He had yet to learn these things.

As soon as Ayla woke, she threw her swimmers on, ran down the track to the beach and dived into an oncoming wave. Relaxing her body, she let the push and pull of the surf tumble her around, hoping the fizz and pop of white froth would wash away the sad visions from last night.

She emerged to flump on the sand. Glad for the first time that Grappa never anchored off Mud Rock. He avoided the open sea, preferring the sheltered bays of Hibiscus and Three Mile, or out beyond the mangroves if the easterlies blew. He was the last person she wanted to see today.

Her mother appeared from the track with two mugs of tea and handed her one.

'Thanks.'

'Thought you were staying on the mainland?'

'Changed my mind.'

'Woman's prerogative.'

A large wave crashed against the shore.

'Jip's dead.'

'Yes, I heard. Harley's claiming he was baited.'

Ayla clicked her tongue. 'I told him it looked viral.' She kicked at the sand. 'Poor Jip.' The piece of pumice stone in her hand was so light, when she tossed it toward the shoreline, it landed at her feet. The failure to throw it further brought tears.

Her mother wiped them from her cheek. 'Hey, hey, hey, Aylee. It's not your fault. You did everything you could.'

'No, I didn't. Everything I attempt, I fail at.'

'That is not true.'

'Then why aren't I at uni? Why am I back here, hiding away, cleaning houses?'

'You deferred because you wanted a break, not because you were failing. God Ayla, get some perspective. You were top of your course. It was that vile narcissist, Harry. He broke your heart. If I ever get a chance to, I'm going to give him a piece of my mind. Selfish bastard.'

'Wasn't just him. Even last night...it was lovely to see all my friends, but I still felt like I was observing everything from outside. I can't explain it –'

'Once you start back at uni that will change.'

'Will it? Feels like I don't belong anywhere.'

'You belong here.'

'No, I don't.'

'You were born here. Literally. I didn't even make it to the boat, remember? If anyone belongs here, you do.'

'No. Aunty Dora does, Rayleen does, Mandy does. We don't.'

'Codswallop. On my mother's side, you are fifth-generation Australian. How many generations back do we need to go before we can call a place home?'

'We're still aliens here though. It's not our ancestral home.'

Her mother looked stunned. 'You're being far too intellectual about this. As Aunty Dora would say, you're thinking too much in white feller terms. You can't honestly say you don't feel a strong connection to the island?'

'I thought I did when I was a kid, but now...' Ayla couldn't stop the new wave of tears.

Her mother put her arm around her. They touched heads.

'You've just lost yourself for a moment, Aylee. I have full faith in you. You'll get there. It doesn't help having Grappa fill your head with so much nonsense. When you were little, you believed him with all your soul. I knew this day would come.'

'What day?'

'When the universe he created for you would collapse. Grappa was your world. You always took his word over mine. That really annoyed me.'

'He's the annoying one. Sick of the way he carries on.'

Her mother blew on her tea. 'He dropped by earlier. Said I wasn't to let you out of my sight.'

Ayla buried her feet in the sand. 'Did he tell you how he left that poor guy stranded there, all night?'

'Who? The dark-haired agent of the faery queen? The son of the changeling in the guise of a woman that's moved into the old Johnston house?'

'Mum, it's not funny. He's humiliating.'

'He shouldn't drink so much.' Her mother's voice was steeped in disappointment. 'He has a good heart and loves you beyond words. You have to remember that.'

Ayla groaned.

'Why don't you visit the young man and apologise? Tell him your grandfather's a little mad. I'm sure he'll understand.'

Ayla wriggled her toes so the sand around her buried feet caved in. 'I feel so embarrassed. I don't know how to explain Grappa.'

Her mother's arm around her wet body felt safe and warm. An image of Riley standing mystified on the end of the jetty in the moonlight came to her, making her jump up. She helped her mother to her feet.

'You're right. I should make sure he got home, at least.' They hugged. 'Thanks Mum.'

She brushed the sand from Ayla's back. 'You should go see Grappa, make amends.'

'Too angry with him.'

'Fair enough.'

They walked into the house, quietly going their separate ways, linked by mutual love and frustration for that silly old man bobbing about in his boat somewhere beyond the island.

By the time Ayla walked past Harley's, there was a mound of fresh dirt in the front yard and a makeshift cross on top with the first hibiscus flowers of the season scattered around the base. Harley, Trev and June were sitting on the verandah, drinking. Ayla was relieved to see Harley had his sunglasses on. She tried to rid herself of the memory of his tiny red eyes, too close together.

He called out. 'Want a beer, man? Trev bought a slab.'

Ayla opened the gate. 'No thanks, Harl. Just wanted to say how sorry I am. Wish I could have saved him.'

'No one could save him. Damage had already been done. Fucking bitch.'

'Harley thinks he knows who did it.' June looked apologetic.

'If he'd been poisoned he would have been vomiting, Harley. He didn't vomit once, did he?'

'Nup.' He turned to June. 'It was like his heart just fuckin' seized up on him.' June patted Harley while he struggled to speak. 'Was good as gold couple of days ago. No dog gets that sick overnight unless some fucker's done something to him.'

The violence with which Harley said this disturbed Ayla. 'No one would want to hurt Jip.'

'Unless his barking got to them...not that he barked that much. He was a one bark kind of dog.' Trev punctuated this with a burp.

'Just because that woman complained, doesn't mean anything, Harley.'

'Yeah? Well, I haven't told you this bit – I caught a lift home with Tilly the day Jip got sick and that bitch was in the car. When we pulled up and Jip didn't run to greet me, that bitch smiled, a real knowing look she had on her face.'

'The woman smiled, not Tilly,' added June.

'And when June saw her walk by earlier that morning, she swears that bitch looked over at Jip lying there and laughed, man. Laughed. June remembers, 'cause she wondered what the fuck she was laughing about. Who would laugh at a fucking dying dog?'

'Maybe it was a coincidence Harl? Maybe she was thinking of something funny at the time?' June said hopefully, always trying to see the best in people.

'June's right, without proof, you can't go accusing her.'

'My dog is dead. How much more fuckin' proof do you need?' Harley grabbed his shirt and wiped his face with it, almost knocking his sunglasses off in the process. There was a lull in the conversation as they stared at the grave. Ayla stood to leave.

'Sorry about the language, Ayla. Not meself today. Don't usually drink.'

'Get yourself a puppy. That'll be the best way to get over Jip.'

'That's what we've been saying to him,' Trev and June almost cheered in agreement.

'Nup. No one can replace Jip.' His pursed lips and jutted jaw ended the conversation.

Ayla walked down Long Street and turned into the dirt road that led to the mangrove swamp. Her stomach flipped, remembering the feel of Riley's skin when they touched hands.

The house had a graveyard silence. It had been years since she had come near this place. All the macabre stories attached to it assailed her. What acts had those Johnston brothers committed here, where no one but the mud crabs could hear them? Were there really human remains buried under the house, or was that island gossip? She took a breath and knocked lightly on the door, the dead stench from the mangroves filling her head with gruesome thoughts.

The place was too quiet. All she could hear was the whine of mosquitoes, circling. As she turned to leave, his mother opened the door. Ayla was struck by her beauty. The brown of her eyes so deep it was almost black. The same almond shape as her son's eyes. She didn't look like a changeling or a dog murderer.

'Yes?' The woman whispered.

'Um, I was wondering if Riley was home?'

She looked indignant now. 'How do you know him?'

Ayla couldn't place her slight accent. 'We met on the jetty last night.'

She examined Ayla like something in a Petri dish. 'He's asleep.'

'Good. Just wanted to make sure he got home.' Ayla turned to leave.

'Why aren't you killing them?'

'Pardon?'

'The mosquitoes. You're brushing them away, not killing them.'

'They have as much right to live on this planet as the rest of us.' Ayla shrugged, not wanting to explain how, as a child, Grappa had told her the Nor folk probably use the mosquitoes as spies, information gatherers from the human realm, so from an early age she had developed a habit of not killing them.

The woman looked at Ayla as if she was an angel fallen from the sky to land on her doorstep. 'Good for you. I'll make sure to tell him you dropped by.' She shut the door.

Ayla decided there was a definite aloofness about his mother that wouldn't endear her to people, but once she warmed to you, she seemed lovely.

She intended to walk her favourite way home via the beach, until she saw Little Beaudy anchored in the bay. She darted down Hibiscus Beach Drive instead, to cut through the bushland behind Mud Rock. Anything to avoid Grappa. The sight of his boat sent her awash with anger and guilt, creating a dull ache in her chest. She realised the dream walls of her childhood were made of sand. Grappa had built them around her so high her view had been obscured. In her mind's eye, she could see him now, pouring booze over them, melting them away to a sodden mess.

9.

Riley was exhausted. He slept into the night and most of the next day. When he woke, his mother was sitting by the bed, watching. He hated it when she did this. He had asked her not to once, because he found it creepy. She had screamed, 'Now I'm creepy, am I?' and stormed off, refusing to speak to him for the rest of the day.

'You must be hungry. I'll fix you lunch.' She brushed the hair from his forehead.

He should try not speaking to her for a day, see how she liked it, he thought, following her into the kitchen.

She kept her back to him while making a sandwich and asked too casually, 'That money...did David give it to you?'

'Earned it myself.'

She turned, 'How?'

'Our weekly trips to the Sunday markets, we weren't only buying food. I set up a stall, sold my flutes, busked.' He relished the shock this produced.

'If you ever need money, just ask me.'

'It was David's idea. He organized everything. Said I should know that what I created was worth something.' The more he talked about David, the more pain he inflicted. 'He insisted we go behind your back because he knew you wouldn't allow it.'

'I see.' She handed him the sandwich.

'I made friends at those markets. David encouraged it.'

'I've never stopped you having friends.'

She sounded so indignant, believing her own lie.

'In fact, a young woman dropped by asking for you yesterday. Pretty little thing. I thought she was very nice.'

He stopped chewing and studied the chair leg. 'What did she say?'

'Wanted to know if you made it home safely.' She opened the cupboard and reached for a can. 'I'm glad you've made a friend on the island. When you've finished lunch, you should go catch up with her.'

Riley watched as she opened a can of pineapple. His mother had never encouraged any form of friendship and destroyed his one attempt at making a friend.

'It's about time you got out there and met people. David was right. You need to live your own life now.' She burst into tears. 'I don't know why I've opened a can of pineapple.'

He hugged her. She was too small, too easily broken. It came out as a whisper, 'Mum, my father...' He gently turned her face so he could read her eyes. 'You really don't know where he is?'

She shook her head and looked away. 'Go and find that young woman. She wanted to talk to you urgently.'

'Urgently?'

She went into her laboratory and shut the door.

Riley spent too long trying to make himself presentable, wincing every time he recalled his smell and dishevelled appearance on the jetty. Staring at the things on the ends of his legs, he remembered the first time he thought about his feet. His mother, examining them in disappointment, had withered. 'You have your father's feet.'

He loathed wearing shoes, but after what Ayla's grandfather said about his feet, he thought it best to cover them, pulling on his only pair of shoes: black patent leather numbers his mother had bought him for David's funeral. They felt slimy without socks.

He grabbed the largest of his flutes – thinking if Ayla wasn't home he would get some practice in – and started for the beach, tripping in the hard, foreign things imprisoning his feet.

In the bay was the same red wooden boat, anchored now in a different spot. It looked like her cranky grandfather's vessel. He wondered if Ayla was on board. There appeared to be no sign of life.

He walked to the headland on the point and climbed, with difficulty in his cumbersome shoes, until he could see the length of the surf beach curving around to the next spit in a half smile. Apart from a man and woman with three young children at the far end, the beach was empty. From this position, he had a clear view of the 'No Trespassers' sign.

As the waves crashed on the rocks below, a new tune crept into him, rising out of the cliff itself. He tried to change the melody to something less brutal, but his fingers weren't his own anymore, they moved beyond him as a strange melancholia seeped into his soul, torturing and twisting it. Harnessing all his strength, he pulled the flute from his mouth. Disturbed by where the music had taken him, he scrambled off the rock and headed toward her track, faltering when he arrived at the sign. If he walked up the path and knocked on her door, she would know how he had discovered where she lived. She would have heard his flute the other morning and guess he had seen her naked.

Undecided, he trudged further up the beach and sat in the shade of a tree, feeling ridiculous in shoes now full of sand.

On the brink of abandoning his vigil, she came along the track, dressed in a bikini. As she threw her towel down, she spied him standing in his goofy shoes. 'Riley.'

'Gosh, fancy running into you here. I was just passing by. What a coincidence.' He cringed at the idiocy pouring out of his mouth and tried not to stare at her skimpily clad body.

Her big warm smile brought a sun-filled melody into his head.

An unshakeable cloud of misery had settled over Grappa, and Ayla, his cloud buster, was nowhere in sight. He felt suspended in time waiting for her to come to the beach and wave, his signal to row in and collect her for a cup of tea. Or, sometimes, they would stroll around the island. If he could only talk to her, describe the dream, then she would understand and his world could spin freely again. The earth could revolve around the sun, and the moon could revolve around the earth, and all would be as it should be. He couldn't sleep with the thought of her in the company of that creature.

He moored his boat on the western side of Hibiscus, where, through a gap in the trees, he could see the dirt track leading to the Johnston house. He watched for two days and a night, cursing every time he dozed off. Towards the end of the second day, he caught sight of Far Dorocha striding boldly onto the beach to glare at Little Beaudy.

Jesus Christ, Son of Mary. Grappa ducked, craning his neck to peer out. The creature turned and marched toward Mud Rock, wearing shoes this time to hide his unearthly hooves. Grappa noted how he had groomed himself to appear more human. But worst of all, his instrument with the strange markings had magically tripled in length. Grappa knew this was a bad omen as he watched the fiend head in the direction of Ayla's house.

He scrambled into the dinghy and rowed to shore as quickly and quietly as his age would allow. The thing had climbed to the top of the Rock and was playing a tune that came from another world, mesmerising Grappa.

'Concentrate, you fool.' Dragging himself out of his stupor, Grappa ran for cover, scanning the undergrowth for a stick large enough to attack with. No point wasting a good oar. The music stopped mid-flight. He saw the beast leap from the rock.

Staying hidden in the shade of the cottonwood trees, Grappa

scrambled through the scrub behind the headland and past the bent she-oaks, towards Ayla's house.

He watched the creature approach the track, stop and circle, then walk further up the beach to sit and wait for its prey.

Grappa picked up a thick piece of driftwood and moved silently to position himself behind the fiend, just in time to see Ayla unknowingly amble down the path. The beast stood and accosted her, pretending he happened to be passing, rather than lurking in wait. Ayla was captivated, her eyes ablaze with longing.

God, the Son and the Holy Ghost.

Riley didn't know where to look as Ayla came forward, the blood rising in her cheeks. 'I want to apologise for the other night —'

Before she could finish, her grandfather jumped from the scrub, waving a club above his head, screaming.

'Run, Riley.'

Riley bolted down the beach past the startled family, falling over in his stupid footwear. He could hear Ayla shouting and looked back to see another woman emerge from the track to take hold of the old man, berating him.

Ayla ran to catch up. 'Follow me.'

Riley sprinted after her ponderously through the sand in his hard shoes, around the point to a beach full of dead trees. They both doubled over, catching their breath.

'I'm sorry, Grappa...He's...totally lost it.'

'He seems very possessive of you.'

'That's not the half of it. I know where we can hide in case Mum can't talk sense into him.'

She led him over and around and sometimes through the sun-bleached skeletons of trees to a track which zigzagged up a cliff. She ducked behind a prickly bush, then, on all fours, they scurried through the undergrowth. It was hard to concentrate with the way her bikini bottoms rode up her buttocks.

The track opened into an overhang you could almost stand up in. 'This is my secret place,' she said, sitting down in the shade, her back against the cave wall.

He loved her broken voice.

'Promise not to tell anyone?'

'Promise.' He sat at a distance, too shy to look at her directly. He had already glimpsed the full beauty of her breasts. They appeared even more wondrous now, partially hidden. He followed her gaze and a jade coloured ocean with no visible end stole his breath.

'Puts you in your place, doesn't it?'

He could feel her watching as he stretched his legs and sand poured forever out of his ridiculous shoes. If only the cliff he was sitting on would crumble away and take him with it.

'Grappa believes – that's my grandfather – he thinks because you have black hair and play a flute, you are a dark lord from the faery kingdom come to steal me away.'

Riley checked to see if she was serious.

'It's my fault really. I got him going on the notion and now he can't let go of it.' Her frown deepened. 'Actually, it's my great-great-grandmother's fault.'

'Sorry?' She was losing him.

'Grappa's Gran was brought out here from Ireland at the end of her life, against her will, from what I can gather. Her two sons emigrated here and thought she would like it. Think she felt it was her duty before she died, almost like she owed it to the Irish in him, to fill her only grandson's head with all the Irish stories, superstitions and myths she could muster. Grappa's full of them and he lives his life by them, which makes him appear quite mad. Sorry about the way he's acting. He'll get over it, I hope. I've never seen him take things this far. He's becoming worse the older he gets. Do you usually wear shoes on the beach?'

He hesitated, not knowing if he should speak the truth. 'No. I never wear shoes.' He took them off and tipped the rest of the sand out of each one, his toes wiggling, happy to be free.

'Hope it wasn't because of what Grappa said the other night?'

'No I...no, of course not.'

She watched him. 'How do you know where I live?'

'I don't I...um...' He found her directness unnerving.

'You saw me the other morning, didn't you?'

Riley stared at his toes, blushing. She startled him by gently touching his left foot.

'I think they're the most human-looking feet I've ever seen.'

Grappa tried to twist out of his daughter's grip. 'Helen, let go of me.'

'What has gotten into you?'

Befuddled by her rage, he dropped the piece of wood. 'You shouldn't let her run off with him.' He tried to pull himself free but she grabbed his other arm and turned him to face her.

'Dad. Ayla isn't a child anymore. She's a woman. Free to do what she wants. It's her choice. You need to respect that.'

In his daughter's angry face, he saw Nettie. 'You've turned her against me.' To his dismay, he almost broke down at the thought of losing Ayla's love.

Helen's face softened. Before he could stop it, he was lost in the folds of her embrace.

'What are we going to do with you? Come and have a cuppa. We need to get this sorted.' She led him up the path to the little wooden house he had built with his own hands when he and Nettie were newlyweds. He still couldn't stomach the colour Helen had painted the place. Nettie's red geraniums, growing wild now around the back steps, were in full bloom.

The warm cinnamon smell of freshly baked banana bread filled the newly renovated kitchen. The hand painted tiles on the splashback were the one remaining sign of his Nettie. Helen switched the jug on while he sat at the kitchen table watching his shaking hands. He hadn't touched a drop since Ayla had called him a stupid old drunk.

Jesus, Son of Mary, what I'd do now for a snifter.

'Imagine if you had hit that young man with that lump of wood. You could have killed him.'

'He's not a young man.'

'Dad.' She gave him one of her looks, so like Nettie, it was unnerving.

'I wasn't going to hit him. Just trying to frighten him off.'

'You're embarrassing Ayla. Can't you see that?'

'If she would listen to me, give me a moment to explain, damn it.'

'Explain what?'

'The dream I had.'

'That's where all this has come from? Tell me the dream, I might be able to make sense of it for you.'

He was apprehensive. Helen had never truly believed as Ayla had. When Helen was a child, he tried countless times to draw her into the world of the Nor folk but she always angled her chin down, like a doctor studying a patient and said, 'Daddy, you're funny.' Too much of Nettie's common sense in her.

'Just the imaginings of a stupid old drunk.'

Helen put her hand over his. 'Ayla feels bad about calling you that.'

He knew in his heart Ayla was already lost to him, submerged under the flute player's spell. He didn't want to cry in front of his daughter. Above all else, he needed a drink. He stood up.

'Where are you going?' She looked worried.

'Back to the boat. Forget the cuppa.' He couldn't understand why his voice was shaking.

'Here, take some bananas. All the trees have come on at once.'

She walked with him back to the beach. 'From what Ayla told me, he sounds like a nice young man.'

'Not young. Probably thousands of years old.'

'Dad.' She clicked her tongue like Nettie used to. 'And his mother seemed quite normal.'

'You met her?'

'Only briefly.'

'Where?'

'The Resort the other night.'

'Stay away from her. She's bad news.'

'You've been listening to Harley, haven't you?'

'What's Harley got to do with it?'

'He's blaming Jip's death on her.'

Grappa felt the hairs on the back of his ears stand on end. 'Jip's dead then?'

'And Harley's convinced she did it. Poor woman.'

Grappa went back to the boat via a detour to Harley's. When he heard what Harley had to say, his Gran's words from the dream taunted him. 'Always a laugh for other people's misfortunes. Some even said she caused them.'

The memory of the woman laughing on the barge at the child's hurt sat with him as he rowed out to Little Beaudy. He had a bad feeling under his skin. His Gran had never come to him in a dream before. That dream contained a message of incredible importance and it was solely up to him to decipher it. With each pull of the oars, his shoulders ached. The fate of the whole island was resting on them.

Riley wanted to reach out and straighten one of the triangles on Ayla's bikini that had moved, almost exposing her nipple, but he didn't dare.

This close, he saw her skin was the same colour as the honeyed cliff face, and the light sprinkling of freckles across her nose reminded him of the microscopic fragments of shell grit he had found in the sand. Her eyes were the pale green of the distant sea. She's not real. She's carved out of this landscape, he thought, hypnotised, as she inched closer to place her lips on his. Her mouth was the softest thing he had ever tasted. Drinking her up, his hands wandered with a life of their own over her bare back as he drowned in her musky scent and the silky feel of her.

He struggled to pull away. 'I...uh.'

'Wow.'

'I better uh...I just remembered I had to...' He stood, smashing his head on the ceiling of the cave.

'Are you alright?'

He rubbed his crown in pain. 'Yeah, I'm...I just...I need...I promised Mum I would uh...' His arousal made every movement indecisive, even where to place his gaze.

'I'll take you back, in case Grappa's lurking somewhere waiting to ambush.'

He laughed too loudly and followed her down the path, the bump on his scalp throbbing in time with the blood of his erection.

They walked the beach in silence, stealing glances at each other. Still disoriented from her kiss, Riley furiously tried to think of something to say.

By the time they reached the path with the 'No Trespassers' sign, the lavender sky was streaked with yellow in the west where the sun was disappearing, and their silence had grown all sorts of meaning. The old man was nowhere in sight. Riley felt idiotic clutching his over-sized footwear in one hand and the heavy ornate flute in the other.

'Sorry if I came on too strong before,' she blurted. 'I don't know why I kissed –'

'No I...not at all...I...I would like to do it some more...' This time he initiated the kiss, moving in too quickly and dropping one of the patent-leather monstrosities on her foot.

'Ow.'

'Sorry.'

She started hopping. 'Ooooh – caught me on the bone.'

'I'm so sorry.' He leaned down to pick up the shoe as she bent to examine her foot and they smashed heads.

'Sorry.'

'No, I'm sorry.'

'I better leave before I kill you.'

She laughed. 'Might see you tomorrow? I'm usually here swimming most afternoons.'

'Sure, that would be fine...just fine.' Walking backwards, he tripped over a tree root.

'Um, maybe go home via the road, not the beach. I think Grappa's anchored off Hibiscus.'

'Sure.' He got up, waved and marched off, irritated by being so hopeless around this living, breathing island goddess.

By the time he arrived at the dirt road, he was grinning like an idiot and floated like that the rest of the way home. She had kissed him. She had kissed him. Even the old house hanging over the stinking mangroves couldn't steal the stupid smile from his face.

Marlise counted the last of the notes and placed the money back in his flute case. She checked the room was exactly as he had left it.

The hallway swam with the thoughts rolling in her head, forcing her to rest against the architrave. She shut her eyes at the realisation that Riley had enough money to leave the country if he wished.

How long had he and David betrayed her during their weekly trip to the markets? Then there were the cyber cafe visits. Before he died, David revealed he had taken Riley to an internet cafe on a regular basis. Why? What had they searched? Pornography? The thought made her sick. David hadn't been that kind of man. Then again, he was a man. Riley had become a man at some moment when she wasn't paying attention. Men, thick as thieves — thieves of her heart, both of them, laughing together. She always missed the joke, her mind half with her mosquitoes, half listening. She tried to picture herself in their relationship and couldn't see it. Who had she been to David? What was she to Riley?

Her beautiful baby boy would leave her soon to be torn up and spat out by the world. She could feel it. Unless she could help him find happiness here? Happiness was that pretty thing that didn't kill mosquitoes. The perfect distraction to help him forget searching for his father. If Riley found Lorcan, then she would lose him forever. They would communicate through their music, beyond any level she was capable of, beyond her understanding. If Riley found Lorcan, she would be redundant, or worse, the enemy.

She walked into her lab and placed the first of the mud samples under the microscope, content in the knowledge that Riley had eagerly run off to find the lovely one with the pert breasts who conveniently lived on the island. Marlise understood well the power of sexual attraction. Once the girl had revealed her wonders, then all thoughts of leaving would fly out of his mind. She pressed her eye against the lens, entering the microcosm of the minuscule, until the slam of the screen door downstairs.

'Riley?'

'Yeah, only me,' he sounded happy.

She walked into the kitchen where he was busy preparing food.

'You keep working Mum. I'll cook dinner.'

His eyes were shining and his face flushed, all his blood raised to the surface. She could almost smell it, pumping frenziedly around his body, just beneath his skin.

'Caught up with her then?'

'Yeah.' He evaded her gaze, busily chopping onions, then stopped to scratch his abdomen and lifted his shirt. 'What...?'

She examined the beginnings of a welt-like rash on his torso. 'Oh dear...hives.'

'Hives?' He stared as if diagnosed with cancer.

She touched a swelling on the side of his face.

He ran to the hallway mirror. 'No. No. Why?'

'It's a nervous thing with you. You got them every time I tried you at a new school. It was easier to homeschool in the end.'

'It's the same thing that happened last year, when David took me...'

'Busking and selling flutes?'

His look reminded her of the time he had denied opening the jar of honey, with the tell-tale traces of stickiness plastered around his four-year-old mouth.

'Now I understand why a simple trip to the markets brought you out in hives.'

'Only the first time.' He was still at the mirror.

'What's brought it on this time?'

'The swelling's getting worse, Mum.'

'Don't panic.' She walked into the bathroom. 'We've got some anti-histamine.'

He was right behind her. 'Last time it took days to go away.'

'Can do. Here, take one of these.'

He popped the pill, then checked his face in the bathroom mirror. 'Oh great, just great.'

She had never seen him care about appearance. He's smitten, she thought, suppressing the bubble of laughter in her lungs.

10.

Marlise was woken by the intermittent scuff of footsteps on the dirt road. That wasn't a normal walk. It was sneaking, not wanting to be heard. She jumped out of bed. Where would Riley be skulking off to so early and why would he be wearing shoes? Passing his bedroom, she saw his enormous feet poking out from under the doona. She ran the rest of the way downstairs to unlock the solid wooden door.

Someone had left a note jammed under the security screen, the almost transparent paper ripped from a lined notebook. The writing in black pen was cursive, small and uneven: *Fuck off back to where you came from. You're not welcome here.*

She inched the screen door open. The empty road looked malignant in the ash light of dawn. Torn between fear and a desire to know who had left the threat, Marlise ran part way up the road, the gravel sharp on her bare feet. A peacock and his hens crossed in front of her, the cock blocking her way, the blues and greens of his exotic tail vibrating in the pale light, startling her with his loud cry.

'Vermin.' She waved the piece of paper, trying to move it on so she could pass.

At the bend in the empty road, she pulled her thin satin dressing gown tighter against the chill of early morning as a gust of wind blew dust into her face, and she heard the screen door slam. She walked back to the house, reading the ugly little note again. It had to be the dog owner. If only she hadn't complained about the damn barking.

Riley was standing under the house in a singlet and boxers, shivering, his face lined from sleep. 'The door banged.'

'Just the wind.'

'What were you doing?'

'There were peacocks.' She tucked the note into her dressing gown pocket. No point in upsetting him. 'Your hives are gone.'

'Really?' He felt his face then raced inside.

She observed her disappointment. He had spent the last three days moping, obsessing in front of the mirror, and had allowed her to fuss over him. She had enjoyed revelling in his need, such a rare occurrence these days.

She entered the kitchen and heard the shower in the bathroom turn on. He would be off to find the girl now. At least it would distract him from the idea of his father. Last night she had caught him staring at that photo again, and the day before he had asked to see his birth certificate. She had lied, claiming it had accidentally been thrown out along with hers, years ago. He had scowled for the rest of the day, then asked to use her computer. She had searched the history, later. *How to apply for an American birth certificate.*

She sighed and opened the fridge. They were almost out of milk and Riley had eaten the last of the bread. A trip to the mainland was necessary, which meant walking past that man's house. A car to get around the island would be handy. Tilly had told her, 'Everyone here ends up with two cars, one for the mainland, one for the island – too expensive bringing a car backwards and forwards all the time.' And Marlise had learnt now, you needed to book in advance. She bit her lip. There was no avoiding it. She would be forced to walk past him sitting there, watching from under his dark sunglasses. He was probably waiting for her now, anticipating her reaction. What was he planning? The note was toxic, burning a hole in her pocket. She read it again. 'Arsehole.' she said to no one and felt nauseous. Her head became heavy in her hands as she sat at the kitchen table, effectively a prisoner in her new home. The excitement she had known since moving here curdled into despair. David would have stopped her from complaining about the barking. For the past twelve years, he had managed her, kept her away from people wherever possible, quietly guided her in the most appropriate way to act. If David were here, none of this would be happening.

What if that scar-faced psycho came back at night? In such an isolated corner of the island, no one would hear a scream for help. This thought made the marrow in her bones shrink, made her clutch the table, a child again in the dark, suffocating. She left her body and saw herself sitting fully grown in a kitchen. Her son was on the other side of the wall. The sound of the shower soothing. She took a breath and drifted back into her body, alive and safe.

A panic attack? That hadn't happened in a long while.

All week Ayla had frequented the beach, neglecting cleaning jobs in the hope that they would cross paths but there had been no sign of him, not even the sound of a flute, since the afternoon they had kissed.

She stared at herself in her mother's full-length mirror. The red and white polka dot shorts weren't quite the look she was after, but they were preferable to her usual daggy house-cleaning gear. She began to apply her mother's make-up.

Why would you wear make-up to clean a house, fool?

She washed the gunk off, hating the roundness of her cheeks and her pointy chin.

'Stuff it.'

Grabbing her cleaning trolley, she half ran, half walked, the flip flop of her thongs leaving a trail of dust all the way up the road. At the end of Long Street, she stopped. What if he was cool towards her?

Whatever happens, keep your dignity, Ayla.

Turning onto the dirt road that led to his house, they spotted each other at the same time. A smile lit his face. Ayla felt her heart float up her throat.

'I was ah…just coming to visit you.'

'I was just coming to clean your house.'

'Pardon?'

'Your Mum booked me to clean your house today.'

'My Mum…?'

'I do all sorts of odd jobs for Tilly. Means I don't have to go to the mainland for work.' She kept walking.

'You…you can't clean our house.'

They rounded the bend and nearly ran into his mother. Her hair tied in a knot on top of her head revealed a mosquito tattoo at the base of her neck as she turned to slip a lethal-looking blade into her handbag.

'What are you doing with David's grafting knife?' Riley sounded appalled.

'You frightened me. I didn't know what that noise was. Just your trolley.' She pulled a key on a string out of her bag, placing it around Riley's neck, 'I'm going to the mainland. I've locked the house. This is your key. Don't take it off. Always lock the house when you go out, please.'

Ayla felt sorry for the woman. Had she heard the rumour Harley was spreading about her? Had someone been rude to her? Ayla cringed knowing how some locals were horrendous gossips. If only his mother understood how safe it was living here. Most islanders never locked their houses.

She held out her hand and said, 'Hello again. I'm Ayla, your cleaner.'

His mother's face went blank.

'Since when do we need a cleaner, Mum?'

'I forgot I booked a cleaner.'

'Would you like me to come back another time?'

She hesitated – 'Not at all' – then shook Ayla's hand.

The brief touch of the woman's fingers was cool and limp, like something dead.

'We haven't been here very long, but the house is already a mess. Needs a good clean.'

'You can't let her, Mum. I'll clean the house.'

His mother laughed in disbelief.

'I will. Really, you don't need to clean our house.'

'It's up to her, Riley. If you need the money, you're most welcome, but if you would prefer to delay it, that's fine also. I know Riley's been itching to catch up with you. Literally.' She smirked.

He looked away, annoyed.

'I'm here with my stuff ready to go. Might as well.'

'Settled then.'

'Mum, no.'

His mother called as she walked off. 'Don't worry about my work room, that's out of bounds, even to Riley. And don't move furniture or clean under beds. Vacuum around the beds, please.' Her 'please' sounded more like a command than a request.

'Vacuum around the beds. Got it.'

'I'm not going to let you clean our house.' He had to yell to be heard over the trolley on the gravel.

'I could do with the money.'

'I'm going to help you then.'

'Don't you have something better to do?'

'I've got nothing better to do. I'm…I was…I'm sorry I've…' They were at the front door. He paused, daring to take her hand.

Her heart was beating so hard, her head was thumping. She stared into his open face and realised they were the same height. How perfect was that? She took his other hand. The warm feel of it thrilled her. 'Thought maybe I'd scared you off.'

She felt the pulse at the end of their fingertips racing in time.

'Shall I start with your room?' She teased.

'I'll do my room.'

She followed him as he carried her trolley up the stairs, admiring the curve of his body under his jeans.

Riley parked her trolley in the hallway and raced around, picking things up. She had never been in this house. There was a gloominess that sat heavily in the air, even on a sunlit day like today. Touching the old weatherboards, she remembered after the Johnstons, a young couple had moved in and renovated. When their newborn baby died of cot death, they sold to an investor and moved off. The house then sat on the market for years.

Ayla could see into what looked like the main living area where Riley was throwing pillows onto a couch. He picked up an empty bowl with a spoon left in it and carried it to the kitchen, clearly uncomfortable. 'Let me tidy up a bit first.'

To the right was another door which she opened onto a dank smelling room with benches, a fridge, freezers and a large box like a walk-in wardrobe that was softly humming. She crept into it and realised it was a humidifier full of cages. At the bottom of some were dishes of water filled with little black...what were they? Wrigglers? Yuk, she's breeding mosquitoes. Ayla shuddered and stepped out of the cubicle. On the floor was a giant canister labelled: *caution liquid nitrogen*, and behind a microscope sat a jar of clear liquid marked *chloroform*. Beneath the workbench a metal cupboard emanated a musty smell. She had smelt that smell before. What was it? As she approached the metal locker, his voice surprised her.

'Like Mum said, you don't have to clean this room.' He sounded constricted. 'Please...' He gestured for her to leave. 'She hardly lets me in here.'

Ayla could tell he was upset, the colour of his eyes even seemed darker. 'Sorry.'

'Not your fault.' He slammed the door behind her.

She walked into the lounge area and stared at the array of books lining the shelves. There was also a substantial record collection. 'Wow, someone likes books and music.' She attempted to lighten the mood.

'My step-father, David. He passed away four months ago.'

Knowing that words were useless in the face of death, she stayed silent and followed Riley down the hallway. He entered a room and started picking clothes off the floor, then quickly made his bed. The long shelf in his room was lined with flutes.

'That's quite a collection.'

'I sold them at the markets.'

'We have markets here twice a year.'

'Really?' He looked happier. 'Might set up a stall at the next one.'

'Is that how you make a living?'

'Was trying to.'

'If you need a job, I'll ask Tilly for you. She always knows if there are any jobs going.'

'Thanks. I'd appreciate that.'

She was relieved to see him smile again.

The flutes, varying in size, shape and colour, each had a unique pattern burnt into them. Some had retained parts of the original tree, a knot or the fork in a branch, making them look otherworldly. 'Carved in a realm where wood elves dwelled,' Grappa would say.

'You make these?'

'Burrawang had an endless supply of soft woods.'

'Burrawang?'

'David's property, two hundred hectares of forest, some of it rainforest backing onto a national park.'

'Wow.' She twirled the wooden flute in her hand, feeling the essence of the trees permeating from the wood.

'David got me going on the flutes, then I read a few books, mainly learnt from experimenting.'

'And your bed —' His single bed was wooden. The four pillars which formed a canopy for the mosquito net were intricately carved. 'Don't tell me you made that too?'

'With David's help. It's the only thing we brought with us from the treehouse.'

'Treehouse?'

'When I was fourteen, David and I built a treehouse away from the main house so I could play my flutes without disturbing Mum. I loved it so much, I moved into it permanently. Wish you could have seen it, way up in the trees, like a part of the forest.'

'You must hate this house after living there.'

'I haven't slept well since we've been here. Sounds like there's people walking around all the time, when there isn't.'

Ayla felt the hairline at the back of her neck tingle. Why had the original Johnston built his house here at the end of the mangrove swamp when there was the whole beautiful island to choose from? So he could be hidden away unobserved, with no chance of being disturbed while he carried out atrocities on the native population? Then his descendants, those brothers, what they had done to that poor girl on Mud Rock…Ayla stopped herself. Riley didn't need to know any of it.

'Mum definitely bought on the wrong side of the island. The surf side where you live is much nicer.'

Ayla stared at the snakes, frogs and dragonflies, creatures of the rainforest carved into the four pillars. 'You're really gifted.'

He looked at the bed and a long silence saturated the too intimate space, the presence of the bed dominating the room. They stared at each other and he cleared his throat.

'So, where would you like me to start?' she felt herself blushing.

'Start?'

'Cleaning. What did you think I was talking about?' Smiling at him with her eyes.

Marlise paused at the corner of Long Street, touching the hilt of the grafting knife in her handbag for reassurance. What was the worst he could do? Run at her? A tirade of verbal abuse? If that? His handwriting was too small, too shaky. The spidery scrawl of a coward.

She clutched at her bag and turned the corner. There was a TV blaring, but no sign of him. The couple next door, sitting on their front deck, were watching her. The woman gave a slight nod. Marlise looked away, quickening her pace up the hill. The rot of leaf litter and mud drifted from the paperbark swamp. She inhaled the damp air and felt her head clear. She had done it. She had made it past.

By the time she reached the jetty, her dress was damp with perspiration. She scanned the community notice board in the hope that someone was selling a car, studiously ignoring Sharon's ice-cream booth, still furious at the woman for telling Riley she 'needed her head checked.'

A community meeting flyer in which local council representatives were offering to discuss the resumption of insecticide spraying of the mangroves, sickened her. She made a mental note of the time and place, determined to fight for the rights of the mosquito.

There were no cars for sale, but there was an ad for a scooter. She rang the number and stole a glance at the ice-cream booth. It was empty. The tall shaved-headed guy, Sharon's partner, was cleaning the pool. Marlise watched the muscles on his back working as he scooped leaves and tried to recall his name.

Josh.

'Hello?' The voice on the phone was accented.

'Hello. I'm ringing about the scooter for sale.'

'You come and look. Good bike. Brand new. You will like.'

'Where are you?'

'Big place, near barge ramp. Maria Boccabella's. You ask. Everyone knows,' and the woman hung up.

On the notice board, a small hand-written note flapping in the breeze, caught her eye. It was scrawled on the same kind of paper, in the same messy longhand as the note found under her door. She felt fear run down her spine from the base of her neck where her tattoo sat.

I know who you are. I know what you did. I'm watching you, bitch.

Marlise scanned the area. Only Josh in sight and he still had his back to her. She ripped the note from the board in a flash of anger, tore it into tiny pieces and scattered them to the wind. The act of doing so filled her with resolve. That scar-faced wimp could go hang himself. She refused to be intimidated any more.

As she approached Josh, she realised why Sharon held onto him like a delicious possession, the definition of muscle on his flawless back was impressive.

'Hi, Josh.'

'Shit, scared the daylights out of me. Didn't see you there.'

His chest was equally remarkable. 'I thought Sharon worked here?'

'She does. Three days a week, I do the rest.'

'Do you know where a Maria something or other lives?'

'Maria Boccabella's? Can't miss it. Follow this road towards the mangroves and you'll see it on the left. If you hit the barge ramp you've gone too far. But you'll fall over it. Brick monstrosity...Corinthian columns...the works.'

'Thanks.' She faltered, unable to stop her eyes slithering over his body one last time before walking off. She could feel him watching her and was glad for the sweat that made her dress cling. Instinctively, she swayed her hips more than usual, then stopped herself. What the hell was she thinking? Even though David was dead, she felt like she had betrayed him momentarily.

Josh was right about the house. She had noticed it, set back from the road on a substantial piece of land, dominating the surroundings with its ludicrous size, shape and colour. The white horse from the church stood near the front door as if waiting for someone to let it in. It watched her knock, snorting in approval. Marlise heard shoe heels clacking on tiles. The door opened to reveal the elderly woman who had given her directions to the ferry.

'I'm Marlise. I rang about the scooter.'

'Ah, you are Marlise?'

She watched the woman assess her, deciding if she was a dog murderer or not. '*Si, si*, come in.' The woman nodded, patting the horse, speaking in Italian to it like it was a baby. She turned to Marlise. 'Please. I show you.'

The white tiled house smelt like an Italian bakery. Her senses were assaulted by the gilt and red velvet furniture, overly-dramatic against the white. They stepped down into a large garage containing three Italian sports cars and there, behind a green Maserati, stood a shiny new yellow scooter.

'I bought for my nephew, but he no want to move here now. You no need for bike licence. You ride with car licence. We say $1000?'

Marlise sat on the bike, surprised at how comfortable the seat was. 'Could I try it first?'

'*Si si.*' The woman hit a button on the wall and one of the three roller doors slid up. Marlise turned the key. The bike jerked forward and died.

'No, no, you put in neutral. See?' She showed Marlise the gears.

Marlise started it again, cautiously slipped it into first and drove out of the garage, savouring the high-pitched mosquito whine of the engine. She travelled the perimeter of the paddock that led down to the sea as the horse galloped past and out onto the beach. She headed back and switched it off. 'Sold.'

Maria burst into a torrent of Italian and hugged Marlise almost knocking her off the bike.

'I need to go to the mainland to get the money. I'll come back soon, okay?' She heard the loud scrape of the barge ramp and decided to catch the barge.

'*Si, si.*'

Marlise went to dismount.

'No, no, you take bike. I trust. Besides, I know who you are, where you live.'

'Everyone on this island seems to know who I am and where I live.'

Maria nodded profusely and thumped her on the back but Marlise wasn't amused.

All she could think of were the words scattered in the wind.

I'm watching you, bitch.

In the end, Riley grudgingly allowed Ayla to vacuum, insisting he do the rest as he headed off, sponge in hand, to the bathroom.

His mother's bedroom was the smallest room in the house. The only one painted: bright yellow, with faded stencils of teddy bears in one corner. The room where the baby died.

Ayla vacuumed as fast as she could, deciding she would ask Tilly to offer this job to the other cleaner. This house was too freaky, and Riley was obviously uncomfortable with the arrangement. As she manoeuvred the vacuum under Marlise's bed, it blocked up. She switched it off, but didn't want to look, imagining a mummified foot of a dead baby jammed in the end. It was only a piece of paper.

Dear Marlise,

I hope this letter finds you and my little Riley. I know he is too young to read so please tell him how much I love him and miss him. It's aching me to sleep at night for the want I have to feel his small body in my arms again. I don't miss our squabbling but I miss your wildness. Before Riley you were a wild one. We had the best of times didn't we pet? I miss that. What's happened to you? I'm calling you. You're not answering. Would you not just call me? I would love to hear from you. Why are you not writing me? Didn't you get my last letter? It would go a long way to let me know if you get this or not. I've enclosed a few bob. Hope it eases the burden. Wish I could send you more but things are a bit tight this end. I hope to make it back to America soon as I can afford the ticket. I know you're sick to the guts of me but it's hurting me to all buggery not seeing Riley. He is my son also. I hope you're not planning it in your soul to do anything stupid Marlise

Under the bed was a wooden box which had tipped over, spilling a pile of letters and photos across the floor.

His mother, as a young woman, was stunningly beautiful. The man in the photos looked so like Riley it had to be his father. A tap turned off in the bathroom, she quickly placed everything back in the wooden box, discovering it had a false bottom. She slid the false bottom over the contents, impressed at how the box now appeared empty. Then she remembered Marlise's instruction to not vacuum under the beds. Ashamed, Ayla pushed the box far under the bed where she thought it had been and packed up the vacuum.

Riley was in the kitchen. 'Orange juice?' He handed her a glass.

'Thank you.'

'Would you…I mean…are you free for the rest of the day, or do you have other jobs?'

'I'm all yours.' She hadn't meant to sound coy.

He put his glass down on the sink, almost smashing it in his excitement. 'Maybe you could show me more of the island?'

'I'll need to drop my cleaning stuff home first.'

He insisted on pulling the trolley, and though he went barefoot, his speed and agility on the gravel road was impressive. She smiled at the image of him sitting in the cave with those formal shoes on.

'David would have been fascinated by the plants here. They're smaller than at Burrawang, like they've had to cope with more wind and salt and less rain. Everything grows on a larger scale up there.'

'Was he a botanist?'

'Property developer, originally, mainly retired by the time Mum met him, but a keen gardener.'

'Did he have a favourite plant?'

'Carnivorous.'

'Carnivorous…as in insectivorous?'

Riley nodded. 'He had the largest collection in the southern hemisphere. National Geographic did a story on it. I'll never forget Mum's face when he showed her his collection. She hated those plants because they ate mosquitoes.' His face clouded over. 'She destroyed them before we left. I thought that was nasty. She can be incredibly cruel when she wants.'

Ayla couldn't get the contents of the box out of her mind. She tried to remember what Riley had said about his father on the jetty the other night, something about his mother lying.

'What about your birth father? Do you see him at all?'

Riley's face contorted. She immediately regretted raising the subject.

'Mum told me he died when she was pregnant, but I found this.' He pulled a photo from his pocket. 'If he died, then how can he be holding me as a three-year-old? She admitted she lied, said he didn't want anything to do with me so she let me believe he was dead.'

'The way he's smiling at you, looks like you were the love of his life.'

Riley gazed intently at the photo before slipping it back into his pocket. 'I don't trust her.'

'Do you always carry that around?'

'If Mum gets her hands on it, she'll throw it out. It's all I have of him.'

Ayla knew then, it was imperative she tell him. She was contemplating how to explain the letter, when she became aware he was waiting for an answer to a question he had asked. She hadn't been listening. 'Sorry?'

'What about your father?'

'He drowned at sea seven years ago in a trawler accident. Freak storm. They found the boat but never their bodies.' She was impressed at how unemotional she could sound, as if rattling off a series of news headlines.

They arrived at her front door.

'So, we're both fatherless.' He looked at her like this new fact changed everything.

The rusty croon of Johnny Cash drifted between them, claiming love was a burning thing.

'Who's playing the country and western?'

'Mum. I forgot, she only works a half day today.' Ayla was frozen, trying to decide how to tell him about the box.

'Do you want me to wait here?'

'Of course not. Sorry. Come in.' The moment had passed.

Her mother was painting at the kitchen table.

Ayla turned Johnny Cash down. 'Mum, this is Riley.'

'Pull up a seat, Riley.'

'Won't be a tick.' Ayla left for her bedroom, her head spinning. How could she explain reading such a personal letter? She would hate for him to assume she had been snooping. Standing at her window, she could see between the trees, the waves curling in. On every wave came the same question: why would a mother hide a father's love from her son?

In the kitchen, they were deep in conversation about Johnny Cash.

Her mother turned as she entered. 'Riley's a bit of an expert on country and western, it seems.'

Ayla pulled a face. 'Great.'

'Not an expert. My stepfather had an eclectic collection of records which I slowly absorbed, that's all.'

'Riley builds and carves in wood, Mum. Made his own tree house.'

'A man of many talents.' Her mother was impressed.

'You want to see *my* tree house?' Ayla pretended she had a delicious secret.

He looked intrigued. 'Sure.'

'Ayla, Rayleen rang. Her mother's worried about Grappa. He hasn't been on his walk for days. Why don't you go and see him? Or call him…invite him to dinner tonight.'

'If Aunty Dora's worried, why doesn't she ring?'

'She did. He's not answering. I've tried too. You're his whole world, Aylee.'

'I'm sick of being his whole world. Let's go, Riley.' Ayla shot out the front door, they crossed the road and followed the winding track through the thick scrub. Images of Grappa kept harassing her, the way he laughed so hard he cried, the way he would stop at a certain tree, pointing to a crevice in the trunk, and declare, 'Doorway to their realm.' The way he got so drunk sometimes he passed out. He needed to learn to look after himself. If he couldn't make an effort with Riley, then why should she make an effort with him? It's a two-way street old man.

She looked back at Riley who had stopped in the middle of the Pandanus grove, one foot on a waterfalled root system.

'Pretty special, isn't it?'

In here the pounding of the sea was subdued.

'I've never seen so many palms naturally occurring in one place before.'

'We locals call this the Pandanus Forest.'

For a moment, in the cool green shade fanning out above their heads, she felt she had known him all her life. He dared to remove a leaf from her hair. The lemony tang of the sunlit scrub beside them pervaded. In this palm dappled light, he had stepped from another world. If he was the dark lord of the faeries, she was entirely under his spell.

'Where's your tree house?'

'A bit further.' They continued walking. 'This is a mysterious track. The way back is shorter than the way there. I've even timed it.' She glanced at him, wondering if he would think her mad.

A smile crowded his face. 'I had a track like that in the rainforest at Burrawang.'

They continued until the path opened onto a sandy clearing. Ayla knew no one had been this way all morning because her hair felt covered in spray due to the fine cobwebs she had passed through. They stopped at a grand old ghost gum, white elephant skinned and wrinkled at the joints. She pointed to the cliffs on the left. 'That's where the cave is, and beyond that is the best sand dune hill to roll down. I'll take you there sometime.'

At the circle of Norfolk pines, she jumped over the small fresh water stream that snaked its way down to the beach, reached across it and took his hand. 'You ready?'

Her childlike-self pretended he was Far Dorocha and the Nor folk really existed. A tremor ran through her body as he stepped across the rivulet and she led him into the circle, half expecting the earth to crack open. She hadn't had this much fun in years.

But of course, nothing happened.

As he approached the gigantic fig, she whispered, willing it. 'When he touches the tree, the Nor folk will appear and surround him.'

But again, nothing. She caught the scent of that ever-changing sweetness she always smelt here.

'What a specimen. It's a mother tree for sure.' He stroked the rough trunk, softly, with the back of his hand.

'A mother tree?'

'David showed me this article. Scientists have discovered trees communicate with each other through a complex underground system.'

'I think I read about that…through a symbiotic relationship with fungi in the soil or something?'

He nodded. 'And the largest tree is what is referred to as the mother tree. She sends out warnings, signals, nutrition, whatever is needed, protects and nurtures the younger trees. Sacrifices herself if she has to.'

'Grappa always says humans underestimate trees.' She patted the immense trunk and started to climb, which was simple as most of the branches grew horizontally. As she did so, her head cleared of all emotion. Whenever she had a problem, being in this tree helped solve it.

He needs to know about that box, tell him. The thought was simple and precise.

He followed her to the end of a mammoth limb. Sitting with her back nestled into a vertical branch, so safe it felt like she was snuggled into an armpit, she said, 'My favourite spot on the island.'

He lay on the bough, worn flat through decades of use and went to place his head in her lap, but hesitated.

'Please.' She touched his head so he lowered it to look up through the branches at the sky.

The weight of his head was electrifying. She dared to rest her fingers in his hair. 'When Grappa was a little boy, my great-great-grandmother told him this tree was called the Nor Folk Tree,' she was shocked. The words had tumbled out of their own accord.

'I thought it was some kind of fig?'

'It is.' She had to continue now she had started. He looked up at her as she told him about Grappa's Nor folk and how she thought she had seen one.

'Maybe you're their Queen?'

She looked down at him. 'I know now it was my overactive imagination.'

'Shhh, you don't want them to hear you say that.'

At first, she thought he was teasing, but his face remained open to all kinds of possibilities. Relieved, she shut her eyes and leant against the tree. The Nor Folk were an intrinsic part of her imagination, she hadn't realised how important it was that he didn't ridicule. Her mind fluttered back to the letter. Explain how it happened, the voice in her head insisted.

As the words fell out of her mouth, she felt the dappled light disappear. It was only the sun going behind a cloud, but it spooked her. She described the box and the photos, and felt his body go tense. 'One of the letters got caught in the vacuum. When I was trying to get all the crumples out I read a tiny bit. I'm sorry. I didn't mean to. It just happened.'

'What did it say?' Something had strangled his voice.

'He said how he missed you so much he ached to hold you in his arms again. He wanted her to tell you how much he loved you. He was saving up to come back, to be with you.'

'From where?'

'I...I don't know.'

Riley sat up. 'Knew it.' The words seethed out of him. 'My mother... she...' His gentle face choked with anger.

'Please don't confront her. She'll know I vacuumed under the bed.'

'That's the last thing I plan to do.'

'It's already hard enough with Grappa carrying on.'

'Maybe my father is still alive?' He hung his head as if weighed down by too many new thoughts. The sun came out from behind the clouds and a perfect shaft of light shone on his hair, directly in front of her. In the bright sunlight, up this close, she could see strands of blonde in among the black.

'My God, you don't have pitch-black hair.'

'Sorry?'

'Come on. Quick.' She scrambled down the tree.

'Why?'

'We need to show Grappa.'

'Show him what?'

'Your hair.'

'My hair?'

11.

Grappa had no idea how long he'd been asleep, or what day it was, when the glare from the skylight woke him. He shifted onto his back, watching the thick puffs of cloud float across the sky, remembering how he had laid here in this bed after Nettie died and drank for ten days straight. How he didn't want to die but was scared if he stopped drinking, the hard cold fact that he would never see her again would annihilate him. How the dolphins had woken him out of his drunken stupor by surrounding the boat and calling until he staggered onto the deck, then the way they played until he was laughing, until he was crying. As quickly as they came, they went. The last of them, the one with the propeller scar near his top fin, catching his eye, as if to say, 'wake up to yourself, old feller.'

When he told Ayla, she wasn't surprised. 'The eye of that dolphin, Aylee, it looked into my soul and pulled me out of my grief.'

As quick as a fish on a hook, she'd said, 'They could feel you were in pain, Grappa.'

He loved that she had always understood. Until now.

As he reached for the bottle, a sound startled him. He looked through the porthole. This time it wasn't dolphins. It was Dora, sitting on Hibiscus Beach, hands cupped around her mouth. 'Cooee.'

He poked his head out of the cabin and waved. She signalled for him to come to shore. Not knowing if he was drunk or hungover, he held up five fingers then disappeared to squint at himself in his small square of a mirror, all whiskers and grime. He threw water on his face, changed his shirt then rowed in to be met by her grimness.

'You been sick?'

'Drunk.' He flopped onto the sand beside her; the row in had made his head throb.

'Drunk.' She played with it like a new concept.

The sun was so bright he rested an arm across his face. 'According to Ayla, I'm nothing but a stupid old drunk.'

'Sounds like you're feeling sorry for yourself.' She traced patterns in the sand with her finger.

'Feeling sorry for Ayla. She has no idea what's she's got herself into, hangin' out with those people who bought the old Johnston place.'

'She's a smart girl, your Ayla. She can take care of herself. Ants are going berserk. Must be big rains coming.' They watched them scurry about.

'Dora, the day after they moved to the island, I had a dream about that woman. Remember you told me about that dream you had when you were pregnant with Rayleen?'

Dora stopped tracing in the sand and looked at him.

'It was one of those dreams. Powerful. My Gran was in it. She told me I had to stop that woman.'

'Stop her from what?'

'That's the thing. Don't know. Can't figure it out.'

'So your Gran came to you trying to warn you about something. Doesn't mean you go on a bender. What you've got to do is sit and watch. Watch how the island responds to this new degga. You'll know soon enough what your dream meant.'

'The island's already responding. Have you noticed the birds are all over the place? And I haven't seen the dolphins all week, have you?'

'I meant the people, you bujin.'

'Oh yeah. Them too.'

She was shaking her head now. 'You're such a bujin sometimes.'

'What exactly does that word translate to again?'

'Old fart.' She chuckled and put her arm around him.

The tears rose from nowhere. He choked them back as her hug grew tighter.

'You're the only one who understands me. Know that?' His voice betraying the depth of his emotion embarrassed him.

'If you didn't drink, she couldn't call you a crazy old drunk, you know.' She patted him on the back. 'Could just call you crazy and old.'

They both got the giggles then. By the time they saw Ayla running towards them, Grappa's tears were flowing freely down his face.

'Grappa, guess what?' Ayla's smile vanished when she saw him crying. 'I'm sorry.' She threw herself into him and he hugged her, squeezing out all the memories of all the hugs they had shared. She searched his face. 'You alright?'

'We were just having a bit of a laugh.' Dora groaned as she stood up. 'Sit down and have a yarn with your pop. He needs it.'

Ayla grabbed his hand. 'Far Dorocha has pitch-black hair, doesn't he?'

'As black as the starless night, Gran said.'

'Then Riley can't be your Far Dorocha. His hair isn't pitch-black. Up close, you can see blonde hairs, white even.'

Her little face was so full of hope, he lost his words.

'See for yourself.' She ran back up the beach, waving her arms.

Dora looked quizzical. 'What's she on about? Black, white, what?'

'Maybe I've made a mistake,' he said as the young man stepped from the cottonwood trees. Ayla led him up the beach toward them. The sun went behind a cloud and the world seemed darker. 'Or maybe she's made a mistake,' Grappa struggled to his feet, his heart feeling wonky, standing as tall as his seventy-seven years allowed. At least the creature was without his instrument this time.

'Do you mind?' Ayla asked the thing. It glanced at Grappa before kneeling and bowing its head. Ayla parted the hair, searching intently. Grappa summoned his courage and took a step forward to peer into the thick mass. He had never seen such black hair. Ayla's eyes met his.

'Wait,' she said, looking to the sky. The sun came out from behind the cloud to illuminate two blonde hairs, glistening in among the black strands. They hadn't been dyed, they were the real thing. 'See.' She was triumphant.

'What's the colour of this poor boy's hair got to do with anything?' Dora asked, confused.

Grappa could feel Ayla waiting to see if he would explain. 'Long story,' he muttered.

'Aunty Dora, this is Riley,'

'Welcome, Riley. Hope your Mum isn't finding that old house too gloomy.'

Riley's face filled with rage at the mention of his mother.

'Who cares what she thinks? She needs her head checked.'

So, the boy was against her, not with her.

'Think I owe you an apology son. Mistook you for someone else.' He shook Riley's hand and felt the warmth of human blood in his grip. Relief surged through him, bringing with it the same hopeful anticipation he experienced pulling on the float of a heavy crab pot. Grappa treasured that moment of not yet knowing what lay at the end of the line.

By the time Marlise returned from the mainland and paid for the bike, it was late afternoon. As she rode home, the vibration between her legs made her think of the curve of muscle below Josh's hip line where his torso disappeared into his shorts. She stopped herself, disgusted, hating the uncontrollable desire that rose in her sometimes. She saw lust as her greatest weakness.

She accelerated against a niggling growing fear. What if Ayla had found the box and showed Riley? If only she had remembered booking a cleaner, she would have moved the box. It was all that nasty dog owner's fault, with his grubby threats. The stress of him was making her forgetful and careless. Descending Long Street, she braced herself to pass his house.

He lurked in his doorway like a sun-glassed wraith. Being on the bike gave her courage. She forced her best sugar-coated smile and waved.

He made no response.

Around the corner, she pulled over, rage boiling through her.

How dare he ignore her. He had humiliated her, made her feel pathetic for trying to be friendly. She would go back and abuse him. How dare he threaten her with his pathetic little notes?

She revved the engine, torn as to what to do. Not wanting to give him the opportunity to see how his actions were upsetting her, it took all her strength to stop from turning around and confronting the greasy-haired creep.

Riley's mind kept racing towards the box hidden under his mother's bed: letters from his father, photos of him, the new, shiny truth of it all. He wanted, beyond anything, to run home, but Ayla's hand on his shoulder was enough to hold him. He looked at the old man and woman and felt like he was kneeling before the king and queen of the island, requesting entry into their kingdom.

Then her grandfather was pulling him up, his face friendly now, leaning in so Riley couldn't escape the fume of alcohol.

'Maybe your mother's from another realm, son.'

Riley looked at Ayla for help.

Embarrassed, she led him away, calling out. 'Come for dinner tonight Grappa. Mum said to invite you. Bye, Aunty.'

Riley started running. Why had his mother kept that box hidden from him? Maybe she was already home. This thought compressed his lungs, making him breathe faster, run harder.

He unlocked the door with the key from around his neck and called out. There was no answer.

Ayla nodded. 'Race you to it.' They sprinted up the stairs as Riley's head continued to flood with questions. Why did his father leave them if he ached to see him again? Was he still wandering the world in search of them?

As they entered his mother's bedroom, they heard the high-pitch of a bike motor. Riley crossed the hallway to the bathroom window. 'It's Mum.' The front door opened. They darted into the lounge room. Ayla leapt on the couch to leaf through a *Nature* magazine while he put a record on. They could hear her walking up the stairs. Neil Young singing about creatures at play in a foreign land cut through the air. Riley sprang onto the couch beside Ayla, forcing himself to meet his mother's smile.

'Thought I heard a bike, Mum?'

'I bought a scooter.'

'A scooter?'

They watched as she walked into the kitchen and placed bags of shopping on the bench. She opened her purse and came into the lounge room, impressed.

'Well done. The house looks wonderful. How much do I owe you?'

'You'll have to pay Riley most of it. He hardly let me do anything.'

Marlise made her way to the record player.

Riley leapt up. 'I'll do it.' She had no respect for David's music, always careless with the needle on the vinyl.

'Best to sort the money with Tilly.' Ayla stood up.

'Can't I pay you directly?'

'Tilly prefers to deal with the money. Thanks for a lovely day, Riley.'

The music stopped.

He caught Ayla's eyes. 'I'll walk you out.'

'Thanks again.' His mother was still smiling. Why did she keep smiling like that?

'Bye.' Ayla looked so uncomfortable, he ushered her from the room.

They walked in silence up the dirt road.

'Sometimes I hate her.'

'Don't say that.' She took his hand. 'She's your Mum.'

They stopped at the bend and he kicked his toes hard into the gravel. 'That smile...she's so fake.'

'So are we. It felt wrong then, pretending. She's going to think I'm a sneak.' Doubt dominated her face. 'She explicitly told me not to vacuum under the beds.' Ayla started walking back towards the house. 'This is silly. I'll just explain I forgot. It was an accident. The letter jammed up the vacuum. Wasn't like I was prying on purpose.'

'No, please.' She was going to ruin everything. He grabbed her. 'Give me time to read those letters first.'

'But surely if we're honest –'

'You think she'll happily show me? You don't know what she's like.'

Ayla shook her head and kept heading towards the house. 'It feels wrong.'

'The next time she goes out, I'll look at it all. Then you can tell her, I promise. Please?' He had to hold her tight, surprised at how determined she was.

Her body collapsed into him. 'Then I clear the air with her. I couldn't stand it if your mother hated me.' She held his head in her hands. 'It would make it that much harder for us.' The way she kissed him made him want to push her to the ground and climb on top of her. It took all his willpower for his body to obey his brain and wrench himself away.

Bye. She mouthed the word.

He watched her leave, trying to catch his breath, knowing she was the exact opposite to his mother. Ayla operated from a place of trust.

The way she had assumed there was a soft way into his mother's heart made him want to protect her. She was a sand faery who had lived her life in a place of light, unaware there were people like his mother in the world, so broken and damaged there was no way through to that tender place anymore.

'Did you make mud cakes when you were a child, Mum?' A flash of a memory from before Burrawang.

'I was never a child,' she had replied, pretending to eat his mud creation. He had only noticed her silent tears once the mud began to melt and run down her wrist.

Ayla turned before the corner and they waved at each other.

God help us if she does ever hate you, he thought.

12.

Marlise could hear something human moving through the mangroves. She crept onto the verandah and saw, between moon shadows, a figure sneaking toward the house. A man. The dog owner, wearing sunglasses in the middle of the night.

How the hell can he see?

She turned into a mosquito, flew down and landed on his arm.

He looked at her as if she had spoken. 'I can see. I know what you are, bitch.' His hand came down hard as she woke in fright.

That was the third nightmare since the note had been jammed under her door. A similar dream had woken her last night and early this morning, after which sleep became an enemy. She couldn't continue to live in constant fear. Something must be done. She rolled onto her side. And then there was Riley, politely sullen for days and not leaving the house once. She assumed there had been a falling out with the girl, but when asked, he grunted. 'Not at all.'

The questions about his father infuriated her. The way he casually popped them into the middle of conversations, or from complete silence, flooring her until her brain formed a vague response. If Riley found those letters...the thought made her sick. Shaking, she reached under her bed and pulled out the box. Wrapping her satin dressing gown over her nakedness, she crept past a soundly sleeping Riley and stopped in the kitchen for a box of matches. At the bottom of the stairwell, she switched on the outdoor light and silently opened the door. The night was calm and still in the damp sulphur air rising from the mud. As the mosquitoes swarmed, she gathered sticks to build a small fire in the darkest point under the house where the dirt floor was black and powdery. She stared into the swamp and shivered, unable to shake the feeling of being watched.

A huntsman ran along the ground toward the laundry. She jumped back, stifling a scream. For an entomologist, she had an irrational fear of spiders. With a deep breath, she lit a match and picked up a letter, his signature catching her eye. The round curve of the L and the flatness of the n. 'Yours always, Lorcan.' Her eyes moved further up the letter, picking out sentences. Love crept from between the lines and curled itself through her heart, releasing buried memories – the way he held her, their young naked bodies skin to skin in the middle of the night, the velvet lilt of his voice in her ear when the nightmares overwhelmed, the songs he wrote for her that made her cry.

The match burning her fingertips pulled her back to the present. She sucked the pain away and heard Riley upstairs. She kicked the pile of sticks, scattering them over the dirt floor. Powdery dust covered her legs. A light came on, spilling through the cracks in the floorboards. She ran, searching for somewhere to hide the box. That spider was lurking in the laundry. The scooter? She lifted its padded seat. The box fitted so snugly into the compartment, she almost exclaimed out loud. She heard the toilet flush. As he made his way back to bed, she waited until the light flickered off before creeping upstairs to enter her lab. With adrenaline pumping through her body, it would be impossible to sleep. She decided to collate her test results for the upcoming community meeting. The chemical breakdown of the mud samples from the swamp had proved disappointing. Poetic licence would be needed to support her argument. Hopefully, her credentials would be enough to scare the local council into believing her claims. She stared out of the window into the shadowy mass of mangroves, wondering how far she could stretch the truth to save those poor darlings from being murdered. When that prickly feeling of being watched grew again, she thought she saw a glint of moonlight caught on a pair of sunglasses, and drew the curtains close on the night.

Ayla stood on Mud Rock, surveying Hibiscus Beach, hand cupped above her eyes to block the dazzling sun and soften the sparks of light bouncing off the ocean. Still no sign of Riley, and now Grappa's boat was gone from the bay. The wind hadn't changed so there was no reason for him to have moved it.

'What are you up to old man?' Her voice whisked away on the breeze. He had been suspiciously on his best behaviour last Friday night at dinner, arriving with a small packet of Smarties tucked behind his ear. When she was little, a packet of Smarties would magically appear on some part of him as a surprise gift. On this occasion, it had been a peace offering and all night he had behaved, resisting the inclination to become esoteric or drunk. Her mother hated it when he talked 'gobbledegook' and family gatherings degenerated into heated debates with her mother frustrated, Grappa hurt, and Ayla piggy in the middle. This time they had stayed up late playing Cluedo, merely content in each other's company. But Ayla sensed Grappa had that air about him. He was on a secret mission involving a real-life game of Cluedo. She suspected it had something to do with Riley's mother.

The thought of her made Ayla's heart slump, wondering for the zillionth time if Riley had examined the contents of the box yet. She took one last look up the beach then sat on the rock, hugging her knees to her chest, undecided. She hated being on this headland, but it was the only place that afforded a simultaneous view of Mud Rock Beach and Hibiscus Bay.

A few days ago, aching to see Riley again, she had walked to his house, but at the sight of the scooter parked in the driveway, she turned away, knowing he needed time to sort things with his mother.

She found a cockle shell on the cliff face and picked it up. Maybe he didn't want to see her again? Those old feelings of insecurity and distrust she had felt with Harry came creeping back. Harry had been a shifty fox who played love as a game, continually changing the rules to keep the thrill of the chase alive. But Riley didn't seem like a game player. When she was with him, the attraction felt utterly mutual, as natural and as simple as the cockle shell she held in her hand. She couldn't help thinking about the last time they kissed, the intensity of it.

She dragged her mind to focus on a cormorant that had landed on the rocks below. After Harry, she had promised herself to never allow another human being to hold control over her happiness. 'Get a grip Ayla. You're pathetic.'

The cormorant had a bald patch halfway down its neck. She let out a squeal of delight. 'Buster.' The bird flew off without a glance. She watched until he was a dot on the horizon, rejoicing at the life in him.

Each new wave smashing into the headland sounded more ominous. Frustrated with herself, she threw the cockle shell and watched it disappear into the bubbly white foam below.

She stood to leave and saw Riley at the base of the rock, on Hibiscus. He waved, and she almost somersaulted from the cliff into his arms. He scrambled up and they hugged hard. She couldn't speak for the feel of him, his distinct earthy smell; the sound of his breathing.

He took all of her in. 'You look beautiful.'

She blushed, knowing she had worn this dress for him. 'Did you read the letters?'

'I've been waiting for her to leave the house all week. Her bedroom door squeaks so I don't dare try while she's home. Ever since I found that photo, she's been watching me like a hawk. I gave up. Missed you too much.'

'I was hoping you would come.'

He sat down and pulled her to join him.

'Can't believe I didn't get your mobile number.' She plucked her phone from her pocket.

'I don't have one.'

'Are you for real?'

Riley shrugged. 'I've never had anyone to contact, so it's never mattered.'

'No one at all?'

'I was home schooled from the age of nine. There was a boy, Kelvin. He lived on the property next door. We'd play together nearly every day. He was the closest I ever came to having a friend.'

'Are you still in touch?'

Riley shook his head. 'They moved away when I was thirteen... mainly because of Mum. She manipulated her way into their lives. His mother ended up hating my mother. When I think about it, Mum has destroyed every relationship I've ever had, except with David.'

'I should feel privileged then.'

'Or scared...the way she treats you, it's like...she's selected you.' The sudden violence with which he threw a stone so it smashed on the rocks, unnerved her.

She steered the subject away from his mother. 'Tilly said Dennis, her gardening man, wants to retire. If you come by her office, Dennis will try you out for the day.'

'Really? That would be...I...I always helped David around the property. I think I could do that.'

'Sure...just general maintenance. There's lots of holiday houses here owned by rich people who pay Tilly to keep their gardens looking neat, also rental properties and elderly people Dennis mows lawns for.'

'I could buy a phone...now I've got someone to contact.'

The tips of his fingers on her face felt soft and hard at the same time. She examined them, fascinated by the thick pads formed on the end of each one.

'From playing.' His breath had caught in his throat.

They kissed, and she became tangled up in the want of it, pushing him back against the rock to feel the hardness of the flute in his shirt pocket against her breasts and his own hard length against her thighs. He groaned involuntarily, his hands moving over her, pulling her closer as she melted into him, a wave of rapture surging through her. He wrenched his mouth from hers and sat up.

'God Ayla...' He looked out to sea trying to steady his breathing. 'When I kiss you, I feel like I'm...'

'What?'

'It's too much.' He rubbed his hands over his face and through his hair.

She put her arm around him and felt his heart thudding.

Flustered, he started to play notes which turned to a tune. She watched, hypnotised at the continual crash and suck of the waves on the rocks below. The melody, a slow menacing one, twisting back on itself again and again, flushed her with fear. A sick feeling crept over her as the foamy white water between the rocks swirled with a pink tinge. Blood? Or was she imagining it?

He pulled the flute from his mouth as abruptly as he had interrupted their kiss. 'Last time I sat here that tune came. I don't like it.' He stood up, wanting to flee.

She looked back at the water, clear again now. 'It's this headland.' They climbed down to the surf beach.

'How do you mean, the headland?'

'Most of the islands in this bay have death spots, places where atrocities happened. Mud Rock is the place on this island. It was the biggest of the bay island massacres.'

He blinked. 'Massacres?'

'Men, women, children, even babies. Government soldiers pushed them over the edge. Those that didn't die from smashing against the rocks were eaten by sharks that came in because of the blood. Anyone who tried to swim to shore was shot. Aunty Dora's great-great-grandad was a little boy hiding in the bushes over there…saw the whole thing. Most of the local population won't live on this island because of what happened here, they prefer Big Island, where the mission was.' She pointed to a distant land mass beyond Hibiscus.

'Doesn't Aunty Dora live here?'

'She always jokes about why she moved her family back. Reckons she'd rather live here with the ghosts than put up with all the dramas that happen with the mob on Big Island.' Ayla paused. 'I've heard her sometimes, standing on the edge of Mud Rock, arms out, singing to her ancestors.'

He stopped walking to look back at the ancient formation jutting into the sea, glowing red in the afternoon sun.

'Something else happened on that rock, in the 1980's, before I was born. Two of the Johnston brothers – descendants of the family who built the house you're living in. There were five brothers in all.'

'Five of them all lived in that house together?'

'That was only one generation. Grappa told me the Johnstons lived there for generation after generation, and every generation they got fatter. He describes them as fat white maggots.' Riley's mouth hung slightly open as he listened. 'Two of the last generation of Johnstons that lived there brought an Indigenous girl over from Big Island – she was only fourteen. They took her to the rock and raped her, left her unconscious. The girl was too frightened to go to the police, but when the community learnt what happened, they took the law into their own hands and the Johnstons were driven off.'

'What do you mean driven off?'

'Ostracised, threatened, picked on until they couldn't handle it. The weirdest thing is, my friend Mandy found out that the house was rebuilt in the 1960s. Before that, it was one of the original shacks on the island, built by a man called Samuel Johnston. And get this, Samuel Johnston, nicknamed Buster Johnston, because of his brutality, was the soldier in command that led the Mud Rock massacre. Those Johnston brothers were his descendants.'

Riley shook his head as if trying to rid his mind of everything she had told him. 'No wonder I find it hard to sleep there.'

'I wasn't going to say anything but now you'll be working for Tilly, you'll hear it all. Islanders love passing on the goss, especially if it's awful.'

They had walked all the way to Dead Tree Point. Riley sat on a ghostly limb and played his flute with a trace of the same sad melody, but lighter now, managing to infuse it with hope.

The pale finger of the sand bank stretching before them in the twilight was disappearing on the incoming tide. Ayla didn't know if it was his music, or the swish of her dress around her thighs, or both, but she shut her eyes and let her body lose itself in his rhythm. She danced for him, for his gentle longing, for the way he softly explored her face each time he looked at her.

When the song ended, she realised she had danced to the edge of the sandbank, the water caressing her feet.

He walked to her, eyes bright with wonder.

'It's your music…' She tried to explain but he placed his finger on her lips.

With her head on his shoulder, he held her as if protecting her from all things bad in the world and they laughed at the mullet flipping for joy in the last of the sun.

'Tell me what you can remember of the letter again.'

She did. Then they walked in silence, only the touch of their hands speaking to each other. She could see by the crease in his brow, his thoughts kept returning to the unanswered questions in his head. Arriving at the trespasser's sign, he said quietly, 'Mum's going to a community meeting tomorrow night at six-thirty. That will be my chance. If you're free, could you come over? I'm scared about what I might find.'

'Of course.'

Standing under the angophora, they parted too fast and lightly. She sensed the air between them would burst into sparks and set the old tree on fire if they lingered a moment longer.

13.

Filthy with mosquito bites – the red lumps encompassing his face, neck, arms and ankles – Grappa walked into the rapidly filling community hall. The more casual he tried to behave, the more attention he drew to himself.

Dora took one look, 'Good one. How do you think you're going to help our argument against spraying coming in looking like that, you bujin?'

He sank sheepishly into the chair beside her. Tilly bundled up with a big guffaw. 'Grappa, you're a walking talking advertisement for the fact that the mosquito population on this island is out of control. Well done.'

Ted Hanson, the president of the canoeing club, piped up, 'Put him out front with a label: exhibit A.'

Several people laughed at this.

'Everyone's a comedian,' Grappa muttered.

'What the hell have you been doing?' Dora examined him, taking in the extent of the bites.

'Research.'

'What kind of research?'

Grappa had spent the last two days hidden in the mangroves, watching the old Johnston house through a pair of binoculars. He'd tried to sleep during the day and spy at night. If she were Fey, she'd be more active in the dark, he figured. Unfortunately, that's also when the mosquitoes were more active, and no amount of repellent could keep the little suckers at bay.

He was fascinated when Ayla told him about the box of letters and photos, and how Marlise had lied to Riley. Grappa felt he'd discovered a messed-up jigsaw puzzle. All the pieces were there, he only needed to fit them together.

Why didn't she want Riley to know his father? Maybe the father knew what she was? Was she scared he would tell Riley? Whatever she was, the father was defintely human. The warmth of the boy when Grappa shook his hand proved he wasn't all Fey. The way he played that pipe though, that came from her side, the faery side.

These thoughts kept rattling around in his head as he watched the house from Little Beaudy's hidey-hole in the mangroves. There was one way in and out of the swamp via boat on a low tide: a deep channel known only to the locals, which ended where the mangroves grew impenetrable. The gap to see the house was no bigger than a man's fist. Through his binoculars, he had watched Riley on the verandah several times, with drink or food or a book. Once, he sat carving a piece of wood, whittling it into a new flute until driven inside by mosquitoes.

The first time he saw her was at dusk, when the mosquitoes were at their worst. She stood on the verandah, perfectly still. Why weren't the mosquitoes attacking her? Grappa knew immediately she was up to no good. Was she communing with something? He nearly fell overboard in his excitement to get a closer look.

Energized by what he'd seen, he was determined to watch for the rest of the night, but fell asleep, waking to the sound of a toilet flushing. He caught sight of her under the house as she went back inside. Grappa was livid. What'd he missed? Why'd she been outside in the middle of the night? A light came on upstairs in the front room and she sat at a computer. When she looked straight down the barrel of his binoculars before pulling the curtains shut, he whimpered in terror.

On the second evening, at dusk, she came onto the verandah and communed with something again, but this time she was alone. He'd seen Riley go out earlier. She began speaking to someone who wasn't there. Grappa was too far away to hear the words but could tell by the tone she was soothing something. He had to gulp from his flask to keep the binoculars steady. When she heard the boy walking down the road, she fled into the house. Grappa stayed awake all night on high alert, drinking to keep calm, hoping to discover more, but the place remained eerily still of any movement.

At dusk, she speaks to something...when the boy's around she does it silently, when he's not, she speaks aloud. Mother-of-God. Who, or what, does she speak to?

Dora prodded him, interrupting his thoughts, bringing him back to the present. She pointed to the young council representative making his way towards the stage. Grappa stifled a yawn as he realised it was going to be another long bloody boring community meeting.

Startled at the number of people pouring into the old wooden hall, Marlise parked her scooter beside Tilly's car then made her way onto the bull-nosed verandah. Sharon was among a gaggle of women beside the latticed-worked main entrance. Marlise turned to enter via a side door but Sharon was too quick. 'Marlise. Don't tell me, you've come to stick up for your favourite blood suckers,' she said, noting the documents tucked under Marlise's arm.

'Cute dog,' Marlise ignored her, addressing the white scruffy thing Sharon was holding.

The dog growled, making Sharon smile.

'Must have heard you're not fond of dogs, only mosquitoes,' Sharon said to the other women, who either tittered or looked away, embarrassed.

Sharon's oblique reference confirmed it, Harley had spread his noxious belief around the island – he held her responsible for killing his dog.

'Who told you that?' Marlise feigned confusion.

'You know…island gossip.'

'No, I don't know island gossip. Who's been saying things about me?'

The group went quiet.

Sharon smirked. 'Now you're being paranoid.'

Samantha stepped forward. 'You'll soon learn, on the island, don't believe any of what you hear and none of what you see. If they don't have anything on you, they make it up.' She touched Marlise on the arm. 'If you're free tomorrow, join us. Every Friday a group of us go to the mainland for an outing. Tomorrow we're trying the new café at Rocky Point.'

They all joined in, urging her to come, while Sharon took an overt interest in tying her dog to a verandah pole.

'I can't tomorrow. Maybe another time?' Marlise lied. She couldn't think of anything more tedious than spending time with Sharon and her sycophantic entourage. Marlise remained standing near the doorway to let them enter the hall first, deciding to sit as far from them as possible.

The dog owner, wearing sunglasses under the bright fluorescent lights, materialised out of the crowd. She stopped breathing. He brushed by, the scar on his face loomed, puckered and nasty. She heard, softly but distinctly, the word 'bitch.' He bolted down the verandah, through the car park and into the night. Marlise felt lightheaded. Her ears were hot – all the blood rushing to them. He's gone now. She took solace in the thought. He's gone now.

When her heartbeat slowed to normal, she managed a glance around the room. The dog owner's neighbour was in a seat against the wall by an empty chair. Marlise approached. 'Is anyone sitting here?'

The woman looked trapped, head spinning towards the door. 'A friend was but...I think he's gone home.'

Marlise sat down, surprised at how old the woman was, from a distance her long hair made her seem younger. 'Don't you live at the end of Long Street?'

'Yes.'

'We're almost neighbours.'

The woman smiled like she had bitten down on something sour. Marlise tried to think of how to lead into a conversation about the dog owner, but the president of the Stop Progress Association was asking for quiet.

Riley crept into the room. The stencilled teddy bears on the wall stared with their cot death stare. How did his mother sleep in here? He was surprised to see his hand shaking as he reached to lift the bedspread. Was it excitement, or fear of what he was about to discover? A light tap on the front door made him pause.

'Riley?' It was Ayla's irresistible husky voice.

He ran downstairs, two at a time.

'I was hiding in the bush up the road, waiting for her to go past.'

She was a vision in the twilight: the green material of her dress hugging her like he wanted to. He resisted the urge to touch it. It would lead him to her. 'Thanks for coming. We don't have much time.'

She waited in the doorway of his mother's bedroom while he knelt to retrieve the box. 'There's nothing here.'

She was beside him now. 'It was. I swear.' They sat up at the same time. 'She's moved it.'

'Or destroyed it.' The thought pinned him to the floor.

The last of the day was fading. Ayla snapped on the light and began opening drawers. 'She's put it in a better hiding spot, that's all.'

Together they searched until Riley sat on the edge of the bed, elbows on his knees, head hanging low. Hope quietly slipped out of the room on the ghostly breath of a dead baby.

'Have you said anything that would make her suspect?'

'I've been conscious of that, trying to act as normal as possible while all the time I've wanted to scream at her.'

Ayla sat beside him and put her arm around him. 'There's still the rest of the house to search. What about her work room? Bet you it's in there.' She stood but he held her hand and pulled her back down.

'It's almost dark. You should go. She'll wonder what you're doing here.'

'Those community meetings go for hours. We've got heaps of time.'

He didn't know how to explain his mother's illegal entomological practices. 'It'll be awkward if she finds you here.'

'Aren't I allowed to visit you at night?' she teased, playfully nudging him back to lie on the bed. The feel of her body against him in that dress sent the blood rushing between his legs. Her lips on his neck and down his chest were paralysing.

She sat up. Riley could see her breasts pushing at the thin material. He reached out to touch them. 'Ha,' the sound escaped at the firm softness.

She was watching him. 'You've never felt a woman's breasts before, have you?'

A slight shake of his head and he was kneading the wonderful things in his hands. She shut her eyes, moved toward him and groaned. He thought he had hurt her and leapt up, shocked at the violence of his thoughts. He wanted to rip her dress open and rub himself against her until he squirted like he did with his own hand. Such a gentle girl and he kept picturing being violent with her. Was there something wrong with him? If David were alive he could ask if this was normal, but there was no one.

She was watching from the bed. 'Sorry.'

'Don't be sorry. Mum might be home soon, I...'

She straightened the bedspread. 'There. She'll never know.' She slid past him and he followed her downstairs to open the door for her. 'I forgot. Tilly said to come around in the morning at seven. She'll try you out with the lawn mowing.'

'I'll...I'll be there.'

She looked up the road. He wanted to hold her.

'Can I see you tomorrow?' They said it at the same time.

'I'll come over after you've finished work then?'

'Sure.' He shut the screen door before they could touch. This touching business was dangerous. She was his mango sorbet he wanted to devour until he felt sick.

Ayla looked back and blew him a kiss. He felt it land on his lips and became aroused again.

The stairs squeaked. He switched on the light in the stairwell, wondering if it was the ghosts of the five Johnston brothers that made the house creak so mysteriously, while another part of him was remembering the feel of Ayla's breasts in his hands.

Running up the stairs and throwing open the door to his mother's lab, the knowledge that he had limited time to find the box pushed all other thoughts from his over-excited mind.

Dora nudged Grappa awake. 'You're snoring.'

He tried to focus as the pimply council representative droned on about the history of mosquito spraying in the bay. Tilly caught his attention as she popped outside for a cigarette. That's when he saw her bewitching face, pale against the blackness of her hair, dark eyes shining fiercely. She was sitting near the entrance to the verandah beside June, in the shadows, listening and watching. Suddenly Grappa was very alert, feeling her foul energy, even from where he was in the middle of the room. She stepped forward, her knife-blade voice slicing the air, cutting off the council bloke mid-sentence. Grappa couldn't place her trace of an accent. Ayla had said something about America.

'You moronic little yes man. How dare you stand there boasting about council's routine massacres of mosquitoes. As an entomologist, I've carried out a series of scientific tests only to find the mud surrounding this island is toxic.' A gasp rippled through the audience. 'Those 'harmless' poisons you brag about pumping into their ecosystem on a regular basis...let me tell you...I have found samples of those poisons in mangroves, pipis, fish, crabs, and I'm sure if I tested any one of you, I would find it in you, in your babies. Apparently, a baby died of cot death in the house I am living in, which is situated on the border of the principal mosquito habitat for this island. I'm sure if a further autopsy was carried out on the corpse of that baby, they would discover the cause to be chemical toxicity. Chemical toxicity created by the very poisons you're trying to sell to this community as harmless. How stupid do you think these people are?'

She walked through the hall up to the council officer and shoved some papers at him. 'Here's a report on the results of all the tests I've conducted. I believe the family of that dead baby could sue council if they wanted. Go back to your superiors and tell them that. Might make them think twice about spraying this island anymore. Go on, get out of here, and take your poisons with you.'

She walked back to stand beside Tilly. The poor young council officer fumbled with the papers as a hushed murmur fell. To Grappa's dismay, Dora stood and clapped. A quarter of the audience joined her. Seeing Dora all fired up to let loose, he sank into his chair.

'What this scientist is saying is spot on. As one of the traditional custodians of this land, I vehemently oppose any further spraying. My ancestors lived here for thousands of years in harmony with the mozzies. Why can't we? What makes us any different? Every chemical you spray into the environment affects the whole fragile ecosystem we are all a part of. By poisoning the mozzies, we're effectively poisoning ourselves. Anyone with a half a brain can figure that out. You shouldn't need a scientist to tell you,' Dora nodded at the woman. 'But I'm grateful she's taken the time to do so.'

The woman nodded back. When Dora sat down, Grappa leaned across. 'Don't smile at her.'

'Why not? I like her. She's got balls.'

'That's the woman I had the dream about.'

'You still going on about that dream?' Dora looked at him like he wasn't the full quid.

Sharon stood up. 'I reckon council should send their own scientists here to carry out their own tests. No offence to Marlise, but I know for a fact she has a real fondness for mosquitoes that could make her a tad biased.'

Marlise? What kind of name is that? Grappa felt offended at the sound of her name, especially the way Sharon said it. He liked Sharon but couldn't tolerate her voice. Listening to her speak was like listening to a sick crow dying.

'Most of us have lived on this island for years and have experienced, first hand, how bad the mozzies are in summer.'

A significant hum of agreement spread through the crowd, evoking the buzz of mosquitos on the hunt for blood. Sharon glowed with self-satisfaction as she addressed Marlise.

What the hell was Sharon thinking? She was usually a good judge of character. Couldn't she see the woman was emanating pure hatred? If Sharon knew what was good for her, she'd shut up. Grappa's thoughts were screaming through his head as he tilted his chair back to gain a clear view of Marlise.

Dora hissed at him. 'Didn't they tell you in school it's dangerous to swing on your chair?'

Poor Sharon continued to crucify herself. Mother-of-God, you're playing with fire, girl.

'No offence, Marlise but you're yet to experience a summer here. My kids used to play outside all year, but the last few summers, since council stopped the spraying…last summer, they had to stay indoors the whole bloody school holidays, the mozzies were that fierce. What kind of quality of life is that for our kids? Also, as a small business owner, the summer tourist trade used to keep us afloat for the rest of the year. I don't know if we can cope much longer if the visitor numbers don't pick up. Please, I beg you, resume spraying. Generations of families lived here without any health problems from the spraying. I think she's leaping to big conclusions. Babies die from cot death all the time. I really don't know how legitimate these so called 'findings' are. Resume the spraying. Not only is the lack of mosquito control affecting our quality of life, it's putting us out of business.'

Sharon sat down, pleased with herself as most of the audience clapped and cheered. Maria Boccabella was speaking now, but Grappa wasn't listening, intent on watching Marlise, tilting his chair back further. He saw Tilly lean in and say something. Marlise shook her head in disgust and turned to leave, briefly catching his eye. The sharp stab of her stare from those black pits made him yelp.

'What's wrong with you?' Dora snapped.

'Just got the evil eye.'

'Serves you right for staring, you pea brain,' were the last words he heard before his chair tipped backwards spilling him across the floor, causing the people around to cry out.

Marlise was so incensed, she stood in the middle of the car park, fuming, imitating the sound of Sharon's voice. 'No offence, Marlise.' Sorry Sharon, offence has been taken…bitch. If the council did send their own scientists, they would easily disprove her findings. Where the hell was her scooter?

Circling until remembering she had parked near Tilly, she located the sign on the roof of the car, 'Tilly Little Real Estate. We Make Big Things Happen', and walked towards it, smelling the dog shit before she saw it smeared over the bright yellow vinyl of the scooter's seat.

'Enough is enough,' she screamed to the edge of the car park, where the street light didn't penetrate, where anyone could be hiding in the undergrowth, watching. Harnessing her anger, she ripped a section from the hem of her dress and used it to wipe the turgid sticky mess.

When she rode past the dog owner's house, still reeking of dog faeces, her blood was pumping furiously. She glared at the house in the hope that he was watching. He had pushed her past the end of reason now.

On arriving home, she stormed into the laundry, threw disinfectant on a sponge and viciously scrubbed the seat of the scooter. The more she scrubbed the angrier she became, until she found herself laughing, realising her fear had evaporated. Her anger had empowered her. It was war. She would fight to the death, if necessary.

She remembered the wooden box hidden under the seat and lifted the newly cleaned compartment to see it there, untouched.

Riley was at the screen door.

She dropped the seat.

'What are you doing?'

'I sat in dog poo.'

'Yuk. I can smell it.'

'It's all over the back of my dress.' She returned the cleaning equipment to the laundry.

That was too close. She had to destroy that box.

In the laundry, she slipped out of her soiled clothes, grabbed a towel from the washing pile and wrapped it around her.

He was still at the screen door. 'Tilly tells me you're starting work tomorrow.' She forced herself to sound pleased.

'Yeah.'

'Thought you'd be happy?' She opened the door.

'I am.' He moved to let her pass.

She stood in the stairwell, examining him. 'Riley, have I done something to upset you?'

'No. Better get to bed. Early start. Night.'

'Night. I'll be up in a minute to tuck you in.'

'Please don't. I'm too old for that now, Mum.'

'But you know I like to.'

He was all hunched over as he walked away.

'Love you.'

He didn't answer.

What was she going to do about him? She clung to the idea that this new job would snap him out of it. The hard ball of anger from the evening's events began to churn as she tried to ignore what was solidifying in her mind: she had made a fatal mistake moving them to this island.

14.

The shower had made the ringing in Riley's ears from mowing lawns all morning worse, not better. He would buy himself ear muffs, as Tilly suggested.

Flopping onto his bed, he shut his eyes and imagined Ayla dancing naked on a beach made of mango sorbet. His mother's voice in the hallway caused him to spring up, using the towel to cover his arousal.

'I'm off now. What's wrong?'

'Nothing.' She was dressed in a sarong. 'Where are you going?'

'Thought I might do some laps at the pool.'

'Laps?'

'My new hobby.' She disappeared.

Riley was baffled. As far as he could remember, his mother hated swimming. At the sound of her scooter fading down the road, he pulled on a singlet and jeans. Then starting in the lounge, he snatched books from the shelves, two at a time, in the hope that the box was hidden in the bookcase. He found his copy of Huckleberry Finn given to him by David on his twelfth birthday, and opened it to read the inscription when a knock on the door startled him. He ran downstairs two at a time.

It was Ayla in jeans and a blue t-shirt with 'Say NO to plastic' written across her chest. He nearly knocked her over in a rush to hug.

'Did you find it?'

'Not yet. But Mum's gone out.'

'I'll help you. We can't keep sneaking around behind her back. It's not right.'

'Come on then. Let's empty the book case.'

They worked methodically, side by side as Ayla told Riley about Peach's reaction to being released back into the bush this morning. Riley, in turn, shared how he had befriended a series of monitor lizards and giant tree frogs over the years, sharing his tree house with them, and the funny names he had given his wild pets. He stopped searching to act out each one, portraying their different personalities until Ayla was shaking with laughter.

'Wish you'd been there.' He swallowed the emotion that threatened.

Her eyes turned liquid. 'Wish I'd been there too.'

In silence, they returned to the task at hand, but he couldn't concentrate, every molecule of his being was tuned to her. Was it possible to fall into someone?

Marlise kept shifting the banana lounge into the shade as the sun moved, ensuring she always maintained a clear view of the notice board and jetty. She was pretending to utilize the pool, in the hope that she could meet people in the community and discover more about this Harley. If she confronted him about the note, there was a possibility he would deny it and cast her as a paranoid fool, as Sharon had. At least there were no more nasty hand-written threats on the noticeboard. On arriving, she had checked.

Josh, who was finishing the water aerobics class he had been teaching, looked over as she undid her sarong to reveal her old crocheted swim suit. Lying down, she admired the weave of the crochet against her unblemished skin, the way the stitch became tighter over her nipples.

She was glad now she hadn't thrown it away. This morning when she put it on and looked in the mirror, she noticed her body seemed to have a fresh ripeness to it. When her period had been more regular, there was always a time of the month when her breasts felt beautifully full, when she was quickly aroused. She hadn't had a hot flush in days. Maybe her cycle was returning to normal. She could feel her estrogen rising.

Pulling her sunglasses down to hide under, she was in the perfect position to watch the notice board, and sporadically perve on Josh. Apart from the healthy mosquito population, Josh was the most entrancing feature of the island she had discovered so far. The class was over now and he was saying something to make the old women cackle. He dried himself, tied the towel around his waist, then, bare-chested, headed towards the ice-cream booth.

Marlise dragged her eyes from him to the notice board at the end of the jetty, where a small crowd of people gathered, including the dog owner's lank-haired neighbour.

How perfect, just the woman I was hoping for. The thought tickled Marlise on the lips almost making her smile.

The group was chatting as they walked up the jetty, but Harley's neighbour remained at the notice board.

Was she looking for his pathetic little threat?

Marlise appeared beside her, causing the woman to jump. 'If you're after the ad for the scooter, too late, I already bought it'. She gestured to the bike parked under the palm trees at the pool entrance.

'Oh…I was just…seeing what was on the board.' The woman went to walk away, her brown eyes darting everywhere.

'I'm Marlise by the way.' She pushed her sunglasses to the top of her head and held out her hand.

'June.' She shook Marlise's hand. There was a jitteriness about the older woman Marlise found comforting.

'You live next door to that poor man whose dog just died, don't you?'

'Harley. Yes. He's a bit lost without Jip.'

'I know what he's going through. I lost my dog of fifteen years not so long ago. There's a gaping hole in my life where a big bundle of love used to be.'

Relief flooded June's face. 'I'm so glad to hear that. I mean, I'm not glad your dog died I just…I'll pass on your sympathies to Harley. He's so upset you see…he…he's convinced someone slipped Jip a bait.'

Marlise opened her mouth to portray shock. 'That's abominable. People who do that kind of thing should be hung, drawn and quartered. Who in their right mind would want to hurt a poor, innocent animal?' She dished the clichés out, gratified by the ease with which the conversation was unfolding. 'I was about to have a coffee by the pool. I don't really know anyone here yet. Don't suppose you'd have time for a coffee?'

'I…have to pop across to the mainland…here's my boat. Maybe next time?' She started to walk down the jetty.

'If I'm still here when you get back, come over.' Marlise was making herself sick with the drivel pouring out of her mouth but was determined to talk further about Harley.

'Okay. I will.' June's smile was contagious.

Marlise beamed back, hoping she would find out all she needed before the day was out.

When she returned to her banana lounge, the pool was empty. She waved to Josh in the ice-cream booth. He waved back, peeping over the top of his newspaper as she undid her sarong again. She stretched out and pulled her sunglasses over her face, watching him watch her, and felt sexy lying there with his eyes sliding over her body. She rolled over and released the strings across her back that held her top in place, then rested her head on her arms, aware that Josh would have a perfect view of the side of her breast.

The ferry arrived and left twice, with no sign of June.

She stood to face Josh, slowly lacing up her top, then turned and bent over her bag to search for her purse, giving Josh an eyeful of her backside. Her desire was palpable with him continually watching her. She dawdled towards the ice-cream booth, casually adjusting the crocheted triangles over each breast. 'Hi.'

'How you goin'?'

'I'm hot.'

'You can say that again.'

Flattered at his innuendo, guessing he was at least ten years younger, she said, 'I need something to cool me down.' She was enjoying herself. It had been years since she had flirted. 'Can I have –' she read from the sign, 'a double scoop in a cone, please?'

'What flavours?'

'What would you recommend?'

'Coconut and Pina Colada.'

'Perfect.'

As he fixed her order, she admired the way the towel sat under his hip bone and wondered how firm his body would feel compared to poor David's whose skin was so soft in the end, loosened due to the ravages of time.

'Decided to take the day off, have ya?'

'Trying to work up the courage to jump into your pool. I can't swim, so thought I'd better learn how to stay afloat at least, now I'm living on an island,' she lied.

'I could teach you if you want.'

'Really?'

'As you can see, things are pretty dead during the week.' He went to hand her the ice-cream as she stepped forward and tripped over a cement block. The top of the ice-cream landed in her cleavage.

'I'll make you another.'

'It's fine.' She took what was left of the ice-cream. His gaze felt erotic as he stared at the smear between her breasts. Her arousal had become excruciating.

He picked up a paper serviette from the pile on the counter and held it out to her. 'Here.'

'Would you mind?' She found herself asking, indicating the ice-cream in one hand and her purse in the other.

He held back. The knob of ice-cream slid further between her breasts.

She gasped. 'Cold.'

He awkwardly wiped the ice-cream from her chest. 'There you go.' He wiped for longer than needed.

'Now I'm all sticky.' She held his gaze and slowly licked what was left of her ice-cream.

His lips parted. Something behind her caught his eye. 'Hi, June.' He went to rinse the scoop.

'Hi. Still up for a coffee, Marlise?'

'Sure.' Marlise surreptitiously threw the ice-cream into the bin. She didn't know if it was the artificial sweetness making her sick, or the shock at what she had just tried to do.

'I'll have my usual, thanks, Josh.'

'No worries.' He kept his back to them.

Marlise smiled at the woman, relieved. June had stopped her from committing a dreadful mistake. She promised herself not to go near Josh again. He was a married man. The repercussions would be catastrophic in such a small community.

June insisted on paying for the coffees. 'My gift, to welcome you to the island.'

They sat at one of the poolside tables and chatted about the perfect spring weather. Marlise learnt that June worked part-time as a barmaid on the mainland and that her partner Kev, who was ten years older than her, was retired. Through June's questions, Marlise was forced to explain how her husband had recently passed away. She was amazed to see tears of sympathy forming in June's eyes. This prompted her to describe how lonely she felt not knowing anyone on the island and how she appreciated June taking the time to chat with her.

Marlise didn't know how to react when June said, 'If you ever need someone to talk to, pop around anytime…even if it's the dead of night. Things can seem really bad in the dead of night.'

She longed to move the conversation to Harley, but waited, hoping it would naturally turn in that direction so as not to arouse suspicion. As if she had read Marlise's mind, June stated, 'I said the same thing to Harley. Since Jip's death, me and Trev have been real worried about him. Never seen him this down.'

'Doesn't he have anyone in his life? Anyone special I mean?'

'No. He only has us. Poor bugger'

'He's probably got friends at work that he –'

'Harley doesn't work,' June dropped her voice. 'Sickness benefits. Ex-addict, on the methadone program. That's why we're worried about him. Too much time on his hands. If he gets too down, he could easily OD again.'

'Again?'

'When he first moved to the island…he tried it. Lucky I found him before it was too late and rang the ambulance.'

'What led him to try and kill himself?'

'He fled here from Rocky Point. Said he felt like scum over there.'

'What did he mean…scum?'

'He always talks about how he would be walking up the street on a Sunday and they'd all be cleaning their cars. They were clean, their houses were clean, their children were clean. Said he felt like a piece of filth, dirtying up their neighbourhood, living off the taxes from their hard-earned, squeaky-clean cash and they hated him for it. He was suspicious of the islanders at first, but Jip saved him. People would stop and pat Jip and chat to Harley and he started to feel accepted here. Jip opened up the island to Harley, the community slowly wrapped their arms around him and he came good.'

'So, he feels tolerated here?'

'Not just tolerated, accepted. That's the important thing. He knows everyone knows what he is, and they still take the time to say hello. That means the world to Harley. No one is judging him.'

Marlise was so grateful to June, when it came time to say good-bye, her hug was genuine, even though she knew they would never connect on an intellectual level. It would be impossible to discuss the perfect breeding conditions for the mosquito vector *Aedes vigilax*, for instance. Still, she felt a rarity had occurred in making a new friend.

'Thanks.' June waved from her front gate as Marlise rode off. From the corner of her eye, she saw the shadow of Harley hiding in his doorway and almost felt pity for him.

He's weak and sick, nothing more than an addict. She grasped at this new knowledge in the hope that it would put an end to her nightmares.

Riley was in the bathroom and Ayla in the kitchen when they heard the high-pitched scooter. They met on the lounge. He couldn't hide his disappointment.

'Let's talk to your Mum. It's the only way.'

'No.'

He heard the door downstairs open.

'I'll just explain I was vacuuming and accidentally –'

'That approach won't work.'

His mother was walking up the stairs now.

'But you've searched the whole house –'

'Please Ayla, not yet.'

Marlise came into the room and they looked at her like a pair of possums caught up a tree in daylight.

'You didn't tell me you were planning on having company, Riley.'

'I wasn't. Ayla dropped by unexpectedly.'

'Really? Is that why you're wearing your best jeans?' She threw her bag down. 'Please don't lie to me. Ayla is welcome anytime, but please don't lie. You know I can't stand liars.'

Something exploded in him. He jumped up, spitting words. 'You can't talk. Don't you talk to me about lying, you hypocrite.'

'My God, Riley –'

Ayla tried to save the situation. 'It's my fault Marlise. The other day I was…I didn't mean to but I –'

'No,' he screamed at her. She was going to ruin his chances of reading those letters.

'The other day you didn't mean to what?' His mother was intrigued now.

Ayla stared at him in shock, but his anger was too raw. 'Fuck.' He said it under his breath, menacing enough to make her elfin face crumple before racing downstairs. 'Ayla.'

'What didn't you mean to do?' his mother called after them.

'Ayla. Stop.' She was fast. It took him to the corner of Long to catch her. 'I'm sorry.' He tugged her elbow, turning her, astonished to see how fierce she was under the tears.

'Confront her about it. This sneaking around and lying is making us sink to her level. Can't you see that?'

'You don't understand the way she operates –'

'I understand.' She yanked her elbow out of his hand. 'Let me know if you ever get things sorted with your mother.' She went to walk off but he pulled her towards him, twisting her arm in the process, making her cry out in pain.

'Sorry.' He let her go. She held her arm, not looking back.

He hadn't meant to hurt her. How badly had he hurt her? She was still holding her arm as she disappeared around the bend, like one of the injured birds she had told him about, the baby tern with the broken wing. His mouth went dry. Why had he grabbed her like that?

As he walked back to the house, the picture of his mother, grafting knife in hand, viciously chopping into David's treasured plants, hounded him, her face distorted from screaming with eyes as red as the sap which had splattered all over her.

When angered, she always became physical. The amount of times David was forced to hold her as she hit out at him in pure rage. Then there was the morning she casually mentioned she suspected she had the ability to transform into a mosquito, and that each time it happened it felt like a dream, but she knew 'it was more than a dream.' Riley had laughed so much she hit him, hard enough for his jaw to remain swollen for two days. After that, whenever she spoke of her 'transformative mosquito dreams', he was careful to remain expressionless. David too had learnt to keep his face empty of emotion from fear of being hit. It struck Riley that he might be inherently violent like his mother. Was it genetic in some way? He had hurt Ayla. What kind of person was he to harm someone so gentle when she had only been trying to do what was right and honest? His bellow of heartbreak sent the first of the curlews quiet.

As he climbed the stairs, he heard his mother in her lab printing something from her computer. Crawling onto his bed, he buried his head in his pillow to block the picture of himself smashing his fist into his mother's face until it was a mushy pulp. The printer ceased. In the silence that followed, the butterfly of a thought landed lightly on the top of his head – the box isn't in the house. There were all the shelves and nooks and crannies outside, under the house and in the laundry.

She crept into his room. 'What was it you didn't want her to tell me?'

She sighed and picked up one of his flutes, examining it like she had never seen it before. 'I'm sorry if you're having a bad time here.' She placed the flute back on the shelf. 'We could always move somewhere else, somewhere less crowded...start again?'

She rubbed her eyes. He noticed her hands were shaking. She was in a bad way, not handling it here with all these people. It would only be a matter of time before something unpleasant happened. It was always the way. Watching his mother was like watching the truck crash he had witnessed on the drive here from Burrawang. There was a certain point when Riley knew the crash was inevitable. He'd never forget how time lost momentum as the truck rolled in slow motion through the red dust.

She was hovering now. He sprang back instinctively. The tears rolling down her face made him feel nothing.

'Why did you call me a liar?'

He shut his eyes in the hope that she would leave.

'I love you.'

She had been saying those three words a lot lately. He hated the way she made them sound, her tone pleading, begging him to say it back. He turned away from her.

'All I want is for you to be happy,' she whispered and left.

Her love for him was undeniable. Why was there a part of him that hated her for it?

15.

Ayla savoured the burnt, sweet aroma of freshly brewed coffee as she watched the rain pelt down on the peak hour spectacle outside. The gutters overflowing dishwater brown as pedestrians, hidden under umbrellas, waited for traffic lights to change.

'It's not like he actually hurt my arm. I just wanted to make him feel bad for man-handling me. Maybe I did overreact?'

Mandy pushed the coffee plunger down without answering. Ayla had voiced that question so many times in the last two weeks, she was even boring herself.

'Sorry, Mand.'

Mandy looked at her over the top of her coffee mug with a naughty twist to her face.

'You really think he's a virgin?'

'Shh, mum's the word.'

'From what you've told me, Mum's the problem.'

They erupted in laughter, flooding Ayla with gratitude for Mandy's friendship. She had phoned at the right moment and invited Ayla to stay. 'My flatmates are away for two weeks. We'll have the whole house to ourselves.' Such serendipity always happened between them, they were no longer surprised by it.

Once at Mandy's, with Riley in the distance, Ayla gained some perspective on the situation. She was scared by how deep her feelings ran for him and realised she needed to slow things down, but it felt like trying to hold back a river.

'If he's been Tarzan boy, living alone with mad Mum in a tree house with lizards and frogs most of his life.'

'And his step-dad.'

'I thought he was dead?'

'Only recently.'

'He's still grieving then.'

They exchanged a look.

'Yeah, for the rest of his life.'

The death of their fathers had linked Mandy and Ayla in an unspoken understanding unique to their friendship. At the time of the deaths, they could appreciate the flood of pity from the island community but mutually hated it too, making an unspoken pact to stand tall and proud in the face of it.

'You're right, though, his grief is still fresh, and he's only just found out his real father may be alive...anyone would be an emotional mess.'

Mandy reached for Ayla's hand when she saw her eyes brimming. 'Hey.'

'I like him so much, it frightens me, Mand.'

'Good to be frightened. Least you know you're alive.'

The land line pierced the room, causing Mandy to jump for the phone. 'Hello?....Hi Helen, how – yeah she is...'

Ayla wondered why her Mum had called the house phone rather than texting as usual. When she heard the way Mandy repeated the name, 'Harley Mangleson,' she knew the answer.

'I'll put her on.' Mandy held the phone out.

Ayla didn't take it. She didn't need to. 'Harley's dead, isn't he.'

Grappa hated the way it could bucket down for days without end. Life on a boat was miserable without an occasional break in the rain. Everything was damp and smelly, and the sight of water, fresh or salt, became intolerable. It was impossible to see with binoculars through such a deluge, so there was nothing to do but shelter in Hibiscus and wait.

Between drinks, he worked his way through the meagre collection of books on Changelings and Shapeshifters he'd ordered from the library on the mainland and then started on the 5000 piece jigsaw puzzle Dora had given him for his birthday. When he heard a foreign sound over the constant drum of the downpour, he peered through the round window and saw Riley standing on the beach, arms waving like a wind sock in a southerly. Grappa climbed on deck and called through the rain.

It was hopeless.

Cursing, he clambered into his dinghy and rowed in, his heart pumping too hard. Last night, over the roar of falling water, he thought he heard the banshee wailing. His Gran had told him the banshee's wail signalled death, so part of him was waiting to hear who'd died. Riley waded out to meet him. They had to yell to be heard through the deluge. 'What's wrong, boy? Is it Ayla?'

'Do you know where she is?'

'Last I heard she'd gone back to the city. Why?' The poor boy couldn't speak. Grappa had seen that broken-hearted look on a man many a time. 'You two have a blue?'

The boy nodded.

'Bloody hell, I'm gettin' soaked. Jump in.'

Riley stumbled into the boat and they rowed through the pouring rain back to Little Beaudy.

'Tie off on the end there. Not there...here. Use the ladder to climb up.' Jesus Christ, he was a clumsy thing with those big feet. Once inside the cabin, Grappa cleared a space and threw him a towel. 'Dry yourself. Want a drink?'

Grappa took the silence to be a yes and poured them both a straight scotch. 'This'll dry you out from the inside.' He tried not to stare at Riley's feet. They were the ugliest feet he'd seen on anyone. The boy was leafing through the library books. 'Know what a changeling is?'

'I read about them in my stepfather's *Faeries and Other Wondrous Beings* book. What is this?' He held his glass out in disgust.

'Scotch. Drink up. Good for you. Did your stepfather have lots of books like that?'

'David seemed to have a book on everything, and if he didn't, he would order it. I was home schooled, so he thought it was important I learn about all the wonders of the world, real or not.'

'Don't think changelings are real then?'

The boy held his gaze. 'I certainly think there's more to life than greets the eye.'

'And what about your mother?'

'What about her?'

'Did she think it was important you learn about such things?'

'My mother thought it was important I keep out of her way and not interrupt her research.'

'But when she home schooled you, did she –'

'She didn't. David did. Her idea of homeschooling was to leave me to my own devices. David picked up the pieces. He wanted to send me to school, but she wouldn't allow it. Did Ayla say if she was coming back?'

'Didn't speak to her. Helen told me she'd gone to the city. She upset with you?'

A slight nod.

'Want to talk about it?'

He shook his head, but as the scotch softened him, he began to speak of the box, producing the picture of his father, in a plastic zip-lock bag to protect it from the rain. Grappa could see verbal communication wasn't something that came easily to the boy.

'I didn't mean to get so angry…I just didn't want her to tell Mum. I know what my mother's like.'

'What's she like?' Grappa stopped himself from leaning forward in excitement, now the conversation had returned to the woman.

'She lives in her own version of the truth. Doesn't even know when she's lying half the time because she does it that often she believes her own lies. She's incredibly convincing. I've seen her make people doubt their sanity. Ayla thinks if we're honest, she'll be honest back. But Ayla has no idea what she's dealing with when it comes to my mother.'

'No.'

'That's not the worst of it.'

'What's the worst?' Grappa almost wet himself in eagerness.

'She gets these bouts of…I don't know what you'd call it… depression? Doesn't get out of bed for days, stops eating. It's like all the life goes out of her. David always referred to it as her illness.'

'Illness?'

'Like sometimes she can be really unpredictable, get mad over nothing – and I mean really mad. David would always say 'Don't worry mate, that's just her illness.'

'Fascinating.'

'As suddenly as it started, she's back to normal. I wouldn't even call it normal, more like obsessing about something, usually her mosquitoes.' He laughed a bitter laugh for someone so young and finished off his scotch. Grappa poured him another. It was starting to loosen the boy's tongue.

'What country's your Mum from, son?'

A long pause as uncertainty swept over the boy. 'I was born in America but she's not from there. My grandmother came from –'

'Ireland?'

'How did you know?'

'Had a feeling your mother was Irish.' Grappa almost burst into a leprechaun's jig but restrained himself. Didn't want the boy thinking he was daft. 'What part of Ireland, do you know?'

'My grandmother, she lived with us in America. She looked after me because Mum would tour and give lectures. She was like a young prodigy. We were always moving. I remember my grandmother talking about home, and how she was going to take me there one day and how cold it was. She spoke funny. There were words she said that I couldn't understand. She had a strong accent.'

'Can you contact her? Do you have an address for her in Ireland?'

'No. She and Mum had a big fight. I was about seven by then. A year later Mum met David and we moved to Australia. Mum calls herself Australian now. Scotch does warm you up, doesn't it?'

'So, your grandmother never rings? Never sends birthday cards? Christmas presents?'

'Not that I know of. When we first got to Australia, I kept asking Mum if she was going to visit, and Mum said she was dead. But I don't believe that.' The boy's mahogany eyes were all turmoil. 'I don't believe anything she says since I found this.' He painstakingly wrapped the photo back up then took another swig. 'Wouldn't be surprised if I never see her again.'

'Who? Your mother?'

'No. Ayla.'

Now the words were pouring out of the boy's mouth so fast, he couldn't keep up.

'Oh God, I hope I haven't blown it with her.'

'Who? Ayla? Or your mother?'

The boy began to cry like an inconsolable child. Bewildered, Grappa patted him on the back and poured them both another drink.

Riley couldn't remember ever feeling so horrendous. It even hurt to turn his head. He sat at the kitchen table, sipping on his glass of water, wondering if he had more vomit left in him. The constant drops of rain hitting the tin roof were like hot needles piercing his skull.

His mother still hadn't surfaced. If David were here, he would say, 'Hope she hasn't gone into one of her spirals.' That was always the first sign, not getting out of bed. David had always spoken in terms of her 'illness' secretly to Riley, never in front of her. She would eventually materialise, happily refreshed, full of manic energy, and no one would mention the fact she had been bedridden.

There was something disturbing Ayla's grandfather had said about his mother last night. Riley couldn't quite remember. It was a nasty misgiving sitting in the back of his mind. There was a lot of last night he couldn't remember. He had a vague recollection of falling overboard and almost drowning while the old man sat in the row boat, cackling.

He thought he heard a car door slam over the sound of the rain. A loud knock on the front wall of the house confirmed it. Head pounding, he crept downstairs and opened the door.

'Hi, love. Mum home?'

'Hey, Till.'

'Still pissing down. You may never work again.' She took her dripping raincoat off, smiling at the look on his face. 'You do know I'm having you on. Once the sun comes out after all this rain, you'll be mowing your cute arse off. Mum home?'

'She's still in bed.'

'At this time of day? What, she sick?'

'I'm fine. I was just resting,' Ghost-like, Marlise stood at the top of the stairs, her skin paler than her nightie.

'Shit, you look like death warmed up, love.'

'Haven't been sleeping well, that's all.'

'Came to tell you the goss on the council decision about the mozzie spraying,' Tilly waddled upstairs, reaching the top, out of breath.

'Riley, fetch Tilly a glass of water.' Her voice sounded as pinched as her face. She sat at the kitchen table, waiting for Tilly's coughing to subside. He had the urge to touch his Mum on the hand, to check if she was alright, like David would. As usual, he couldn't bring himself to. He knew she craved more shows of physical affection, but something always held him back. The umbilical cord between them was no longer soft and malleable, it had stiffened and dried-out with the blood of distrust. He fetched the water quietly like an obedient child in the hope this would suffice.

'Your findings sure put the wind up them. Their initial decision was not to resume spraying, even though it was obvious most of the community wanted it. When Maria Boccabella found out though... far out, you should have seen her. Talk about a crazed woman. You know Maria, the Italian who lives in the monstrosity near the barge ramp?'

'Yes.' The sharp tone of impatience made him study her. She was too still, extremely agitated, ready to snap.

Tilly was oblivious. 'She stormed into the council chambers and disrupted a meeting, threw things around. Had to restrain her, I heard. Anyway, cut a long story short, she got the decision overturned.'

'How?' His mother was sitting on the edge of her chair, ready to attack.

'Maria had a big hand in the Mayor's last election campaign, basically funded it. She owns five houses on this island and half of Rocky Point. That's an exaggeration but you get what I mean, she's loaded. Claimed if they didn't resume spraying, the return on her rental portfolio would be so poor she would have no choice but to pull the plug on all future cash donations, including the Mayor's next electoral campaign. Threatened to fund a smear campaign instead.' Tilly pulled her cigarettes out. 'Thought I'd let you know the whole story so you don't feel too bad. Your report almost worked. But money talks in the end, as always.'

His mother was gazing into the linoleum as if the secret of the universe was hidden in the pattern. 'Doesn't that Boccabella woman have a heart? Is money all she cares about?' Her eyes flashed, wet and black.

'Nah, Maria's a good stick. Loves that horse, and she's very generous with her cash. Just came back from Bali and bought me a fancy jewel encrusted ashtray. Personally, I'm not upset about the decision. Holiday rentals and house sales have dropped since they stopped spraying. All got to make a living somehow.' Tilly pulled her lighter out.

'Bali? There are all sorts of killer mosquito-borne diseases rampant in Bali. Let's hope she hasn't brought one back with her.' His mother emptied her face of emotion.

He had no rational reason to feel frightened for that old lady he had seen on the horse the other morning, but he did.

Tilly gave his mother a tentative look. 'Mind if I smoke in here, love?'

'Yes.' The seething was evident in her voice.

Tilly widened her eyes at Riley. He knew she wanted to ask: 'What's up her bum?' It made him smile.

She scrutinised Marlise. 'Sure you're okay, love?'

'I'm fine.' One of her hands was gripping the edge of the kitchen table so hard the fingernails bent back.

Tilly unpeeled herself from the small wooden chair, releasing it from her vastness. 'Better get going. Got a funeral to organize. Poor Harley Mangleson's gone and killed himself. Knew he was upset about his dog but didn't know things were that bad with him. Never can tell with people, can you?'

At the name Harley Mangleson and the mention of the dog, what Grappa had said about his mother last night came back to him: 'His dog Jip was poisoned just after you moved in. Harley swears it was your mother. Know anything about that, son?'

Watching her reaction to the news of Harley's death, Riley's stomach turned over. He reached the toilet in time to find his vomit still tasted of scotch, which made him start all over again. He could hear his mother seeing Tilly out. He remembered her mentioning the dog several times the day they arrived, how its barking irritated her. She had all sorts of chemicals and poisons in her laboratory. It wouldn't be hard, with her scientific knowledge, to concoct something. An image rushed at him, his childhood friend Kelvin, sitting with his dead dog, Buddy, Kelvin's tear stained face confused and full of rage. 'My Mum reckons your Mum killed him. Why would she do that? I'm not allowed to play with you anymore.'

He was dry retching now. Surely, he had nothing left in his stomach.

'Are you ill?'

He hadn't heard her come back upstairs. She was so pale, even her lips looked bloodless.

'Self-inflicted.' It hurt his throat to speak.

She teemed with disappointment. He couldn't hold her gaze. When he looked up again, the question forming on his lips left him. She had gone. Only the slam of her bedroom door indicated where.

So, he was dead.

Marlise sank onto her bed and cried from relief. She might be able to sleep tonight without waking at the slightest sound, imagining the sunglass-clad, drugged-out psycho slinking down the hall, machete in hand.

Last night, when she did manage to fall asleep, she dreamt she was a mosquito captured in a jar and he proceeded to pull her wings off, one by one. She shuddered at the memory and stood up.

The view through her rain soaked window defeated her today. The mangroves looked forlorn standing bedraggled in the muddy water, the mess of their root systems as twisted as her emotions.

He was dead.

Why didn't she feel elated? It was disheartening that Riley was ruining himself with liquor over some flaky girl he scarcely knew, but the genocide about to be inflicted on the poor mosquito population was intolerable. Of course she would fight the decision. This was what incapacitated her. There was always something here in their newly found paradise she had to battle with. All too exhausting. She lay on her bed and realised she hadn't eaten all day. No wonder she was feeling so tired. But the thought of food was repulsive. She turned over and willed herself to sleep.

She didn't know what time it was when she entered her laboratory but through the glass door, she could see the wet swamp glittering in the bright moonlight.

Too perfect a night not to work.

In the insectary, the putridity of the dead rodent hit her at once. She pulled a latex glove from the packet and peered into the cage full of fat well-fed mosquitoes, congratulating herself on her timing. The rotting mouse lying on the floor of their cage was pale and bloodless. Six days ago, she had taken a syringe and extracted the frozen pathogens from a cryotube plucked from her canister of liquid nitrogen. Then, selecting the plumpest of the baby mice, she had injected its brain with the live pathogen. Two days later, when the mouse was showing visible signs of infection, she had placed it in the cage for her darlings to feed on. They had done a wonderful job sucking every last drop from the creature. She tried to pick it up but it stuck slightly so she had to scrape at it, leaving a stain on the cage floor. This displeased her. Usually, she would remove the dead mouse after a few hours but with all the Harley trouble and lack of sleep, she had forgotten. Revolted, she threw it into the swamp for the crows to feed on. Taking a jar from the shelf, she undid the lid, then pricked her thumb and let a drop of blood fall into the bottom of the vessel. She undid the knotted fabric covering the opening in the cage, and placed the jar in the hole. The cloth opening had been cut so the jar fitted exactly.

'Starving…poor darlings.' They swarmed to her blood at the base of the jar and drank, not enough to fill them up but to give them a taste. She screwed the lid on and admired her hard-working vectors, one ear always tuned to Riley's steady breathing. The gutters outside were dripping. The rain had finally stopped so she crept downstairs, leaving the heavy front door ajar.

The full moon hovered above the house like an old friend waiting in the dark. She looked up for too long and became dizzy. Feeling faint, she staggered to the bench under the house at the edge of the swamp to lay down. Unsure if she fell asleep or passed out, when she woke up she was exhilarated, as light as a shadow flying into the night, burning with hunger, directly to Maria Boccabella's house.

The night smelt deliciously dank and mildewed after the rain. She gulped as she almost flew under a dripping branch. One drop of water on her wings could ground her. She relaxed into it. This was her favourite part, the flying. She soared and dipped, somersaulting around the sparkling drops of salt hanging in the moonlit air. Burrawang lacked these crystal salt particles, was her last thought before the human world fell away to only the sound of her wings as she flew through the diamonds in the night.

The Italian woman's house was in darkness but for the fluorescent blue lights hanging from the balcony, zapping moths by the hundreds and many poor mosquitoes that strayed too close. The sound and sight of those electrified lights killing her kind, filled Marlise with venom, venom full of deadly live pathogens. She swished the saliva around in her mouth and felt them brewing. How convenient the woman had been to Bali recently. The authorities wouldn't suspect a thing.

On her fourth lap, she realised there was no way in. The house was a fortress, every door and window screened, all potential gaps sealed. She screamed angrily into the night, which emerged as an unsatisfying faint buzz.

Flying toward the horse asleep under a Jacaranda tree, she marvelled at the talent of the pathogen carrying mosquito, harbouring the ability to kill so many different species.

The glowing whiteness of the horse made it look carved from the moon, but its skin was soft and easily penetrated. Even though she was starving, she tried not to over feed, which wasn't difficult – horse was her least favourite blood. She knew if she over-fed she would lose the excess later in human form through abdominal cramping, which she loathed.

The horse slept until she pulled out, when it swished its tail, flinging her into the coming dawn. She regained her balance, changed direction and flew west toward the swamp and home to Riley, who she guessed was sleeping with a sore head and bruised heart.

It was midday when Marlise woke from the sun pouring in through the window of her room. Her first proper sleep in weeks and her appetite had returned.

'I could eat a horse.' She remembered her vivid dream and laughed. The nightmares had been replaced with such delicious wonder.

She stretched languidly on the bed. Hopefully now the rain had stopped, Riley would return to work instead of moping around looking like he wanted to skin her alive and feed her to the murder of crows frequenting the back deck.

His new job was a terrific development, she realised yesterday when she heard him relating to Tilly, how natural he was, how at ease. Maybe a new life here was possible? She had even made a friend. June seemed full of potential.

'All you need in life is one good friend,' her mother always said when Marlise came home from school crying, claiming no one liked her.

But best of all, that nasty dog owner was no longer a threat. She ticked off all the blessings in her head, her grateful list.

Energized after such a good sleep, she rolled over and fantasised she was covered in ice-cream and Josh was licking her clean. She knew if she went down to the pool for her swimming lesson, they would end up fucking hard and fast on the dirty cement floor of his ice-cream booth, hidden like rats. If no one ever found out, what harm could there be?

She groaned in frustration and felt between her legs. Disturbed at how wet she was, she pulled the sheet back and saw blood.

Then the cramping began. She raced and sat on the toilet, shocked, as the dark syrupy liquid dripped from between her legs. She hadn't bled since the arrival of the hot flushes. The subtle vile odour wafted up in clumps. She caught her reflection in the mirror and all thoughts of visiting Josh vanished as she watched herself shrivelling, drying up. The voluptuousness she had been feeling disappeared. She looked old and spent, and smelt like a dead animal.

16.

Once the rain clouds dispersed, Grappa spent a day on the boat cleaning, whistling as he worked. At least the two small tanks he'd rigged to catch runoff from the roof were full.

The following morning, he rowed to the island and heard the news that Harley Mangleson had overdosed the night of the Banshee wail. He was saddened by Harley's death, but the timing with the Banshee was food for his soul. How had the boy put it? 'There's more to life than meets the eye.'

So much more son, you have no idea. Only a matter of watching for the signs, then all is revealed.

Grappa was so excited by the confirmation that the Banshee's wail had been real and not the imaginings of a 'crazy old drunk,' he spent the day on the island stretching his cabin cramped legs, chatting to anyone who'd listen.

It was late afternoon when he noticed Toto – the magnificent horse belonging to Maria Boccabella – trying to walk up the beach near the barge ramp. It staggered and shook its head. As Grappa drew closer, he saw the neck muscles twitching.

'Hey there, Toto.' Usually the horse would approach him, but it skittered in the opposite direction. He followed Toto into Maria's yard, concerned by the fact that its front legs were starting to give way. The horse pressed its head against the jacaranda tree. When it collapsed into a kneeling position, Grappa raced to the house and dragged Maria from her plasma screen.

By the time they returned, Maria's slippers flapping as she ran, poor Toto was on the ground, convulsing. The woman went hysterical in Italian, throwing herself over the horse.

He yelled to be heard. 'Ring a vet. You need a vet.'

'*Si, si.* I ring Stan.'

'Stan's away. You need to ring a mainland vet. Go.'

'*Si, si.*' She ran back to the house as fast as the flip, flop of her slippers would allow.

When a curlew cried three times and the jacaranda flowers fluttered down in slow motion, Grappa knew that death was upon them. The image of that glorious beast as it lay in its death bead of lilac rain would stay with him to the end of his days. The liquid brown eye, sad but calm, conveyed a knowledge beyond human comprehension, before life trickled out of it.

Grappa felt the island hold its breath. A curlew skittered across his vision and screamed, bloodcurdling in the fading light. How many more deaths would there be? Jip, then Harley, now Toto. A darkness that had clung to the island since that first day he had seen her on the barge engulfed him. It was no coincidence the deaths had started soon after she arrived. He was certain she was the cause of it all, somehow. The taste of fear sucked his mouth dry.

'Can't start blaming her for everything, you moron. Harley overdosed, and the way Toto acted...didn't look like poison.' The sound of Maria's slippers ceased his muttering. He could hear her on her cordless phone, talking to the vet.

'Yesterday I notice he not his usual self. He not eats the apple I try to give –'

When she saw the horse was dead, she collapsed, crying out in her mother tongue. Grappa rescued the phone and answered the vet's questions as well as he could. The man explained it was too late to shift the carcass but would come across now to take tests. 'Most important thing is that neither of you leave the property.'

'But I don't live here. I was –'

'Don't care. You were with the horse when it died. You touched the horse. I'll need to alert the authorities. There are procedures in place now. You're both in quarantine until we know more.'

'Quarantine? For what?'

'There's been two outbreaks of Hendra in the last month on the mainland, one right here at Rocky Point. Can't take any chances. Are there any fruit trees that attract bats on the property?'

Grappa stared at the forest of bananas and pawpaws along the fence line and cleared his throat. 'A couple.'

Grappa didn't like the way the vet let out a breath. 'Has anyone else been near the horse? Is anyone on the property with you, apart from the owner?'

'Not that I know of.'

'Don't let anyone enter the property. Neither of you are to leave the property. On my way now.'

Grappa felt a genuine sadness for the little Italian woman as he pried her off Toto. Half carrying her back to the monolithic house to wait for the vet, the ferocity of her sobs made him wonder how much more grief one island could endure.

Ayla hunched beside her mother, looking around the wake, silently toasting Harley with the beer Trev had given her. Harley would have been astounded – almost half the island was here. His brother, squatting on the front steps of Trev and June's house, was so identical to him it was eerie. He and some second cousin were the only members of Harley's family who had bothered attending.

His grey fibro house seemed tomb-like all shut up and had started to grow mould down the shady side, from all the rain. The lawn needed a mow and Jip's grave looked lonelier than ever. 'Harley and Jip should be buried together, not apart.'

Her mother patted her on the knee in answer, distracted by Aunty Dora and Rayleen who were sitting with a group of ladies from the island Art and Craft Club. Dora's laugh rang out, her face turned to the bright sky, guffawing so hard she had to wipe tears.

'Think Dora just heard about Grappa's quarantine.' Her mother sounded wicked.

'Can you imagine him, being stuck there with Maria? They have nothing in common.'

'I know.' Her mother couldn't stop chuckling as she went to join the women and have a good laugh at Grappa's expense.

Mandy was sitting beside Rayleen, who had her arm firmly around her daughter with no intention of removing it. Mandy caught Ayla's gaze and mouthed, 'save me.'

The wake was buzzing with the news of Toto's death.

'Third death in a row.'

'That'll be it now. Always happens in threes.'

'Hope that fucking dog killing bitch feels guilty for what she did to Jip. Poor Harley paid the price.' It was Steve Tyson who ran the fishing club.

'It wasn't her, Steve. Harley got it wrong,' June was emphatic.

'Seemed fucking certain last time I spoke to him.'

'I met her...had coffee with her. She was very concerned about Harley. Asked all kinds of questions to check if he was okay.' June's make-up didn't hide the fresh bruise under her cheek bone. She tilted her head so her hair fell over her face.

'Trev not coping too well, hey June?' Steve's voice caught with emotion.

'Trev found him. Hasn't stopped drinking since. Anybody need a beer?' She walked away without waiting for an answer, collecting empty cans on the way. Trev, who was frightened of Aunty Dora, was nowhere to be seen. Ayla pulled the letter out of her pocket and read it again, savouring each word.

Dear Ayla,

I am truly sorry for losing my temper. It was mortally wrong to grab you like that. I was a monster. Now you have seen the worst in me — my awful temper, and you were only trying to do what was honest and correct, honourable lady that you are. This situation with my mother is very involved. I applaud you for running from it. Now I have employment (thanks to you), I can search for a place of my own. I can't live with her anymore. I understand if you don't want anything further to do with me, but please know I can't stop thinking about you. The thought that I may never see you again is unbearable. I am sorry for any distress or physical harm I have caused you.

Your Riley.

She touched the ink marks. Plain blue writing on white paper had never emanated such charm.

'How many times are you going to read that thing? Go and see him.' Mandy poked her shoulder.

'Mum said he looked dreadful when he dropped it off, like he hadn't slept for days.'

'He's around at Mrs Watson's, mowing her lawn.'

'How do you know?'

'Just heard Mrs Watson and Tilly talking about him. Sounded like a couple of old cougars. I'd come with you to suss him out if Mum would let me out of her sight.' Rayleen was calling her.

'Maybe if you visited more, she wouldn't be so full on.'

'You kidding? She'd be worse.'

'True.'

'God almighty Mum, give me a break,' she screamed across the party as only Mandy could. 'Have fun making up with virgin boy,' she teased, as she headed back to her mother.

Ayla drained the last of her beer for Dutch courage and opened the front gate. Her heart raced ahead of itself as she walked up the hill in the direction of Mrs Watson's. It had been weeks since she had seen him, but nothing had changed. The thought of him still made her hold her breath. Breathe, stupid. What are you scared of?

Riley was pushing a mower into the shed at the side of the large brick house, wearing only an old pair of shorts. She had never seen so much of his body exposed. It had a natural beauty to it, unlike the fake sculpted look Harry had gained from working out. Harry's muscles were artificially inflated, like his ego. Everything about Riley, including muscle definition, was real. Ayla stopped herself, annoyed. She knew she was always comparing out of fear of being hurt again, but would it ever end? She didn't want Harry in her psyche anymore.

Riley was locking the door to the shed. The way his shoulders slumped made him look worn out and sad. Was it because of her?

'Hi.'

He spun around.

She moved toward him, but he took a step back. 'I stink. I've been mowing lawns all day...'

'Don't worry, I smell of beer.' She stepped into him.

He hugged her hard.

'Thank you for your letter.'

He pulled her in tighter and they stood for a long time feeling each other breathe.

'Let's go for a swim.' She slipped her sandals off and held them in her hands. 'Last one there.' She was off. He overtook her on the gravel but once they hit the beach she had the lead. 'You lose.'

They flopped onto the sand, panting. Between breaths, he said, 'You know I can't swim?'

She checked to see if he was joking. 'I'll teach you.' Stripping down to matching bra and pants, she ran into an oncoming wave.

He pulled his shorts off to reveal white y-fronts.

His mother must still buy his underwear. How cute.

He remained in the shallows. 'Come on!' she called.

He's frightened of waves. That's even cuter.

'Dive under the next one that comes at you. Like this,' she shot under a wave and surfaced further out. 'See? You come out the other side.' Three waves passed before he worked up the courage. She went to him and held his hand. 'Let's do the next one together.' They dived four times until clear of the breakers.

He looked toward the beach. 'We're so far out but I can still touch.'

'Isn't it the best?' She disappeared, emerging beside him, pressing her slippery body against his. She kissed his salty mouth and felt it explode with desire. Their mouths became one, hands wild for each other. Her legs wrapped around him, lost in the want of him, rubbing herself against his erection, coming in her pants as he did. The strangled noise he made, entrancing.

He looked horrified. 'Sorry.'

'I'm not.' She kissed him and whispered in his ear. 'I'd love to feel you inside me.'

Still breathless, he let out an indistinct sound, half word, half laugh.

Ayla felt a blush rising, so she dived under and headed toward the beach.

They dried themselves with their clothes, avoiding eye contact. She tried to think of something to say as the silence between them hardened. 'You need a phone. Why don't we go to the mainland tomorrow and buy you one?'

'Sure.'

'I've got to clean in the morning, but I could meet you at the jetty for the two o'clock? Are you working tomorrow?' She walked towards the track to her front yard. He looked so uncomfortable, standing shivering in his wet y-fronts, she wanted to let him be.

'I need to trim a hedge, that's all.' He mumbled, backing away and tripping over the same tree root that brought him down last time. 'See you at two then.'

She waved like an idiot, wanting to smash her head on the angophora as she passed it. Harry had taught her to talk dirty. 'I'd love to feel me inside you.' One of Harry's operating lines. Cringe factor. Talk about awkward. Good one Ayla. She realised she was fumbling into new territory here, groping her way in the dark, learning to start all over again.

17.

Starving after cleaning all morning, Ayla stood at the end of the jetty, watching for Riley and gobbling the last of the ice-cream like she was breathing it in.

Shane, the decky, stood in the doorway of the ferry. 'Shit, you were hungry.'

She couldn't answer because her mouth was too full.

'You catching this one, Aylee?' Shane had his hand on the rope about to untie.

She saw Riley running, and nodded as she stepped onto the boat. Riley dived on behind, ready to hug. She grabbed his hand instead. 'Let's go upstairs.' Every goggled eye in the boat was upon them.

'Hi, Aylee.'

'Hi, Mrs Parkes.'

'How you going, Aylee?'

'Good thanks, Sammy.'

'Ayla, can you tell your mother that the geranium cutting she gave me took beautifully.'

'Sure thing, Beryl.'

'Is your grandfather still in quarantine?'

'Don't know actually, Tina.'

As they climbed the ladder, she heard them gossiping about the death of Toto and the suspected cause.

They had the top deck to themselves. 'You know everyone,' he said, hugging her freely now.

'Did you see them checking you out? It'll be all over the island – Ayla's got a boyfriend.'

At the word 'boyfriend' he dared to put his head on her chest. 'I couldn't stop thinking about you all morning.'

'Thought you were trimming hedges?'

'While I was trimming hedges.' He kissed her neck. 'Even last night I couldn't stop thinking about you. I hardly slept.' He kissed her mouth. 'My God. You taste like mango sorbet.'

She pulled away, smiling at his eagerness. 'Shane will be up in a minute.'

He became visibly nervous.

'I was so happy to see you yesterday, I forgot to ask…did you find the box?'

At the mention of it, he sank into himself. 'I've searched everywhere…every time she goes out…even under the house.'

Shane popped his head up and Ayla held out her multi-ticket.

Flustered, Riley pulled a thick roll of money from his pocket.

'Wow mate, you rob a bank?'

'Um…return please.'

She noticed how uncomfortable Riley looked as he counted the correct money.

Shane gave her a 'who's this weirdo?' look but said, 'Guess who I saw yesterday, Aylee?'

'Mandy?'

'Gee, she's looking hot. She still only into women?'

'Yep. Sorry Shane.'

'Just my luck.' He climbed down the ladder.

'How come you brought so much money?'

'I didn't know how much a phone would cost.' He looked confused.

'Won't cost that much. Don't you have a wallet or something?

'No.'

'You should put it in a bank. That's too much to be carrying around.'

He held up the thick wad of notes. 'Money is a strange thing, isn't it? What is this? Solidified energy from my flutes, my music, the gardening...if I tossed this overboard –' He went to and she screamed, grabbing his hand.

'Put it away, please?'

He shoved it back in his pocket, the smile dropping from his face. 'My mother married David for his money. The day I met him...the way she primed me...'

'What do you mean, 'primed you'?'

'We were waiting at the airport. She was all jumpy. Kept bending down and holding my shoulders, repeating, 'He's rich. He's going to take care of us. He's filthy rich, so don't be rude to him.'

'Were you?'

'Of course.'

As the afternoon progressed, Ayla became intrigued by Riley's quirkiness, revealing how isolated his upbringing had been, and he seemed fascinated that she found his reactions to things funny. In the bus to the shopping centre, he asked where the seat-belts were, embarrassed to admit he had never caught a bus before. He hated the slimy feel of the shopping centre linoleum on his bare feet and walked on his heels which made her laugh so much she got the hiccups. Watching him discover the phones and their myriad of functions was like watching a child eating lollies for the first time.

'Didn't David have a phone, or your mother?'

'The reception was so bad we relied on the land line. When we were packing up, I found an old phone of David's. Mum rang the company and they talked her through connecting it, but it's nothing like this. It's more like that one.' He pointed to a phone on the display stand.

'A senior's phone.' The sales assistant said with disdain.

By the time they caught the ferry home, he was obsessed with his new toy.

'I'm starting to get jealous of that thing.'

He fought a yawn. Ayla thought of him lying awake all night, thinking of her, and gestured for him to put his head in her lap.

'Shut your eyes.' She massaged his scalp.

She assumed he had fallen asleep when he said, 'I want to try your idea of being honest. She likes you. It might work.' He stared at the flame pink clouds hanging low over the horizon as if trying to tell the future by them. 'Besides, I have no options left.'

'Grappa always says life unfolds in a circle. The seasons circle in on each other. The moon and the sun are circles. The earth is a circle. Every action we do in life will circle back on us in some way. His Gran lived by that belief. She told him that's why the Irish cross has a circle around it, to remind us of this. Maybe your mum knows you need to see that box, to learn about your father, complete the circle? Maybe that's why she's kept it all these years? But she hasn't been ready to face it?'

'Maybe.' He didn't sound convinced.

By the time they approached the house, Ayla didn't feel so confident. Her mouth dried when she saw the old wooden place; a giant long-legged insect standing crookedly over the swamp.

Marlise was sitting on the verandah, statue-like, staring across the mangroves to some distant point beyond life itself.

'Hi, Mum.'

She looked down on them. Ayla thought she looked ill.

'Hi, Ayla.'

'Hi.'

He ushered Ayla upstairs, 'Would you like a glass of water?'

'Yes please.' She followed him into the kitchen and sat at the table, wondering why they were whispering.

'Would you like a glass of water or something, Mum?' he called, holding the fridge door open.

His mother materialised, her skin paler than Ayla remembered, with black shadows under her eyes. 'That's the first conversation he's initiated in days,' Her sadness made Ayla feel guilty. 'Hope you don't treat your mother like that? I don't even get a 'bye Mum' when he leaves the house anymore. Maybe it's a boy thing.'

Ayla didn't know how to reply.

His mother collapsed into a chair, as if the act of standing took all her energy.

Riley sat opposite. 'I'm sorry I've been angry with you Mum...if you hadn't lied about Dad –'

Marlise cut him off with an audible sigh.

'When I cleaned your house the other week, I accidentally knocked over a box under your bed. One of the letters got caught in the vacuum. I read part of it and told Riley about it.'

His mother's face was a mask, too hard to read.

'I know you were probably waiting for the right time to show him that box yourself, but either way, it's done now and he knows about it, even though he hasn't seen it because when we went back it was gone. I know you told me not to vacuum under the bed. I'm sorry. I forgot.' She said in one breath.

'A box? What box? I don't know what you're talking about.' Marlise looked genuinely surprised.

'Mum, please...I just want to know where he is. What country is he living in?'

'What box is she talking about?' His mother's confusion seemed to be growing.

'It was wooden with carvings on the lid. It had a false bottom full of letters from Riley's father and photos of him with you and Riley.'

'I have no idea what she's talking about.'

'Mum, please? Stop lying.'

'Lying? I'm not the one lying here. She's the liar.'

Now it was Ayla's turn to be confounded. 'Why would I make it up?'

'No doubt you showed her the photo you found —'

'Mum'.

She turned to Ayla, her wild eyes black with emotion. 'Did he show you that photo and tell you the sob story of how angry he is because I lied to him?'

Ayla nodded, wondering where this was heading.

'I lied only to protect you Riley. She has fabricated this box of other photos to feed your anger toward me. That's why you haven't seen it. Because she is making it up. Can't you see what she's doing?' She swung back to Ayla, cold now. 'You're trying to turn him against me. He hasn't spoken to me in days. My own son. My only son. Now I know why.'

The phone in the lounge room rang. They all ignored it. On the sixth ring, Marlise stormed out.

'Remarkable, isn't she?' The contempt on his face made Ayla nauseous.

Marlise stomped into the room. 'It's Tilly, Riley, can't find the key to her tool shed.' She continued to the large kitchen window, ripped open the curtains and stared out at the swamp.

As soon as Riley left, she was in Ayla's face, bent close, her breath repulsive. 'Please say you made it up. You'll turn him against me. Don't do this to me.'

'I...I can't lie to him.'

The madness in Marlise's eyes frightened her.

'I thought you were the one for him. If you turn him from me I'll... who knows what I'm capable of? I'm warning you,' she hissed.

Riley walked into the room, watching his mother. Deflated, he sank into a chair. 'Forget about the box. I just want to know where he is.'

The deadness in the way he said it made Ayla want to shake Marlise. Why was she doing this to him?

'I have no idea where he is.' Marlise's voice was controlled, but

Ayla noticed one of her knee caps undergoing a wild spasm.

'What's his first name then?' Riley asked.

The shape of her mouth as his mother left the room made Ayla think Marlise was going to spit on her.

'I don't even know his name,' he cried out.

Ayla moved her chair to his and hugged him.

'You should go.'

'Do you want to come back to my place?'

He studied her face like he might never see it again. 'I can't. I've started this now. I need to pursue it.'

'Let's catch up for dinner at least. Mandy wants to meet you. We were thinking of having a fire up near the cave...cook up a damper or something?'

His eyes held no hope as he touched her face. 'Sure. Why not?'

She waited, trying to say something comforting, but kept coming up empty.

'I'll walk you to the corner.'

'No, need. Stay and talk to her.' She stood up. 'I'll text you where and when, now I've got your number.' She managed a smile and left.

The image of him slumped at the table, broken, stayed with her all the way to Hibiscus where she intercepted Grappa dragging his row boat down to the water. 'You're alive.' She hugged him. 'How was quarantine?'

'Don't want to talk about it.' He seemed short-tempered.

'So, it wasn't Hendra?'

'No. The horse died of MV something or other.'

'MV?'

'Can't remember what the bloody hell it was. Wasn't Hendra. That's all I care about.' He sure was grumpy.

'How did you and Maria get along?'

He gave her a suffering look then changed the subject. 'Want you to know I like Riley. I was wrong about him. Make up with him, will you? Never seen a boy so miserable. Drank me dry he did.'

'I was just over there.'

Grappa froze. 'Don't go there. Hear me? You tell him to come to yours or meet somewhere else. I don't trust that woman.'

'Sure is a piece of work.' Ayla looked toward the mangrove swamp and told Grappa what had occurred. When she relayed how Marlise had threatened her, Grappa almost dropped one of his oars in the water.

'Sweet Jesus.' He sat in his row boat, oars poised, lost in thought. 'I need to know what we're dealing with. Do you know her surname?'

'Legros.'

'French? Thought she was Irish?'

'I thought she was American?'

'Legros? Sure that's her name?'

'That's her dead husband's name. David Legros.'

'I need her name, her maiden name.'

'I'll ask Riley.'

'What's his last name?'

She had seen him write it twice today when he was signing for his phone. 'Gallaher.' At the time, he had said, 'Apart from the photo, that's all I have of my father.'

She spelt it out for Grappa.

He secured the oars. 'Don't go anywhere near her. You got that?'

'Grappa, I can take care of myself. Please don't do anything stupid.'

'Listen to me. All these deaths on the island, it's no coincidence.'

She began to walk as the mozzies gathered, ignoring his overblown sense of drama.

He called as he rowed. 'Don't cross her. Stay away from her. Go straight home.'

'I am.' She blew him a kiss.

The lack of a breeze amplified the sound of the oars slapping against the water, echoing it around the bay. The humidity of the coming summer, already thick in the air, felt oppressive. But it wasn't only the weather. Marlise's glacial eyes, devoid of human warmth, kept flashing into her mind.

Eventually Riley gave up pleading through the locked laboratory door and went to shower. The intensity of her silence was maddening.

When he emerged, cleanly shaven and dressed, he found her in the kitchen, cooking. 'Look darling, risotto, your favourite.' She was radiant, as if nothing had happened.

'Ayla's already invited me for dinner.'

She kept stirring the rice as her eyes filled.

'Please, Mum? I won't be angry, I promise. I just want to read his letters.'

'I don't know why she's making up stories. She's trying to take you away from me.'

'Mum, it's not going to work. I'm not thirteen anymore.'

'Thirteen?'

'What happened with Kelvin –'

'They moved away. You can't blame me for that.' Her voice rose in a choked pitch.

'I do.'

A curious lonely sound detached itself from her. She held onto the kitchen bench as if it was about to fly away. 'You've been so unhappy here –'

'I'm the happiest I've ever been.'

'Maybe we should go somewhere less populated, somewhere –' she went to touch him but he stepped back.

'I like it here.'

She turned toward the sink again and picked up a glass of water. He could see the liquid vibrating.

'Obviously you're fucking her already.'

The vehemence in her voice set off an alarm in him to protect Ayla. He tried a different tactic. 'Maybe I'd consider moving somewhere new if you were willing to be honest with me about my Dad?'

She spun around, eyes flashing in anger. 'Why this obsession? You haven't mentioned him in years and now you –'

'I thought he was dead.'

All the fight seemed to go out of her. 'It makes no difference, you know. I never knew my father.'

And look how stuffed up you are, he thought, placing his tongue against the back of his teeth to stop from speaking the words.

'He was a stranger. An American just passing through. Gone before my mother even realised she was pregnant.'

'Is that why you ended up in America? Searching for him?'

Before she looked away, he saw he had guessed the truth.

'I didn't even have a name. The only thing she could tell me was he had a brown birthmark in the shape of a heart on the side of his neck. It didn't take me long to realise it would be impossible to ever find him. Once I accepted that fact, life became much easier.' She drank from the glass, crying.

He softened his tone. 'I miss David, Mum. I miss him so much it hurts.'

'You think I don't miss him?' A sob interrupting the middle of her question.

He hugged her.

'We need to get off this island, make a new start. It's not right here for us.'

He didn't answer but continued to hold her. It was his duty. She was his mother. He was all she had. Suffocated by this thought, he pulled away. 'Got to go.'

'Please? A quick bite? I've gone to all this effort.'

His phone beeped.

'Where did you get that?'

'I bought it.'

'When?'

'Today.'

'How?'

'Went to the mainland with Ayla.'

'You went to the mainland?'

'It's a short ferry ride, Mum.'

'But...you don't need a phone. We've got a land line.'

'I've got a job now. I need a mobile.'

'You can borrow mine. I don't use it.'

He opened the message. 'No need, have my own now.' He left the room without looking at her, ran downstairs and slammed the screen door.

He heard her come down behind him but didn't hear the door. He could feel her watching him. As he got to the bend, she cried out softly like a wounded animal in a cage. 'I love you.'

He refused to look back.

Marlise stood lost in the kitchen, a painted bowl in her hand. If she had the energy, she would start packing their belongings back into the boxes she had yet to throw away. What an atrocious mistake she had made bringing them to this overcrowded hellhole. It was vital they leave as quickly as possible. She needed to get Riley away from that girl. That little minx had taken him to the mainland and bought him a phone. Who did she think she was, his mother? And Riley had gone without telling her. How many times had he done that? What else had he been doing without her knowledge? That little tart was leading him astray, teaching him how to be deceptive. She looked innocent, but Marlise knew now she was intent on destroying his relationship with his own mother, wanting him all to herself. She had even told him about the box for fuck's sake. Marlise pelted the ceramic bowl so it smashed against the floor.

She took another bowl and dished some risotto, trying to think methodically. This time she would not be so hasty in her decision. Choosing a house via the internet had been idiotic. Who would have thought it would turn out like this, living under a microscope with a bunch of mosquito-hating imbeciles? She had learnt her lesson. This time they would rent for six months and then buy, only if it were suitable.

He knew about the box. My God, he knew about the box. Her brain kept jumping back to it. She gulped for air. Her hands felt numb as she carried the bowl of risotto to her computer.

'Calm down, Marlise.' David's voice, a soothing balm. She remembered the feel of him, the way he stroked the back of her neck.

Of course…Riley hadn't seen the box. It was her word against Ayla's. Once she had convinced Riley that slag of a girl was lying, he would see her for the little manipulator she was, trying to steal him away from his own mother.

Marlise stabbed at the computer so it came to life. At least this time she didn't need to drive hours to an internet cafe. She could trawl the web all night, if necessary.

The memory of the way Riley looked at her when she denied the existence of the box flipped her stomach. She pushed the steaming bowl of gluggy undercooked risotto away. The fear that he would stop loving her had shrivelled up her appetite.

Grappa was so exalted to be home in the cramped comfort of Little Beaudy, he kissed her walls several times. Fussing around the cabin, checking all was as he left it, gave him infinite pleasure. He put the kettle on and fired up the battered old laptop Helen had given him years ago. One bar of battery left.

'Blast.'

He typed the name Gallaher into the search engine and read, 'surname commonly found in the south of Ireland,' before the screen died. His mind ran over everything his Gran had taught him. And the dream. He kept returning to the dream.

The south is where the Fey are most active. Marlise would've been a young woman when she met this Gallaher, a young woman living in the south of Ireland? Was Riley's father from her village? As a child, was she whisked away by the Fey? Did this twist her in some way? Give her the power to curse? Or is she one of them, replaced? Maybe she's not from there at all? Maybe only the grandmother is Irish? His mind raced in circles.

Weary at the thought of the long night ahead, he made himself a potent cup of coffee then fired up the engine. Impressed she caught first go, he kissed her again.

'You little beaudy.'

Grappa steered out of the bay and found the hidden channel into the mangroves, killed the motor, drifted to his hidey-hole and lowered the anchor. The view from the deck was clearer but the drone of the mosquitos kept him in the cabin, propped against the circular window with his binoculars, where he watched and waited. There was light in the front room. He could see her sitting at a computer, the remainder of the house in darkness. After half an hour, he lay back to rest a moment.

'Nothing like your own bed.'

The loud buzz of his snores soon brought the crabs complaining from their holes in the mudflats. They clicked their claws in unison, organising themselves into a protest march, but Grappa snored on obliviously.

Riley was starving. The two sausages they fed him had only increased his appetite and the baked crusty smell of the damper Ayla was pulling from the fire grew torturous.

Maybe I should have eaten some of Mum's risotto, he thought, his guilt sedating him. Though, her gluggy mess always turned out nothing like David's. He tried not to picture her at home alone, waiting for him. Why did she make things so difficult?

'Throw me the cloth, Mand.'

'It's on your shoulder. Duuh.'

Watching the way the two girls related, Riley was acutely aware of lacking a long term friend. He had felt the same with the young people at the markets; the assumption and casualness they had with each other spoke of years of shared experience.

Now the damper was out, he stoked the fire. The night was warm, but a fresh breeze blew in off the ocean. Mandy lifted the blackened alfoil and the smell set his taste buds weeping. From her backpack, Ayla produced a wad of butter, another plate and a knife.

'What else you got in there, the kitchen sink?' Mandy teased.

'Shut up and start buttering.'

Spellbound, he tried not to stare at Ayla. In the firelight reflected against the cave wall, she had moved beyond the realms of earthly beauty.

'Careful, it's hot.' Her soft eyes locked with his, checking him over, comforting him.

The damper was fluffy and buttery, melting in his mouth, demanding their full attention. Even Mandy fell silent.

He stole another glance at Ayla who was looking out to sea, searching the horizon. 'Did you see the last painting Mum did? She's turned them into mermen.'

The unexpected sorrow on her face seemed to encompass all the oceans of the world.

Mandy followed Ayla's haunting gaze. 'Yeah…who knows, hey…

never found their bodies. Maybe they are swimming around out there, not a care in the world.'

Part of the drunken night on the boat with the old man, returned to him. He remembered how Grappa's blurry eyes lit up as he spoke of his granddaughter. 'The night her Dad went missing, I took her to the old fig in the circle of pines –'

'The Nor Folk Tree?'

'She told you about it?'

'She took me there.'

'That's a good sign, son. She never took Harry there.'

'Who's Harry?'

'A dead head who broke her heart. No one important. So, what did you think?'

'Of what?'

'The Nor folk? What did you say to her when she told you about them?'

'Said, "I think you're the queen of them,"' Riley raised his glass.

The old man leaned in. 'She is. The night her father went missing, we hugged the tree and prayed for him and Reg to be found alive, and I swear to God, when I opened my eyes, the circle of trees was lit up from within, from the base of the fig. I could see the root system extend under the earth, spreading out to the circle of pines. And Ayla...she was a part of it. She had her eyes shut, still praying, but I swear on my dead Gran's soul, Ayla can commune with the spirits of the land.' The old man hiccupped, and Riley realised how drunk he was.

Mandy's voice cut through his memory. 'If this water was permanent' – she was washing the dishes in a trickle of water coming over the rock – 'then this would've been the island birthing place for sure. Imagine it? You'd be sitting on the site of the birth place of generations of babies. Generations of mothers' blood spilt into this very earth. A sacred site, thousands of years old.'

'You've never told me this.' Ayla looked upset.

'Calm down. I said "if". This water's only here because of all the rain we've had. You think heavily pregnant women would've climbed up this hill?' She threw the tea towel at Ayla. 'Get real.' She feigned a yawn. 'Well, I better get back before Mum sends a search party, or worse, starts calling, "Moo Moo." I can hear her already. Swear the whole Island knows I'm back. Can't take one step without the holler, "Moo Moo."' Mandy, mimicking her mother, disturbed an owl that crashed through the trees below then dropped out of sight.

Riley stood. 'We'll walk you back then.'

They looked at him as if a flower had sprouted from the top of his head.

'Lived here my whole life, mate. No need to walk me home.' She ambled toward the track. 'This is my country. I know it by heart,' she said, and tripped, falling into the bush. 'Ow. Got a torch I can borrow, Aylee?' She got the giggles.

Ayla had already produced one from her backpack and passed it to her friend. They could hear Mandy swearing as she kept walking into things. Ayla knew she was acting the clown to make them laugh, which they did.

Finally, there was silence. They sat, eyes drawn to each other.

'Are you cold?' He went to move the picnic rug spread beneath them.

'Leave that. There's a blanket in the pack.'

'Mandy's right, you did bring everything.'

'Only the essentials.' She sat beside him and draped the blanket over them. 'It's a good spot here because it's high. You don't get the mozzies with the breeze from the sea...and if it rains you can move into the cave...I thought maybe we could sleep here for the night? I mean, if you want...if you didn't have to get back...we don't have to...just thought you might like a break from your mum...and –'

He answered her with a kiss and they lay back beside the fire.

'Your letter...I want you to know...I think I feel the same...I mean, I don't think, I know…I –' He shut her up with another kiss, beginning to feel confident with this kissing thing. When she kissed him back, he knew it was possible to fall into someone.

She pulled away. 'Should I take my dress off?' He had never heard her sound so shy.

Not trusting his voice, he nodded and watched as she stood and lifted her dress over her head. She let out a nervous laugh, not her usual laugh. Dumbfounded as to what to do, he did what he knew best and began to play a song of desire for her. His longing made her sway for him in the firelight. She shut her eyes and danced for herself, away from him. He saw that he could pull her toward him with his music and she danced back to him. He felt the night sky falling down as she knelt beside him. The flute dropped and an owl cried out as he put his mouth to her breasts. The feel of her flesh beneath his lips was so intoxicating, he didn't notice she had unbuttoned his shirt. It was only when she unzipped his jeans he realised he was almost naked. He lifted himself so she could pull his pants off and they paused, taking each other in, catching their breath. When she stroked his erection, an electric current shot through him, making him grab at her, wanting to get inside her. Lost in the touch and feel, a slave to a primal longing, he didn't hear her at first.

'Wait,' she said again and gently held him at bay. She went to her backpack, but the sight of her naked from behind was too much. He lunged at her, his mouth discovering her tender shape, fingers exploring the wet mystery between her legs. He heard her again, that same shy laugh as she rolled something over his erection. He stopped and looked at it. A prophylactic. He had read about them in David's *Professor Lang's Essential Guide to Sexual Health in Men.*

'Condom, so we don't make a baby,' she whispered.

He was glad he hadn't used the archaic term out loud.

As she guided him inside her, he came. 'Sorry.' Disappointed in himself, he wanted to make her pant as she had in the water. She lay beside him and pulled the blanket over them, cuddling into him. 'We've got all night,' she said between kisses, and taught him other ways to pleasure.

With the alluring smell of her on the ends of his fingers and the feel of her against him, the stars danced in the endless night to the sound of the surf on the wind. Riley knew this was the happiest moment of his strange and lonely life.

He drifted into sleep and into her, then they woke to explore each other again. She laughed her deep throated laugh as he opened a condom packet with his teeth, 'I'm glad I brought more than one,' she said, guiding him into her softness. He loved it most when he made her gasp. He made her gasp so much she cried out and he thought he had hurt her, but she sighed contentedly and kissed him on the eyelids.

'Who's Harry?' he asked, and she told him about her recent life.

In turn, he talked of the friends he had made at the markets, and the girl, Bliss, who had kissed him behind the toilet blocks and how he couldn't speak to her after that.

She fell asleep on his arm in the breaking dawn, so he let it go numb for fear of waking her. A lone mosquito buzzed around them, making him think of his mother. Had she changed her mind? Would he arrive home to find the box waiting on his bed?

'Doubt it,' he caught himself whispering.

Watching Ayla sleep while a crimson sun peeked over the ocean, bathing her face with pink light, the pain in his arm became as unbearable as the love he felt for this gentle being who had finally relieved him of his virginity.

18.

When Grappa woke with the sides of his mouth crusted shut, the sun was high in the sky and there was a dent in his head where the binoculars had slept. He scrambled to focus them. She was a blur in the kitchen, then a flash of a white dress before coming into view downstairs, where she fussed around with a scooter. The drone of the engine penetrated the mangrove swamp as she drove off, disturbing a flock of sulphur-crested cockatoos. Their larrikin squawks deafening as they swooped low over the boat.

'Rack off, you mongrels.'

He opened a can of chick peas and ate straight from the tin. Where was she off to? The memory that she'd threatened Ayla made the chalky gunk stick in his throat.

He puttered out of the mangroves into Hibiscus, threw out the anchor and rowed to shore for his daily walk, heading straight for the tree to ask once more for protection for Ayla. It was all he knew to do, feeling flaccid in the face of the woman. Thumping along in the hot sand, memories perforated his skull: Jip on the beach shivering and whimpering, Harley lost and broken, swearing she was responsible, and Toto's sad eye trying to communicate a malicious power was amongst them, a power that needed to be thwarted or the banshee would be hoarse from wailing.

It came to him in a flicker of sunlight. What kind of woman could live in the old Johnston house anyway? Grappa had never entered that house. He approached it once, years ago when it was abandoned and the cobwebs had grown, but turned away full of trepidation, the sweat of fear trickling down his neck.

She was strong this woman. Ayla said she slept in the dead baby's room. Holy Mother. How twisted was that? No wonder her son had issues with her. Maybe she feeds on the souls of dead babies? This thought made him swallow before he'd even unscrewed the lid of his flask.

Marlise couldn't comprehend what was happening with her body. She felt depleted but unable to relax. At least the bleeding had stopped, as quickly as it started. She suspected it was the shock of discovering Riley knew about the box. The headache, from lack of sleep, intensified with the high-pitched whine of the scooter as she rode around the island, her tired eyes continually searching. He was with that girl, she was certain. Now he had a phone, he could ring at least, let her know he was still alive. He probably tried to, but the girl had stopped him. She was a piece of work that one. Just the kind of thing she would do. Box-finding little trollop.

His money hadn't been in his flute case. Had they left the island to search for his father? Marlise glimpsed the ferry moving away from the jetty, too far out to see who was on it. She accelerated, heading towards the barge, which was due any minute.

The unloading was in progress as she skidded to a halt. Sharon sat at the driver's wheel of one of the waiting cars. Marlise ran up to her. 'You haven't seen Riley, have you?'

'Took off again has he? That's what you get for not letting him eat ice-cream,' Sharon had that self-satisfied grin. 'I've never denied my kids anything because I know the first thing they'll do, first chance they get, is the exact thing I banned them from. It's common sense.

Not too smart for a scientist, are you?' Sharon's nasally voice lingered in the morning air.

Marlise resisted the urge to spit on the woman. She spied Grunter on the barge. 'Grunter, you haven't seen my son, have you?'

'Hey, just the girl I was looking for. I'm off tomorrow. Up for a fish?'

'He didn't come home last night.'

'Probably off bonking some chick or getting drunk with his mates on the beach. Don't worry about him.'

The driver in the tower blew his horn. Grunter gave him a filthy look. 'Jesus, I hate it when he does that,' he signalled the first car to drive on. 'So, we fishing tomorrow?'

'I have to find Riley.'

'He's a grown man for fuck's sake, let him be.'

Marlise looked at Grunter's sunburnt face and felt repulsed. 'You know I'm never going to sleep with you, don't you? You're not my type. Besides, Tilly told me about your venereal disease.'

Grunter's red face went beetroot. 'What?' He stabbed at the air, signalling Sharon to drive forward.

Marlise walked off, catching Sharon laughing in her peripheral vision. That woman had publicly humiliated her once too often.

You'll need *your* head checked when I've finished with you, bitch.

Marlise smiled for the first time that day as she started the scooter and headed for Josh conveniently tucked away in his ice-cream bunker. From a young age, she had learnt there were two types of men in this world: those who were ruled by lust and those who could rise above it. Lorcan and David fell into the latter category. Marlise harboured disdain for men who couldn't contain their desire. She was certain, by the way Josh had wiped the ice-cream from her breasts, he lacked self-control.

She stopped not far from the Boccabella woman's place, in an isolated part of the road surrounded by bushland, and looked at the time. She needed to seduce Josh between ferries, when there was an absence of people. The thought of what she was about to do lifted her spirits. Sexual revenge was the only activity momentarily capable of granting her relief from her worry over Riley. She ran her hands down her snug-fitting cotton dress and took pleasure in the fact she had no bra on. She peeled her knickers off, threw them into the bushland and climbed back on the bike. With the anticipation of what was about to occur, the vibration between her legs felt exquisite.

Walking up Mud Rock Beach with the sun beating down on his bare back, Grappa's sweat made his shorts stick to him. He turned into Dead Tree Point to spot Dora swimming off the sandbank and waded out to her.

'Heard you'd been released. Did Maria behave herself?'

'Had to beat her off with a big stick.'

'Sandy and Carol and the three kids saw you trying to beat someone with a big stick on Mud Rock Beach. It's all over the island.'

'That was before I got to know Riley.'

'Poor kid. Wonder he's still talking to you.'

Grappa dived under the water. When he popped up, Dora looked mischievous. 'Don't know why you and Maria didn't hit it off. She's a very attractive lady.'

'If you're into Telly Tubbies.'

He liked it best when he cracked her up. After she regained some composure, she said, 'You know you're a mega star? There was big money going 'round. Odds were nine to one you had Hendra.'

'How much did you lose?'

He loved her laugh which came deep from her belly. He swam to her and they embraced. 'Come to dinner tonight?'

'Can't. Got to go to Big Island. Cousin's birthday.'

'Tomorrow night?'

'Could do.'

'Cooee. If I'm not off Hibiscus, I'm around the corner in the mangroves. I'll hear you.'

She lay back and floated in the water. 'Thought I'd see you walking this morning?'

'Slept in. Worn out from trying to figure out what that woman's up to.'

'What woman?'

'The boy's mother. The one in the dream.'

'Mosquito woman? I like her. She put that council feller in his place, that's for sure.'

'I don't trust her. She's up to something. I've been watching her.'

'What do you mean, you been watching her?'

'Been hidin' in the mangroves, watching her through the binoculars.'

Dora's face got that fierce look he didn't like. She stood up in the water. 'You have no right. Who do you think you are, spying on people? That's called stalking, that's what that is. I should report you.'

'Settle down, I was just –'

'Don't you tell me to settle down, you pervert, spying on a poor innocent woman. What's got into you? That's disgraceful behaviour.'

'Hey –'

'Don't come near me. You disgust me, and don't expect me for dinner. When are you going to wake up to yourself?' She swam away down the beach and hopped out, not looking back.

Dora, you hot head.

The scrub swallowed her up. He waded out and cimbed over dead trees towards Three Mile, focusing on the tops of the Norfolk pines he could see in the distance, trying to push the fight with Dora from his mind.

She'll come right. He was accustomed to her flying off the handle over things and knew it was only a matter of time before Marlise exposed herself. Where Dora was concerned, he could be as patient as a pipi waiting for the tide to turn if he had to.

The ancient stand of trees looked cool and inviting in the white glare of day. He had a custom of removing his hat before entering the circle of dappled light. Grappa knew he was stepping into a sacred room. He was enraged to see two discarded beer bottles lying on the ground, then a plastic bag and a chip packet stuffed into the nooks of the tree. He unravelled the bag and crammed the rubbish into it, clutching it to his chest, trying to hide the blasphemy, disgusted with his fellow human beings.

'So sorry.'

He collapsed into the base of the fig in his preferred spot between the folds of the roots, with his back against its old body. That familiar sweetness drifted over him. He swore he could feel the old tree osmosing in time with his breathing.

'*Dia dhuit.*'

He closed his eyes.

'Please put a ring of protection around our Ayla.'

He opened his eyes to see a blue dragonfly land on his knee. Watching it fly off and disappear into the mess of branches above, he giggled like a school boy. 'Thank you. Last time I was here you gave me a sign in the shape of a dream. If you could give me something more, I would greatly appreciate it.'

He shut his eyes. At first nothing came. Then the image of Marlise and the scooter this morning as he had seen it through the binoculars flashed into his head, on replay. He took a deep breath and the sequence slowed down. He realised what he had seen. In a fluid series of actions, she had checked over her shoulder, turned back to the bike, flipped the lid of the seat, lifted up a box, opened the lid of the box, then replaced it under the scooter seat.

It had all happened so fast, he didn't comprehend it at the time.

Grappa's eyes snapped open. 'Bloody hell.' He needed to tell the boy. He hugged the trunk of the tree. *'Maith thu.'*

Half running up Dead Tree Point, the plastic bag of rubbish clinking by his side, his glee overflowed when he saw the moon hanging in the broad day sky.

'Should have known.' Good things happen on a sun moon day. The Nor folk had provided once again.

Josh was alone, scooping the pool for leaves when Marlise pulled up.

'Might take you up on that offer of a swimming lesson.'

He nodded. 'As you can see, the place is swarming with tourists.'

'Thought I might need to book ahead. I didn't bring my swimmers.'

'Next time then.'

'Suppose I could swim in my dress. Could you lend me a towel?'

'We could manage that. Jump in.'

He placed the scoop down, dragged a box of swimming implements beside the pool, ripped his shirt off, then dived in.

She worked her way down the ladder. The smell of chlorine stung her nostrils and the coldness made her wince. She hated being submerged in water.

He grabbed a child's yellow kick board. 'First up, want you to hold onto this, like so. Body nice and straight and kick your legs all the way to the other side of the pool.' He demonstrated then handed it to her.

She feebly attempted what he had asked, giving up when she reached the deep end.

'Need to keep your body straight like this.' He put his hand on her belly to push her up, but she clung to him.

'I want to get out. I can't touch the bottom.' She nearly pushed him under as he grabbed for the kick board. 'Please.' She wrapped herself around him, pressing her body into him.

'Don't panic. I got you.' He carried her to the edge. 'My fault. Should have kept you in the shallow…' His voice faltered when she climbed out and sat on the side of the pool, fully aware her thin white dress was see-through now.

With his head level to her knees, she parted her legs so he could see up her dress. 'Can I borrow a towel? It's freezing.'

He swam to a far ladder to get out. 'They're in the booth.' He cleared his throat.

She watched the droplets of water run down his tanned back as she followed him, relishing the sensation of undoing the buttons that ran down the front of her frock.

He turned before she had finished, and saw her dress half open. He threw the towel at her. 'What the fuck? Everyone can see you.'

She went down on all fours to spread the towel on the cement floor. 'Now they can't.'

Panicked, he pulled the roller door down to the counter. 'What the fuck are you doing? Get up.' He stood over her.

She knelt, so close she felt heat radiating from him. His wet board shorts clung to his crotch, inches from her face. She looked up at him. The drip of pool water on cement and their breath the only sounds. As if the spring on a trap was released, they moved at the same time. He grabbed her by the hair, pushing her face into him as she yanked his pants down. Her dress was ripped, buttons flew into the air as they became a mess of limbs on cold concrete. He bit into her, she cried out, straddling him, coming hard and fast, riding the wave of his orgasm.

Removing herself, she stood up and buttoned what remained of her dress. 'Thank you.' She felt rejuvenated, powerful and in control once again.

He lay there mortified, hand over his face.

'Maybe you should get up.'

'I'm married,' he croaked.

'This can be our little secret. No one need know. If I were you, I'd pull your pants on in case someone walks in.'

He did, not looking at her. She could see by the expression on his face he was disgusted with himself.

'Don't know why you're so worried. Sharon knows all about you and Samantha.'

He was aghast. 'How do you...?'

'Sharon told me, she's waiting for you to grow the balls and admit it to her yourself. The whole island knows.'

She pulled the roller door up and left the booth, amazed at how energised she felt. 'Thanks for the swimming lesson,' she called, spotting the ferry pulling in. She longed to ask the ferryman if he had seen Riley, but her dress was gaping open.

Maybe Riley was home by now, she hoped, driving as fast as the bike would allow. The breeze against her wet dress felt arctic, but the lingering warmth between her legs more than made up for it.

Ayla had already suspected it would be a sun moon day when she spotted the pale moon, a chunk of quartz in the sapphire sky. She manoeuvred the foil wrapped potatoes out of the coals then sat so her body shadowed Riley's face from the brightness and checked the time on her phone. Almost midday. Wow, he was tired.

She savoured being able to watch him unashamedly and couldn't decide if he was more handsome asleep or awake as she studied every inch of him: the blackness of his lashes, the shape of his lips. She restrained herself from leaning forward and kissing them. But it was the cut of his jaw and neck and shoulders that entranced her, they spoke of strength and loyalty. Riley was someone she could trust with her heart. It was there in the rise of his Adam's apple, the line of his clavicle. At this thought, he opened his eyes.

'Afternoon, sleepy head.'

He pulled her into him, nuzzling the nape of her neck. 'Love the way you smell.'

'I pong. I'm dying for a swim.' She kissed him and extricated herself to dish out the potatoes.

He lay on his side, propped on his elbow, smiling at her.

'What?' She said, passing him a potato.

'You.'

'Me, what?'

'Just, you.'

She kissed him and told him to eat, after which they packed up and climbed across to the sand dunes so they could roll down, laughing so hard Riley spat sand.

'Want to skinny dip?'

'What if someone comes?' She liked the way he asked this, his sandy lip twisted in a naughty curl. An expression she had never seen on him before.

'You just have to be quick.' She pulled her dress off, sand flying everywhere, and ran into the oncoming wave.

He stripped and ran after her, calling out before he dived in. 'The first time I saw you, you were naked.'

'I knew it,' she splashed water at him. 'I knew you saw me that morning.' She wouldn't stop splashing him. He grabbed her, holding her arms down. 'Let go of me, you perv,' she teased.

'You're mine now…trapped forever.' He did an atrocious version of a wicked laugh as Ayla saw a figure coming around Dead Tree Point.

'Grappa.'

They scrambled for their clothes. By the time Grappa reached them, Riley had his jeans on and Ayla's dress was stuck to her still wet body.

Grappa was trying to catch his breath. 'In her scooter.'

'Pardon?' Riley frowned.

'It's in her scooter…the box…a compartment under the seat.'

'How do you know?' Ayla heard the excitement in her own voice.

'The Nor folk told me.'

She looked at Riley, disappointed, but he wasn't deterred. 'Worth a try.' He took off.

'Wait,' Ayla and Grappa called, simultaneously. Riley turned back.

'I'll lend you my push bike. It'll be quicker.'

'Promise me something, son?'

'Sure.'

'Don't let your mother see you take it. Sneak a look then put it back without her knowing. She's already blaming Ayla. Please don't upset her any further.'

'I'll do my best.'

Grappa put his hand on Riley's shoulder. 'You're a soldier about to enter the frontline. Good luck, son.'

Grappa was overdramatising the situation, caught up in another one of his fantasies. She hoped Riley wouldn't be too heartbroken when he found the box wasn't there.

'You'll be right. It's a sun moon day,' Grappa called after them.

She had to run periodically to keep up with Riley. 'Don't get too hopeful. Grappa has a tendency to make things up sometimes to add to the drama of it all.'

'It's the only place I haven't looked.'

Ayla decided not to say anything more. The squeak of his feet in the sand sounded determined.

Riley hid Ayla's bicycle behind the large bloodwood tree at the edge of the mangroves. Where he rested the handle, there was an explosion of sap: solidified blood from a wound on the tree. He broke a length off, snapping it as he walked up the dirt road until all that remained was a ruby globule in the palm of his hand.

Tilly's car was parked outside the house. Her loud voice floated down from the kitchen. When he saw the bright yellow scooter, it looked to him like something divine blazing out of the gloomy backdrop. He quietly flipped the seat and his heart whirled in delirium at the sight of the box. The carved wooden lid felt familiar.

Tilly sounded upset. He crept to the screen door.

'Wouldn't even let me on the barge. Said people who spread vicious rumours aren't welcome on this service. What on earth possessed you to tell him I said that?'

'But I didn't. I mean…I didn't say it was you.' His mother was flustered. 'He guessed it was you. Who else do I know here? I told him, it didn't matter who it was. I just wanted him to leave me alone. I panicked. I'm sorry.'

'Marlise, golden rule to surviving a small community: it's fine to repeat gossip but never to the person who the gossip is actually about. Don't know how I'm going to mend this. Grunter is one stubborn cookie.'

'I wouldn't worry about him after what he said about you.'

'What did he say about me?'

'What about your golden rule?'

'Forget it. What did he say?'

'Promise not to tell him I told you? I don't want any more trouble.'

Riley held his breath. What was his mother up to? He really liked Tilly.

'Of course I won't. What did he say?'

'If you didn't have such a problem with alcohol, you'd be a good real estate agent.'

'What? I like a drink on a Friday night, that's it. He can't talk. He's down at the resort every chance he gets, drinking the place dry. I'm a bloody good real estate agent. He's talking through his arse. Bloody dickhead. That's it. He's blown it with me.'

Riley heard a kitchen chair scrape across linoleum as someone stood up. He ran to Ayla's bicycle as quickly and as lightly as his bare feet could carry him over the sharp gravel. With the box firmly under one arm, he steered with the other, pedalling with all his heart towards the thought of his father.

Ayla was waiting at her front gate. 'How did Grappa know?' Her face ecstatic.

'Is there somewhere we can go? If she discovers it's gone, she might follow me here.'

'The tree?'

'Jump on.'

She grabbed a cushion from the verandah and placed it on the bike rack to sit on, then put the box in front of her under the seat, using the ocky strap to keep it in place. 'All set.'

They wobbled at first, but once he gained speed they were off. With Ayla's arms wrapped around him and his father's words tucked safely beneath him, he had a sense of journeying into a new life.

On reaching the tree, Ayla released the box, presenting it to him as the ambrosia scent drifted over them. The tranquillity inside the grove felt sacred.

He felt ashamed at his trembling as he studied the wooden carvings on the lid. 'I remember now. When I was little, she kept this on her dresser with jewellery in it.' The anticipation made his legs contract. He sat down.

With Ayla beside him, he lifted the lid of the box. His heart stopped. There was nothing in it.

'She probably kept her jewellery here, but look.' She slid a thin piece of wood from the side of the box, revealing letters and photos. 'A false bottom.'

She handed him, piece by piece, the story of his father. It was the images that held him first. He looked so like his Dad it was uncanny. Ayla pointed to the baby Riley, in the arms of his father beside a sign: Yellowstone National Park. 'Too cute.'

'I look happy. We all do, even Mum.'

'They look very in love.'

Riley tore himself from the photos to work his way through the letters. Ayla suggested they read them in chronological order and arranged them by the post dates on the envelopes.

By the time he had finished, he knew many things about Lorcan Gallaher. He was Irish, and a musician. 'Like me.' Riley couldn't stop thinking of this. 'I wonder if he plays the flute?' His smile disappeared at the next thought. 'I wonder if that's why Mum hates music? Because of him?'

The story of the break up unfolded like a faded and torn newspaper with bits missing. They looked over the letters again, trying to piece the history together.

'I must have been what? Three when he left?'

'He left you and your Mum in America to go back to Ireland for someone's funeral.'

'His Dad's. Look he says so…here. So weird…we have similar handwriting.'

'There was some problem with money. He was forced to cover the funeral costs with the cash he had for his flight home.'

'He got stuck over there trying to make enough money to get back to America. So what? Why did that upset her so much?'

'I don't know. But it was during that time she must have sent a "Dear John" letter.'

'But what did he do to make her do that? I don't understand.'

'Sounds like she gave no explanation. Listen to this…how shocked he is.' Riley's mouth hung open in confusion as Ayla reread the letter.

Marlise, your letter knocked the bejesus out of me. Where did all this come from? What's going on with you now? I'm busting my gut here, working three jobs to get the money to get out of here. A couple more weeks and I'll be there. Just hang in there. I love you pet. Just hang on for another while. I'm sorry you're finding it hard with Riley and your work and stuff – that's why I wanted to take him with me. But you wouldn't have it. I'm not lying to you, I'm coming back. Why have you had the phone cut off? Why won't you ring me? I'm going mad from the silence and now your letter, it's tipped me over the edge. Jesus Christ woman you and Riley are my world. You cannot be doing this to me.

Riley's head felt on fire with all this new information.

'I wonder what he tried to do when he did get back to America, for her to take a DVO out on him?'

'Nothing. Doesn't he say somewhere about her lawyer friend inventing facts to destroy him, to ensure he never obtains access to me again?'

'This one,' Ayla hands him a letter.

'Listen to how angry he is.'

You fuckin lying bitch. Why? Why are you making up these lies? What have I done to deserve this? I have a right to see my son, Goddamn you.

'So out of character from the other letters.'

'I'd be angry if someone stole my child and wouldn't let me see them.' Riley felt crushing pity for his father at the hands of his mother.

'Did you notice toward the end, the letters don't start, 'Dear Marlise'? They address you instead. Look –' Ayla leafed through them. 'My dear son. My dear son…and without fail he always mentions the amount of money enclosed.'

'Their falling out might have been over money.'

'What makes you think that?'

'Here. Look.' Riley found a letter.

If money is so important to you why did you have a child with a musician? You should have had one with a fuckin doctor.

'Look at the return address on this. He must have given up and gone back to Ireland, eventually.'

'But that didn't stop him. He kept writing until I was...' He found the last letter and calculated from the post date. 'Eight.'

Riley reread the letter but couldn't finish it from the tears blurring his sight.

On the envelope was written: 'Do not open until Christmas.'

My dear son,

I'd give my right arm to be there with you to hand you this tin whistle in person. As a little one you had the love for music. Hope you still have. Hope she hasn't killed the music in you, son? I hope to God you're getting these letters. The fact that you've never written back makes me think you've not received a single one. I'll keep writing you until I reach the grave. Without hope we have nothing. Don't be angry at your mother for keeping you from me. I blame myself for leaving you both. She begged me not to leave. I should have seen the signs. Going back to Ireland for my Da's funeral was the biggest mistake of me life. Your mother has done good for herself considering the shit she had to put up with from her own mother. She dragged herself up out of the gutter and taught herself all that fancy stuff about bugs. You should be very proud of her. Everyone important in her life gave up on her at some point. I should have known she wouldn't have trusted me to return. I should have known she didn't know my love for you and her ran deeper than life itself.

Nollaig Shona Duit, mo buachaill. (Merry Christmas, my son)

'Sometimes it's more like he's writing to her in a way, isn't it? Like he knows she won't pass them on to you?'

'He said he would never stop writing. But he did.'

'Maybe he didn't.' Ayla pointed to the envelopes. 'It's the same post box he was sending them to. She had them forwarded to wherever you were living.'

'We moved to Australia when I was eight. Maybe she didn't bother then?'

'Because she didn't need the money anymore,' they said it at the same time.

'In that post office in America, I bet there'll be a whole lot of letters waiting for you.'

He couldn't speak for the truth of knowing now how much his father wanted him, feeling it jumping out of the words on the paper, the smiling face in the photos. Riley stroked the letters as if the essence of the trees was alive in the paper and his father's love was seeping into him via osmosis.

She was crying now too.

'Hey...'

'Just imagining how it would feel. You think your Dad's dead all these years then you find out he's alive. Always been my greatest wish.'

He touched her cheek. 'If he's still alive.'

'You could write to this address in Ireland.' She turned over an envelope.

That thought gathered in him like a tight knot of hope as he studied the photos again, until the shadows grew so long they merged into one.

'I promised I'd let Grappa know your mother's maiden name if I found out.' Ayla started texting. 'Marlise Griffin. God knows why he wants it. That's Grappa for you, always concocting.'

'I had no idea that was her name. It's like she's tried to destroy all trace of who she really is.' He reread a letter and shook his head. 'She almost destroyed my father.'

'We should go.'

'I can't face her.'

'You don't have to. Stay at my place for the night.'

Without speaking, they rode back to Ayla's, his father's words nourishing him with a new-found sense of worth.

He took the box into the house with him. 'May I keep these here tonight? At least I know they'll be safe.'

'Let's put them in my room.'

He followed her into her bedroom which was dominated by a window with a view of the track to the beach. Through the paperbarks, in the fading light, he could make out the moody hue of the sea. There was a bookshelf lined with science and veterinary textbooks, and clothes strewn everywhere.

'Sorry,' she said, picking things up. 'Since I've started cleaning houses my bedroom never gets cleaned.'

She opened her cupboard and then her underwear drawer. 'Here. Hide it under my bras and knickers.'

He looked at her and neither of them could keep a straight face. 'Lucky Dad,' he said and they fell onto the bed in hysterics. Their mirth turned to kissing as memories from last night swam through him.

The front screen door slammed. He sprang up, thinking it was his mother.

'Ayla?' Helen called out.

'Hi, Mum.' She stood up.

'You go. I'll be with you in a minute.' He indicated the lump bulging through his jeans. They tried to suppress their giggles.

Once she left, his thoughts turned to his mother and anger seethed out of him; a noxious vapour leaking into the peaceful solitude of Ayla's room. He was shocked to discover he had her pillow between his hands, twisting it like a neck, wringing the life out of it. He knew there was no way he could go home tonight. How would he react to the sight of her, the presence of her, now he knew what he knew? He did his best to shake the tension from his body before walking out to join Ayla.

'You hungry Riley?' Helen's warmth helped him unfurl.

Together they prepared a simple meal of garden picked salad, fresh fish (courtesy of Grappa), and baked potatoes. Riley was acutely aware of the way Ayla and her mother communicated from a place of love and respect. He couldn't help comparing it to the volatile relationship with his own mother.

After they had eaten, Ayla washed up and he helped Helen dry the dishes, surprised by how at ease he felt.

This is what it would be like to be part of a regular family, he thought, before his mind jumped back to the sad story of his parents' break-up and the anguished tone of his father's voice in the letters.

He caught Helen watching him. 'You okay?' She asked.

'Today Riley had confirmation that his father might be alive. His mother told him he was dead.'

Helen didn't speak at first. After a while, she announced, 'Sometimes mothers do things, and at the time you don't understand why, but later you realise it was coming from a place of love, or sometimes fear.'

Riley knew now where Ayla's generosity of spirit came from. He tried to contain the fury in his voice. 'I think my father wasn't rich enough for my mother. She saw an opportunity where she could conveniently rid herself of him to find someone with money.'

Ayla tilted her head in contemplation. 'Or maybe she genuinely thought he had abandoned her? She looks so in love in those photos. Maybe the pain of feeling abandoned by him sent her into a spiral of destructive actions out of self-protection? Sounds like she was already damaged from her childhood.'

Both women were looking at him questioningly. How could he explain his mother? Every time he thought he had a clean glimpse of her, she slipped out of sight.

'She'll have her reasons. Don't be too hard on her.' Helen hung up the tea towel. 'Don't know about you two, but I'm done for. Nighty-night.'

Riley watched her hug her daughter. She held Ayla by the chin. In one intangible look, he saw a conversation take place between them.

Helen turned and embraced him. She smelt how a mother should be, warm, spicy and comforting.

In Ayla's bed, Riley and Ayla lay entwined with the events of the day a black ribbon winding through them, tying them together, rendering them silent.

He spread out the letters and photos, studying each one, committing them to memory. 'I want to keep all this. It's all I have of him.'

'I've an idea.' Ayla sat up. 'Today when we rode past Stan's, I noticed his caravan was back. His wife is a photographer. They have a colour photocopier. We can go over first thing in the morning and get them copied. I'm sure they won't mind, especially if we pay for the paper and stuff.'

'I have to work tomorrow.'

'I'll do the copying and then you can sneak the box back when you get a chance.' Ayla's eyes widened at a new thought. 'What do you think your mother will do if she finds it gone?'

'If I go home in the morning before work and act perfectly natural, she will assume all is well. There won't be a need to check, will there?'

'What if she already has?'

'She'd be here, pounding on the door.' Riley didn't like the little frown lines that appeared on her face. 'What?'

'Yesterday, your Mum – when you went out of the room – she said if I turned you against her, she would...'

'She threatened you?' He pressed his lips against her temple, his mind reeling with possibilities.

'The look in her eyes Riley, it frightened me. She looked insane.'

He moved so he could see her face. 'I have a plan. She doesn't like it here. Wants to move away, off the island. She's expecting me to go with her. What if I pretend I'm happy to move away? I'll help her set up in the new place, settle her in and then I'll start to leave, only for a few days, then slowly, bit by bit, increase the time I'm not there, until I leave for good. Hopefully she won't follow me back here. I know it means more deceit, but I think it's the safest way – to leave gradually. Otherwise, she might lash out at you. I...I honestly don't know what she's capable of.'

He pulled her toward him. Riley wanted to lose himself in her velvet wetness and not think about the mother, who, through all these years, had denied him his father's love.

19.

Marlise backed away as the man came towards her. It was too dim to see his face. She turned to flee but he caught her by the hair and smashed her head hard against the kitchen bench.

She woke with her face resting on the table, staring at the bench featured in her dream. She had fallen asleep waiting for Riley. Marlise knew dreams. That one was a premonition, a warning that some man was going to enter this room and slam her head against that bench. At the sound of the screen door, she jumped, grabbing her phone as the footsteps mounted the stairwell.

Riley walked in and embraced her. 'Sorry, should have told you I was staying at Ayla's. Hope you weren't worried?'

'No, I guessed that's where you were,' she lied. It had been another sleepless night imagining him in pursuit of his father. It didn't matter now. He was back and hugging her of his own free will.

'I'll save my number into your phone. Then you can always text me if you're worried.'

She watched him, stunned. He was so warm and – the box – he hadn't mentioned the box. So obsessed with that girl's twat he didn't think to call. Her repressed smile turned into a yawn. Maybe Ayla wasn't that bad after all. He headed to his room and she sank back down. The relief spreading through her body relaxing her so she almost fell asleep again. The night had been a long and lonely trawl through real estate sites, until, in the coldest hour of early morning when the tide was at its lowest, she found a place, a house on a mosquito-infested river, a four-hour drive south. The closest town, with a population of 490 people, was thirty kilometres away via a dirt road. She decided she would take a visit to see how healthy the mosquito colony was.

'Got to get to work.' He was now in his work clothes

'What about breakfast?'

'Had it, at Ayla's.'

'Riley?'

'Hmm?' He was half way out the door.

'I might have found a place. You're not becoming too attached to this girl, are you? I mean, if we move –'

'I'm still young, Mum. Not ready to settle down yet.'

'What about your job?'

'There'll be other jobs. Don't want to mow lawns for the rest of my life.'

He was a wise boy. 'I was thinking of taking a trip to look at the place. Stay in the area for a week or so. See if we could rent the house before we commit to buying. I'm sure you'll love it. It's on a river. When would you like to go?'

'Since all that rain, the jobs have piled up. You go. I'll be fine on my own.'

'I couldn't leave you.'

'Mum, I'll be safe here. Nothing or no one is going to hurt me. Promise.'

Marlise considered. This was an opportunity to regain his trust. And, if he did stay, it would give her a chance to destroy the contents of the box. Every time she had thought about making a fire to burn it, she hadn't pursued it, in case he caught her in the act. Away from him, she could safely do it. The idea was tempting.

'You sure?'

'Mum. How old am I?' He rolled his eyes.

'Okay. The sooner we get off this island the better.'

'You're not going right this minute?'

A wall of fatigue hit her at the thought of the long drive. 'Later. I need to rest first.'

'Can you wait until I get back from work, so I can say good-bye?'

She was touched. 'Of course.'

'Thanks Mum.' He briefly gathered her in his arms, then left.

Another hug. All his aloofness had dropped away. Sex with that girl was working wonders on him.

Marlise sat and imagined their quiet life on the river. Maybe Riley would take up kayaking? The sharp knock on the door startled her. Feeling vulnerable in only her satin dressing gown, she pulled it tighter, then crept out onto the verandah.

There was a bicycle, but no owner. 'Who is it?' Josh emerged from under the house. She didn't like the look on his face. 'What's wrong?'

'Want to talk to you.' His bitterness punctured the air.

She heard him thud upstairs. Tousling her hair and loosening the front of her gown, she met him in the hallway. 'What a lovely surprise. Would you –'

'Who the fuck do you think you are, moving here and fucking round with people's lives, destroying people's lives? Sharon had no fucking idea about me and Samantha. You fucking lied to me.'

She had to think quickly. 'I was trying to save your marriage.'

'Save my marriage? She's fucking kicked me out.' He had her cornered against the wall.

Marlise slipped sideways and backed into the kitchen, toward her phone. 'She was going to find out sooner or later. Isn't it better she heard it from you?'

'It's not fucking better. She won't let me see the fucking kids. Samantha's not talking to me. Who the fuck do you think you are?' He was in her face, a vein under the skin of his shaved head, swollen and throbbing.

'Once Sharon gets over the shock, she'll love you for being honest, you watch.'

'She hates my fucking guts.' He stabbed his finger at her, trapping her against the sink. 'She wants to fucking kill me, you stupid bitch.' He grabbed her by the shoulders.

The déjà vu hit. His next manoeuvre could be her head against the bench. She changed tactic. 'Sharon should understand you can't help it if you're God's gift to women. Look at you. Every woman on the face of this earth should experience a body like yours at least once in their lives. Sharon has no right to deny you to the rest of the world. I can't stop thinking about you.' She skimmed her hands over his crotch. 'Please? I'll do anything.'

She saw his anger disperse. He stood away from her, walked in a circle and stretched his arms over his head, then covered his face. 'Fuck!' he screamed it at the ceiling and stood there motionless. The clock on the wall grew louder. 'I don't understand why I...first Samantha, then you.' He looked dismayed. 'I love Sharon. I honestly love her.' He was about to cry.

If Marlise had been a different kind of woman, she could have felt sorry for him.

'What kind of man am I?'

An easily manipulated one, she wanted to say but the memory of the feel of him inside her, stirred. Now David wasn't around to satisfy her, she had to be resourceful. 'You poor thing, you can't help it if women throw themselves at you. Look at this body.' She lifted his shirt.

He pulled away. 'Don't you get it? I feel nothing for you. You disgust me. I want Sharon back.'

She undid the sash of her gown and let it drop to the floor. 'Do I really disgust you?'

He ran his eyes over her nakedness and looked away. 'I disgust myself,' he muttered.

She moved to him. 'I'm leaving this island. You'll never see me again. She'll never know. I promise.' His smell of chlorine and sweat aroused her sense memory. 'Why not one more time, as a parting gift?' She unzipped his jeans. 'No one will ever know. Please?' She knelt and glanced up at him, fascinated. He had his eyes shut and a pained expression on his face. She knew he was trying to resist what she was doing to him, but his magnificent body had a will of its own.

She slid up his torso and he pushed her back against the table, his glazed eyes not seeing her anymore, wanting flesh. Anyone's flesh. She was nothing to him. No one. He pinned her down and entered her. A reoccurring terror from her twelve-year-old self tried to surface but she conquered it with the thought that Josh was something to her: he was her victim, her obedient fool. I am the one in control, she thought, as she angled herself so he hit that pleasure spot. His grunts in her ear sounded like a desperate animal as he thrust harder and harder.

'Good boy.' She managed to say before the strength of her orgasm took her voice somewhere else.

Mother-of-God.

Grappa nearly dropped his binoculars when he saw what Josh was doing to that woman on her kitchen table. Even from where he was, he heard her cry out. At the sound of her, it seemed the whole swamp came alive with the whine of mosquitoes and the shrill of cicadas.

He watched Josh pull his trousers up.

Josh, you bloody idiot.

He thought he heard a cooee over the ruckus of the insects, listening so hard, his ears hurt.

'Cooee.'

He fired up the engine and manoeuvred out of the swamp. If the wind had been blowing, he wouldn't have heard Dora on Hibiscus.

He rowed in to find her waiting with eggs from her chooks and greens from her garden.

'Bit early for dinner.'

'Shut up.' She climbed into the boat. 'And you can get that look off your face.'

'What look?'

'That smug, I told you so, look.'

'Didn't say a word.'

'Didn't have to.'

'At least tell me why I'm meant to be smug?'

Dora glared. 'You were right about that mosquito woman. She's bad news. The whole island's gone mad. Craft group ladies aren't talking to the barge blokes because Tilly and Grunter had a falling out. The craft ladies have sided with Tilly and the bargemen are supporting Grunter. Samantha and Sharon have had a mighty row. Half the women are on Samantha's side, half are with Sharon. It's out and out war all over the bloody island. The whole community's falling apart. So I've been doing some research of my own. Did some asking around and found out all this quarrelling stems back to her, that mosquito woman. A real trouble maker that one. We're going to have to do something about her. Got any plans? You better not be laughing at me.'

'Grab the rope woman,'

Dora gave him her 'deadly' look as she tied the dinghy off and they climbed aboard Little Beaudy. 'No wonder she likes mosquitos. She is one, buzzing round here and there in people's ears, spreading gossip. Seems to me she likes stirring up trouble, must see it as a form of entertainment.'

'Doesn't just like it Dora, she feeds on it. Her sustenance doesn't come from food. It comes from other people's pain. That's what keeps her alive.'

'Well, I say we go round there and suggest if she doesn't behave herself, she can move somewhere else. This island isn't big enough for the likes of her.'

'That approach won't work.'

'What's your plan then, smarty pants?'

'Let's think on it while I cook us up a feed. I'm starving.'

'So, you got no plan?'

'Nothing's occurred to me yet.' He grabbed a couple of onions out of the cupboard above Dora's head.

'Fish are biting off Pearly, apparently,' she offered as a truce.

'Maybe we should camp there overnight? Be good to have a change of scene.'

'Why don't you turn your bloody phone on now and then, silly man? Tried to ring last night, and this morning. What's the point of having it if you never turn it on?'

'Damn thing. Always forget about it.' He located his phone and switched it on. 'There. Satisfied?'

'No point now, is there? I'm here.'

Grappa's phone signalled a text. 'Blasted thing.' He went to turn it off but saw it was from Ayla, sent yesterday. *True name Marlise Griffin.*

'Griffin…?'

'Hey?'

'Her last name is Griffin. Now we'll know what we're dealing with. You want to chop onions or google?'

'Chop.'

He handed her the knife, went outside, detached his laptop from the solar panels, brought it into the cabin, fired it up and typed 'Surname Griffin' into the search bar.

'Seventy-sixth most popular surname in Ireland.'

'Ireland? That's where your Gran was from.'

'Ah, ha.'

'She's from your country then?'

'Just as I suspected.'

'How can we make it clear she's not welcome on my country?'

Grappa watched as Dora finished chopping the onion. She looked up. 'What?'

'That's it. We should talk to her in her language, her own native tongue. What we need is an ancient curse.' He searched, 'Irish language curses,' and scrolled down until he found the perfect one.

'Imeacht gan teacht ort.'

'What's that mean?'

'May you leave without returning.'

Dora laughed. 'Worth a try, hey? Chuck me the garlic, will you?'

'Imeacht gan teacht ort,' Grappa loved the way the words bounced off his tongue, as if they had been hiding there all his life waiting to be pronounced.

Ayla stared at the time on the computer screen: 7:45am, wondering if it was too early to go to Stan's. She drifted outside and sat on the back steps in the sun amongst the red geraniums as the black Bantam scooted out from under the house, making a ridiculous fuss. The surf rolled in beyond the paperbarks, calling to her. Normally, she would swim, but something niggled at her. Every time she tried to bring it forward as a conscious thought, it scuttled away to hide in the back of her mind.

The letters hadn't clarified Marlise. If anything, they had made her portrait murkier. His mother was a growing conundrum. Once Riley had left this morning, Ayla decided to do an internet search on Marlise Legros.

Doctor Legros, formally known as Doctor Griffin, was a leading expert in mosquito-borne viruses, particularly those belonging to the Flavivirus group. The paper that set her on her pathway to fame was published in the prestigious *Science* journal. It was titled, 'Isolation of the Saint Louis Encephalitis virus (SLEV) in Horses.' While in America, Marlise was the first to discover that SLEV caused fatalities in animals. Once she moved to Australia, her speciality became Murray Valley Encephalitis virus or MVEV, a disease which had produced sporadic outbreaks through many parts of the country and caused multiple human deaths. Ayla discovered several papers written by Marlise on MVEV. One titled: 'Experimental Infection with Murray Valley Encephalitis virus in Pigs, Mice, Birds, Dogs, Kangaroos, and Horses.' She had gone on to write a controversial paper claiming to have genetically engineered a 'hot strain' of the virus with the ability to cause fatality within two days. Marlise's work, from then on, seems to have become contentious in the entomological world, generating major debate and eventually setting her up for ridicule by other renowned entomologists. From what Ayla could discern, scrolling through media reports and journal articles, Marlise developed such a reputation that certain universities formally disassociated themselves from her, one even accusing her of not considering the negative consequences of her research, stating that her deadly strain could be utilised by bioterrorism groups. Marlise's counter argument remained the same: with established cases of viruses naturally mutating in the field to become highly pathogenic, her investigations could help researchers discover ways to combat such occurrences. She was simply trying to obtain a greater understanding of the way a hot virus behaved.

Ayla's phone signalled a message from Riley: *copied yet?*

leaving now, she replied back.

She fetched the box and Riley sent another: *text me when done please hurry*.

Had something happened? She jumped on her pushbike and rode as fast as she could.

When she pulled up, Stan was so focused on cleaning the mud off his treasured caravan, he didn't notice her. 'Hi Stan.'

'Aylee.'

'Welcome back,' Ayla had a real fondness for Stan. Even though he was retired, he still functioned as the island vet, only taking payment if it was in the form of a gift from the vegetable garden or home baked goodies. When Ayla had come to him at sixteen and shared her dream of going to university to study veterinary science, Stan had made it his singular mission to pass on as much knowledge as he could. He had taken it personally when Ayla deferred.

'Good to be back, Stan?'

'Seems to be a bit of angst going on. Everyone I run into has a bad word to say about someone, or their back up about something. Not the friendly little peaceful place I remember.'

'You know the island, always some drama going on.'

'True.'

'Stan, could I borrow your photocopier?'

'Sure, come in. Nancy's down the road, chin wagging.' He led her into the sun room and switched on the copier. 'All yours.'

Ayla worked her way through the box and refused an offer of a cup of tea, and Stan declined the offer of money, as she suspected he would.

'Thanks, Stan.' She placed the copies on top of the originals and sent Riley a text: *done x*

Stan followed her outside. 'Heard you had a couple of fatalities while I've been away?'

Ayla knew he wasn't referring to Harley. Stan always thought in terms of the animal kingdom.

'Poor Jip took a bait, hey?'

'Wanted your opinion about that, actually.' She picked up her bike, detailing Jip's symptoms and how Harley had described the onset.

'If he was pressing his head...sounds like swelling of the brain tissue. Hard to say...certainly doesn't sound like poisoning.'

'That's what I thought.' She strapped the box to her bike.

Stan was still pondering. 'The outcome of the test results on Toto's death were interesting: MVEV.'

'Murray Valley Encephalitis virus?'

'That year at uni did teach you something.'

'No, I...' She couldn't finish the sentence.

He scratched his ear. 'MVEV is mosquito-borne...causes swelling of the brain tissue. Wondering now if Jip died of the same thing? If it can kill horses, no reason it can't kill dogs. I was in two minds about it, but maybe it's a good thing, the spraying of the swamps.'

Ayla's heart leapt around with each new thought. 'Liquid nitrogen canisters in laboratories, what do they use them for, Stan?'

'Depends. Liquid nitrogen is useful for keeping things alive.'

'Like virus-carrying pathogens?'

'Sure.'

'And what about chloroform?'

'Chloroform can sedate animals, and people for that matter. Why?'

'Just wondering.' Her thoughts were dominoes, rapidly falling into one another. Harley swore Marlise killed Jip because she didn't like his barking, and most people on the island were lauding Maria as a hero for pressuring the council into resuming the spraying. Riley said his mother was ropeable about the fact. Could she have targeted Toto in revenge to hurt Maria? She could picture Marlise sneaking in the dead of night with a jar full of live mosquitoes, taken from those spooky cages in her lab. Mosquitoes full of live virus-carrying pathogens which she had bred to be fast-acting, vicious and brutal. She would knock the animal out with chloroform, hold the jar against the poor creature and let those mosquitoes suck, leaving a strange circular welt, like the one on Jip's abdomen. 'Stan, you're a genius.' She jumped on her bike.

He called after her. 'You'd be a genius if you went back to uni and finished that course.'

She waved as the bile from her stomach rose up her throat. Had Marlise already discovered the box was missing? Would she try and harm her in some way? She imagined Marlise cutting a hole in the flyscreen of her bedroom window and emptying a jar of killer mosquitoes into her room while she slept. The image made her pedal fiercely.

Riley was sitting on her front verandah, waiting, covered in grass seed and dust.

'What's happened?'

'Nothing, but she's leaving the island today, which means she'll be taking the scooter.'

'Here. Take my bike.' She took the copies and handed him the box with the originals. But Riley opened the box and switched the originals for the copies. 'Do you think that's safe? She might notice?'

'It's all I have of him.' He hugged her, smelling of petrol and dirt. 'What's wrong?'

'Nothing.' She didn't have the heart to tell him. By the way, not only is your mother a psychopathic liar, I suspect she's also an animal killer. Besides, she had no proof, only a repulsive growing suspicion.

'She's leaving the island for a week, maybe more, to look at a possible place.' He sounded happy at the prospect.

'Text me when it's done.'

The bike tyres left a thin trail of dust in the air.

A couple of Pacific Black ducks and their five ducklings waddled from the bushland into the front yard. They made Ayla think of Grappa. He knew where the box was hidden. The Nor folk had told him. He claimed Marlise was responsible for all the deaths. All? Not Harley's. But how had Grappa known about Jip and Toto? She almost burst into tears, remembering she had called him a stupid old drunk.

Ayla didn't know how long she stood there watching the ducks, but she felt the old magic from her childhood returning. Trusting in the knowledge that Grappa had infused in her, the natural world of the island would always guide her if she was sensitive and patient enough. Like the time a cottonwood flower had dropped from the tree to be caught in her hair. Grappa knew it had been sent as a gift. A thank you from another realm.

Her phone beeped. *Done. She was fast asleep. Return bike after work* *xxxxxxxx!*

One of the ducklings sat on another duckling's head and Ayla giggled. They were there to remind her his mother was leaving the island to search for a new place to live.

'I don't like the idea of you being here all alone,' Marlise took her bag from Riley and placed it in the luggage compartment on the back of the scooter.

'I won't be. I'll be at work or with Ayla.'

She looked him over like she used to when he was little and she had just cleaned his face. 'I've never left you before.'

'Mum. Please? You're going to miss the barge.'

She climbed on the scooter. 'I don't know how long this will take. I want to stay and get a feel for the area. Not going to rush into buying the wrong place again. Mind you, we need to be gone from here before they start spraying.'

'Take as long as you want. I'll feed the mice like you showed me.'

'And the mosquitoes with the sugar solution, don't forget the mosquitoes.'

'I won't. Go.'

'I'll ring every day.'

'Ayla said that texts are more reliable here.'

'I'll text you every day then.'

'And I'll text back, promise.'

She couldn't bring herself to leave him. 'Make sure you lock the doors. Tuck yourself in at night. Keep yourself safe.'

'Mum. The barge.' He pecked her on the cheek and hugged her.

Three hugs in one day. He was like a different person.

'I love you,' she said, riding off. She thought he might have responded but couldn't quite hear over the scooter.

All the cars were loaded by the time Marlise rode onto the barge and the ramp was raised. She was relieved to see Grunter wasn't on shift. The boat was crawling with people, none of whom she recognised. How could one small island sustain so many human beings? No one smiled at her. They all seemed to be talking about her though, whispering, pointing.

Mosquito hating imbeciles, the lot of you, she abused them in her head.

David would claim she was being paranoid, but Marlise knew people. They were saying monstrous things. The loud group sitting under the driver's tower roaring with laughter had made a joke at her expense. She knew by the way the fat woman in the floral dress glanced over. The quicker she and Riley escaped from here, the better.

At her car on the mainland, in the undercover parking area, she locked the scooter and waited for the place to empty. Once alone, she grabbed the contents of the box and headed for a silver rubbish bin two bays from her car. Purposely not looking at what was in her hands, she scattered the whole lot into the bin, struck a match and threw it in. There was no sign of smoke. She leaned over the bin and the entire contents, including the plastic liner, burst into flames, almost singeing her hair. The black smoke spread quickly through the space, making her cough. A man in a business suit ran towards her.

'Someone must have thrown a cigarette in there,' she lied.

He flapped his coat at the bin. 'You need to get out of here.'

Marlise stumbled into her car and drove out into the open, cranking up the air conditioning as a hot flush overcame her. She was forced to pull over onto the side of the road as emotions racked her body. So many years of secrets and memories, her last link with Lorcan, now nothing more than a curling wisp of black smoke drifting from a car park. The dark cloud rising into the sky became Lorcan's face. He stared at her with pity and love. She stumbled out of the car and ran towards him, calling. 'Lorcan. Riley has grown...into you. I wish you could see him.' Lorcan's face twisted in pain, warped and drifted into a flowering eucalypt, causing two kookaburras to take flight.

She returned to her car and sobbed into the steering wheel. The tears so profuse, she wiped and wiped at her eyes before she could see to drive again.

20.

The island seemed lighter with Marlise gone from it. The community had stopped bickering and bitching. Sharon had let Josh move back home, conditionally. Tilly and Grunter had apologised to each other. Grappa said the birds were less jittery, and the fish and crabs were biting once more.

The day after Marlise left, Ayla felt the tension weighing her down roll away with the waves, sucked out on the tide. But the biggest change was in Riley. He had a certain seriousness tinging his edges – still grieving for his stepfather, she assumed – but with his mother physically out of his life, he relaxed and opened up. It was like watching the solitary daisy in their vegetable patch unfolding in the morning sun to reveal its bright centre.

He avoided the Johnston house. They only left each other's side if necessary, spending most afternoons meandering out on the beach. Ayla tried to teach Riley to swim, amazed at how unnatural he was in the water, and he attempted to teach her the flute, concluding with a grin, 'I didn't know it was possible for one of my flutes to sound so bad.'

Two days after his mother's departure, Ayla took him by the hand and led him through a stand of grass trees at the side of Helen's house, down a path that opened onto a clearing. She was impressed to see the honeysuckle vine that had started to strangle everything had been cleared. Aunty Dora and Ray, who had bought the block next door, in the hope that Mandy would return one day to settle down, had been hard at work clearing the weedy vine. The fruit trees were thriving, and Ayla had forgotten how the two large mango trees dominated the rear of the block. All the grevilleas were in full bloom, and down toward the beach, an old blue gum reached for the sky. Now the honeysuckle was under control, it was a perfect blend of natives and exotics living side by side.

In one corner was an old shed.

'This was my parents' piece of land.'

She opened the cobwebbed door and disturbed a fat carpet snake. It languidly slithered between them into the surrounding bushland, looking peeved.

Riley stepped inside the shed full of timber.

'We lived here in a caravan for a while when I was a kid.'

'So much wood' he said, lifting a beam. 'Good solid stuff, hardwood.'

'Dad was collecting it to build a house. But Mum hasn't set foot on the place for years. Can't bring herself to. After he died, Grappa gave Mum his house, and she gave me this block.'

'Look at your fruit trees. You're rich in citrus, bananas, paw paws and mangoes, Ms Finlay.' He bowed before her.

'Arise my dark lord and kiss me quick.'

He did, and they held hands as they explored.

'If you trimmed a few of these branches, you would have an excellent view of the water.'

'It wouldn't take much to clear a path down to the beach either.'

'Let's do it now.'

She turned to face him. 'After you went to bed last night, Mum suggested I ask you to help me build a tree house with all this wood before it rots away. I mean, only if you wanted to. If you don't want to, that's fine also. I —'

He kissed her. 'It would be my honour to build a fortress for my love.'

'The best thing is Mum works in the building department at Council. She said if I call it a shed, she can obtain approval overnight.' She grinned. 'I'm game if you're game.'

'I'm game.' And, he was working his way through the wood, pulling it out piece by piece, laying it down, planning. 'We could start with a low platform here, then we could build a floor between the two mangoes? We could have three levels? What do you think?'

Her elation rendered her silent, blurred her vision. He picked her up, spun her around in the air thick with orange blossom. They lay in the long grass together as a pair of lorikeets, their rainbow colours bleeding into each other, landed on an acacia tree to hang upside down and stare. She could feel the island beneath them, breathing.

Riley looked Grappa in the eye, 'On the count of three: one, two –' They lifted the door frame into position. The old man's face had gone red with the effort. 'You alright?'

'Right as rain.'

But Riley saw he was struggling to catch his breath. He kept watch until Grappa's colour returned to normal. 'If you could keep a firm hold while I hammer these brackets down?'

Once it was solid, they stood back and admired the carved archway: dolphins and waves emerging and sinking into the wood.

'Makes a grand entrance. You are one talented young man.'

The admiration he could see in Grappa's gaze made him proud and shy all at once. 'Hope she likes it.'

With Grappa's help, Riley had been able to secretly work on the carving as a surprise for Ayla.

'She'll swoon, you watch.'

Riley stretched out in the sun. All the wedding bush, as Ayla called it, had blossomed overnight. The tendrils of white flowers danced in the honeyed breeze. He had never worked so hard in his life and never felt so content. By helping Ayla build her 'castle,' he had started to believe he could make his way in the world, that he had something to offer: the ability to provide and nurture, and love.

The only blip in his life came in the form of regular texts from his mother, the tone of which changed from day to day. Sometimes she sounded positive and swore she had, *at last found a place where we could be happy*, then other days her texts were short and sharp. *Everyone here is backward.* One day she wrote: *There is no way we are moving to this place.* Within an hour, another text arrived: *You're going to love it here darling boy. People live on boats in the river.*

Riley felt guilty for misleading his mother, but his heart was growing roots which spread deep into the island and deeper into Ayla. As each day unfolded, the more impressed he became by her. She knew what creature made which markings in the sand and could read the water like he could read her moods. When that little frown appeared, he stayed silent or played his flute to make her happy.

One day they had been sitting on the beach together and she said, 'See that rough patch on the sea where it looks like the breeze is rustling the water?'

'Yeah?'

'Keep watching it.'

He had been rewarded by a school of small fish jumping together, creating a silver dragon's tail snaking in the sun.

He realised that the old man had asked him something. 'Sorry?'

'You're always off with the birds, boy.'

'Actually, I was off with the fish.'

Grappa nodded as if to say fair enough. 'I said, when do you expect her back?'

'Who? Ayla?'

'No, your mother.'

'Soon, I imagine.'

'She's actually moving off?'

'Who knows? My mother's renowned for changing her mind.'

The old man took a swig from his flask, then offered him a drink. 'No thanks, not after last time.'

Grappa cackled.

The more time Riley spent in his company, the more intrigued he became. 'Did the Nor folk really tell you where the box was?'

'Let's just say, they made me aware of knowledge I already had.' Grappa looked omniscient.

Riley enjoyed the way he spoke in riddles. 'Ayla said your Gran came here from Ireland? She was the one who taught you about the Nor folk.'

'That's right. The little folk are big over there.' The old man looked confused by what he'd said. 'If you get what I mean. Where is she?'

'Who? My mother?'

'No, Ayla.' Grappa shook his head at the reoccurring motif within their conversations.

'At a cleaning job she's been putting off all week.'

'Harley's place?'

Riley nodded and smoothed his hand over the back of one of the dolphins, the voluptuous curve of the wood reminding him of her body.

Ayla wished Harley's brother had removed more possessions from the house. The worst moment was finding the comb in the bathroom cabinet with Harley's long black hairs stuck in it.

She was cleaning the last of the windows when she discovered his sunglasses on the floor of the lounge room, hidden under the curtains. The sad silence of the house became deafening as she turned the glasses over and over in her hands, wondering if Trev had flicked them from

Harley's face to land under the curtains when he found him dead. Or had Harley done it as he lay down to die?

The walls closed in as a vision of Harley walking, head bowed, apologising to the world for his existence made her rush outside into the fresh air.

June was at the Hills Hoist next door, hanging out washing. 'Hey Aylee.'

Ayla held the glasses up in way of an answer. June came over and the two women hugged, June's tears dampening Ayla's neck.

'It doesn't make sense. He had plans to go to the animal shelter that Thursday to buy a new dog.'

'Wish I had taken Jip to a vet. Then they might both still be alive.'

'Don't you dare think like that. Harley killing himself had nothing to do with Jip's death. That morning of the day he died, Trev and I spoke to him, he was acting very strange, claiming half the island hated him. He was saying ridiculous things like the people on the island only tolerated him because of Jip, but now Jip was dead they wanted him gone. That they thought he was a scum bucket and a bludger living off their hard-earned tax dollars. We tried to calm him down, but he claimed he had proof. Some anonymous letter from a group of island residents.'

'What?'

'We didn't believe it either, so we asked to see the letter, but he said he'd already burnt it. He wasn't himself. He was acting very paranoid.'

'There's no group of people who hated him. If there was, we'd know about it in such a small community.'

'Exactly. Everyone on the island loved Harley because of his work at the youth hut.'

'I know, Ajax, who I went to school with, says he wouldn't be alive if it wasn't for Harley.'

'He said the letter made no mention of his youth hut work. He was very angry about that. He'd been smoking a lot of dope so Trev told him to lay off the stuff. We begged him to come for dinner but he 'wanted to chill', he said. That night Trev went to check on him, but of course...' June couldn't finish.

They both stared at the sunglasses in the hope that Harley would emerge from them, laughing his shot gun laugh, full of life.

'What should I do with these?'

'Trev might like them, as a keepsake.' June put the glasses in her pocket. 'I hear you've got a new boyfriend. Good for you. If he's anything like his mum, he must be a real sweetheart.'

'I heard you had a coffee with her.'

'I wish people would stop claiming she killed Jip. Harley did her a real injustice there. She recently lost her dog of fifteen years, so she knew how Harley was feeling. She was very concerned about him.'

Riley had never owned a dog. He had always wanted one. Ayla's instincts prickled. 'In what way was she concerned?'

When June finished recounting the conversation, Ayla had a sickening suspicion who had written the letter. 'You didn't tell Marlise about Harley's youth hut work?'

'No, but...' June looked askance. 'I'm sure she had nothing to do with...'

'Of course not.' Ayla lied, staring up into the spindly branches of the spotted gum hanging over the house. Poor June would blame herself if she realised the truth.

'You okay, Aylee?'

'Just sick of cleaning. Sick of uncovering all the dirt, all the sad secrets of other people's lives.' She gave June a quick hug. 'I better get back to it. You've got new neighbours arriving tomorrow.'

Worry spread across June's face. 'I hope they're....' she couldn't find the word.

'Nice?'

'Harley was so tolerant, you know...non-judgmental. Such a good neighbour. Can't believe he's...' Unable to speak, June hurried across to her yard.

Ayla took a steady breath, entered the back door, made a quick call to Tilly, packed up her cleaning trolley and thumped home as quickly as her legs would accommodate her rage.

The official take on Harley's death was accidental overdose, but Trev claimed Harley knew what he was doing when it came to opiates. According to Trev, Harley had committed suicide. A letter of that kind would have been enough to tip him over the edge. A wave of repulsion hit as she thought about the letter Harley had burnt, trying to reduce its power, but the sinister words would already have done their damage, locked in his memory, torturing him.

'I thought I heard your trolley,' Riley said, sliding the back-door open. 'I've got a surprise for you.'

'I've got a surprise for you, too.' She failed to keep the bitterness out of her voice.

The smile left his face.

'Your mother told June she could sympathise with Harley because her dog had just died.'

Riley grunted. 'Obviously Mum's attempt to stop the rumours that she killed his dog.'

'She had heard the rumours then?'

'Grappa told me that's what people were saying about her.'

'Do you think she killed Jip?'

He shrugged and looked out the window, his jaw clenched. 'The day we moved in, she kept complaining about its barking.'

'I'm sorry Riley, I think Harley was right. She did do it.'

He glanced at her, the shame evident on his face.

'Not only that, but...'

'What?'

She didn't know how to start.

'Ayla?'

As she told him of her conversation with June, he stood in silence, listening, eyes downcast.

'Do you think a letter would have been enough to make this guy kill himself?'

'His self-esteem was pretty low. I don't know. We have no proof, but I can tell you now, there's no group of residents who had banded together to write a letter. I checked with Tilly. If anyone would have heard a whisper of such a thing, it would be Till. She said it was a load of baloney.' Ayla paused, pained by what she was about to say. 'And... there was a horse that died on the island. I think your mother might have had something to do with that too.'

Riley remembered the expression on his mother's face when she found out Maria was the one to overturn the council decision. He slid down the kitchen cupboard and sat on the floor, his head hung between his raised knees. 'I'm sorry Ayla. We should never have moved here.'

'You have no need to be sorry. If she is responsible, these are her actions, nothing to do with you.' She sat beside him, sensing the years of torment he had lived through.

Riley knew this was the beginning of the end. His mother had done it again. It would only be a matter of time before all this happiness would be ripped from him. What shocked him most was his lack of surprise. It was almost a relief she had exposed herself. He no longer needed to maintain the facade. 'She's psychotic.'

'I'm guessing. I have no proof.'

'It was Mum. I know it was. She's vindictive.' Vindictive. The word exploded in his mouth. It felt good to spit it out.

Grappa appeared on the back deck.

Ayla threw herself into his arms. 'I'm sorry I ever doubted you. You were right. I think she did cause all three deaths.'

Riley's throat constricted. He stared at what Ayla was drawing in Helen's large sketch pad on the table, trying to make sense of the deaths by creating a rough time line.

She turned to Grappa and detailed the evidence. Grappa's set of his face said it all. Pointing to her notes in the sketch pad, she said. 'Let me know, Riley, if any of this is wrong. This was the day you moved to the island? You said your mother complained about Jip's barking. Three days later...Jip was dead. Then, around here...according to June, this was the day she grilled her about Harley. So, I guess she dropped the letter off between this date and the day Harley killed himself. The whole island was abuzz with the gossip that Maria caused council to resume spraying on this date. I remember because Mum said it was all anyone was talking about, and here, two days later, Toto is dead. Stan's pretty confident both animals died of MVEV, a mosquito-borne virus. All those mozzies she breeds in those cages –' She stopped at the look on Riley's face.

'Nice detective work,' the old man said, nodding.

Riley felt like he was asphyxiating in the truth of it, the humiliation making his voice small and tight. 'I have no doubt it was Mum.'

'I have no doubt it was her either. But she didn't do it by any scientific means,' Grappa stated matter-of-factly.

Ayla shook her head. 'Grappa.'

'There's more to your mother than meets the eye, boy.' The old man leaned over the time line and picked up the pencil. 'See...day she moved to the island was a king tide. Full moon...I remember 'cause I went crabbing that night.' He drew a circle above the date. 'And the morning I found Toto, that was two days after a full moon. I remember 'cause when the rain stopped, I moored off Three Mile. The light was that bright you could see the cars on the mainland. Remember thinking it was a sun moon night.' Grappa drew another circle and didn't flinch under Ayla's cynical glare.

'A what night?' Riley asked.

'Grappa's name for a particularly bright full moon.'

'Not just bright. It's when the moonlight is that luminous it feels like sunlight. As if the sun is hiding in the moon. Mark my words, not all full moons are sun moon nights, but the ones that are…well let's just say, bad things happen on a sun moon night.' Grappa fiddled with the pen. 'If she's Fey, she'd be guided by the cycles of the moon and the earth to draw on her power.' He re-circled his circles.

The word Fey whirled in Riley's ears as he stared at the moon symbols the old man had pencilled, remembering the dead pigs, birds and pademelons he and David had found walking the perimeters of Burrawang over the years, and how David remarked once, 'Strange. Always seems to happen around a full moon.'

Something foreboding clicked in his head. Before he knew what he was saying, it came out: 'My mother told me once, she has these dreams where she turns into a mosquito…but she doesn't think they're dreams. She actually believes she becomes a mosquito.'

Grappa looked at him. 'That confirms it then.' It felt like the world stood still. Riley knew it wasn't logical, but he experienced a rush of relief, as if an unspeakable burden had been lifted from him.

The old man understood, reaching out and touching him on the shoulder. 'Good you told us, son.'

Riley saw disbelief invade Ayla's face. He wanted to tell her not to worry. Like David said, 'there's always a logical explanation for everything.' But the last few weeks spent in the company of the old man, Riley felt a growing respect for Grappa's wisdom. It was as ancient as the sea and came from the earth itself. He seemed to be at one with all creatures, from the tiniest ghost crab to a passing dugong. The way he was guided by the natural world inspired Riley.

And so it came that Riley found himself caught between their gazes, not knowing who to side with. As far as his mother was concerned, anything was possible.

21.

Grappa was on his regular dawn walk when he came across the grizzly maze of dead and dying mutton birds on Mud Rock Beach. The big winds last night had blown the exhausted birds in. Now the winds were gone, the fetid smell of death bled into the air as the flies began to gather with the approaching day. He picked his way through the gruesome sight, which had never frightened him before, not like this time. The words 'bad omen' sat on his tongue all the way around Dead Tree and along Three Mile to the mangrove swamp where he found the boobook owl hanging from a blackbutt, swaying in the breezeless air. The fishing wire, a macabre bow wrapped around its throat. He checked the poor creature's pulse: still warm, but dead.

'Sweet Jesus.'

Had that mosquito woman returned?

When he heard the scrape of the barge ramp on the cement platform, a shadow passed overhead. He headed back toward the barge.

The sun was still drowning in the watery horizon but the dawn was already filthy with heat. He waved at Ranga, who was signalling the garbage truck to disembark.

'How's it hanging, old man?'

'Much traffic?'

'Nup. Normal people don't get up at sparrow's fart.' Ranga lifted his baseball cap and wiped the sweat. 'Sun's not even up. Gonna be a stinker.'

'Bureau of Meteorology predicts 42.'

'I heard 46. Don't go away, got something for you.' Ranga walked off.

The garbage truck reversed, revealing the woman's yellow scooter parked on the barge under the driver's tower. Grappa's heart skipped a beat.

'Here you go, know all.' Ranga passed him a bottle of scotch.

'What for?'

'Didn't catch one snapper all weekend.'

Grappa remembered then, Ranga had been boasting about the amount of snapper he was planning on catching, but Grappa was adamant the snapper had moved on. The argument had escalated into Ranga placing a bet.

'Thanks, mate. Nice brand this one.'

'Should have known better than to get into an argument with you over fish.'

'Where's the owner of that scooter?'

'The good-looker? Just missed her.'

'Why'd she leave her bike?'

'Spluttered and carked it, out of petrol. Should have seen her carrying on. Thought her head was gonna fly off. I said she could leave it, come back later and deal with it.'

Grappa took off in the direction of the road.

'Thought you said she was trouble?'

'She is,' Grappa called over his shoulder.

'*Imeacht gan teacht ort.*' He practised it as he walked.

May you leave without returning.

When he arrived at the old house on the swamp, he could hear the shower running. The creak of the screen door as he opened it made him jump. 'Don't be a coward, you stupid old fart,' he told himself. 'You can do this.' He crept upstairs, repeating the Irish words in his head like a prayer of protection. He saw a woman's handbag on the kitchen table but ignored it to search the lounge room lined with books for a clue of some kind, evidence that would expose her...but what? *Ancient Celtic Folklore and Mythical Beings*, torn and well used. He flipped to the index and searched S for Shapeshifter...page 89. There was an underlined section.

The Puca is a mythological faery and ultimate shapeshifter, a legendary creature found most notably in the West of Scotland, Wales and Ireland. Renowned for confusing and terrifying humans and capable of assuming a variety of forms including a horse, goat, rabbit, goblin or dog.

Someone had written in pencil in the margin the word, *Mosquito?* Then, below this, *Puca, Irish for ghost.* Had she written this trying to understand what she was?

Grappa dropped the bottle of scotch. It bounced along the wooden floor and he scrambled to retrieve it. The shower turned off. Trembling, he put the book back. The scrape of a shower curtain sent him running into the room beside the lounge room. The laboratory was as Ayla had described it. Marlise was coming down the hall. He was light-headed, his worn-out heart beating too fast. He willed it to slow down. The bottle of scotch felt like a weapon. He didn't want to scare her. He needed to draw on the knowledge of his grandmother and her mother and all the mothers before. He knew a curse required the inner formidable strength of a woman. He placed the bottle beside the computer and wiped his sweaty palms on his shorts.

She walked past and onto the verandah where he saw her through the glass door, bending to dry her hair. She wrapped it in a towel on the top of her head, revealing the tattoo of a mosquito at the back of her neck above her dressing gown. She surveyed the swamp, turned and screamed.

The words jammed in his voice box.

She slid the door open. 'Who the hell are you? Get out.'

He saw his Gran rise out of her chair and lift her head. '*Imeacht gan teacht ort,'* he bellowed, casting a spell. The ancient phrase echoed through the mangroves beyond. Marlise lost composure, grabbing at the door to steady herself.

'Get out.' Her fierceness returned.

'Imeacht gan teacht ort,' he repeated less convincingly and darted through the hallway and down the stairs. The heat of her black rage singed his neck as he slammed the screen door in her face and ran, not daring to look back.

'Imeacht gan teacht ort.' Those words had made an impact. She had almost collapsed at the sound of them. Hopefully it was enough to make her leave without returning. At the corner of Long, he giggled.

Mad old bastard.

His mirth dried up when he thought of his thirst and his missing scotch.

'Shit a brick.'

Marlise watched him running up the dirt road. The local lunatic. There was always one. Memories of her mother were unleashed with the sound of those strange words. Her mother was leading her through a field to an isolated tree on the top of a hill. 'Mammy? Where are we going?'

Darkness was falling when her Mammy told her to wait. 'Don't you go moving from here. I'll be back shortly.'

She remembered how close the grey skull of a moon came rising over the hill as the afternoon turned to night, how frightened and cold she was when the mossy trunk grew too damp to lean against, how she tried not to look at the black gnarled and twisting branches above her transforming into faceless creatures of the night. She never knew what happened after that.

She ripped the towel from her head and rubbed viciously at her hair trying to rid herself of her mother. Was the selfish old hag still alive? The hot flush forced her to lie on the steps. She had to find the cool. 'Damn it.' The temperature of the air was warm enough without her body contributing. The heat brought an image of herself as a teenager, watching her drunken mother rolling around the bathroom floor in her own vomit. Her mother's various boyfriends leered towards her. She snapped her mind shut.

Marlise breathed in her fury, slammed the front door, locked it, and clumped upstairs. The house was stuffy and smelt musty. Riley had hardly been here. Her mice had lost weight and her mozzies were dead. Those still alive were starving.

Poor darlings. How could he be so cruel? She had driven half the night and raced for the first barge to surprise him before he left for work, and he wasn't even home.

She took her handbag into her room, collapsed on her bed, fished out a packet of paracetamol and swallowed two. It was still early morning but the night couldn't come fast enough. She hadn't slept in days.

The new day slipping through the cracks of the house, already hot enough to prickle her skin, pulled her into a fitful sleep where tortured souls drifted up from beneath the house and stood in the shadows of her room, watching.

Riley guessed there was one hour of daylight left. If the heat wasn't too crippling, he and Ayla could finish work on the first of the treehouse platforms by sundown. A few more planks to hammer and it was complete. Because of the full moon tonight, they had planned a bonfire to burn the scrap wood piled on the block. He had second thoughts now about the fire. It was so swelteringly hot the idea melted his brain. But Ayla had bought a bottle of champagne to mark the occasion and he had never tasted champagne.

As if thinking about her made her materialise, she came around the corner on her bike.

'Where do you go to my lovely?' He had taken to speaking to her in bad song lyrics for the reward of her smile.

'Picking my pay up from Tilly.' She jumped off her bike.

'I need to do that.'

'I'll walk with you.'

'Might pop back to Mum's first, grab some clothes. This heat...I'm burning up for your love,' he sang, and kissed her on the neck.

'Don't tell me you're finally going to change your clothes.'

He pinched her bottom. 'That's enough from you. Give us your bike for a sec.' He sat on it. 'Jump up.'

'On the handle bars?'

'Kelvin and I used to do it. Trust me, it's fun.'

They wobbled off down the road, Riley singing, 'You looked so pretty as you were riding along,' and pretended to lose control of the bike to make her scream. By the time they got to the house, his chest hurt from laughing.

'You're nasty and cruel.' She play-slapped him.

'Just like my mother.' He feigned a wicked laugh, took the key from where he had hidden it on top of the power box and unlocked the door.

Marlise's eyes snapped open at the sound of Riley's voice.

'How did you work in this heat?' That was the girl. She was with him, coming up the stairwell.

'I was digging a pond for Mrs Boyd under the shade of her mulberry tree. I kept hosing myself down, and she kept bringing me iced drinks.'

'Bet she did. She's sweet for you. All those old ducks are.'

'Are not.'

'Are too. God'

'What?'

'This house. Gives me the creeps. When do you think your Mum will be back?'

'Who cares? Haven't felt this free, ever. I know it's because she's not here.'

Marlise's hands clamped across her mouth tasted of shampoo.

'Do you really think your plan will work?'

'What plan?'

They were in the hallway. She sat up.

'To move to the new place then sneak back? What if she follows you back and gets...gets nasty?'

She stood, clutching at the wall. They were so close now, across the hall in his room.

'If she becomes impossible, we go to the police with the story of the letter. I don't know.'

What is he talking about?

'The official take on Harley's death is accidental overdose, so even if we could prove she wrote a letter, I don't know if they would charge her with anything.'

'Can we try my plan first?'

'The authorities might be interested in the deaths of Toto and Jip though, and what she's breeding in her homemade laboratory.'

Vindictive little bitch, spreading lies. She needs her tongue cut out.

They heard it at the same time, the door of Marlise's room opening. She appeared. A vile apparition, darkening the doorway of his bedroom.

He had never seen his mother so wretched. She had lost weight and the black rings under her eyes, deep as ruts, made her old and shrivelled. Her wet hair stuck to her head, but it was the hatred in her face that sent his blood still.

'Mum? I didn't know you were home.'

'Obviously.' Her voice was dead.

'I didn't see the scooter. Mum?'

Her smile twisted, but she remained focused on Ayla.

He moved to protect Ayla, but she stepped forward. 'Riley loves you Marlise. You're his mother…of course he loves you, but he wants to live his own life now. He's not –'

'You can't do this,' she screamed with such force, he knew being reasonable would be pointless.

His brave Ayla grew taller. 'I know what you did…to Harley… Toto…Jip. You don't frighten me.'

'Lies. She's full of lies. Can't you see what she's doing?' His mother was shouting so hard she had spit in the corners of her mouth.

He stepped in front of Ayla. 'Mum. I love you. No one can ever take that away. You're my Mum.'

She looked at him like she didn't recognise him, then she reached to touch him. 'Riley –'

'But I'm not moving off with you. I'm staying.'

'No. You're not.'

'I read all the letters. His name is Lorcan Gallaher. He's a musician. You stole me away from him. Why did you do that?'

'No.' Her head wouldn't stop shaking. 'She's lying.'

'I love you, but I'm an adult now. I'm not going with you.'

'No. No. No.' She slid to the floor like someone had sucked the air out of her.

She struggled to get up. He went to help, but she pushed him away. 'Don't touch me.' Her face streaming tears and snot.

He saw it before it happened. His mother pulled the whittling knife from his half-made flute on the table near the door and lunged at Ayla. She dived out of the way as he tackled his mother, knocking her to the ground. Ayla grabbed the knife. He pinned his mother down, sitting on top of her as she fought to get free bellowing over and over. 'I have to kill her.' He looked into her distorted face and the words turned into something else, his mother howling as she chopped into David's cherished plants with his grafting knife. 'You left me no choice!' Chop. 'I had to!' Slash.

Had to what?

The words he heard that day had been squashed in his memory, compacted, too horrifying to comprehend. A series of images besieged him: his mother sitting with David, smiling as he lay dying. Kelvin hugging his dead dog. His mother, naked, running through the rainforest as David tackled her, wrapping her tightly in a sheet while she screamed and screamed.

He stared into her disfigured face. 'David...' He was scarcely audible, but it silenced her. The flicker of fear in her eyes confirmed the truth for him.

He didn't know how his hands got from her wrists to her throat but became fascinated by the fact that he could feel her windpipe bending. Her pleading eyes bulged.

Ayla's voice came from far away. 'Riley, stop.'

He looked up through a tunnel and saw his beloved standing pale in the corner of his room, a whittling knife in her hand. His grip relaxed, and his mother sucked in air. He watched her, the shock dropping his body temperature, and knew there was only one course of action left. He spoke before he changed his mind.

'Please go.'

Ayla stood immobilised.

He couldn't talk for the pain of it. 'I can't see you again.'

'What?' She didn't notice the knife drop from her hand.

He helped his mother to her feet and hugged her to him as she sobbed into his chest. 'She needs me. I'm all she's got. Please go.'

Ayla's mouth opened, but no words formed.

'Please? Can't you see what happened? I...I tried to kill her. This... us...it's not going to work.'

Ayla wouldn't move. Unable to bear the hurt he was inflicting, he started to yell. 'I said, go. What don't you get about that? Are you deaf? Leave us alone. Fucking leave us alone!'

Her face shattered. He gouged his heart out and offered it to her. It lay there twisting and writhing in the palm of his hand. A drop of blood landed on her foot between her sandal straps. She fled. He waited until he heard the screen door slam, then collapsed onto his bed, sobbing unrestrainedly.

Someone touched him on the shoulder. He turned to see a blotchy face with red eyes and scraggly hair, smiling at him.

'Poor baby.'

Her touch made his stomach churn. 'I'm going to move off with you and never see her again, so there's no cause to hurt her now. Is there? Mum?'

'Sleep, poor baby. You look so tired.'

He curled into a foetal position away from her. 'Promise me. Mum? You're not going to hurt Ayla.'

'I promise.'

The end of the bed sank as she sat. The rustle of the mosquito net being tied into a knot above him. Why didn't she go? Why did she keep stroking the back of his head like that? He shivered. Had she killed the man she loved? What was she?

He sat up too late, vomiting onto the Persian rug.

'Poor baby. You've had too much sun.' She folded the mat to contain the soupy mess. 'Can't believe Tilly made you work in this heat. I'll bring you a glass of water,' she carried the rug out carefully.

His head was throbbing from the heat, from the heartbreak, from a possibility too horrific to say out loud. He shut his eyes and hoped to never wake. To die in sleep, that would be best. The ghost of a dead baby drifted down and curled into him.

Ayla pedalled through syrup. Her legs had turned to rope and she couldn't breathe from the cramp in her lungs. Her lungs surrounding her heart, designed to protect her heart. Nothing can protect a heart.

Where was she riding to? The memory of his words burning into her marrow made the earth spin off its axis and flung her out into the atmosphere where she floated like an empty husk with no direction, no purpose. She could ride off the end of the island and into the ocean. She could ride along the bottom of the sea and meet her father who would take her in his arms and hold her. Simply hold her.

The moon rising over the tops of the trees was so immense it was going to fall down. To be crushed by the weight of it, what a relief that would be. To be killed by the moon is preferable to living with the memory of him.

Someone called and waved, but the liquid in her eyes blurred the light of the colossal moon. She rode toward its glow until her bike turned to jelly and became tangled in her body. How hard the earth was and where did this blood on her knee come from? She found herself in her front yard. Something important to her hit the ground and cracked but she didn't stop. Nothing was important now.

'Mum?'

Her Mum would put a band-aid on her knee. Her Mum would cry for the wound she knew was too big to bandage, the wound wedged behind her lungs, where her heart once was.

'Mum?'

The house was empty. She sank into her bed, the despair made her bones too heavy as the sun was eaten by the moon. Grappa had known all along, Riley was Far Dorocha. He had played and she had danced, willingly following him into the abyss where nothing but sorrow grew, wild and free.

Twilight. Her favourite time. The sun was low in the swamp. It hit the window and set the scotch ablaze. She sat by her computer and stared at the pretty colours in the bottle. Riley knew her rule about alcohol in the house. Another sign of his betrayal. The swelling bruises on her throat where he had tried to squeeze the life out of her made her reach for the bottle, unscrew the lid, sniff it and take a swig. The liquid set her on fire. It had been too, too long between drinks. She gulped until her head was buzzing, until the grafting knife on the bench was in her hand. She sliced it savagely through the air. Ayla has such a pretty face. If she was disfigured, Riley wouldn't find her half as attractive. He wouldn't be tempted to run back to her. Or if she was dead, there would be no her to run to. Ever. She popped the knife into her dressing gown pocket and reached for her phone.

Tilly answered directly. 'Hello love, heard you were back. How was your break away?'

'I'm running late, Tilly. Sweet little Ayla invited me for dinner and I forgot to ask the address. I can't get hold of Riley on his mobile.'

'Seabreeze, down the end, last house in the street...can't miss it... its bright purple.'

'Thanks.'

'Might pop over in the morning and –'

Marlise disconnected.

Sorry Tilly, no time for small talk.

She had noticed Seabreeze Crescent: the street on the left, at the top of the hill, not far from where puny sunglass man once lived. What a non-event he had turned out to be. She had been prepared to write several letters and it had only taken one. No fun.

Maybe she would miss this island after all? She had created some lovely memories in the short time she had been here. She sucked again from the bottle and tiptoed down the hall. He was asleep now. Why he had wasted so many tears on that little bitch would always be a mystery to her. She quietly shut his door, went into her bedroom, opened her wardrobe and took another swig. The darling mosquitoes outside were calling for blood. After such a big rain and with this heat, their numbers were magnificent.

She pushed against the fly screen of the window until it popped out, landing upright, stuck in the shiny mud below. She found the sight of it hilarious. The brown liquid fire had lifted her mood considerably. She could feel the pull of the full moon rising as the mosquitoes started to swarm and suck.

'Hello, my darlings. What a perfect night to feed.'

Grappa knew it was a king tide, but even he was shocked at the size of the pink moon rising over the island. Dora watched it fill the tangerine sky, threw the pot overboard and said, 'Good night for crabbing.'

Grappa didn't like how there were two rings around the moon. 'Pity it's so bloody hot.'

'Broke the record, hottest day ever, they reckon.'

They both stared as a cloud of bats smudged the sky, leaving the island in their hundreds.

'That's odd.'

'Maybe the heat?'

They were accustomed to seeing bats from Big Island flying in. Neither of them had ever seen the local colony fly out towards the west collectively like that.

Grappa handed her another chunk of raw meat to tie into the next pot. Dora jumped when the dugong surfaced beside the boat. It observed them then sank down to come up moments later in the same spot. It looked at Dora, tilted its head then disappeared below the surface.

'Almost like old man dugong was trying to tell us something then,' Dora said.

A bat dropped into the boat, flapped around disoriented, then flew off. Grappa stared at the black mass of mangroves at the rear of the island. 'That woman's back and all the animals are acting up again.'

'Thought you said you spoke to her.'

'I did. Might take more than words but...'

Grappa puttered around the sandbank closer in to the island, killed the engine and let Little Beaudy drift as Dora threw another pot. A pod of dolphins swam towards the boat, circling and leaping. Dora watched them. 'They're not playing. Something's upset them.'

Grappa was trying to ring Ayla. There was no answer. He tried again. 'Shit.'

'What?'

'Ayla always has her phone on her.'

'Maybe she's out of range.'

He rang Helen but the home phone rang out. 'I've gotta check on Ayla,' as he said this, one of the dolphins hit the water hard, splashing the boat. 'Alright, already. I'm going. I'm going.' He started the engine and headed toward the island. The dolphins trailed in the wake.

'Something big's happening, old man.'

He took in the brightness of the moon. The world felt too grim.

She wiped the sweat from her face and scanned the still horizon. 'Hope to God it's not a tsunami.'

Ayla was woken by the whine of mosquitoes and pinpricks on her skin. The phone in the kitchen was ringing. Switching on her light to find her room swarming with mosquitos, she screamed and hit out.

'Thought you said they have as much right to be on this planet as we do?'

The voice from nowhere made her spin around. Marlise was standing outside her window beside a gaping hole in the fly screen.

'Should have known from that first meeting what a liar you were,' she said, and slashed at the screen with a knife.

Ayla ran through the house screaming, 'Mum!'

Her mother still wasn't home.

Marlise was on the back verandah now, knife in hand, opening the sliding door. The weirdest smile on her face as she gaped at the bloody cut on Ayla's knee. Ayla grabbed the broom from beside the fridge and ran at Marlise. It was like hitting a wall. Marlise yanked the broom from Ayla and threw it clean across the room with the strength of ten men. The woman had entered some sort of psychosis. Ayla scrambled out the front door, slamming it behind her.

The only light in the street was Edna Ferguson's. Marlise could easily hurt frail Edna, who used a walking frame now. Ayla didn't think twice, she ran away from the safety of the light into the cover of the bushland across the road, stumbling along the track lit by the moon as fast as she had ever run. If she could make it to Three Mile, Len Pike's house was the second from the end. The burly leader of the volunteer firefighters could easily help her overpower Marlise. Not daring to look back, Ayla ran until she reached the Pandanus palms, where she stole a glance over her shoulder. She stopped and listened, trying to catch her breath.

Silence.

Maybe Marlise hadn't seen her go into the bushland? Had she gone to old Edna Ferguson's, who would open her door to anyone? Ayla had to save Edna. She went to run back but a tawny frogmouth flew down and landed on the path, staring with his piercing yellow eyes. Any other instance, Ayla would have been delighted by the sight of this rare nocturnal creature but she had no time to stop and look at birds.

There were footfalls. Someone was running towards her. Ayla snuck off the beaten path into the bush, thick with acacias, wattles and native frangipani. She had the advantage of knowing the island intimately, but still, each rustle of a branch or crack of a twig was deafening. She squatted behind a grevilia and waited, spotting two creamy, speckled curlew eggs, camouflaged in the undergrowth. She knew curlews never left their eggs for long. They would return soon and hiss and carry on and give her away. The frogmouth on the track flew onto a low angophora limb to keep watch. Her saviour had stopped her long enough to hear Marlise approaching. It looked like Greedy, who she had nursed when she was sixteen.

Marlise ran past in sinister determination, continuing along the track, the blade of the knife glinting in the cold blue light of the moon.

Ayla waited, too frightened to wipe the sweat that dripped or swipe at the gathering sand-flies. The only time she stirred was to kill a mosquito that landed on the gash of her knee. She never knew terror would make her feel so clear headed.

When she thought it safe, she pushed her way through the thick scrub, but a large golden orb spider, as bright as day in the moonlight, dropped in front of her and commenced weaving a golden web. She heard soft footfalls and sprang down, peering at the track.

Marlise was retracing her steps, slowly, searching the bushland to each side of her, holding the knife out as if expecting an attack.

Why had she turned back? Could she smell her?

As Ayla thought this, Marlise stopped and pointed the blade toward her.

Could she sense her?

Ayla held her breath. The spider above her stopped spinning. She felt the pulse of the earth beneath her quicken.

Marlise reached into the leather satchel slung diagonally across her abdomen, pulled out a bottle of scotch and took a slug.

Riley said his mother didn't drink?

She dropped the bottle back into the satchel. Ayla heard it clink. What else did she have in there? Jars full of killer mosquitoes? A flask full of chloroform to knock her out with?

Marlise left the track and crept toward her, the knife poised in readiness, chanting a child's nursery rhyme. 'Round and round the island, like a teddy bear. One step, two step. I'll find you anywhere.' The whites of her eyes too bright against the mad pupils.

Ayla couldn't tell if Marlise ran into the web or if the spider jumped, but the sticky golden orb scurried down the middle of the woman's face before flying to safety on a glistening strand. Marlise was screaming, nearly slashing herself with the knife, believing the spider was still on her. The two curlew parents appeared, lifting their wings and hissing, snake like, at Marlise. She ran backwards, shaking and cursing until she was on the track again. She turned up the path to the lagoon, brushing at her head and arms.

That path was a dead end. Marlise would be back soon. Ayla could hear her still mewling in fright as she crept to the track and ran towards the Nor Folk Tree. Not far from the tree, up Three Mile, were houses full of people who had known her all her life. People who loved her: big Len who would help her, Rachel Pinkerton with her three cats, Otto and Marg who ran the bush care group, Matt Bateman who lived with his elderly Mum and liked to crochet. The hundreds of people who lived here quietly stood together in her mind. She would protect them and they would protect her. Marlise didn't stand a chance. This was Ayla's community. This was her home.

In the dark, on his bed, where he had cried himself to sleep, Riley woke with pain in his hip from lying on the flute in his pocket. The memory of what he had done to Ayla twisted through him, spreading the ache to every part of his body.

The clock on his bedside table came into focus. He had slept only thirty minutes, but it felt like an eternity to wake into a life without Ayla.

'Mum?' He opened her bedroom door to find her moonlit room full of mosquitoes, the unscreened window wide open. His mother's handbag on the floor, her purse, keys, phone, everything still in it.

'Mum?' He raced through the house then downstairs into the swamp. 'Mum?' The mozzies attacked.

His heart jumped into his mouth. He felt it beating wildly under his tongue. 'Oh, Jesus. Ayla...' He ran until his legs burnt and then faster, willing his body to catch fire. This is what he deserved for the pain he had inflicted on her.

He turned into her street and a car tailed him, the headlights blinding. 'Want a lift?' It was Helen.

He jumped in and asked where Ayla was, trying to keep the panic out of his voice.

'I haven't been home yet. Popped in to see a friend. Caught the last barge. Thought I'd bring the car over, needs a good clean.' Helen went to pull into her driveway, but Ayla's mangled bike was there.

Riley was out of the car. In the light from the headlights, he found Ayla's phone smashed on the ground.

Helen was beside him now, worried. 'Riley, what's happened?'

He raced into the house, Helen shadowing him. Ayla's room was full of mozzies, her flyscreen slashed.

'Riley, what's going on?'

'Ring the police.'

'Why? Where's Ayla?

'Tell them she's missing,' he shouted as he raced next door to the beginnings of the tree house.

Everything was as they had left it, the half-built wooden platform and Grappa's tools, all clear and distinct in the luminous night. He could hear Helen screaming for him but ignored her to run onto the beach.

No trace of Ayla. The waves crashing on shore seemed too savage and the stench of the rotting mutton birds turned his stomach. The sight of the radiant moon chilled him in the sweltering night. What had the old man said? 'Bad things happen on a sun moon night.'

'Ayla?' he shouted as he scrambled up the rock to see if Grappa was moored in the bay. 'She's with Grappa. She's with Grappa,' he repeated like a mantra. There was no sign of the boat. 'What have I done?'

He reached for the flute in his back pocket. If he stood on this rock and played the love song he had written for her, she would hear it and come, she would know then that his love for her was as constant as the turning of the tides. He faced away from the ocean, toward the island, so the sound would travel across the land, playing without thinking. Her song began to bleed into another melody. Fed by his own grief and fear, the tune he always heard on this rock took hold of him. He tried to back away from it, but it pulled him under and rode over him like a wave. A fourteen-year-old girl, pinned down, whimpering in pain; a mother bellowing, watching her baby smash against the rocks; a young man, shot in the back of the head. The brutal memories of the place drifted up through every crevice and wrapped themselves around him, trapping him, compelling him to play.

Grappa was the first to hear it over the engine noise, but Dora was the first to see him. She couldn't speak, just pointed to Riley on top of Mud Rock, playing the flute, inching his way backwards towards the precipice. Grappa pulled into the bay as close to the rock as possible, cut the engine and hollered, 'Riley.'

Riley took another step backwards.

'Bloody idiot. What's he doing?'

'It's not him. It's them,' Dora was gaping, her brown face pale. 'See them? My people.' She had tears in her eyes, her face glowing.

Grappa had no doubt she could see something. 'Bloody fool. He's called the spirits up.' He looked again, but all he saw was Riley dangerously close to the edge. The dolphins were circling the base of the rock.

'Row me to shore, quick.' She was already hauling the dinghy in. Half way to shore, she jumped out and swam. Riley was too close to the edge, his flute frenetic now.

Grappa rowed in and dragged the boat up the beach as Dora finally reached the top. Riley took another step back and she ripped the flute from his mouth, pulling him to safety. He collapsed, dazed. She turned to her ancestors and spoke in their language. The ancient song hung in the air. To Grappa it appeared that time stopped for a moment, resting on the shoulders of his noble Dora as she tried to catch her breath.

They all waited for something.

When Grappa heard an old woman's wail come from the direction of the mangroves, his heart hiccupped. The Banshee. Or a bird's scream? Either way, he felt it. Someone was about to die.

A breeze blew along the tops of the trees and the spell was broken. Dora helped Riley to his feet. They spoke together as they climbed down. Grappa clambered to meet them.

'Where's Ayla, son?' He asked, the banshee's wail still ringing in his ears.

'I broke her heart. Now I can't find her, or my mother.'

Grappa felt a sharp pain in his chest. 'When she was little, if she was upset, she'd run to the tree. Bet that's where she is.' The boy was already off. 'Riley, do you have a phone?'

'No.'

Grappa fished his from his pocket and threw it to him. 'We'll go to Helen's and put the word out. Text Helen's mobile as soon as you find her.'

The boy was running again, so he had to yell. 'Whatever happens, make sure she stays at the tree. She'll be safe there.' Grappa believed that was the one place on the island Marlise would be powerless to penetrate.

Dora started to shake.

He put his arms around her. 'It's shock.'

'You should have seen them, standing there.' The tears ran into her wrinkles. 'So proud, so strong.'

'Like you.' He held her and felt generations of pain alive in the air they were breathing.

Where was that little slut hiding?

Marlise was disoriented, melting in the feverish heat where the bush was thick and sharp and kept grabbing at her. The more she drank, the thirstier she became. The night was sticky, making her clothes bake. She needed to strip before she burnt up.

There...far more pleasant being naked.

As if she summoned him with her body, Lorcan materialised, stepping out from behind a ghostly trunk. She tried to speak his name, but it was lost on an intake of breath. He hadn't aged, but his hatred had grown. She could taste it sweltering in the air, enveloping her as he moved forward, spitting the words. 'I hate you. I wish you were dead.'

When his fist met her jaw, the world spun around and the earth came to meet her. He was a black shadow standing over her. 'Put your clothes on, Mum. Go home.'

Mum? 'Riley.'

It was the scent of Ayla somewhere to the southeast that woke her. How long had she passed out? Only a moment. She could still hear her cherished son who wished her dead, in the undergrowth heading toward the beach. She stretched her wings and flew through the hot night air. A whiff of Ayla's deliciousness, enough to keep her flying in the right direction, smelt very real. The poor little dear thing had cut herself on the knee, the trace of her blood fresh and open. Marlise's mouth watered. She swished the deadly pathogens around in her mucous, searching for a path out of the trees. A perfect night; there was no wind to battle and the moon shadows were sharp, visibility superb.

Via a gap in the foliage, she saw the beach with her darling son running through a pattern of rotting birds, a pod of dolphins trailing behind him.

Running to his sweetheart. And you promised Mummy you would never see her again. Tsk tsk, naughty boy. Lucky Mummy knows you now for what you are: a liar and a sneak.

He would lead her to the meddling little bitch. Marlise began her ascent, her thirst raging.

Riley peered into the grove of pines to find it empty. His heart sank as he pulled the old man's phone out and wrote: *she's not at tree.*

Glancing into the topmost branches of the fig, he recognised her familiar feet, deleted the *not* and sent the text. He tiptoed into what felt like hallowed ground. There was a gash on her knee with a dry trickle of blood snaking around her calf. She was watching from the shadows, ashen. 'What do you want?'

Shocked at the sharpness of her voice, his own broke with love. 'I'm sorry. I didn't mean any of it. I wanted her to believe I hated you so she wouldn't hurt you.'

He went to climb, but within a heartbeat she had descended. Neither could speak at first for crying.

'I thought you were her, so I hid.' He could feel her heart thudding. The way she was whispering and shaking, he had never known her so frightened.

'Oh God, what have I brought on you?' He looked her over, stopping at her bloody knee.

'I fell.' Her eyes kept darting wildly to beyond the circle of trees.

'We're safer with two of us: one to tackle, one to grab the knife.'

He pulled the knife from his pocket. 'I told her to go home.'

She sobbed in relief.

Riley ripped his lips from hers when he heard the whine of a mosquito. 'Look out. There's a mozzie.' He scanned her body.

Ayla examined him, searching his soul for madness. 'You don't believe Grappa, do you? The silly stuff he said about your mother?'

'I don't know. He knew where the box was.'

They both heard it at the same time. The noise sucked the air out of Ayla's words. 'Sounds like...'

They walked to the edge of the circle of trees. The moon had turned black. The cloud of mosquitoes so large, it ate the stars in its path.

'They'll eat us alive,' she whispered in his ear.

He pushed her back into the protection and cover of the old tree.

'No.' Ayla's voice cracked in terror.

He could feel his mother's presence.

'We have to run.' She was struggling to break free.

'Stop.' He gripped her. 'We can't outrun that swarm.'

The sound was frightening. He pressed her into the folds of the tree. 'It's better we hide. They'll fly straight over. Trust me.'

She kept struggling. 'They'll smell us.'

'Ayla. Please. Trust me.'

She stopped.

He spoke fast. 'Turn around and hug the tree. Shut your eyes and talk to the Nor folk. Ask for their protection.'

Part of him said this to keep her calm, another part was desperate, deciding to place his trust in Grappa, grasping for belief in the old man's Nor folk while intrinsically knowing, 'there's a logical explanation for everything.' His gut contracted as his heart and brain fought each other.

She whispered fast into a gnarly opening in the trunk, a circular chant. 'It's me, your Ayla, I'm here, I'm with you, I feel you, I know you, I love you, I need you. I need you to protect us, oh please protect us. I am your Ayla. I'm here. I'm with you...'

The swarm was closing in. Their reverberating drone made him cover every inch of her body with his, while twisting his neck to look over his shoulder, expecting his mother to step into the circle.

As Ayla chanted, he remembered Grappa's story about her and the tree. He didn't know if it was the moon suddenly exposed again, or if it came out of his imagination as if he willed it to happen, but the tree appeared to glow, starting at the base and spreading beneath the earth. He could see the root system shining under the soil, reaching above into the branches towards the circle of pines. It was so subtle. Was it real? Or was it just the moonlight against the shadowed pattern of the trees? Either way, he held his breath at the possibility of magic.

As Ayla spoke into the dark crevice of the tree, the doorway to their realm, she squeezed her eyes shut. Her terror took her beyond herself where the Nor folk appeared as she had always envisaged them, decorated with silver butterfly dust and seashells adorning their heads. The whole tribe gathered: men, women, children, and babies. So many babies alive and well, asleep at their mothers' breasts. They quietly linked hands, even with the babies, and they hummed. They hummed until the hum of them turned into the drone of millions of mosquitoes.

As the swarm passed overhead, the vision faded. Ayla opened her eyes in the silence and secretly thanked her grandfather for the power of her imagination.

They peeked from the circle and saw the luminous moon, a giant search light beaming down once more.

The phone in his pocket buzzed. 'Grappa and your mum are almost here. They're just parking. Whole community knows you're missing, all out looking for you.'

'How embarrassing.'

Riley walked back to the tree. 'She protected us.' He tried to hug its trunk, both arms stretching around the bulk of it, not even reaching half way round its expanse.

Ayla laughed. 'You look like a little boy with his mother.'

His face contorted as he turned to rest his forehead on the tree.

She searched for the best way to say it. 'You can't carry the burden of her on your own anymore. There's a mental health unit that comes to the island once a month. She...she needs help, Riley.'

'She needs to...' He swallowed the word and threw his head back to stare through the branches. The night so bright, he could have been standing in sunshine. A kaleidoscope of emotion ran across his face as he shut his eyes on the moon.

Marlise wanted to fly toward the incandescence but her sisters, her daughters, were calling. She saw them in their billions, pregnant mothers-to-be rising out of the mangroves, entreating her to come. If only she could find Ayla. She could smell that gash on her knee but couldn't get to her. Her darling mosquitos were frantic now, surrounding her. She had never felt such love, so wanted, safe and happy in this place where she belonged. Too tired and thirsty, she let them carry her in the pack. As they reached the swamp, they clustered around, hungry, wanting to suck from every part of her, obscuring her vision. She flew too close to the ground. There was mud on her legs. She tried to wipe it off but they were pressing down on her now, hurting her. No. Her body was on fire with their stinging betrayal. 'Help,' she screamed, trying to escape, flying into the sludge again. Her wings covered, she was trapped, falling forward, her face hitting the mud which slid down her throat and into her lungs.

'Mammy.'

Why had she called for a mother who had never been there? A memory of being held and rocked drifted through her. Her mother had almost been a child herself when she had borne her. This thought bubbled up through the mud and settled in her heart as forgiveness. Forgiveness. David? She sensed him there, standing in the shadows amongst the twisted roots, flanked by a pack of dogs, waiting with their low growls for David to give the signal. Would he? Or would he remember their love? David. Her voice was gone. She couldn't move. Life was trickling out of her. The warm mud cooling now. From the depths of the earth, a horse was galloping toward her, the smell of revenge in its sweat. Her scream was stopped by the appearance of a little boy. Riley, as a toddler, one of the buckles on his red corduroy overalls had come undone. He was running to Lorcan who threw him into the air. Her little Riley laughed so hard she thought her heart would burst with love at the sound of him. Lorcan set him on the ground and he was running to her now, the buckle on his overalls flying free, arms outstretched, reaching for her, calling to her. No one could ever take that moment from them. This thought calmed her as she pressed his strong little body, squirming with life, against her still heart.

22.

Grappa felt as if he had stepped into a painting. Marlise's naked body shone from within the mangroves, the blackness of the mud against her pale skin in the early morning light looked surreal. The waves lapped against her body, which, as he drew closer, he saw was swollen with mosquito bites. Every inch of her was bitten, even between her toes. Her hair, like tentacles, floated out from her head in the water. Her hair in his dream, he realised.

The crowd of islanders standing quietly, whispering on the edge of the swamp, held their tongues as Riley pushed past. The swamp itself became still. No breeze and, curiously, not one mosquito. The murder of crows on the verandah rail twitched in the cloying septic smell.

When Riley saw his mother lying face down in the water, the noise that uncaged itself wasn't human.

'Can't touch the body, son.' The boy was too powerful. He pushed Grappa off, making that unearthly bellow as he tried to turn the body over.

When Henry Pickler – the know-all who was on the phone to the police – saw what Riley was doing, he screamed. 'This is a potential crime scene. Step away from the body. I command you to step away from the body now.'

'It's his mother for Christ sakes. Show some compassion.' Grappa grabbed the phone off Henry. 'Constable, the woman's son just turned up. He's a bit upset. As you can hear. He's touched the body.'

Josh grabbed a sheet off the line under the old house and waded out to place it respectfully over the corpse. Grappa thought Josh was crying, but it was hard to tell as he kept his head low. Did Josh have something to do with the events of last night?

Grappa was only half listening to the irate police officer. He could hear Henry big-noting himself, explaining to the crowd of onlookers that the police were on their way. They'd been held up because of a fatal shark attack at Big Island. A woman swimming with her dog off the point, where the sand bar drops away to the reef, was mauled by a pack of bull sharks. All that was left was her torso and no sign of the dog.

Tilly, who'd discovered Marlise's body, was sitting on a log, looking as if someone had slapped her hard across the face.

The police officer was speaking in legal jargon now.

'Yes, I understand constable, but it's his mother.' Grappa remembered his find this morning, his new bottle of scotch discarded in the pandanus forest, empty, with the cap still on. Ayla had said Marlise had been drinking straight from the bottle. 'I don't think it was suspicious constable. Looks like she was drunk, wandered into the swamp, got stuck in the mud. You know the scenario.'

Every couple of years there was a fatality on one of the islands, someone wandering drunk into the mangroves and getting caught in the slippery deep sludge. But where were her clothes? What had she been doing out here naked? And what the hell had she done to the mosquitoes to make them swarm like that? The authorities were claiming a combination of factors to do with global warming: the recent heavy rainfall, the king tide and the unusually hot temperatures. But Grappa knew Marlise had been the final ingredient in the equation.

'Constable? The tide is coming in fast. You might lose the body if it floats away – getting deep enough to swim in now.'

The constable changed his tone and granted permission to move the body to the shoreline.

Henry Pickler snatched his phone back, dropping it into the water in a rush to assert his authority, abusing Grappa in the process.

Grappa saw Ayla arrive on her bike, her face riddled with anxiety. She began to wade out, petrified by the noise coming from Riley, but was blocked by Henry Pickler. Grappa signalled for her to wait. He placed his hand on Riley's shoulder. 'Cops said we can move her out of the water, son.'

Riley struggled to stand with the body. Josh and Grappa helped him to his feet, Josh all the time fixing the sheet so it covered the corpse. Grappa felt a sense of fatherly pride as the now silent and stoic Riley held his head high to carry his mother's body out of the swamp.

The crowd moved away out of respect.

Riley was almost at the shoreline when he saw Ayla. Violent, uncontrollable waves of shock registered through his body. She ducked out of Henry's grasp and ran to Riley.

A ragged old cormorant with a bald patch of missing feathers halfway down its neck landed on the balcony of the crooked house, causing the crows to fly off. Their spectral caws drooping in the listless air.

Grappa thought it was uncanny, the old cormorant watching the proceedings looked like it belonged to the house, or the house belonged to the bird. He couldn't make up his mind which.

23.

Riley stared at the wad of legal documents in his lap. Who would have thought there would be so much paperwork? The results of the autopsy confused him. His mother died of suffocation from falling face down into the mud, but it was the almost lethal blood alcohol level he couldn't understand. As far as he was aware, she never drank.

Ayla held their tickets out for the ferryman. As usual, Riley hadn't seen the man approach. Life kept happening around him, from a distance, as if he were one step removed. Like the woman at the bank today, demanding answers, placing papers in front of him to sign. Riley blushed at the memory of his own ignorance. Luckily, Ayla had been there to guide and interpret. She had been his lifeline in the endless interviews with the police. He knew, if it had not been for Ayla and the evidence from the rest of the island community, he may have been charged with his mother's murder. The bruises on her throat and jaw, all proof of his anger and hatred. He held back the ocean of guilt by reaching for Ayla's hand, grateful once again for her presence. There was something in the way she was staring uncomfortably ahead that made him aware of the conversation occurring behind them.

'Weren't you here the night of the mozzie plague?'

'Nah mate, been in the Territory.'

'She wandered into the mangroves, drunk. They found her dead the next day. Stark naked she was.'

'Heard she was starkers.'

'I saw her mate. Streaked right past me front door, arms flapping like a bird, not a stitch on. I ran and told Suze, but she wouldn't believe me. Reckoned I'd pulled too many cones.'

'Typical.'

'That Mosquito Woman was a bit of a goer, quite the cougar. Heard one night she got on the turps and serviced all the barge boys.'

'In one night?'

'Except Grunter, wouldn't touch Grunter apparently.'

'Don't blame her.'

Ayla stood up. 'Neville, I thought you knew better. Come on, Riley.'

Neville turned. 'Shit Ayla, sorry…didn't know he was there.'

As Riley followed her up the ladder onto the open-air deck, he heard someone murmur. 'Mosquito Woman's son.'

He was impressed. She had already become a legend. They had even given her a name.

Ayla put the documents in her bag. 'Sorry. They're a bunch of gossipmongers – disgusts me sometimes.'

'They don't mean any harm.' He shrugged, touched by the warmth he had received from this tiny community since his mother's death.

Ayla sat down and sighed.

From his far-off place, he sensed her frustration. 'I'm sorry, Ayla.'

'You have nothing to be sorry for…' She took his hand.

He tried to think of something comforting to say, but words had become foreign as he struggled against drowning in guilt. He wanted to explain how he had wished his mother dead, and now she was dead he was fighting to stay afloat as the words bubbled around him in the wrong order. It was easier not to speak.

They waited for everyone to disembark before leaving the boat. As they climbed the hill the mood between them grew heavier. The guilt pressed down, making him stop when they reached the church at the top of the rise. 'You go. I'll be there soon.'

As she turned the corner, he saw the little hop in her step had vanished and he wanted to cry.

Staring once again at the plaque in the brick wall with his mother's name on it, he tried to comprehend that she had been reduced to this.

'Don't know if I'd like to be stuck in a box in a wall. Would you?' Aunty Dora's voice at his shoulder made him jump.

They both watched the plaque as if waiting for something to happen.

'Why don't you take her ashes and scatter them down in the mangroves? Have a private ceremony. Say what you need to say to her.'

She walked across the road with Riley following. There was something comforting about Aunty Dora that made him crave her company. He realised as she continued to speak that she was the only one who talked to him openly about his mother.

'I'll never forget her standing her ground in that community meeting, passionately fighting for her mosquitoes. In my language, this island, Moondarrawah, means mosquito. Know what I reckon, son? I think the island claimed your mother. Maybe it recognised she belonged with the mosquitoes. She wasn't at peace when she was alive. She's at peace now.'

They had reached the old lady's front gate.

'You been back there yet?'

'Back where?'

'The old Johnston house? The swamp?'

He shook his head.

'Need to go back then. Make peace with the place.'

He shut the gate behind her and watched her climb the stairs onto her front verandah. 'What are you waiting for, boy? Christmas?'

Riley ran down the hill and into the dirt road that led to the old house. The flap of the police tape kept time with the beating of his heart. The door was unlocked. At the bottom of the stairwell the smell almost disembowelled him. Something decomposing, rancid, flesh putrefying. He forced himself up the stairs, following the vileness to the cage of dead mice crawling with maggots. A symbol of everything secretive and rotten within his mother. He howled and kicked at the possibility she had killed David until there was a mess of stinking gunk squirming over the floor. He moved then, through the house, their possessions overwhelming him with memories of her fierce love, the way her beautiful face came to life every time she saw him. In the kitchen, her coffee cup sat on the bench, but she was gone and he could never explain that he hadn't meant those last dreadful words. He crept down the hallway toward her room. The sight of her satin dressing gown folded him in half. He could never say sorry for hitting her. She had died thinking he hated her. As he picked the garment up, her smell flooded him with the memory of her voice.

'Riley Smiley, time for sleep. Riley Smiley, not a peep.' The ditty she had chanted every night of his childhood as she tucked him in. Even when he was older and lived in the tree house, she would walk out by torch light to say good-night. Sometimes they would sing the old rhyme together as a joke. Sometimes she would almost tell him what it was that haunted her.

His heart tripped over itself. 'I love you.' He sobbed for all the times she had said that to him and he had answered with silence.

24.

Ayla stopped sawing to watch Grappa through the trees, down on the beach, searching the sand with a large magnifying glass, occasionally bending to pick something up. Collecting shells for the Nor folk, she suspected. When she told him about the vision that had come to her during the mosquito swarm, he had been fascinated.

'They wore shells as hats?'

'Yes. You know the circular mollusc shells shaped like little bowls?' she found one in the sand. 'Like this.'

'How appropriate.' His eyebrows raised in wonderment.

'You know I didn't actually see them. I had my eyes shut. It was my imagination.'

'How many times do I have to tell you? You see better with your eyes shut.' He made a sweeping gesture with his arm, taking in the whole world. 'All an illusion, merely reflected light. Even the scientists will tell you that.'

Ayla watched him move further along the beach. The last time she had visited the old fig, she had found a pile of tiny mollusc shells at the base within the folds of its roots. She had taken them and buried them in the sand, knowing he would be pleased to see they were gone, assuming the Nor folk had made use of his gift.

The hammering behind her had ceased. She turned to see Jonathon, a pelican she recently disentangled from a plastic bag, had landed where Riley was working, demanding something to eat.

'No, Jonathon. You can feed yourself now. Come on, out of here. This way. There's a good boy.' Ayla led the disgruntled bird down the beach track. He looked back one last time then waddled off to the water.

Riley was leaning against the door frame, arms folded, watching her. 'You have a natural way with animals. Your Mum's right. You should go back to uni and finish your course.'

'I will next semester. I've been thinking about the polar bears and what will happen to them when all the ice melts. I'll have a better chance of helping them, if I'm a vet.'

'When does the semester start?'

'Ages away. I've missed the cut-off for this term.'

He took her hand and kissed it. 'Sit down a minute?'

They sat together on a driftwood log.

'I want to try and find my father.'

'You've got enough money for a ticket to Ireland.'

'I've got enough for two. We could be back before your semester starts.'

She looked through the trees and beyond to the horizon, wondering how much ocean you would need to cross to get to Ireland.

'I keep having this dream, I'm there playing my flute, and you're there too, dancing.'

'I can dance on the sandbar at Dead Tree Point. Don't know if I could dance on the streets of Ireland.'

'Just shut your eyes and pretend you're dancing on the sandbar.'

There was a dead butterfly lying on the end of the bench. He felt the softness of it.

'Don't.' She stopped his hand. 'Grappa always told me you should never touch freshly dead butterfly wings.'

'Why?'

'Look,' she showed him the end of his finger. 'See? Silver dust.' She rubbed it on the inside of his wrist and it left a shimmering streak. 'He said his Gran told him the Nor folk use the dust to paint themselves for celebrations. They need it. We shouldn't waste it.'

Riley rubbed his finger down the tip of her nose. 'There's Nor Folk Trees everywhere in Ireland apparently.'

She imagined the spirit of her great-great-grandmother taking her by the hand and walking with her through an ancient green expanse, pointing out features of the foreign landscape, whispering local tales passed down through centuries.

He pulled her to her feet. She laughed when he jumped onto the log and started to play an Irish jig.

In the music, she felt her ancestors pulling her over the water, far away from the tea-tree filling her head with the scent of love for this, her heartland.

Acknowledgements

Firstly, thank you Arts Queensland and Redland City Council for the Regional Arts Development Fund grant which enabled the birth of this work.

Thank you to the phenomenal Nicola O'Shea for taking that initial 'spew draft' and restructuring it into the book it is today. I felt like I swallowed a mountain of knowledge working with you, which I am still digesting.

Thank you Uncle Bob Anderson for the generous sharing of your wisdom, history and language. It is always an honour and a privilege to sit and yarn with you. And a big thank you to Cathy Boyle for your wise guidance, answering of endless emails and helping to co-ordinate meetings. I feel blessed to have you both in my life.

Thank you to Varuna, the National Writer's House for granting a Litlink residency which allowed valuable time and space to develop the manuscript and facilitated a mentorship with the insightful Kim Swivel. Thank you Kim for your continued friendship, generosity and advice.

Thank you to the wonderful team of remarkable women at MidnightSun, my publisher Anna Solding, editor Lauren Butterworth, publicist Brooke Lloyd and Kim Lock for the fabulous cover. A special thank you to Lynette Washington who plucked my manuscript out of the slush pile.

Thank you Jenny Darling for your reader's reports. They were invaluable in the development of the manuscript. I will always be grateful for your interest in my work.

Thank you to my favourite entomologist Stephen Dogget for educating me on the mosquito and tolerating my poetic license.

Thank you David Paxton (Coochiemudlo's Stan), Kathy Gibson and Caitlin MacRae for all things veterinary.

Thank you to all my manuscript readers, each one of you helped to improve the work in different ways – Desmond Kelly, Trish Cation, Joye Spink, Jo Kaspari, Phil Halpin, Amanda Kane, Rozulmo Dedovič and Georgie McClean.

Thank you Elisabeth Gondwe from the North Stradbroke Island Historical Museum for your support and insight into the history of the treatment of the original inhabitants of Quandamooka.

Thank you Elaine and Patrick Barron for your Irish expertise. A special thank you to Craig MacPherson for sharing your personal knowledge and experience with me.

Thank you Margarite Lack for taking the time to walk through the coastal scrub with me to check names and behaviour of all the Quandamooka flora mentioned in the book. Any mistakes are mine.

Thank you Nunka Wulew Nunukel and Petrina Walker for generously allowing the use of your grandmother's precious words.

Thank you Gevan Cole for your beautiful music inspired by the book, and thank you to the talented Renee Judd for building such a kick arse website to promote the book.

Thank you to my dear network of family and friends for your unfailing belief in my ability, particularly those in the island communities I have known over the years – Coochie, Macleay and Straddie. Please see this book as a gift of love to you and the islands you inhabit. And apologies to all the wonderful ferry and bargemen, the gatekeepers who work the boats of the Moreton Bay islands. I have never heard any of you be sexist like the boat boys depicted in the novel, but hey… that's why it's called fiction.

Thank you, Garth Cameron, for filling my childhood with wild imaginings – it was you who taught me how to tell stories – and thank you, Judy Cameron, for instilling in me such a strong work ethic. I wouldn't be writing novels if it wasn't for the example of discipline you ingrained in me.

Thank you to the bright stars in my life, Bodhi and Lily, for tolerating a mum who 'is always writing', and a big thank you to Lily for your wonderful book trailer.

Lastly, thank you to my first reader and love, Loomis Hayes. I remember you when we met, too many years ago now, always with a flute in your pocket, ready to whip out a quick tune and place me under a spell. I am so grateful for all that you do. This book would still be an idea whispering to me on the wind without your constant, unassuming support.

About the Author

Originally an actress, debut novelist D.M. Cameron is an AWGIE nominated radio dramatist, award-winning playwright and celebrated short film writer. She received funding to begin work on her first novel and was then selected for a Varuna Litlink residency to further develop this initial draft into what became *Beneath the Mother Tree*.

www.dmcameron.com

Photo: Una Davis

MidnightSun Publishing

We are a small, independent publisher based in Adelaide, South Australia. Since publishing our first novel, Anna Solding's *The Hum of Concrete* in 2012, MidnightSun has gone from strength to strength.

We create books that are beautifully produced, unusual, sexy, funny and poignant. Books that challenge, excite, enrage and overwhelm. When readers tell us they have lost themselves in our stories, we rejoice in a job well done.

MidnightSun Publishing aims to reach new readers every year by consistently publishing excellent books. Welcome to the family!

midnightsunpublishing.com

Publishing Brilliance